Highlander of My Heart

by

Donna Fletcher

No part of this publication may be used or reproduced in any manner whatsoever, including but not limited to being stored in a retrieval system or transmitted in any form or by any means, electronic, mechanical, photocopying, recording or otherwise without permission of the author.

This is a book of fiction. Names, characters, places, and incidents are either the product of the author's imagination or are used fictitiously, and any resemblance to actual persons, living or dead, business establishments, events or locales is entirely coincidental.

Highlander of My Heart
All rights reserved.
Copyright March 2019 by Donna Fletcher

Cover art
Kim Killion Group

Visit Donna's Web site
www.donnafletcher.com
http://www.facebook.com/donna.fletcher.author

Chapter One

13th century Scotland, the Highlands

"Who did this to you?" Sorrell demanded, fisting her hands at her sides as she tried to contain her anger.

Her younger sister Snow's one cheek was smeared with mud and mud stained her green tunic at her chest and stomach. Mud balls. Someone had thrown mud balls at her. It was enough to make Sorrell want to kill the person. It was malicious and downright rotten to sling mud at a blind woman.

Snow wasn't completely blind, though she might as well have been since she was barely able to see shadows, leaving her far too vulnerable. She had no way of protecting herself against what she couldn't see. With a slight improvement in her vision, after a fire had completely blinded her months ago, there was hope that she would one day fully regain her sight. Until then, Sorrell and Willow had made sure to be their youngest sister's eyes as best they could.

"That is something we can discuss later, after we see to tending Snow," Willow said.

Sorrell ignored the slight shake of Willow's head, warning her that now was not the time for such a question. Sorrell didn't agree.

She approached her two sisters, her anger mounting when she spotted the spreading red blotch beneath the mud Willow was cleaning off Snow's face with a gentle wipe of a wet cloth.

"Not later… now," Sorrell insisted, stopping by the bed where Snow stood. "If whoever did this to Snow is not taken to task for it, he will feel free to do it again."

Sorrell often wondered how Willow could remain calm and reasonable under circumstances that obviously called for immediate retribution. She always appeared unruffled, taking in all that went on and approaching it with a sway and bend like the willow tree she was named after. No matter what storm hit, Willow remained solid and strong, doing what she felt best after considering the circumstances.

It could be that she was the oldest of the three of them and some would say the wisest. Or was it that she stood a good head over Sorrell and Snow, something not difficult to do since they were both petite, taking after their mother. Whereas, Willow got what height she had over them from their da. However, it was Sorrell who got his commanding nature. Willow had plain, gentle features while Snow was the beauty out of the three of them. Sweet and eager to help others, Snow was loved by everyone in the clan, though now there was a cautiousness about her that had not been there before. But how could she not be more cautious when she could see only shadows? A place where dangers lurked.

Danger had certainly lurked there today and Sorrell had every intention of finding that shadow and beating it senseless.

"It was Peter from the Clan MacLoon," Snow said, bringing an end to the disagreement between Willow and Sorrell. "He called out his usual taunts, but I was stunned when I felt the first blow."

"No one stepped up to help you?" Sorrell asked. "And what were you doing out alone?"

"You know better than to condemn anyone, Sorrell. There isn't one in the clan who wouldn't come to Snow's defense," Willow chided.

"Then why didn't someone step forward?" Sorrell demanded. "And again, why were you alone?"

Snow's chin dipped a bit, her glance going to her feet to avoid looking at her sisters even though she couldn't see them.

Sorrow filled Willow's eyes and Sorrell regretted that she had asked.

"You went to Mum and Da's graves again, didn't you?" Sorrell said softly.

Snow raised her head. "I felt the need."

Willow slipped her arm around Snow and Sorrell joined in the hug, the three lassies holding on tight to one another as they had done since losing their parents. They had lost their mum shortly after the fire and their da months later. It still was difficult to accept the fact that both were gone, but they had one another. They would always have one another.

Sorrell laid a gentle hand briefly on Snow's red glowing cheek after seeing it up close and grew angrier when she felt the heat that stung it. She wished the simple touch could take away her sister's suffering. "That must have hurt."

"It stung. At first, I had no idea what Peter had thrown at me." She paused briefly and reluctantly admitted, "I heard him laugh."

"Laugh? He laughed after hitting you?" Sorrell asked, heat rushing up to stain her cheeks as bright red as her sister's.

"Something he has done many times," Snow reminded. "After a few moments, I saw a shadow draw close and I raised my hands to protect my face, but that time the mud ball hit my chest. The third blow followed soon after. Then someone yelled, 'Leave her alone, Peter.'"

Willow turned to Sorrell. "You should go inform James. He will see that Peter is made to pay for this."

Sorrell doubted that. There were moments she still had trouble trusting James, but her mum had insisted he was a good man, and she always had been a good judge of a person's true nature. It didn't help that James was her da's bastard son and that her da had given him leadership of the clan before he died. But so far he was proving to be a good chieftain and he treated her and her sisters good as well. She couldn't fault him when it came to Snow. He was protective of her. It would upset him when he learned what happened. Though, he might find it difficult to get any results since he was in a dispute with Walsh MacLoon, chieftain of the clan, who could prove reluctant to reprimand one of his own.

That left only one thing for Sorrell to do… see for herself that Peter got what he deserved.

Sorrell headed to the bedchamber door.

"Let James deal with this, Sorrell," Willow cautioned.

"I'll let him know," Sorrell said and hurried out the door. And she would, after she was done with Peter.

What she lacked in stature, being far too petite to her liking, she made up for in her determined nature. When she set her mind to something, there was no stopping her. Peter might be larger than her, nearly a full grown man at ten and four years, not that he acted like one, but she wasn't afraid to confront him. A mud ball or two, maybe three, in the face might have him thinking differently.

The chill of autumn hit Sorrell as she walked out of the keep, her own fault, since she hadn't bothered to grab her cloak. The days had been far too chilly and the nights far colder than usual, sure signs that winter would arrive early this year.

She hurried her way through the village, anxious for revenge, when sorrow suddenly tugged at her. The Clan Macardle had always been a strong, thriving clan. Now, however, it was small compared to the surrounding clans, a fault of her father's, though not intentionally. She and most others realized too late that her father was not of sound mind as he once had been. By the time it was realized and addressed, her father had caused several insurmountable problems that James continued to work hard to rectify. He was doing his best, but Sorrell feared it might not be enough or that another more power-hungry clan might seize the opportunity to attack and conquer them.

Whatever the future held, she would stand and fight for her clan and protect her sisters as she was doing now for Snow.

Peter could often be found in the woods that connected MacLoon land to Macardle land. He and his cohorts would assemble there and create whatever havoc they could. It wasn't far from the plot of land where her parents were buried, the land presently in dispute between the Clan MacLoon and Macardle.

Sorrell pushed the strands of her unruly red hair out of her face, squared her slim shoulders and rushed her steps. Her anger had been mounting steadily, thinking of Snow and the fear she must have suffered being struck again and again, not being able to defend herself, not knowing what or who had hit her or when it would stop.

She could almost taste revenge on her tongue, and it tasted sweet.

Sorrell came to an abrupt stop when she spotted Peter on the fringes of Macardle land. He was a good head and a half taller than her and bulky in size. His features still lingered between that of a lad, soft in spots, and manhood, muscles in other spots, and his foolish actions attested to that.

She didn't wait. She scooped up a handful of mud, last night's rain had produced, shouted out his name in a challenging manner and when he turned, she threw the mud ball with a force that one would not expect from such a petite lass.

It hit him right between the eyes, splattering in his eyes and causing him to stumble around blindly.

Once again Sorrell didn't wait. She formed another mud ball and gave it a solid toss, hitting Peter in the side of his head just as he found his footing and sent him stumbling once again. Another mud ball followed that one and slammed into his cheek. By the time she finished, Peter's face was covered with mud as well as his shirt.

"Only a coward throws mud at a blind woman," Sorrell called out. "Attack my sister again and you'll find yourself eating the mud."

Peter wiped the mud from his face, the whites of his eyes glaring and his nostrils flaring with such anger that he looked ready to explode.

Sorrell didn't care. He hadn't gotten half of what he deserved and she was ready to finish it and pummel him senseless.

Peter heaved a heavy breath, snorted, clenched his fists, and stomped toward Sorrell.

"That's it, Peter, let your friends see how a wee lass beats you senseless," Sorrell yelled out, never once thinking it would not end well for her.

Even the closer he got, Sorrell showed not an ounce of fear. All she could think of was what he had done to Snow, and she wanted revenge.

"Come on, coward," she taunted with a wave of her hand. "You're as slow as a crippled old man or is it fear that makes you dawdle?"

Peter sped forward and Sorrell hurried and reached down to scoop up two sizeable rocks off the ground. She eyed the exact spots where she intended to hit Peter and that would cause him the most pain, and grinned. Sorrell never missed her mark.

She tossed one rock in the air and caught it in her hand with ease, and smirked. This one was going to leave him with a reminder of why he should never bother Snow again.

Peter stopped so abruptly that he almost tripped over his booted-feet. After righting himself, he glared at Sorrell with a mixture of anger and fear, though more fear, his eyes going so wide, she thought they'd pop right out of his head. He knew she'd be the victor in this confrontation and how in the end he'd look the fool.

He took a step back, turned, and, with a wave for his cohorts to follow, disappeared into the woods.

"Run you coward, run," Sorrell yelled, "and don't ever come back here again!"

She waited until she didn't see hide nor hair of him, dropped the rocks, then spun around with a flourish of satisfaction and slammed into something solid, stunning her. It took her a moment to regain her senses and realize it was a male chest she had collided with, an extremely broad and hard muscled chest. She raised her head, her eyes having to travel a distance upward before meeting the bold blue eyes of a man the size and width of a mountain.

Chapter Two

"Do you have a death wish, lass?"

Sorrell glared in the bold, yet icy blue eyes of a man so large that he seemed to consume the space around her. Half his face was hidden by a dark bushy beard and his dark hair hung down a distance past his broad shoulders. His green plaid with slim yellow lines running through it was faded and worn in spots as was the shirt he wore beneath. She was quick to spot the sword handle behind his left shoulder, warning her that a sword was strapped to his back. A quick glance down spotted another weapon... the handle of a dagger protruding from where it rested inside his boot.

What troubled and warned the most, though, was the iron shackle attached to his right wrist. It cautioned louder than words... *prisoner.*

"Who are you and what do you want here, giant?" Sorrell demanded, ignoring his query.

"Your tongue is sharp and demanding for a wee woman."

Sorrell took a hasty step back, planted her muddy hands on her hips, and with a slight tilt of her head spoke with a stinging tongue. "You're on my land, giant, and not by invitation, so watch your tongue with me."

Sorrell couldn't be sure of how he'd respond, since the huge man simply stared at her, not a scowl or warning, just a stare that told her nothing.

She had often been told that her mum had named her well since it was the sorrel plant she was named after and while sorrel could be refreshing it could also prove venomous. Many in the clan would attest to that. Rub her the wrong way, harm her family, and Sorrell struck with a vengeance. Usually a look and a stinging barb was enough, but not so with this man.

"What do you want here?" she asked again when he remained silent.

"Shelter and food for a few days, if you would be so kind."

The deep tone to his voice was not at all threatening or commanding, but rather even-tempered, something that didn't seem to fit his size. That led Sorrell to wonder what he was hiding, even more so that he wore a shackle on his wrist.

"Your name?" she asked.

"John."

Sorrell doubted he gave his true name, but there was little she could do about that, except not trust him. The shackle was a different thing.

"The shackle?" she asked with a nod at his wrist.

"That concerns only me."

"Not if you want us to be hospitable," Sorrell warned.

His arm shot out so fast, Sorrell had no time to defend herself. It wrapped around her like the iron shackle attached to his wrist and she found herself smashed against his chest as he turned sharply. He released her with haste and swerved around, keeping his body in front of her like a shield.

Sorrell understood why when she spotted the splat of mud on the sheath of his sword attached to his back. He had seen the mud ball ready to hit her and had taken the blow meant for her.

Sorrell hurried around him and yelled out, "You prove once again what a coward you are, not showing yourself, Peter."

She could have sworn she heard a muffled oath as the giant's body once again wrapped around her and hugged her tight to him, shielding her from not one but two mud balls.

This time when the giant unfurled him from Sorrell, he kept a firm hand on her arm, not letting her step past him.

"Throw another and it will be the last you ever throw," John called out in a tone that left no room for doubt.

Sorrell had to admire the huge man. He remained as he was, not moving out of range of Peter, but staying put and showing not an ounce of fear.

After a few moments, when nothing more happened, John let go of Sorrell. Though he stepped around her, shielding her once again.

"This is not the end of it. He is angry. You embarrassed him in front of his mates."

"I care not what he thinks. He pelted my blind sister with mud balls and laughed as he did. He deserves more than what I gave him."

"You're too wee of a lass to go up against him," John warned.

"Do not underestimate me, giant," Sorrell snapped and stepped away from him. "Go to the kitchen," —Sorrell pointed to the building to the side of the keep— "and tell Dorrit, the cook, that Sorrell said to feed you or I'll hunt her down. And say it like that or she will give you nothing. You can find temporary shelter in one of the stables."

"Thank you for your generosity," John said with a bob of his head.

"Don't make me regret it, giant," Sorrell said and walked away.

It wasn't until she had taken a few steps that she realized he had never explained about the shackle. She shrugged, thinking he wouldn't be here long, so what difference did it make?

Sorrell headed to the keep only to see James approach. He was of fair height and had their father's dark hair and eyes. He had good features, though not the fine features of their father but perhaps it was because of the crook in his nose caused by an injury he had suffered when he was a lad. He was slim, though muscled, and he carried himself like their father had, with confidence.

"Who is that man?" James asked with a nod toward John when they reached each other.

"His name is John and he seeks shelter and food for a few days before continuing on his journey," Sorrell said, not feeling the need to explain more than that.

She could see by the way James stared after the giant that he would find time to speak with him and see for himself if there was any cause to worry.

The thought had her thinking that perhaps it was better he knew more than she had thought to tell him. "The giant came to my aid against Peter."

James rolled his eyes. "What did you do, Sorrell?"

Sorrell boldly explained it all.

"Willow was right in coming to me. I only wish it had been sooner so I could have prevented your altercation with Peter."

Sorrell knew her sister well and understood that by going to James, Willow felt she was protecting Sorrell just as Sorrell felt she was protecting Snow by confronting Peter.

"You should have come to me. I would have seen that Peter was made to—"

"What? Apologize only to have him do it again?" She shook her head. "Walsh MacLoon is too busy trying to claim a parcel of our land to give any thought to what he no doubt would consider a minor incident."

"Perhaps, but that is for me to consider not you. However, there is something I wish to discuss with you." He pointed to the keep. "Let's talk in my solar."

Sorrell almost rushed her hand to her stomach, hoping that somehow it would prevent it from clenching with worry, but stopped when she realized it was covered in mud. It would have done little good anyway, since her stomach tightened like a clenched fist. She hated when it did that. It was like a forewarning that something was going to happen that she didn't like.

"Let me clean my hands first," she said. "I'll meet you there."

He nodded. "This is important, Sorrell."

"I'll hurry," she said, understanding he was letting her know she was not to ignore him and go off and do as she pleased.

She was done quick enough, having cleaned her hands in a bucket of water filled from the rain barrel by the kitchen. And while she took hasty steps to James' solar, she felt as if her boots slogged with every step she took, the sense of being led to her execution weighing heavily upon her.

Upon entering the solar, she took the seat James offered concerned her trembling legs would give way with worry. She was also glad she sat near the hearth, its warmth chasing the chill that had suddenly washed over her. She knew what James wished to discuss with her. He had eluded to it time and again to all three sisters.

Arranged marriages.

Not so much for Snow, thankfully. Her blindness protected her from that, no man wanting such a burdensome wife. But both Sorrell and Willow had hopes of choosing their own husbands, something her mum had agreed with. Unfortunately, her parents' death had changed everything, and it seemed now that she and Sorrell might not have a choice.

James remained standing as he spoke. "I am sure you are already aware that our father's illness took a toll on the clan. We have had a poor harvest and hunting has not gone well. The food sheds are near empty. Several cottages are in desperate need of repair as is the keep." He steeled himself to deliver the dire news. "Unfortunately, the coffers are empty. If we do not get help before winter sets in, I fear that many in the clan, particularly the old and young, will not survive the winter."

Sorrell held her tongue, though it wasn't easy. Instead of duty, he was using guilt to get her to agree to an arranged marriage. How could she possibly let her clan starve or let the old and young die when she could save them? But she was just as good at playing the guilt game.

"I heard you give Father your word, with my own ears, that you would keep us safe," Sorrell accused.

James was not surprised to see her soft green eyes flare with a fiery spark. He had learned over the last few months that it was a sure sign that her temper was on the rise. Even her flaming abundance of red curls that a strip of plaid had trouble keeping contained seemed to blaze in fiery anger. She was definitely ready to argue.

James attempted to explain. "Aye, I did promise our father I would see the three of you safe and I am doing just that by arranging good marriages for you and Willow."

"You have no right to arrange anything. Father was not in his right mind when he made you heir to the Clan Macardle. That should have gone to Willow, his first born daughter as my da once promised, not his bastard son."

She was right about one thing. Their father, Angus Macardle, had not been in his right mind, but that had been going on for months, perhaps even longer, before James had been summoned by Sorrell's mother, Lady Belle. She had been aware that her husband's mind was not what it once had been and that it had been growing worse. And during Angus's lucid moments, he had realized it as well. In one of those coherent moments, Angus had asked for James' word to keep Willow, Sorrell, and Snow safe and he had gladly promised his father.

He did not know if the riding accident that had taken Angus's life had truly been an accident or if he, in a lucid moment, had decided he could no longer continue on, no longer let his daughters watch as his mind deteriorated more and more each day. In the end, it had been a blessing, but still a heartache.

"Perhaps, Sorrell, but our father made a decision and it is done and cannot be undone. I do what is necessary for family, for the clan. You and your sisters have suffered enough and—"

"So you make us suffer even more by wedding me and Willow to strangers, separating us, sending us away from the only home we have ever known, away from Snow who needs us now more than ever and at a time the three of us need each other the most?"

"You will not be far from each other and I do wish I could give you more time. I wish even more that the choice could be yours as your mother wished. Unfortunately, I have no options left to me to see the clan safe."

"So what you are saying is that I am to be sacrificed for the benefit of the clan."

James held his tongue, since he could not deny her words. In a way, she truly was being sacrificed.

"What if I do not care for the man you choose to be my husband?"

"I pray you will find him acceptable," James said. "You will have a few weeks to get to know him and be wed in two months' time."

Her worry had slowly turned to anger as she imagined her life being taken out of her hands, decisions made for her without regard to her own wants.

"Why such a hasty marriage? Is there something besides the dire circumstances you outlined for me that you are not telling me?"

"I didn't want to burden you or your sisters with clan matters," James said.

"We are family. We share the burden together."

Sometimes, James did not know what to make of Sorrell. One minute she reminded him that he was their father's bastard son and on the other she called him family. In time, he hoped the latter would prove truer.

Sorrell's brow scrunched tight. "Wait. How is it this clan agrees to a marriage arrangement when we have nothing to offer in exchange, except..." Her eyes shot wide. "Our land and where it sits, adjacent to the Lord of Fire, Tarass of the Clan MacFiere. Don't tell me that the Lord of Fire has something to do with this arrangement."

Sorrell was far too intelligent for her own good. She could figure out problems with the snap of her fingers and he envied that about her.

"The Lord of Fire is offering a substantial sum for this union."

"Why?" Sorrell shook her head, not needing an answer and understanding why. "This union will benefit him. But how?" she demanded, then shook her head once again realizing the answer. "It must have something to do with a nearby clan who will pledge their fealty to him and strengthen his forces in the area." She closed her eyes a moment and when she opened them they were fiery hot with anger. "Do not tell me you made arrangements for me to marry into the Clan MacLoon, for if you did, both you and the Lord of Fire can go to hell."

"No, no," James said ready to assure her. "It is not the Clan MacLoon the arrangement has been made with."

"Then who is to be my husband?" Sorrell asked, her brow narrowing as she tried to think of possibilities.

James braced himself for her response as he said, "Seth of the Clan MacCannish."

"*No*! Absolutely not! Never! He dictates and drinks until drunk. I'd kill him before our wedding day has ended."

"His father assures me that he will treat you well and dictate only when necessary."

"Dictate only when necessary?" Sorrell asked with a hardy laugh. "Not likely. I will not wed Seth MacCannish."

James rubbed the back of his neck and scrunched his face as he said, "The arrangement has been made, the document signed. It is done. Nothing can undo it."

Sorrell stood and though she was a wee one as the giant had pointed out, when she took a stance on something she appeared taller and more intimidating than the giant himself.

"I tell you now, James, and take it as my word. I will not now or ever wed Seth MacCannish."

James watched Sorrell leave his solar, her head high, her shoulders back and a defiant lift of her chin, and he shook his head. There was no stopping Sorrell when she set her mind to something and that meant she'd find a way to get out of this marriage arrangement, and he couldn't let that happen.

Sorrell had no choice. She had to wed Seth MacCannish, and he would see that she did.

Chapter Three

John sat in a dark, quiet corner of the stable enjoying the small feast Dorrit, the cook, had given him. The short, skinny woman with wiry gray hair that belied her youthful appearance had been wary of him, until he repeated what Sorrell had told him.

The gray-haired woman had laughed and said, "That's our Sorrell."

Dorrit had been more than generous with food and drink and since it had been almost a day since he had last eaten, he appreciated every delicious bite.

He also found himself not being able to get the wee, spitfire of a woman off his mind. He had known strong, independent women, traits found in most Highland women, but none as petite and fiery as Sorrell. How she had the courage to go up against the lad Peter, who was three times or more her size was a wonder. When he had come upon the scene, he had watched with amusement, until he realized the wee woman meant to conquer the lad, though how she would have accomplished that feat had been a mystery to him.

He had stepped forward, intending to give aid to the woman, but the size of him had frightened the lad off, though not for long. He had been wise enough to hide upon his return and John suspected it wasn't the last time Sorrell would see Peter. It made him wonder how she would ever be able to truly protect herself against the angry lad.

He drank from the pitcher of ale Dorrit had given him, and she told him if he returned the pitcher to her, she'd refill it for him. He intended to take her up on her offer.

He rubbed at his beard, a habit of late. How long had it been since he felt his face without it? How long had it been since he had heard his given name spoken? How long had it been since the lies had stolen his life?

He dropped his head back against the stable wall and shut his eyes for a moment. He didn't want to remember, but his left hand drifted over to rub at the shackle on his right wrist. He could rid himself of it, but it wasn't time yet. Someday it would be, but not today.

Today, he wanted nothing other than to sit in the shadows of this corner in peace and quiet and think of nothing, not the past or the future, just this moment of solitude. That was all he wanted, nothing more.

The door to the stable flew open and Sorrell stomped in and went to one of the stalls and began pacing in front of it.

John watched her. She was a tiny one. When she had turned and slammed into him earlier, the top of her head had barely reached his chest. Somehow, though, she seemed taller or maybe it was the way she carried herself, her shoulders drawn back and a slight lift of her chin. She had the loveliest face, not stunning, but fine features that caught the eye and held it. Then there was her red hair that looked as if it blazed one minute and was a deeper red the next and damn if that slim piece of plaid cloth couldn't contain the frenzied curls that fell well past her shoulders. He also couldn't help but take note that even though she was slim, she curved in all the right places. A sudden image caught in his mind of his hands hugging the curves of her waist, catching him off guard, and he was quick to banish it.

He turned his thoughts empty once more, though not for long. The black horse stomped his hooves in agitation, gaining his attention.

"I'm annoyed too, Prince," Sorrell said and stopped pacing long enough to soothe the horse with a gentle touch to his face. "How could James do this to me? Wed me off to an arse of a man who claims he will dictate to me only when necessary. It's horrifying."

So, she was being wed off like many chieftains and lords did with their daughters. It was a daughter's lot to do her duty whether she liked it or not. Evidently, Sorrell didn't like it. It would be a shame to see her spirited nature subdued. But it didn't concern him. He would be here three days at the most, then he'd be gone.

"I want to decide who I wed," Sorrell went on explaining to the horse. "It should be my choice who I spend the rest of my life with, whose bed I share and whose bairns I carry and birth, and who I love with all my heart."

Love. It disappointed, if it at all existed, and he chuckled at her wishful thinking.

"Who's there?" Sorrell demanded, swerving around.

John cursed silently, annoyed that he had made her aware of his presence.

"I found the shelter you offered here," he said, not bothering to stand and show himself.

It didn't matter, Sorrell followed the sound of his voice to the darkened corner.

"What do you hide from?" she asked, squinting her eyes to try and see him.

"It isn't what I hide from, it is what I seek."

"And that is?"

"Solitude."

"Are you telling me to go away and leave you be?" she asked with a tinge of annoyance.

"I believe I made myself clear."

She wished she could see him better. With the shadows hugging him so close, he was barely visible. Peoples' faces expressed so much more than their words.

She continued with her chatter, making it clear she wasn't ready to leave yet. "Have you eaten?"

"I have and again I appreciate your generosity."

"Do you not like people?"

"I prefer to be alone."

"Another hint to leave you be?" she asked, not caring if he wanted her to leave or not.

"I told you what you wished to know."

"You are a strange man."

"How so?"

"You don't give a direct answer."

"I think I made myself quite clear."

She said it more bluntly than he did. "You want to be left alone."

"See how clear I've been." He was glad she couldn't see the smile that touched his lips.

"I will leave you to your solitude," Sorrell said with some regret. He might be an odd man to talk with, but that was what made speaking with him interesting. She turned to leave.

"Sorrell."

Her name falling with such strength from his lips sent a slight tremble through her.

"Aye," she said as she turned around.

"You are a kind woman."

Sorrell gave a hardy laugh. "You will find none here who would agree with that."

"I care not what others think."

"Now there is something we both agree on. Have a good night, John," Sorrell said and closed the stable door behind her.

Dusk was near and with it a sharper chill to the air. Sorrell wasted no time in returning to the keep. She had gone to the stable to calm her anger before delivering the news of her impending wedding to her sisters. She had only grown angrier talking to her horse, Prince. It wasn't until she talked with John that she calmed.

It seemed he had saved her twice today, once from Peter and once from herself.

Sorrell found her two sisters sitting at one of the tables closest to the large hearth when she entered the Great Hall. It saddened her to see how the once Great Hall that so proudly had held splendid banquets, entertained visiting chieftains, and celebrated clan achievements now sat barely used. The many trestle tables and benches had seen little use in this last year and she couldn't recall the last time minstrels had performed here.

She missed those days of friendly chatter, laughter, and fun with family and friends. They seemed to have disappeared overnight and her heart ached at the memories.

"Who is the strange man Dorrit says you sent to her to feed," Willow asked when Sorrell joined her and Snow at the table.

"Someone of no importance. He is just passing through," Sorrell said. "Besides, I have a more important matter to discuss." She paused not believing herself what she was about to tell her sisters and kept her voice low when she spoke. "James has arranged a marriage for me to Seth MacCannish."

Snow was quick to object. "You cannot marry him. He will not suit you."

That Snow knew how wrong the match was, made Sorrell grateful to have a sister who understood her so well.

"My thoughts as well," Willow said. "I am not one to decide or judge quickly, but in this situation there is no question about it. Seth MacCannish is all wrong for you. You would kill him before your wedding day is done."

Sorrell had to laugh. "I voiced the same to James."

She was pleased her sisters agreed, but she hadn't doubted they would. She could count on them… always.

"You informed James you would not agree to the marriage," Snow said, certain Sorrell had done just that.

"I did, but he said it was done and could not be undone."

"Nonsense. We must think on it and find a way to get you out of it," Snow said, Willow squeezing her wrist too late to alert her to hold her tongue.

"There is nothing you can do," James said, hearing their conversation as he approached the table where they sat. "This marriage will benefit the clan and with the documents already signed by both parties, it would take something drastic to void the agreement. I truly am sorry, but I had little choice in the matter."

"Seth MacCannish is not a suitable husband for Sorrell," Snow said. "Why didn't you discuss this matter with her before making a decision? And will you do the same to us? Marry us off to whoever you please?"

"I take no pleasure in this decision or ones to come," James said.

"Ones to come?" Sorrell snapped. "What ones to come?"

"Sit and talk with us, James," Willow offered, ignoring the scowl Sorrell shot her.

"Talk about what?" Sorrell turned a deeper scowl on James. "He's already made his decisions. So, who will be the man you sacrifice Willow to? Or will the Lord of Fire decide that?"

"The Lord of Fire is trying to keep peace in the area. It is more complicated than first thought. Walsh MacLoon remains adamant about the land dispute. He has even gone as far as to request help from a distant relative, lord of a powerful clan.

"That won't sit well with the Lord of Fire," Sorrell said, then gave a short chuckle. "Now I understand and it is a good strategy to strengthen his power and increase his warriors."

"What are you talking about?" Willow asked.

"Think about it, Willow," Sorrell encouraged. "The Clan MacCannish is a good size and their warriors are a hardy bunch and skilled in battle. The Lord of Fire is building his forces, but why?" Sorrell turned to James. "Who is the distant relative that Walsh MacLoon reached out to?"

"No one knows."

"Perhaps it is all a ruse," Snow said, "Walsh MacLoon has been known to tell tall tales."

"I hope this is one of those tall tales," James said, "but in the meantime it is wise to be prepared and wise to see that neighboring clans stay friendly and loyal to one another."

"Through forced marriages?" Sorrell questioned with distaste.

"Through duty," James corrected and stood. "Seth MacCannish will visit with you sometime next week, at least give him a chance."

Sorrell made no effort to respond to James and said not a word until he left the Great Hall.

"I'll not wed him," Sorrell said and no doubt she would reiterate those words often, though she feared they would do little good. The trap had been laid and sprung and she didn't know how she'd escape it.

Snow reached out in search of Willow's hand and Willow took hold of it. "There must be something that can be done."

"The document is signed. It would take something drastic for the agreement to be broken," Willow said, then looked to Sorrell. "Don't get angry with me, but you should consider the benefits of this union along with the downside."

"There are none," Sorrell said calmly, having expected this of Willow. It was in her nature to weigh all sides and Sorrell took no offense to her suggestion.

"I can think of one extremely important one," Willow said.

"Sorrell would remain close by," Snow said with a tender smile that displayed relief. "You would be a short ride away."

"And no one would go hungry," Sorrell said, the thought having weighed heavily upon her.

"It might be a lean winter for food," Willow said. "I've checked the storage sheds and I've seen what is left of the fields to harvest. While low, we will do what we must to get through the winter. Remember, James is not familiar with the workings of our clan, though it is good that he worries. It shows that he truly cares for the clan."

"And I don't?" Sorrell snapped.

Willow reached out to take hold of Sorrell's hand. "That was never a thought, Sorrell."

Sorrell sighed and squeezed her sister's hand. "I know. I'm sorry. I'm just so torn."

"Perhaps Seth MacCannish won't be as bad as we think," Snow said and the three of them laughed.

"We will think on this and see what we can do." Willow took hold of Sorrell's hand and the three sisters held tightly to each other. "We are together, always here for each other, and that's what matters the most."

***

John favored the night. It was quiet, no one about. The air was crisp and the night sky dark, barely a sliver of a moon. He walked through the village, his steps silent for a large man, but then he had learned to walk gently and make little sound.

He had hoped to find an abandoned cottage by now, a place to be alone, to think on his next step. Unfortunately, he hadn't been successful and so he stopped at various clans along the way seeking shelter and food for a night or two before moving on. He hadn't wanted to head north, at least not yet, but it was imperative he remain on the path his search took him.

He stopped a minute and dropped his head back, then rolled his neck around, hearing the creaks and cracks. The past two years had been anything but easy, especially since he had found no answers to his nightmare. Not that he would stop searching, not until he found the person responsible for the hell he'd been living.

He continued walking, enjoying the cold night air that nipped at his cheeks and the silence that surrounded him like a comforting blanket.

Don't you like people?

He almost stopped upon hearing Sorrell's voice in his head.

He had liked people... once. Had trusted them as well, though no more. Not a one. Not for two years now.

Now he held his tongue, let others talk. Though, he had spoken some to Sorrell. Had he a choice? She had chatted away and oddly enough he hadn't minded. He had actually regretted when she had taken her leave.

Maybe it was her blunt nature. She didn't hide anything. She didn't censor her words. She spoke as she felt. He also admired the fact that she wanted to fall in love. He had thought he was loved, a love that could never be challenged. In the end, he had questioned if love even existed.

He shook away the troubling thoughts and continued his walk. He had noticed some of the cottages were in need of repair and the storage sheds as well. Sorrell had been generous with food and drink. Tomorrow he would offer to help with repairs in exchange for the food and shelter provided. Then in no more than two days' time he would take his leave.

Sorrell's lovely face popped into his head and he shook it away. He had no time to favor a woman. Ale would settle that, and he had a good amount left after Dorrit had refilled the pitcher for him. He turned and headed back to the stable.

"It is time to come home."

John stopped at the sound of the familiar voice. He reached down and grabbed the dagger from his boot and looked to see a figure emerge from the side of a cottage, though he remained in the shadows. It didn't matter. He didn't need to see his face to know who he was.

"I have no home," John said.

"Your father commands it."

Anger marked John's words. "I have no father."

"He has had a change of heart."

"The man has no heart."

The voice in the shadows grew annoyed. "Regardless of what you think, he commands your return."

"It will take more than a command for me to return," John warned.

"What will it take?"

"His word he will not kill me would be a good start," John said bitterly.

"He does not want you dead."

"You mean he *no longer* wants me dead," John accused, the pain of what his father had done to him as hurtful as the day it had happened.

"He wants you home."

Curiosity had John asking, "What has changed his mind?

A moment of silence passed before the voice said, "He is dying."

"Good, then let the devil take his wretched soul."

Chapter Four

John stepped out of the stable the next morning, his thoughts as cloudy as the gloomy sky. He knew it wasn't the last he'd hear from Erland, his father's closest confidante. It would be what happened next that made the difference in what he himself would do.

"John."

He turned at his name being called, used to answering to the name he had assumed these past two years, and saw a man of fair height and dark hair approach with a gait of authority.

"James, Chieftain of the Clan Macardle," James said, stopping in front of him and having to tilt his head back to look the giant of a man in the eye. "Sorrell told me how you came to her aid yesterday and I wished to thank you for helping her."

"It was the right thing to do," John said.

"Aye, and a good man would know that."

Good man. He hadn't been a good man in some time, but James Macardle didn't need to know that.

"The shackle?" James asked with a nod toward it.

"A reminder of what lies can do to a good man."

"I know the feeling," James said. "How long will you be with us?"

"A day or two if that is all right, and while here I offer any help you may need."

James was quick to take him up on his offer. "Roofs need repairing."

"I would be pleased to help."

"Good," James said, delighted with the extra help. "Seek out Melvin. He's in charge of the repairs, though I must warn you that Sorrell dictates the repairs more than Melvin. My sister has her hand in everything." He scratched his head. "And damn if she isn't better at it than those supposedly in charge."

A smile caught at the corner of John's mouth.

"You appear a good man, though the size of you can warn otherwise. Don't give me cause to think differently," James said and after a brief nod walked away.

He respected James for being cautious, since if it was his own clan, his warning would have been more threatening.

Eager to be busy on a solitary project, John rolled his sleeves up, found a short strip of leather in the stable and used it to tie his hair back, then he went in search of Melvin.

He walked through the village surprised to see no work being done on any of the cottages. It was past sunrise, work on the roofs should have started by now.

"Get your lazy arse out there and get to work!"

John halted, hearing Sorrell's voice and watched as a skinny man, his short, red hair sticking out in all directions from his head, came stumbling out of a small cottage, appearing as if he'd been dragged from his bed.

"I don't feel well. I need to rest."

"You need to stop drinking," Sorrell scolded. "And I care not how you feel. Your chores need doing. And where's Dole?" She held up her hand. "Wait. Don't tell me. He's needs rest today too."

"One day of rest won't hurt," Melvin argued.

"Do you see the sky?" Sorrell asked, pointing at it and Melvin leaned to the side to look up, and appeared about to tip over as he followed her finger. "You're lucky if you get one roof repaired before it rains. And with how cold it's been, it looks like winter will be upon us early. The holes in the roofs need to be repaired before then."

"Have a heart, Sorrell, my head is pounding," Melvin pleaded.

"I have a heart just not for you. Now get to work," Sorrell ordered.

Melvin turned pale, gagged, and just before he spewed the contents of his stomach straight at Sorrell, John's arm shot out, grabbed hers, and yanked her away.

Melvin gagged and spit, then turned to Sorrell. "I told you I needed to rest."

John's arm snaked around Sorrell's narrow waist when she lunged at Melvin and kept tight hold of her.

Melvin wisely scurried off into his cottage, quickly closing the door behind him.

Sorrell turned angry eyes on John. "You should have let me give him what he deserved, a boot in the butt."

"He gets what he deserves, a stomach that will continue to revolt and a head that pounds endlessly."

"You know that from experience?" Sorrell asked and eased herself out of his arm, a slight chill rippling through her as she lost the warmth of his body.

"I've had my share of too much drink a time or two."

"Melvin has had his share more than a time or two."

"That's obvious."

Sorrell turned her head to look over the village. "The roof repairs will never get done."

"I spoke with James and offered my help in return for your generosity."

Sorrell grinned. "I thought you wanted solitude, to be alone, away from people."

Her grin teased and sparked the green of her eyes and damn if his manhood didn't inch toward arousal.

He strenuously ignored it. "Thatching a roof doesn't involve people. It is a solitary chore. Show me what needs to be done."

***

Sorrell watched John from a distance. He had worked at a steady pace and had finished repairs to three roofs and it was only mid-day. Gray clouds still crowded the sky, but rain had yet to fall. At the pace he was going, there was a good chance he would complete all the roof repairs today.

"Now I see why you refer to him as a giant."

Sorrell turned with a smile to see Willow coming up behind her, her hair falling in lovely waves around her head and down over her shoulders. She was always jealous of Willow's hair. Its dark red color was so much more attractive than her own blazing red hair and Willow's waves more manageable than her stubborn red curls that did whatever they pleased. She had complained to her mum once and she had assured her that her own red color was just as lovely as Willow's and suited her perfectly. But then even Snow's light red and straight hair, not a curl in sight, was more attractive than her fiery red.

Thinking of Snow and seeing she wasn't with Willow had her asking, "Where's Snow?"

"She insisted she was chilled and wanted nothing more than to sit by the fire in her bedchamber. I didn't believe her for one minute."

"She's feeling she's a burden again," Sorrell said, sadness stealing her smile. "I hate that this has happened to her. She had been so vibrant, always busy doing something, and helping however she could. Now it's as if she's a prisoner."

"I wonder if that isn't partially our fault," Willow said.

"What do you mean?"

"We're always there right on top of her. We never let her be, let her find her way in the shadows," Willow said.

"She needs our help," Sorrell argued.

"And what will she do when we are gone, off to live with husbands James has chosen for us? Who will help her then? If we don't encourage her to be more independent, how will she ever survive?"

"You're right," Sorrell agreed, regretting she hadn't realized it herself. "What do we do?"

"Let her be when she attempts to be independent. She will learn. She has learned in spite of our constant help and—"

Sorrell watched as a smile spread across her sister's face and her eyes widened, and she looked to see what she had found so pleasing.

Sorrell didn't smile, but her mouth dropped open when she saw what had her sister smiling. John had gotten down off the roof and had slipped his shirt off to shake the thatch from it. His naked chest was a sight impossible to ignore, broad and hard with muscles that extended down along his arms, and his midriff looked as hard as iron. She had seen men's naked chests before but never had she seen such a fine one. Nor had she ever experienced such pleasure in seeing one as she did John's.

Other women agreed, since the women nearby couldn't take their eyes off him.

"He's an exceptional man," Willow said, still staring at him and was surprised when Sorrell marched, with determined steps, past her, heading straight to the giant of a man, and Willow's smile grew.

"Put your shirt on," Sorrell ordered. "It's too cold to go without it."

"It's just for a moment. I wanted to get rid of the thatch poking me."

"You have more roofs to do. You can rid yourself of the thatch when you're done with them."

John was familiar with that spark in a woman's eye when she finds a man appealing, having seen it often enough. He wondered, though, if Sorrell recognized it in herself. While he didn't mind seeing it there in her green eyes, it could prove a problem.

"You're a hard taskmaster, Sorrell. I was hoping for a bite to eat, since I've eaten nothing since waking."

The spark left her eyes to his disappointment, though, to his surprise, it was replaced with concern.

"You should have said something sooner. No one goes hungry here if we can help it." She reached out and grabbed his hand, hugging it tight. "Come, I will get you food and drink."

"My shirt," he said and she let go of his hand and disappointment poked at him one again.

She caught him off guard when after slipping his shirt on, she reached out and took hold of his hand again with the same possessive determination as before.

Instinct, common response, or just because he wanted to, he closed his hand firmly around hers. It felt small and delicate in his large one, yet she grasped his with a strength he hadn't expected. He followed along as she directed them to the keep.

She had him sit at a table near the hearth and ordered food and drink brought to the table, and he was glad that she joined him, sliding onto the bench across from him.

"I'll finish the other roofs after I'm done eating."

"You've done quite a bit today. The others can wait until tomorrow… unless you plan to take your leave tomorrow," she said, a bit anxiously.

Her green eyes shined with anticipation and she gave a quick nibble to her bottom lip. And he found his manhood reminding him how long, far too long, he had been celibate. He was glad when a servant sat a pitcher of ale on the table and filled a tankard for him.

"I'll be here at least another day or so," he said, then took a generous swig of ale.

"Where will you go from here?"

He thought a moment. He should continue his search for the person who had rained hell down upon him, but with his father supposedly dying and demanding his return home, he wasn't sure where he'd go next.

"I honestly don't know."

"You need a home," Sorrell said as if she decided for him.

Home.

He had had a home, a good, loving home, or so he had thought.

"But I forgot, you don't like people. You prefer solitude so a home might not be good for you, too much talk and laughter. Perhaps the monastic life would fit you better. There is a friary not far from here."

He laughed, as he speared a piece of meat, with a knife, from the platter on the table in front of him. "The celibate life is not for me."

"Then you wish a wife someday?"

"You ask far too many questions."

"That's right. You prefer to be alone." Sorrell stood. "I will leave you to eat in solitude."

He didn't want that. He wanted her to stay. He enjoyed talking with her and that thought troubled him. Sorrell wasn't the type of woman to warm his bed for a day or two, the only kind he'd been interested in these past two years. She was to be wed to a man chosen for her and he was to take his leave soon, matters of his own to see to.

"That would be good," he said.

"Sorrell, is that you I hear?"

She turned to see Snow making her way through the Great Hall. Instinct had her ready to go guide her sister through the maze of tables, but recalling Willow's words of how they needed to help their sister become more independent, stopped her.

"Here, Snow, I'm where we usually sit," Sorrell called out.

Snow smiled and stretched her hands out to her sides as she felt her way past the tables, bumping into one now and again, but her smile remained bright as she did.

Sorrell couldn't stop herself from taking a few steps to Snow when she drew near and reaching for her hand.

"Someone is with you," Snow said.

"How do you know?" Sorrell asked surprised.

"His scent. He smells of," —Snow sniffed the air— "thatch, I think."

"That's me," John said, having gotten to his feet.

Snow turned in the direction of his voice, seeing an overpowering shadow. "You are huge. Oh, you must be the giant Sorrell told us about."

"I am, though it is easy to be a giant when standing next to Sorrell," John said.

Snow chuckled. "And me as well since Sorrell and I get our petite size from our mother, whereas Willow has some height over us thanks to our da. What parent do you favor?"

"My mum," John said, though offered no more on it.

"I was just about to take my leave, since he likes to eat alone," Sorrell said.

"Nonsense, no one likes to eat alone," Snow said, and reaching out to feel for the edge of the table made her way onto the bench. "You don't mind do you," —she paused a moment— "John, I believe Sorrell said your name was John, though I would have thought it Giant since she refers often to you that way."

"Giant suits him," Sorrell said in her defense of her description of him as she slid in beside her sister to sit.

"If names were to truly match us, Sorrell, then you would be called Chatty—no wait—Dictator." Snow chuckled.

Sorrell joined in with a laugh. "Aye, Dictator, that's me."

"And what name would suit you, Snow?' John asked.

"Angelic," Sorrell said and quickly changed her mind, "no... Determined."

"Aye, Determined," Snow agreed and reached out to squeeze Sorrell's hand, pleased her sister thought that of her.

"What of Willow?"

Sorrell and Snow both scrunched their brows.

"Sensible," they both said at once and laughed.

John had forgotten what it was like to have a loving family and he had forgotten how much he missed having one. Or was it that the memories were just too painful to recall? He had had no siblings, but he had had a good friend, Hugh, who had become more like a brother to him. They had been inseparable. John's parents' love had provided a solid family bond. Or so he had thought. And the clan had also been his family, a clan he had been trained to lead one day. That was why it had been so heartbreaking when his da had turned against him.

"What of you, John?" Snow asked. "What would your name be?"

"Giant," Sorrell said, sending a grin his way. "No wait, it would be... Solitude."

Snow looked toward the large blurry shadow that to her was John. "You don't truly wish to be alone, do you?"

"He doesn't like people," Sorrell said.

"Someone must have hurt you badly to feel that way," Snow said.

John understood why Sorrell called her angelic. He could hear the sadness in her voice for him. His hurt truly disturbed her.

"Did someone hurt you badly?" Sorrell more demanded than asked.

She sounded as though she was ready to go out and hunt the person down as she had done to Peter for her sister, and now here she was willing to do it for him.

Sorrell's eye went to the shackle. "Does that shackle on your wrist have anything to do with it?"

"Shackle? You have a shackle on your wrist?" Snow asked. "May I touch it?"

John never let anyone touch it. It was personal to him, but somehow he didn't mind if Snow touched it.

"May I take your hand?" he asked of Snow, and she hurried to stretch it out to him.

Her hand was as small as Sorrell's, though somehow it seemed more delicate. He lifted it gently and placed it on the shackle attached to his wrist.

Snow ran her fingers over the thick, rough iron. "Does it hurt you?"

"Not anymore," John said.

"You should rid yourself of it. You are free now," Sorrell said, it disturbing to her to see it on him.

"One day, but not today," John said, feeling he was yet to be entirely free.

Willow burst into the Great Hall. "Get James! Seth MacCannish and a troop of his warriors approach.

Chapter Five

"What is Seth MacCannish doing here? You told me it would be a few days before he paid a visit," Sorrell demanded of James when he entered the Great Hall.

"I don't know," James said.

"I won't see him. He can't show up completely unannounced and expect me to be available to him," Sorrell insisted.

"Sorrell is right," Snow said. "It isn't proper or considerate."

"Whether proper or considerate, he's here and we shall be hospitable," James said, leaving them no recourse. "I will go greet him and give you time to collect yourself and receive him properly."

Snow grabbed Sorrell's arm to stop her from going after James. "Let him go," she whispered. "We will think of something."

"I should take my leave. There are more roofs to repair," John said, not his place to be part of this. Though, he had the overpowering urge to remain in case Sorrell should need him, since she always seemed to, somehow, be in need of aid.

Sorrell stood. "I will go with you."

"You can't go with him. Your intended is here and you must meet with him," Willow said.

"He should have sent word of his intentions," Sorrell said. "Come, John, we have work to do."

Willow approached her sister. "You know this will create a problem."

Sensible.

Sorrell thought the name truly did fit her sister. She always looked to be reasonable and many times it had proven the wise thing to do, but not this time.

"I will not bend to Seth MacCannish's whims," Sorrell snapped sharply, leaving no doubt she meant it.

"You will have to meet with him sooner or later," Willow said.

"Later will do," Sorrell said and looked to John. "Follow me."

He followed her through the narrow stone passageway to the kitchen, Dorrit sending him a grin as they passed through the kitchen and out the door.

"There's a cottage near the woods whose roof needs immediate repair," Sorrell said and led the way.

He wondered why if it needed immediate repair she hadn't set him to the task earlier, but it was not for him to say. He went and gathered the thatch and the ladder and got busy, though he kept an eye on Sorrell. She paced alongside the cottage, peering out from around the side now and again.

"He's speaking with your brother," John said, leaning over the side of the cottage.

"Does he remain on his horse?"

"No, he has dismounted and he looks around as if—"

"Searching for me?"

"That would be my guess," John said and watched in the distance. "I think you may have a problem."

"Why?" Sorrell asked anxiously.

"Melvin just staggered over to James and Seth and he's pointing in my direction."

"The little weasel. He's getting his revenge on me."

John didn't agree. "He probably thinks he's being helpful and it will get him in your good graces."

"That would take a miracle," Sorrell said and hurried to the ladder, hoisting the hem of her garments as she prepared to climb it.

"What are you doing?" John demanded.

"I'm coming up there by you. If Seth comes this way, I don't want to be anywhere near him."

"You're not coming up here. It's too dangerous," John said in a command more suited to a lord of a clan than a peasant.

Sorrell turned a scowl on him. "That's not for you to decide. You'll take your orders from me."

John swore beneath his breath. He had no choice but to do as she said, especially since he spotted Seth and James heading their way.

"Give me your hand. They're headed straight for you," he said, leaning over the edge of the roof.

Sorrell was quick to stretch out her hand once she was close enough on the rungs to reach it. She was a bit shocked when he took her hand and practically pulled her up along the remaining rungs of the ladder. His arm went around her waist when she drew near enough for him to reach it.

"You'll stay by my side," he ordered and this time she agreed with a nod.

Sorrell watched her brother and Seth walk toward the cottage. James caught sight of her first and when Seth saw her, his eyes nearly popped out of his head and he quickened his steps.

Seth MacCannish was a man of good features and of average height. He was a bit thick around the middle and he had thick arms and legs, and all were firm. He kept his long, bright red hair braided at the sides and his beard trimmed. He was a skilled warrior and he never shied away from a fight. But he enjoyed being in command and demanded far too much obedience from everyone to Sorrell's way of thinking.

Seth stopped at the front of the cottage and looked at her with a deep scowl. "What are you doing up there. Get down immediately."

"You're not my husband yet, Seth MacCannish, you can't tell me what to do," Sorrell shouted at him.

His face flushed red, the color almost matching his beard, and he raised his fist, shaking it at John. "You'll answer for letting her up there."

"I don't take orders from him or you," Sorrell snapped.

"I'll not tell you again, woman, get down from there," Seth yelled up at her.

"And I'll not tell you again, I don't take orders from you," Sorrell yelled back and stepped forward, shaking her fist at him.

John grabbed her around the waist. "Watch where you step."

"Take your hands off my intended," Seth warned with an angry shout.

"He's keeping me safe, you fool," Sorrell called out.

"That's for me to do, not him," Seth argued. "Now get down from there or I'll come up and drag you down."

Sorrell took a hasty step forward.

John tightened his hold around her waist and warned, "Don't take another—"

John never got to finish. They went crashing through the roof together, landing in the narrow bed, that broke under their weight. John had made sure to take the brunt of the fall and Sorrell had wisely and quickly thrown her arms around his neck to remain tucked tightly against him.

The door swung open, pounding into the wall.

"Get your hands off my woman," Seth yelled and lunged forward, his hand closing in a tight fist and his arm getting ready to swing.

John lifted Sorrell off himself and got to his feet.

Sorrell moved just as fast. She scrambled to her feet and put herself between the two men in a flash.

Seth had no time to slow his fist meant for John.

John yanked Sorrell out of the way, but it wasn't fast enough to miss Seth's meaty fist entirely. It grazed the top of her cheek and had enough power to send her reeling. John caught her in his arms as she collapsed against him.

"What the hell, Seth?" James shouted, giving the man a rough shove and rushing over to his sister.

Sorrell was stunned, pain radiated along the whole side of her face, and the only reason she remained on her feet was because John had hold of her. But as soon as her strength returned, she was going to launch herself at Seth and land a punch of her own to his nose.

"Don't even think of it," John warned with a whisper.

She glared up at him. How did he know what she was thinking? His next whisper settled it for her.

"I can see it in your eyes, their glaring an angry green."

James' fury grew when he saw the bruise already beginning to form around the corner of her eye and the top of her cheek. "I'll get you back to the keep so Willow can tend you." He reached out to take her from John.

"No," she said quickly and winced. "John will take me."

John didn't give anyone a chance to object, he scooped her up in his arms.

"I'll be carrying my intended, not you," Seth said, blocking the open door.

"No, John will take me," Sorrell all but commanded. "Now get out of our way."

"Do as she says, Seth," James ordered. "You've caused her enough pain today. And you'll inform me of when you wish to visit with Sorrell the next time or you won't be welcomed here. Now take your leave."

Seth looked ready to take up arms and battle. "Sorrell is my intended, so see that you keep your hands to yourself, giant, or I'll cut them off." He turned and stomped out of the cottage.

"See her to the keep while I see that he takes his leave," James ordered and rushed off after Seth.

Sorrell kept her head rested on John's chest, though it was hard with muscle, it was comfortable. She had felt him grow tense through the ordeal, his muscles expanding and growing harder. A tiny twitch still pulsed at the corner of his one eye as if he was trying to contain his anger. Through it all, he had kept a tight hold on her, kept her safe, as he continued to do now.

"I'll get you to your sisters," John said and was relieved to feel her relax in his arms as he stepped out of the cottage, the anxiousness that had rippled through her finally fading.

He had wanted to reach out and snap Seth's neck for laying a hand on Sorrell, accidentally or not, and he would have if he hadn't had Sorrell in his arms. The more he thought about Sorrell marrying the fool, the angrier he got. But it wasn't for him to say and that angered him all the more.

"What happened?" Willow asked, rushing toward John when he entered the Great Hall with Sorrell in his arms.

"What is it? What's wrong?" Snow asked anxiously, hurrying off the bench with a bit of a struggle.

"After we fell through the roof together and landed on the bed in the cottage, your sister took a punch from Seth meant for me," John said.

Sorrell worried when neither of her sisters responded. They simply stared at her in silence. "I'll explain it all."

"I, for one, can't wait," Snow said with a smile as she sat. "Falling through a roof and landing on a bed with the giant, you always have the most exciting things happen to you, Sorrell."

"Exciting?" Willow questioned with a shake of her head. "You mean foolish, and now this will be the third black eye she's suffered and a bruised cheek along with this one."

"Oh my, are you all right," Snow asked, anxiously.

"I'm fine, nothing to concern yourself with," Sorrell assured Snow.

John wondered how she got the other two black eyes, the wee woman certainly had courage, though her tenaciousness could have had something to do with it as well.

"Please put her down, so I can tend to her cheek and eye," Willow said, seeing how the giant was reluctant to let her go and, if she wasn't mistaken, she didn't think her sister wanted him to.

"I'll put her down next to you, Snow," John said.

"How thoughtful of you." Snow was quick to reach out to Sorrell as soon as she felt her next to her.

Sorrell took her hand and reached her other hand out to take hold of John's arm as he went to turn away.

"Thank you. You kept me safe," Sorrell said and reluctantly let go of him.

"No more roofs," he said and tapped her nose gently.

She smiled and he did to, then he turned and left the Great Hall.

"Be careful, Sorrell," Willow said. "I think you more than like the giant."

"That's nonsense," Sorrell argued. "I barely know him. He has been kind to me, that's all."

"I have to agree with Willow, Sorrell," Snow said. "I could feel how reluctant you were to let him go."

"Ridiculous. Now tend to my face, I have work to see to," Sorrell ordered and her two sisters grinned.

James entered the Great Hall just as Sorrell was about to leave.

"A moment of your time, Sorrell… in my solar," James said and extended his hand out for her to lead the way.

Sorrell did as he asked and, once in his solar, stood in silent defiance.

"Seth extends his apology for accidently hitting you. He made it clear he intended the punch for John. He has requested to meet with you in two days' time. I told him I would speak with you first."

"Three days' time," Sorrell countered. "I'd rather not see him too soon."

James nodded, pleased she had not flatly refused. "I will notify him."

"Is that all?"

"Will it do me any good to tell you to stay off the roofs?" he asked, wondering why he even bothered.

"No," she said bluntly.

"One day, Sorrell, you're going to do something that you can't get yourself out of," James warned.

"Perhaps or perhaps not. Are we done now?"

"Does it hurt?"

For a moment, she didn't know what he meant and then it dawned on her. She raised her hand to gently touch her bruised cheek. "Somewhat, but it will heal."

"I'm sorry and, while it was an accident, I did warn Seth that if he ever intentionally raised a hand to you before or after your wedding, he would regret it, and that you have my word on."

"Thank you, James, I appreciate that," she said and meant it. He had been good to her and her sisters from the moment he had arrived here, except for the forced marriage. Though, to him he had had little choice. His duty, first and foremost, was to the clan.

Seeing how swollen her cheek and eye had grown and how dark the bruising, James said, "Go rest. Thunder rumbles in the distance and rain will be here soon."

"I have one thing I must do, then I will do as you say."

James' mouth fell agape for a moment. "You're actually going to obey me?" Then he gave a quick chuckle.

"Very funny, James," Sorrell said. "I do obey on occ—"

"Rarely," he finished for her. "Not since I've known you have I seen you obey anyone, and I'm grateful that you are obeying me when it comes to this marriage. You do your clan proud."

Sorrell nodded and took her leave without responding. She couldn't imagine spending the rest of her life with a man who allowed his temper to rule him. But how did she escape it when so much depended on her going through with it?

She hurried along through the keep and stepped outside just as a roll of thunder rumbled. She kept a hasty pace. She had to do this. She would not feel right until she did.

She found John stepping off the ladder, repairs finished to the roof they had fallen through.

When she neared him, the first splatter of rain hit her.

John leaned his large body over hers to shield her from the rain, slipped his arm around her, and hurried her into the cottage.

"What are you doing here? You should be in the keep resting," he scolded, taking a gentle hold of her chin to turn her head so he could take a better look at her injury. "That is going to get worse."

"It will heal," she said, curious that he touched her without thought, as if it was his right.

"Like the last two black eyes you got?" he asked, releasing her face.

"I was young. One was an accident and one I got fighting someone bigger than myself."

"And you didn't learn then not to fight someone larger than you?"

She laughed and winced, the side of her face painful. "Learn what? I may have suffered a black eye, but I won the fight."

He should have known it. Sorrell was not one to give up or give in. "You should go rest. I'll clean up in here, hopefully before the person who lives here returns for the day."

"It's not occupied. That's what I came to tell you and to thank you again for protecting me the way you did," she said, only realizing how close they stood, her tunic brushing his shirt.

"I failed to protect you, otherwise I would have saved you from Seth's punch."

"It would have been much worse if you hadn't yanked me away and for that I'm grateful. So, to me you didn't fail. You kept me from suffering a far worse injury."

A damn strong desire to kiss her caught him off guard and he silently cursed his rising manhood for joining in. He forced himself to step away from her. His glance fell on the splintered bed and crushed mattress and he was glad for it. Or else it would tempt him to do something he shouldn't even be thinking of doing.

He shook his head, the image too clear of them naked and his manhood buried deep inside her, and he was relieved for the sudden thought that interrupted his musing. "Why did you have me repair the roof to this place if no one lives here?"

Sorrell spoke rapidly. "I thought if you should stay a few extra days you could use it for yourself. It's better than sleeping in the stable and it will provide you with a modicum of solitude. It's up to you, do as you will."

With that she turned and fled the cottage.

John went to the open door and watched her run off in the rain. She was offering him more than a cottage of solitude. She was offering him a home. She was telling him, in her own way, that he could stay permanently if he wanted to.

That wasn't possible.

Necessity dictated that he would take his leave sooner or later and duty to her clan would have Sorrell abide by the marriage agreement to that wretched man. The thought chewed at his gut, annoyed that he couldn't save her from it.

He turned away and was closing the door when something had him turning back around. He peered outside and caught sight of a figure darting along the cottages, as if he didn't want to be seen, as he followed Sorrell's path.

John rushed out, ready to confront the person, when he spotted John heading toward him and, in a flash, disappeared between two cottages. Though, John gave chase, he stopped when it brought him to the edge of the woods. It was pointless to follow him, the rain growing heavier.

He returned to the cottage and lit a fire in the small fireplace to chase the chill and dry his garments. It troubled him that someone had followed Sorrell. Had this been the first time or had the person been following her for a while, and why? Could she be in danger? Or had that fool Seth sent someone to keep watch on her?

Possibilities kept swirling in his head, continuing to trouble him as he pulled a chair in front of the hearth, reaching out to warm his hands, never realizing he was settling himself in the cottage.

Chapter Six

"I don't care if you don't like it, Melvin, you'll take orders from John or I'll find a new chore for you, cleaning out the fish guts and entails' buckets in the kitchen at the top of my list," Sorrell said.

"But he's not part of this clan," Melvin protested with a wrinkle to his nose as if he could smell the stink of the new chore.

"And yet, he does more chores in a day than you do in a week. Now what will it be? Take orders from John or clean the fish gut and entails' buckets."

"He best not be ordering me about all the time," Melvin said.

"John is a man of few words," Sorrell said.

John did talk with her, but then she gave him little choice. She noticed he said few if any words to others. In the last two days, he had spent most of the day on the chores she had assigned him. He took his morning meal alone and ate supper in the Great Hall sometimes alone and sometimes with her and her sisters. He never said much, a word here or there, but she had noticed how well he listened, smiling or chuckling just when you thought he had drifted off and had been paying no heed to the conversation.

She was also glad he had yet to take his leave. She enjoyed talking with him. He was a man of intelligence and it made her continue to wonder about him. Who was he? Where did he come from? Was he hiding something? Where had the shackle come from? The shackle bothered her every time she looked at it. It didn't belong on him and she itched to remove it. But it wasn't her place, though maybe he needed a little encouragement.

Melvin brought her out of her musings.

"You're right about that. He hardly speaks a word," Melvin said, scratching his head. "I wonder why?"

"Why don't you ask him," Sorrell suggested.

Melvin shook his head. "No. No. The man has a right to his privacy."

Sorrell grinned. Melvin was afraid of John and she was good with that, since Melvin worked when he was with John, too fearful not to.

"Go find John and see what chores he has for you today," Sorrell said.

Melvin turned, mumbling beneath his breath, his gait slow and reluctant.

Sorrell knew where John was… at the smithy, seeing to sharpening some of the tools.

"Melvin doesn't appear eager to do his chores."

Sorrell turned and smiled at James. There were days when she looked quick at him that she could see their father in him and not just in his features, but the way he walked with distinction and purpose that was so like their da. It was those times she was glad her mum had welcomed him into the family, and even though she argued with him on occasion, she was glad to have him as her brother.

"Melvin is never happy to do his chores, but he'll do them now that John is giving the orders," Sorrell said.

"I wish John would remain with us. He works hard and never complains and he's probably good with a weapon. He would be an asset to the clan. Unfortunately, I don't think he's ready to settle down. He seems like a man searching for something."

Sorrell thought the same, though hadn't wanted to admit it. He may have taken shelter in the cottage, but he hadn't done anything to make it truly his, nothing to call it home.

"I came bearing good news," James said.

"Do I dare hope you decided against my marriage to Seth MacCannish?"

"If only there was another way, I would gladly see it done," James said. "At least, you have a reprieve from receiving your intended tomorrow. He will not be able to see you. He must go away for a few days and he will send notice upon his return."

Sorrell folded her hands in prayer, kissed them, then raised them to the heavens. "Prayers do get answered."

"Aye, sometimes they do," James agreed and gave a nod, his eyes on her injury. "Your bruise heals well and fast."

"Thanks to John. If it hadn't been for his quick action, Seth could have shattered my cheek," she said, pleased that the bruising was already beginning to fade and she suffered little pain.

"Another reason, I'll be sorry to see him leave. He often saves you from yourself." James chuckled as he walked off.

"Funny, James, funny," Sorrell called after him and his chuckle turned to a hardy laugh.

Talking about John, she decided it would be wise to see that Melvin had followed her orders. Although, she wouldn't mind the opportunity to see John. He hadn't been at supper last night and when she had checked with Dorrit this morning, she had told her that he had collected supper to take to his cottage and the same with the morning meal. She had been relieved to learn that, since she worried he might have left without a word.

Maybe it would be better that way, when the time came. She didn't know what she would say to him when he bid her good-bye. She had grown accustomed to having him around the last few days and looked forward to seeing him.

You're growing to care for him.

Her sisters had told her that more than a few times and maybe she was, but he was a good man and why wouldn't she care what happened to a good man? It was nothing more than that. She couldn't let herself think it could be more than that. While she wanted to believe that somehow this union with Seth MacCannish could be avoided, it wasn't likely. This was one time she feared her fate was sealed.

She approached the smithy's place. It was set apart from the cottages, the blazing fires making it too dangerous to sit close to other structures for fear of catching fire. She spotted John using the grinding wheel to sharpen an axe. His sleeves were rolled up and his forearms and face held a fine sheen of sweat.

She sometimes wondered what he would look like without the bushy beard, since the rest of his features were striking on their own, especially his blue eyes, so intense in color, though at times icy as if he himself had turned cold.

The grinding wheel slowed and John turned. "Is there something you want, Sorrell?"

It wasn't lost on her that his hearing was good, knowing when someone approached, but it might be more exceptional since he had heard her over the sound of the grinding wheel.

"I wanted to make sure Melvin came to you to learn what chores you assigned him today," she said, entering the smithy's domain and looking around. Not that she wasn't familiar with it, having been there a few times.

"He did and I sent him to repair the stable fence, a minor chore."

He stood and took the sharpened axe and placed it on the bench with several tools that looked to have already been sharpened. It was when he drew his hand away that she noticed the iron shackle had rubbed a section of his skin red.

"You need to rid yourself of that thing," she said, pointing to the shackle.

"In time."

"It's rubbed your skin raw."

"The skin isn't rubbed raw, just irritated."

"A good enough reason to rid yourself of it," she insisted.

"Let it be, Sorrell."

The commanding authority in his voice surprised her, but then she had reminded him about the shackle several times. She should let it be, but she hated to see that it had rubbed his skin red and would turn raw soon if he continued this work. Besides, she was curious how it had come to be on his wrist.

"One good whack on the pin and the shackle would be gone," she said and reached out with two hands for the hammer on the nearby table.

She lifted it with a quick force and her eyes went wide as the weight of the solid hammer sent her tumbling back.

John lunged forward, his arm shooting down to slip beneath her back and stop her from hitting the ground as his other hand grabbed the hammer so that it wouldn't pound against her chest when she came to an abrupt halt.

"That's a heavy hammer," she said as John took it from her and placed it on the ground.

He leaned forward, his nose nearly touching hers, his blue eyes intent on her green ones.

His breath was warm and smelled of mint and his lips peeked out from his bushy beard and all she could think was… how his lips would feel on hers. The thought sent a mixture of excitement and fear through her. Could it be possible? Did she care more for him than she had thought? Her heart skipped a beat or two as she waited, or did she hope he would kiss her?

"You are a danger to yourself, woman," he said and brought her to her feet.

He turned away annoyed with himself for almost losing his senses and kissing her. He should have never brought his face so close to hers. Her lips tempted, particularly the bottom one. It was plumper than the top one and he ached to nip at it.

"Sorrell."

She turned to see Willow hurrying toward her.

"Is something wrong? Is Snow all right?" Sorrell asked hurrying to her sister.

"Nothing is wrong. Snow actually expressed interest in making some wreaths for the keep. Something she used to love to do. Would you have time to collect some branches for her?"

"Of course, I'll go get them now," Sorrell said.

"Good, she'll be glad to hear it," Willow said and hurried off.

"I'll take you," John said, walking toward her.

"It's not necessary. Finish your chores."

"You're not going into the woods alone," he said unable to stop the command in his voice.

"I don't recall you having the authority to tell me what I can and cannot do," she said.

"You're right, I don't, but since you have a propensity for getting yourself into difficult situations, I think it's best if I go with you."

"What trouble can I get into gathering branches?"

He grinned and shook his head. "I don't know, but with you anything is possible."

"John, we've got a problem."

John and Sorrell turned to see Melvin walking their way.

"What problem?" John asked.

"The fence broke while I was fixing it and one of the cows got out."

John scratched his head. "The fence broke while you were fixing it?"

"Fell right apart," Melvin said, nodding to confirm it twice. "And that cow just ambled on off."

"And you didn't go after her?" Sorrell asked.

"I came and got John, since he's the one who I take orders from, just like you told me," Melvin said with a smirk.

John's hand closed around Sorrell's arm when she went to rush past him, and Melvin wisely took a couple of steps back.

"Show me where the cow ambled off to," he said to Melvin, then stepped in front of Sorrell. "Wait for me here and I'll go with you into the woods." He turned a stern eye on her. "Don't dare go without me."

He released her and followed Melvin, calling back, "Heed my words, Sorrell."

Heed his words? Who did he think he was talking to her as if she should obey him? He wasn't her husband and even if he was she wouldn't be obeying him. She wasn't good at taking orders from anyone. Her father had grown frustrated with her through the years when she had continued to do as she pleased. She had known at times she should have obeyed her da, yet she hadn't, and she didn't know why. It was as if she had to find things out for herself, see things for herself, learn for herself.

John wanted to see her kept safe, she understood that, but she had gone into the woods by herself countless times without incident. She wasn't about to wait for an escort now. It was only a few branches she was going to collect. She would probably be back before he returned.

She took off for the woods, eager to see the chore done.

Chapter Seven

"What's the rush?" Melvin complained.

John was ready to strangle Melvin. He now understood why Sorrell called him a lazy arse. The man barely moved. He'd walk, stop, scratch his straggly beard, then take a few more steps. And John knew why the fence fell apart. Melvin hadn't paid heed to his instructions and had caused the collapse of a whole side of fencing.

With the cow returned to the pen, if he left Melvin alone to complete the chore, the cow would probably escape once again. He couldn't have that, and yet, he was worried about Sorrell. He had no doubt that she would pay no attention to what he had told her, and why should she? He had no say over her, from what he saw, no one did. However, his concern had grown when he had seen that figure following her the other day. He hadn't seen anyone following her since, but that didn't mean the person who shadowed her wasn't still around.

She was vulnerable in the woods alone and he didn't like that thought.

"Hurry and finish this with me and you're done for the day," John said.

"No more chores after this?" Melvin asked skeptical, but hopeful.

"Not if you don't hurry and get this done with me," John confirmed and was actually surprised at how fast Melvin could move.

He'd get it finished quickly and be off to find Sorrell, since there was not a chance in hell she hadn't gone into the woods.

***

Sorrell had a good pile of slim branches and twigs collected. It hadn't taken long even with the few times she had stopped to enjoy the peacefulness and the rich autumn scent of the forest. The trees that dropped their leaves were nearly bare, providing a winter blanket for the ground. The squirrels were still busy rushing about collecting and storing food, which was a sure sign that it would be a cold winter.

She was glad she had worn her wool cloak, the autumn air growing colder by the day, another sure sign of winter's early arrival. She rubbed her arms to chase away the chill and was about to gather what she had collected and be on her way, keeping with her plan to return before John found her gone. Melvin would have kept him busy with his slow gait and manner, giving her plenty of time to get done. She stopped just before leaning over to snatch up the pile of branches when she spied a slim branch that had broken off and lay dangling off a larger one. Snow would love it, since it would make a beautiful wreath.

A quick tug would free it, since it was already dangling off the larger branch. Sorrell walked over to it and realized it was a bit higher off the ground than she had thought. For anyone else it would be an easy reach, for her short height, not so much.

She smiled when she thought how easily John could pluck it down and almost regretted not waiting for him. But she was used to doing for herself, not depending on others, and she'd do so now.

Sorrell looked around, giving her options thought, and after seeing a good-sized boulder not far off, worked out a plan. If she gave herself a running start, jumped on the boulder and lunged at the branch from it, she should be able to reach the dangling branch. All she had to do was roll when she hit the ground, and she should be fine. She had done something similar before, so this shouldn't prove difficult.

She took off her cloak and dropped it by the pile of branches, gave one last thought to her plan and took off running. She grinned as her hand reached out and caught the dangling branch with ease, but her grin vanished in a flash as the big branch, the slim one dangled from, not only came crashing down along with her but landed on her one leg, trapping it beneath it.

Thankfully, she hadn't hit the ground too hard, though she had felt a jolt rock her body and she worried what kind of damage the branch might have done to her leg, though she felt no pain.

After resting for a moment and gathering her strength, she raised her free leg, positioning her foot against the branch and giving it a shove, but it wouldn't budge. She tried again and again until she was breathless. Annoyed, and fatigued from her attempt to free herself, she raised herself up on her elbows to see if something could possibly be blocking the branch.

"The branch is caught on a rock. You're not moving it, lass."

Sorrell startled at the sound of an unfamiliar voice and tensed when the man came into view. One look told her that he wasn't one to trust. His garments needed washing, as did the rest of him, particularly his hands, grime covered both sides and dirt was caked thick under his nails. His hair had been sheared and she suspected it was that way due to a bout with lice. It was his face that told her the most. He wore a snickering smile and he licked his lips as his eyes roamed over her.

"You got yourself in a fine way," he said.

"Could you move the branch off me?" she asked, hoping that he would at least free her. That way she had a good chance to defend herself.

He stepped closer and sat on the big branch near her leg and rubbed at his chin, thick with stubble, no doubt the lice having gotten to his beard that had to have been cut off along with his hair.

"I don't know about that. I haven't had a woman in a while and never have I had a fine woman like you. I think I'll have some fun with you first and poke you a couple of times."

Sorrell still had hold of the branch that had gotten her into this mess and she whipped it up, swinging it back and forth in his face. He fell back off the branch when she caught his cheek with one of the swipes, leaving a red welt on it.

"I was going to be nice and treat you gentle, but not now," he said, getting to his feet and turning an angry sneer on her.

She swung the branch again. "Come near me and I'll bite that tiny cock of yours right off in one chomp."

"I ain't got no tiny cock," he said affronted.

"Right you are, since I'll be the one who took it from you," Sorrell threatened and demonstrated with a strong chomp of her teeth.

"I'd run if I were you. She's got a mighty mean bite."

Sorrell was relieved to hear John's voice. Even though she was confident she could handle the situation, she wasn't sure about freeing herself of the branch.

The man stared at John for a minute, his eyes intent on him, then he took off running, and Sorrell smiled.

John dropped down on one knee beside her, though he looked in the distance now and again to make sure the dastardly man hadn't returned.

"Are you hurt?" he asked, gently brushing dried leaves and twigs out of her hair, the mass of stubborn red curls having escaped from its strip of cloth.

"I don't think so. I'm not in any pain."

"You couldn't wait, could you?" he asked, sounding as if he lightly scolded.

She grinned. "I'm stubborn."

"On that we agree. Now lie still until I tell you otherwise. Can you do that?"

"I'll do as you say."

"Your word on it?" he asked.

"You have my word," she agreed, deciding that his time, she was better off being wise rather than foolish.

John stood and walked around the fallen branch. He squatted down in a spot close to her trapped leg and studied it a moment. Then stood again, leaned over, and with one swift lift and toss with his two hands, he had the branch off her.

Sorrell breathed a sigh of relief that she was sure he heard.

"I'm going to touch your leg. Tell me if you feel any pain," John said and squatted down on his haunches.

"Aye," she said and tensed when she felt his finger gently stroke her leg.

"That hurts?"

"No, your hand has a slight chill," she said, thankful for the excuse, since it was his fingers caressing her leg so gently that had brought on the response.

Never had a man touched her naked skin and she imagined she would be in trouble if her intended found out, but she didn't care. She enjoyed the feel of his tender touch. She doubted Seth MacCannish would be that tender.

"You were lucky," John said. "Your leg landed in a sizeable gap in the ground and saved it from being crushed. I'm going to help you to stand. Tell me if you feel any pain anywhere." He eased his arm underneath her and, as he raised her gently, said, "Grab onto my arm."

She curled her slim arm around his thick one and rested her cheek against it when a dizzy spell struck her.

"What's wrong?"

"A bit lightheaded that's all."

"It's enough," he said and laid her back down. He went and retrieved her cloak from where she had dropped it on the ground, raised her up again, and draped her cloak over her shoulders.

The next thing Sorrell knew, she was up in his muscled arms and tucked snugly against his chest.

"I'm going to get you home so your sisters can look after you and make sure you suffered no harm."

Sorrell didn't argue, since she remained a bit lightheaded, but as he carried her through the woods, it gradually dissipated.

"Feeling all right?" he asked, casting a glance down at her.

She wasn't sure, since she wanted to reach up and trace his lips with her finger and feel their warmth and smoothness. She was about to shake her head and chase the thought away when she recalled the question and changed it to a nod, as if she also confirmed to herself that it was a perfectly natural thing to want to touch his lips.

"Tell me something," he said. "Would you really have bitten the fellow's tiny cock off?"

"Without hesitation, though I doubt he would have gotten close enough for me to do that. But I would have waited until he whipped out his manhood and the branch I held would have made a perfect spear. I would have jabbed it hard right in his—"

"I get the picture." John winced, then smiled and shook his head. "I was right. Anything is possible with you."

***

"What happened this time?" Willow asked when John entered the Great Hall carrying Sorrell.

"Sorrell got hurt again?" Snow asked, aware of who Willow inquired about. "Is she all right?"

"I'll let you explain. I have work to do," he whispered and set her on the bench next to Snow and bid the sisters good day.

"I'm good. There's nothing to worry about, a little mishap that's all," Sorrell explained, not wanting her sisters to worry needlessly and cast a quick glance at John's retreating back.

Willow summoned one of the servants. "Some hot cider." She settled herself on the bench across the table from her two sisters. "Tell us what happened."

The telling took some time, since questions and laughter interrupted Sorrell's words.

"It sounds funny now and thank God we can laugh about it," Willow said. "Are you sure you suffered no injury?"

"The abundance of fallen leaves on the ground cushioned my fall and the gap in the ground saved my leg from serious injury. I may have a few aches later but that's about it."

"You should have listened to John when he told you to wait for him," Willow scolded lightly.

"I've been in the woods countless times and nothing has happened," Sorrell reminded.

"Because Father had had enough warriors to post sentries and we usually went into the woods together. Things aren't the same now, Sorrell, even as much as we want them to be." Her glance drifted to Snow as did Sorrell's.

"I know you are both looking at me and I'll not have your sympathy," Snow warned. "It is not easy being blind, but having no choice, I either do my best or surrender to limitations and that I will never do."

"If only—"

"No, Willow, there are no if only. There is only now," Snow said. "What we have now is what matters, nothing else. And the most important thing we have is... one another. And while I wish arranged marriages weren't necessary for either of you, I am pleased that James intends to keep you both close so that we may see each other often. I'm also pleased that there'll be no arranged marriage for me. I would be so terrified to wed a man, a stranger, and whose face I couldn't see."

"That will not happen, Snow," Sorrell said. "James feels you will be safe and protected here in your home. You need not worry about such a fate."

"I make it easy for James, since no one would want a blind wife," Snow said, "and for that I'm relieved. But I must know one thing, Sorrell."

"What is that?"

"Where do you get the courage to do the things you do?" Snow asked, her head turned to her sister as if she could see her clearly.

"It's not about courage. It's about surviving. Remember how relieved and pleased Mum was that we all survived the fire and how she told us to survive no matter what or we'd never have a chance to have a good life she knew we were all destined to have."

"That's right, she did say that," Willow said, recalling the memory.

"So, we'll survive and someway, somehow, destiny will find us," Sorrell said and squeezed both sisters' hands.

***

"Please. Please. I won't say a word. I will tell no one who you are, my—"

John's fist pounded into the man's face and he heard a crack. Blood ran from his now crooked nose.

"It is what you intended to do to the woman that got you a beating. Though, I would advise you not tell a soul who or where I am or I will hunt you down as I did today and kill you."

The man turned frightened eyes on John and he spit out the blood that had run into his mouth from his nose. "I will tell no one. You have my word. No one, but it makes little difference since your father rescinded the reward for any knowledge as to your whereabouts or for you to be returned to him, alive or dead, about a month ago."

John didn't know if he should trust that bit of information, even though Erland had told him the same thing. "So you missed your chance to gain a hefty sum, Daggit."

Daggit looked away, not saying a word, as if by doing so he wouldn't have to admit his guilt.

"You will leave here and never show your face again," John ordered, thinking it seemed far too coincidental that a common thief, known to his clan, should suddenly show up here. And it was pointless to try and get any credible information from the man, since Daggit could weave a tale of lies with ease.

"Aye, aye, my—"

John struck him again and the back of the man's head flew back and hit the trunk of the tree he was tied to, knocking him unconscious.

John looked at his bloody swollen knuckles and went to the small stream, a few short steps from the tree, and washed them clean. He let his hands linger in the running water for a few moments, the cold numbing the soreness.

He returned to the tree to find the man still hadn't come to. It hadn't taken him long to track Daggit down. He'd been more furious at the thought of what the man had intended to do to Sorrell, than that he had recognized him. It wasn't lost to John that Daggit would somehow use seeing him here to his advantage. The man would sell his soul for a coin if possible.

He freed Daggit of the ties, letting his body drop to the ground. He heard him moan and nudged his slumped body with his booted-foot.

"Be warned, if you don't do as I say, you'll not live to see another sunrise."

***

"It is me. John," he said, not wanting to startle Snow when he entered the Great Hall and saw that she sat alone at a table, staring at the hearth as if mesmerized by the flames.

"You have a light step for a giant," Snow said, turning in his direction.

"A skill I acquired," he said, stopping in front of her.

"Out of necessity?"

"You might say that," he said and placed the bundle of branches he held on the table in front of her. "These are for you. The branches Sorrell had collected. Is she feeling well?"

Snow's face lit with delight. "You went and got them, and aye, she is fine." She reached her hand out and touched his arm, her hand traveling down to take hold of his hand to thank him.

A wince escaped him before he could stop it, though it didn't matter since Snow was exploring his swollen hands with delicate touches.

"That must pain you," she said, her face grimacing. "Though, I dare say the other fellow probably suffered far worse." She tilted her head back and stared up at him. "You went after him, didn't you?"

"You're observant for one who is blind."

"Even those with sight can be blind," Snow said.

John thought of his father. "Another wise observation."

"Sorrell will bombard you with questions when she sees that hand."

"When doesn't she bombard me with questions or chatter?"

"Not many men can tolerate her…" Snow scrunched her brow as she searched for a way to describe her sister.

"Powerfully independent spirit," John said, having no trouble finding the words.

Snow smiled. "An accurate description of Sorrell. She has always been that way, even as a child. She often drove our mum and da crazy with worry. It was as if she had to learn for herself, no one could tell her anything. She had to experience it all on her own. The more she learned the more independent she grew. Mum would often say that it would take a strong man to love Sorrell, and she hadn't meant in the physical sense."

"Seth MacCannish isn't that man," John said before he realized it was not his place to say.

"No, he's not," Snow agreed. "I pray that destiny finds that man my mum spoke of before a dreadful mistake is made."

"I should go. I have work to finish," John said.

"Thank you for retrieving the branches and thank you for looking after my sister. I worry far less about her with you around," Snow said.

Her words rang in his head as he stepped out of the keep to find a light snow falling. Winter was eager to arrive and he certainly couldn't be here when it did. But if he wasn't, who would keep Sorrell safe?

He cursed himself for letting himself feel for Sorrell. He had felt for no one these past two years, trusted no one. How was it he felt for Sorrell more than he wanted to? How had she made him care? When he had come upon her and Daggit in the woods and had heard what he intended to do to her, rage had soared in him until he had all he could do to keep from lunging at the man and killing him.

It was recognizing Daggit that had stopped him, and the courage Sorrell had displayed. She hadn't shown an ounce of fear. She had thought all along that she would escape the man, though how she would have freed her leg was another matter. He had purposely let Daggit go with every intention of hunting him down and beating him senseless.

He walked to the smithy's place and gathered the tools he had sharpened and took them to the shed where they were kept. By the time he was done, the snow had turned a bit heavier and the wind had picked up, swirling the abundant flakes around him.

No more work would get done today and with that thought in mind he headed to his cottage. He hoped Sorrell was tucked safe in the keep, resting, but somehow he doubted that.

He was proven right when he opened the door and found her in his cottage.

Chapter Eight

"Where have you been?" Sorrell demanded. "I have been searching all over for you and everyone I asked had not seen you since earlier."

He had never seen fear in Sorrell's eyes. Not once, in any situation she had faced, had she shown an ounce of it. But he saw it now, her green eyes overflowed with it. Fear had gripped her when she had failed to find him.

Did she care that much for him? And was he going to keep denying to himself that as much as he shouldn't, there was something that stirred feelings in him for this wee woman?

"It's snowing?" she asked, realizing his cloak was dusted with it. She hurried over to him and pulled off his cloak, tossing it on the chest near the door. "Sit by the fire and warm yourself, then you will tell me where you've been."

She wouldn't let go of it. She would beat him with endless questions until she got what she wanted. He found her determination was one of the things he admired about her, since he understood it, possessing the trait himself.

Sorrell gave him a light shove toward the hearth. "Get over there and get warm."

John went, letting only the slightest smile escape, and sat on the chair near the hearth.

"What happened to your hand?" Sorrell demanded, when she spotted the swelling. She reached out and took his hand gently in hers, looking closely at his injury.

Her fingers ran over his swollen knuckles so faintly it felt like a feather being brushed across them and he had to fight to keep his passion at a low stir. Unfortunately, it was a losing battle, since he foolishly spread his legs when she stepped to move closer to him, and she slipped between them as she continued to examine his hand more closely.

He cautioned himself to send her away now before it was too late, before he did something he had no right to do, but he ignored his warning. He wanted her close where he could easily see the swell of her breasts, their size a perfect fit for his hands and the way her hard nipples pressed against the wool cloth. He could almost taste the hard buds in his mouth and how his tongue would roll over them.

"You went after him, didn't you?" Sorrell asked in a whisper.

Her question chased away the tempting images to his relief and also his disappointment. "He deserved more than the beating I gave him."

"You didn't have to do that."

"Aye, I did," John said, not able to take his eyes off her lips, particularly the plump one. He so badly wanted to tease it with a few nips before kissing her senseless.

"You are a good man, John," Sorrell said, softly and released his hand.

Not wise, John, not wise.

He didn't listen to the warning in his head, he raised his hands and rested both of them on her narrow waist, though he had the sense to warn her. "Make no mistake, Sorrell, I'm not a good man."

She pressed her fingers to his lips. "I won't hear that from you. I know in my heart you are a good man and nothing you say will change that."

"Then maybe you need to see it for yourself." He gave her a gentle yank and she stumbled against him, her face coming to rest close to his. So close that all he had to do…

His teeth caught her plump bottom lip and he nipped along it softly, tugging and teasing, relishing every playful nip before finally claiming her lips in a kiss that flamed his senses and aroused his manhood much too fast.

He stole the breath from her and Sorrell didn't care. She had never been kissed and had never dreamed it could be so wonderful. The way his teeth had played with her bottom lip had sent a crazy rush of flutters through her and settled a dampness between her legs that she hadn't expected. Nor had she expected it to go from damp to wet when he kissed her.

She should stop him. She should leave and not look back, then his tongue slid into her mouth. Instinct and desire took over and she cupped the back of his head and held tight as she welcomed him and joined in the kiss, tentative at first, but not for long. She found it natural to respond to him, to let her desire take flight and simply enjoy.

His hands roamed down along the gentle curve of her hips and around to her backside, cupping her cheeks and giving them a squeeze. They were firm and her waist narrow and though she was petite there was a strength he could feel in her. And the way she eagerly returned his kisses let him know she would be equally eager to join with him.

Stop this madness, John. Stop it before it's too late.

The warning in his head went unheeded.

He wanted Sorrell with a heated desire he had never felt for any woman. He wanted to strip her bare, carry her to the bed and couple with her, and once he did she would belong to him forever. He'd never let her go.

The thought returned some sanity to him. She was promised to another. She had a duty to do. He had no right. And that's what troubled him the most. He had no right to Sorrell and he had to let these foolish thoughts go, and Sorrell as well. He eased his mouth off hers and rested his brow to her chest, not a wise choice, feeling her breasts brush his heated cheeks. Thank God they weren't bare or he would feast on them.

She rested her face on the top of his head and felt a heavy sadness descend over her. Intimacy with him could never be and the thought brought a sheen of tears to her eyes.

"Sorrell," he whispered and raised his head and his stomach plunged seeing her green eyes glisten with unshed tears. Was she sorry for what had just happened between them?

She cupped his jaw, her small fingers disappearing into his thick beard. "How I wish things were different. How I wish I wer…"

"No," John said, pushing her away, thinking how this could feel so right, yet be all wrong.

He could just poke her and be done with it. That's what he had done these past two years with women who had wanted to warm his bed. But Sorrell was different. She wasn't a quick poke and he wasn't ready nor was it the time for anything more.

He did what he had to do. "I'm no good for you, Sorrell. I'm not who you think I am. I want nothing more at this moment than to strip you bare and take you to my bed and poke you until you're too weak to stand. Leave now before it's too late." He pointed to the door.

She stared at him, not moving. "I'd rather it be you who took my virginity than Seth MacCannish."

Her words were like a well-placed punch to his gut and a stimulant to his manhood. A low growl rumbled in his throat as he got to his feet. The woman had no good sense and no fear. He stepped close to her, lowering his face to hers until their noses almost touched. "If I took your virginity, you'd be mine and no other would ever touch you. And you would obey me." He took a step back. "Now get out before you make a mistake you will long regret."

Sorrell went to the door and opened it and before stepping out she turned to him. "Will you long regret sending me away?" She didn't wait for an answer, she left and didn't look back.

John regretted it the instant she walked out the door. He long ago stopped wishing and hoping things would be different. Things were what they were and you either dealt with them or let them beat you down. His life had been hell these past two years and he wasn't sure what future, if any, he had. And he wouldn't drag Sorrell down into the fiery pit to suffer with him. She had a loving family and he couldn't give her that. He couldn't give her anything. He wasn't even sure if he could give her love.

It was time for him to leave.

***

Sorrell rarely shed a tear even when young, though she had shed several when each of her parents died. The thought of never seeing and talking to her parents again had been unbearable and while time had helped ease the pain, it never truly went away.

She felt that way now about John. He would go away and she would never see him again and her heart felt as if it shattered into thousands of pieces that she would never be able to put back together again. He was a good man, and though he tried hard to convince her otherwise, he never would. From the first moment they met he had protected her and he did so now, sending her away before she could make a mistake she would regret.

But would she?

Somehow, in some crazy way, she had come to care for this man she barely knew. That was one thing he'd been right about. She didn't know him. He was still a stranger, and yet, he did not feel like one. It felt more like they had known each other for some time. Trusted each other. Loved each other.

Love?
One didn't find love that fast.
A preposterous notion. Simply not possible.
"Sorrell, are you all right?"
Sorrell shut her eyes briefly. At the moment, she wasn't interested in hearing Willow sprout sensible advice.
"I heard you crying as you rushed in here to Mum's solar. You so rarely cry, I was worried."
Guilt tore at Sorrell for feeling that way about Willow when she was concerned for her. She wiped at her eyes, annoyed at herself for crying, and turned to Willow.
"I'm fine."
Willow hurried over to her, sitting on the footstool in front of Sorrell's chair. "You're not fine if you've been crying. What's wrong?"
Willow so reminded Sorrell of their mum, always concerned for others, always able to see both sides of things, always able to comfort, and a voice so soft and soothing that for a moment she thought her mum sat in front of her.
"I think I have feelings for John," she confessed to her own disbelief.
Willow turned a gentle smile on her sister. "I think you do too."
Sorrell drew her head back, surprised. "You do? Why?"
"Do you remember Mum telling us that love was impossible to hide?"
"I do, since I told her I could hide anything and it not be found."
"And Mum found everything you ever hid," Willow said with a chuckle.
"But I'm not talking about love. I only realized—admitted to you—that I had feelings for him."
"A prelude to love, and just because you have only realized it, doesn't mean that it hasn't shown on you."

"I don't understand. I didn't do anything different. I've been me all along," Sorrell argued.

"Let me tell you how you've been *you* since his arrival. You seek him out every day—"

"To tell him what chores need doing."

"And do you need to stay with him while he does them and talk endlessly with him? Or give him a cottage to use while here? Or tell Dorrit to feed him well? Or worry when you haven't seen him for a couple of hours? Or talk endlessly about him to me and Snow? Or smile more than you've smiled in quite a while? Or look at him with eyes that—"

"He kissed me and I didn't stop him. I didn't want to stop him. And I liked it so very, very much."

A sadness filled Willow's heart for her sister. "I wish—"

"I know. I wish the same," Sorrell said and a lone tear slipped down her cheek.

Willow stood and squeezed in the chair with Sorrell, wrapping her arm around her, and the two snuggled together.

"I'm so sorry, Sorrell."

"I would prefer John to be my destiny, rather than Seth. But he chases me away for my own good, so he says, and maybe it is so. I don't know anything about him. He warns me he's not a kind man. Instinct tells me he is, but, I wonder if I am blind to him because I feel something for this man. Something I have never felt before. Something that aches and tugs at me and won't let go. And yet, there is no point to pursuing it when my fate is already sealed."

Willow hugged her tight. "It doesn't hurt to have hope."

Sorrell laughed lightly. "You, the sensible one, telling me there might be hope, when James has made it clear how dire it is that you and I wed the men chosen for us?"

"I like to think what Mum said was true. That destiny would find us one day and we'd have a good life. Maybe destiny brought John here and somehow destiny will find a way to bring you both together."

"I expected only sensible advice from you," Sorrell admitted, grateful her sister had given her words of hope, even if that hope would never see fruition.

"I'm not sensible. I adapt because most of the time there isn't any recourse, but that doesn't mean I can't dream or hope for myself and others."

"You've always been so unselfish."

"I've had no choice. I'm the oldest and Mum depended on me to help. With you and Snow not even two years apart, and me six years, it was simply expected of me. And you, dear sister, were a handful."

For the first time, Sorrell realized how little freedom Willow had had when they were young. She had been like a second mother to her and Snow.

"But this isn't about me. It's about you and John," Willow said.

"There is no John and me. I am to wed Seth MacCannish." Sorrell scrunched her face and stuck out her tongue.

Willow laughed.

"What am I missing?" Snow asked as she appeared in the open doorway and felt her way in with her hands.

"Sorrell thinks she is falling in love," Willow said, joy filling her every word.

"It's John. I knew it," Snow said and Willow hurried out of the chair to help Snow to sit in the one next to Sorrell. She went to return to the footstool, but Sorrell waved her over to share her chair once again.

"Shhh, no one can know," Sorrell ordered. "And I don't know what it is I feel for him."

"He kissed her," Willow whispered.

"Oh my, how did it feel?" Snow asked, eager to hear.

"It was magical," Sorrell said with a dramatic sigh.

"I'm so pleased for you," Snow said, her wide smile proof of it.

Willow and Sorrell looked at each other, both feeling for Snow, since they both knew it was unlikely she would ever know what it was like to be kissed. And that thought hurt both of them.

"What will you do?" Snow asked.

"There's nothing I can do. I'm duty-bound to wed Seth MacCannish, and nothing will change that, no matter how much I object."

"You never know what might happen," Snow said, hoping for a miracle for Sorrell.

"Destiny may step in," Willow encouraged.

"Miracles do happen," Snow said with a grin. "One just did. Willow said something that was not at all sensible."

The three sisters laughed and Sorrell thanked the heavens for them. She could never survive the heartache of this ordeal without them.

***

The next morning, she thought to avoid John, but she was braver than that. She would not hide from him. Besides, she tried to convince herself that what she felt for him was probably nothing more than a young woman's fancy. After all, no man had ever attempted to kiss her. That wasn't completely true. When she was young there was a lad who thought to try, though later she had learned it was a challenge he had accepted. He had suffered a split lip when he had tried and when she found out it had been a challenge; she gave him a bloody nose.

She would get over this as she had done with many things. What choice did she have? She would be sensible and adapt as Willow always did.

The air was chilled as she walked through the village, and she was glad she wore her wool cloak. She intended to find John and see that the work on the new shed was well on the way to being done.

Her steps slowed when she spotted him working. The shed was the last of the two to be rebuilt that had been destroyed in a mysterious fire. Her heart began to thump faster and a flutter settled in her stomach. She hadn't expected to feel this thrilled to see him.

If she felt such joy after only having seen him last night, how would she feel if she never got to see him again? Her stomach roiled so badly she thought she would lose her breakfast.

"Are you all right, Sorrell? You're pale. Come sit down," John said and took hold of her arm to walk her to a bench by the storage shed.

Sorrell hadn't even heard John approach, though she had felt the gentleness of his touch and she welcomed it. Sure signs this was no passing fancy she felt for him.

Sorrell was never one to hide from a difficult situation. She had always faced them straight on and so she spoke bluntly and honestly as she always did. "I enjoyed the brief kiss we shared and it upsets me to think we'll never share another. It is a truth I must face, and you were right to send me away. It is proof you are a good man, though you stubbornly refuse to acknowledge it. However, I need you to know something. I will never regret that kiss. I will tuck the lovely memory away to think on when I need it the most."

He had never expected that from her, but then he should have known better than to think she would have handled it any other way. She'd been blunt and honest about everything since the day he had met her. It had taken a bit getting used to since he was accustomed to lies slipping off tongues far too easily. It made spending time with her that more desirable.

The problem was… how would he ever see and talk with Sorrell day in and day out without kissing her again, and remain sane? He couldn't. He would wind up taking her to his bed and whether she intended it or not, her words had let him know that she wouldn't refuse him.

"I will take my leave soon," he said.

"You don't have to leave, unless you want to."

I want you far too much. A dangerous thought and a good reason to leave.

"It's time for me to go," he said. It would do him no good to stay. Besides, she was honest with him, but he was far from honest with her. "I will finish the shed, since Melvin will never get it done before winter sets in, then I will take my leave. Two days, no more."

"As you wish," she said and stood and walked off, annoyed that an empty hollow ache settled in her heart and tears tickled at her eyes. This was for the best. It had to be this way. So why did she feel as though she had just lost someone she loved?

Chapter Nine

Sorrell kept herself busy. It was the only way to keep John out of her thoughts, and that she had to fight to do that annoyed her. And that her stomach churned every time she thought about him leaving annoyed her even more. If this was love, she wasn't good with it. Love should be simple not complex. But this situation was anything but simple.

It wouldn't be if she wasn't obligated to wed Seth MacCannish. Or would it? She didn't know if John felt the same about her as she did him. And how did she truly feel about him? He may have kissed her, but she wasn't foolish enough to believe one kiss meant you were in love. She might not have any experience when it came to men, but she knew enough to know that a man often favored a poke but nothing beyond that.

Was that what John looked for... a quick poke and nothing more?

She groaned at her endless thoughts that got her nowhere and at the aches in her body. It was mid-afternoon and she was feeling the consequences of the tasks she had set for herself. Her arms ached terribly from digging in the kitchen garden, though she had more pounded away at the soil than dug. Then there was the vigorous rub down she had given Prince, her horse, who had thoroughly enjoyed it. After that she had decided to see that a bed was brought to John's cottage. It would be there and ready for anyone to use once he left, and he'd have use of it until he did. There was some talk of a couple of marriages soon to take place and she hoped a recently wed couple would move in it and start a good life together, raise a fine family, and be happy.

She had gotten hold of Melvin and Dole for the task, both complaining the whole way as they carried a bed from an empty cottage to John's place. Their complaints and whining continued as they struggled to get the bed into the cottage and when they finally did, they stood heaving hefty breaths as if they had just moved a mountain.

"I need you to get the mattress now," Sorrell ordered.

You would think she was sending them to suffer the tortures of hell, they moaned and groaned so much.

"This isn't fair, Sorrell," Melvin complained with a drawn out moan. "We were all done with work for the day and you got us working again."

"Aye, Melvin's right," Dole agreed, but then he always agreed with Melvin, though most of the time he didn't know what he was agreeing to.

They didn't stop, on and on they went until Sorrell wanted to strangle the both of them, not wanting to hear their whining a moment longer.

"Stop!" she shouted at the both of them. Get me the mattress and you can go."

Melvin took off, Dole on his heels and they were back with the mattress in no time, dropped it on the floor in the cottage and took off before she had a chance to tell them to put it on the rope that supported the mattress and held the bed together.

"Worthless idiots," she said, staring at the mattress.

This was when she disliked her petite size. A bit more height to her and she wouldn't have a problem getting the mattress on the bed, but with her small size and slim weight it wouldn't be an easy task. Not impossible, but not easy. And she needed to get it done before John returned home, not wanting to be here when he did.

Preparing to tackle the mattress, Sorrell pushed her long sleeves up. She didn't want to drag it along the earth floor and soil it, but the weight and size might not leave her any other choice. Though it was stuffed with straw and sprigs of lavender to give it a pleasant scent, it still had some weight to it.

Not one to ignore a challenge, Sorrell gave it some thought and decided if she could heft it over her head and keep it balanced there, she could get it to the bed without a problem. It took only a bit of a struggle, and a fall or two on her backside, but she finally got it on her head. Keeping it balanced there was the real challenge.

It was only a few steps to the bed and she wobbled with each one she took. When she got near enough, she gave the mattress a shove with her hands and push with her head, and the momentum carried her right along with the mattress.

She found herself caught up in the ropes with the mattress partially covering her. She went to push at the mattress to get it off her and found the rope had coiled around her arm.

"If you wanted in my bed that badly, lass, all you had to do was ask."

Sorrell squeezed her eyes shut for a moment and stifled the angry groan that wanted to break free, hearing John's teasing remark.

John walked over to the bed and squatted down beside it to shake his head. "Just when I think you can't get yourself into any more difficult situations you prove me wrong."

"I don't need your help. I can free myself," she snapped.

"Then I'll just wait here while you do that."

Sorrell turned her head away and gave a tug of her arm to dislodge the rope, but it got tighter, biting into her wrist. She went to move her other arm out from under the mattress and found it was stuck. She gave it a quick yank and the mattress toppled over on her.

It was lifted up quickly, John's face peering down at her with a smile that looked ready to turn into a chuckle.

"Shall I rescue you now?"

She turned a scowl on him. "I don't need to be rescued."

"If you say so," he said, that smile finally turning into a chuckle as he let go of the mattress.

Sorrell silently cursed the man as the mattress landed on her face. She struggled for only a few minutes more before the mattress was lifted off her.

"You are a stubborn woman," John said, shaking his head and lifting his foot over the side board of the bed to plant his booted feet to either side of her waist and let the mattress fall on his broad back.

Sorrell squirmed, trying to free herself.

"Lie still or you'll collapse this bed as well," he ordered.

"I was not the only one who had caused the last bed to collapse," she argued. "*We* collapsed it."

He squatted down over her, reaching out to dislodge the rope around her arm. "Careful, lass, you don't want anyone hearing you say that."

"Why? It's the truth and—" His wicked grin made her realize what he meant and her cheeks heated to a rosy red.

It also made her aware of how they must look with him crouched down over her, and her hands appearing as if she was tied to the bed. And damn if her mind didn't conjure up images of them both naked, and him ready to plunge into her, and her all too willing to welcome him.

Their eyes met and she wondered if the heated desire that smoldered in his eyes were in hers as well.

He lowered his face near hers, his words meant for her alone. "You wouldn't be tied to my bed. I'd want your hands free to touch me, to explore every part of me, to squeeze my swollen manhood and guide it inside you, and to feel your hands cling to me as you explode with pleasure."

Sorrell responded out of instinct. Her head shot up and she captured his lips in a demanding kiss. His hands quickly cupped her face, holding it firm as he returned the kiss with a strength and desire that sent Sorrell's passion swirling out of control.

She didn't realize she was arching her back, pushing up against him until she felt his hard manhood poking between her legs.

He tore his mouth off hers and several oaths flew from it before he said, "This is why I leave. My manhood aches to be inside you."

"John, are you here?"

"Snow," Sorrell whispered a bit breathless as her sister stepped in the open doorway.

"I'm looking for Sorrell," she said her eyes searching the room.

"I'm here," Sorrell said.

"Where?" Snow squinted as if doing so would help her see better. "I can't make out your shadow."

"Your sister got herself into another predicament," John said.

"Not again," Snow said with a chuckle.

"You don't even ask if I'm all right?"

"You're with John, of course, you're all right as well as safe," Snow said.

With his manhood still poking at her, she could debate how safe she was, but then John had been the one to end the kiss. He also had let her know how much he wanted her, not love, wanted. And yet, he had stopped himself, even though she had eagerly welcomed him. Why?

"What happened?" Snow asked.

Sorrell explained while John freed her, and when he was done and helped her to her feet, the heated desire in his eyes just beginning to fade, she gave thought to what might have happened if someone other than Snow had approached the cottage. What would someone have thought if they had seen John crouched over her and them kissing?

"What is it you want?" Sorrell asked.

"James says the pups recently born are weaned off their mum and suggests I should go pick one for myself. He told me of a woman he met who cannot speak and of her dog that protects her. He believes a faithful dog could benefit me as well. Willow waits in the stable to help me pick out a pup, and I thought you would like to join us."

John was familiar with the person James had told Snow about. It was Dawn, the infamous Cree's, Lord of Carrick, wife. He had seen it himself when he had sheltered there for a couple of days. Cree was a powerful warrior and not one to cross, though one to respect. And from what John had seen, Cree loved his wife and family beyond measure.

"I think that's a wise suggestion and I would love to help you pick out a pup," Sorrell said.

"You come too, John, I would like a man's opinion as well," Snow said. She reached a hand out to him, not taking no for an answer. "Besides, I'd love to hear your version of the bed incident."

That had John taking her hand. "And I'd love to tell you."

"It wouldn't be as good as mine," Sorrell said and the three of them laughed.

***

John watched the three sisters talk and laugh as they played with the adorable pups and he envied their close relationship. That they loved one another proved obvious more and more as he had watched them together. And though they were different in many ways, they were the same when it came to loving one another and being protective of one another.

"I think you should pick this fellow. He's all black and has an aggressive nature. He'd protect you," Sorrell said, smiling at the small pup tugging at the end of her garment. "He's a little warrior."

John had his own opinion after watching the pups. There was five of them, the black one, two brown ones, females, with a few patches of black to them that were rolling around and nipping at each other, another female that was completely brown and was playfully nipping at Willow's fingers, and a tiny male, brown with black paws who had taken shelter under Snow's garment as soon as she had sat on the overturned bucket.

The little pup had claimed her. He was the one for Snow.

"This female is a bit aggressive as well," Willow said.

"No, she's playful. This black one is determined," Sorrell said. "And those two brown females rolling around wouldn't benefit Snow."

John liked the way Sorrell and Willow detailed the pups for Snow since she couldn't see them, though he didn't think it mattered to Snow. She had picked up each one, hugged them, and played a moment with them.

"That one that crawled under Snow's garment would be of no help to her. He would scurry off and hide at the sound of laughter," Willow said.

"You're right," Sorrell agreed. He hasn't poked his head out from under there once to see what's going on. It's like he expects Snow to protect him."

Snow reached down and scooped the little pup out from where he had curled himself to sleep on her feet, and rested him against her chest. He looked up at her, yawned, curled against her and went to sleep.

"No, no, no," Sorrell begged. "You can't choose the runt of the litter and one that looks like he'll sleep his life away. You need to choose one who will protect you, not you protect him."

"Thaw and I will do just fine," Snow said.

"She's named him. She'll never let him go now," Willow said.

"Thaw? What did he do melt your heart?" Sorrell asked.

"He did," Snow said with a nod and kissed the top of his small head. "He needs me as much as I need him."

"It's for Snow to choose," John said, taking Snow's side and pleased with her choice.

"Thank you for reminding my sisters of that," Snow said.

"You're no help," Sorrell said, scrunching her nose at him and the little black pup agreed, running over to John and yapping at him.

"Silence," John commanded and the pup stopped yapping, turned, and ran back to Sorrell to tear at her hem once again.

"You command like someone familiar with it," Sorrell said.

"Aye, I've commanded many an animal," John said. "Now I must go and see to the shed."

"You have done enough for the day," Sorrell said.

"There is still light. I will do more."

"Strange," Snow said after he left, "I don't think John was referring to dogs."

"I get the same feeling," Willow said.

Sorrell agreed, but she didn't voice it. There were too many unknowns about John and he made it far too difficult to find out about him, but what did it matter. He would leave in two days or sooner if the shed got finished, and the thought ripped painfully at her heart.

She had hoped to love one day. Now she didn't know if she wanted anything to do with love. It was more painful than joyful.

"Let's get Thaw to the keep," Willow said.

"He will sleep in my bedchamber," Snow said.

Willow was quick to warn, "But not in your bed."

"Why not?' Snow argued as Willow guided her out of the stable, Thaw sound asleep in her arms. "No other male will ever warm my bed."

Sorrell shook her head at Willow when she looked ready to respond. What was the point? Snow was right and if she wanted Thaw in her bed, then so be it.

"As you wish," Willow said and Sorrell smiled at her.

Sorrell left her sisters a while later, making an excuse that she had tasks to see to, when what she wanted to do was see how far John had gotten on the shed. She had been glad when Snow had invited him to the stable to help pick the pup, not that he was of any help siding with Snow, but it kept him from continuing work on the shed, delaying his departure.

She grumbled beneath her breath, berating herself for her constant thoughts and worry over his departure when in all honesty it was probably better he did leave. She hated the back and forth thoughts.

Stay. Leave. Stay. Leave.

She liked her thoughts the way they had been, clear and concise. No questions. No doubts. No madness.

She shook her head and kept walking, coming to an abrupt halt when she spotted John still working on the shed. He had gotten more work done than she had expected. Actually, what needed to be finished, Melvin could do without Dole's help. Not that Melvin would do it without John's prodding. And it was the first time she was grateful for Melvin's laziness.

"You are almost done. One more day will do it," Sorrell said, approaching him.

"One day," John said, putting the tools in the shed for the night. "How is Thaw doing?"

Sorrell had learned quickly that he would change the conversation when he wanted to divert you away from it. She let it be, since she didn't want to talk about his departure either.

"He doesn't leave Snow's arms for long. He curls up in them or on her lap." She shook her head.

"Don't worry. He may not seem like much of a dog that will guard her well, but wait and see. He will surprise you."

"I hope so."

"Thaw sensed her need and her calming nature," John said.

Sorrell laughed. "You don't want to see her when she loses her temper."

"I can't imagine Snow losing her temper. She's so delicate, much like the flakes of falling snow."

Sorrell laughed harder. "Delicate like the snow? What happens when that snow falls fiercely and whips at you? Mum named her perfectly and you don't want to be around when Snow turns into a fierce storm. She'll bury you."

"I can't believe that," he said truly surprised.

Sorrell's smile faded some. "Though, I must admit that I haven't seen her lose her temper since she lost her sight. It's been a struggle for her and I'm pleased that she's fighting to be independent, especially since she will not have me and Willow to depend on once we wed and leave." The thought of leaving Snow on her own upset her, though she didn't let it show. "But I sense that fear still lives strong in her and I can't blame her. She sees only shadows and so much can hide in the shadows."

"Snow is stronger than you think. She will do well."

"You have worked hard today. Please join me and my sisters in the Great Hall for supper tonight," she said and looked up at the sky, the clouds having grown darker and dusk not far off. "With the air chilled and clouds gathering, we could have some snow tonight. A good, hot supper will serve to keep you warm."

"Aye, that it would, and thank you… for everything."

"I will see you then." She turned and walked off, thinking… *one day. One more day.*

***

Sorrell turned every time the door to the Great Hall opened. She and her sisters sat at a table closest to the hearth, the night having turned cold. They were the only ones in the room. James was taking supper in his solar, insisting he had work to do.

Willow and Snow ate, but Sorrell didn't touch anything on the table. Her stomach was troubling her. It had been since she had left John.

One more day.

That's what was left. One more day.

The food had been on the table for a while and there was no sight of John.

"Perhaps something detained him," Snow said, having felt her sister's concern the many times she shifted on the bench beside her.

"Or perhaps he was exhausted from finishing the storage shed and fell asleep," Willow suggested.

Sorrell's eyes went from the door to her sister Willow in a flash. "He hadn't finished it when I saw him. There was still some work to be done."

"Melvin complained to me about how John practically yanked him out of his cottage to continue work on the shed after they had been finished for the day. Melvin told me that John insisted the shed be done today and that he'd have time to rest tomorrow. But Melvin says John will work him just as hard tomorrow," Willow said.

Sorrell stood. "I'm going to go see what's keeping him."

She ignored her sisters' attempts to stop her and hurried out of the keep, grabbing her cloak off the bench where she had dropped it as she went. John had returned to work on the shed after she had left him. That he had finished it and not joined her and her sisters for supper, meant that he intended to take his leave. She should have known it when he had thanked her for everything. He had been saying farewell.

With determined steps, she all but marched through the village toward John's cottage. No one was about, the night too cold, a fine snow falling. She hoped she wasn't too late and he had already left. She wanted to see him one last time and what?

That was the question. What did she want from him before he left? She didn't know, but she'd find out soon enough. She picked up her pace.

He better not had left or she just might hunt him down.

Worry and anger consumed her thoughts and she didn't hear the footsteps that rushed at her, but she felt the blow that knocked her off her feet.

***

John had delayed long enough. He needed to leave. It didn't matter that a light snow fell. It was actually helpful since the snow would cover his tracks if anyone thought to search for him. Something he wouldn't put past Sorrell to do.

Part of him had to smile at the thought, since he wouldn't mind her tracking him down, but the other part of him was practical and knew that wouldn't be good. He supposed he also delayed his departure as long as he did in hopes that she would come looking for him and he might get to kiss her one last time, but that wasn't a wise thought either.

He simply couldn't believe how difficult it was for him to leave Sorrell. He worried what might happen to her without him there to look after her. He also worried how Seth MacCannish would treat her. The thought alone of that man becoming Sorrell's husband sent a burning rage rushing through him. The man didn't deserve her and Sorrell certainly didn't deserve the likes of Seth MacCannish.

Unfortunately, he wasn't in the position to do anything about it. He had his own problems to solve before he was free to do anything. He wanted to rant at Fate for throwing Sorrell in his path. It was not the time or place for a woman in his life. He had to see this matter settled with his father, once and for all.

"Enough," John warned himself, wasting time thinking on it wouldn't get him anyplace. He had to leave now and be done with it.

He gathered what little he had, his sword already in the sheath attached at his back. The wrapped cloth containing food lay in wait on the table. Dorrit had been generous in the amount of food she had given him when he had told her how tired and hungry he was after finishing the storage shed. It would last him several days if he were careful.

He was all set. All he had to do was walk out of the cottage and keep going.

He went to reach for his cloak draped over a chair when he thought he heard someone or something at the door.

The noise came again.

A soft knock, he thought. Or was he imagining things, or hoping?

He went to the door and opened it.

Sorrell swayed in front of him, blood running from a cut just above her left eye down along the side of her face.

"John," she barely uttered, and fell into his arms.

Chapter Ten

John lifted her gently into his arms and her body fell limp against him. He turned to carry her to the bed he had fixed and a tremble rippled through her. It was either from fright or the cold since she wore no cloak, though he wondered if she had lost it when assaulted.

He went to lay her gently on the bed.

"No! No, I don't want to leave your arms, not yet," she said and slipped her slim arm around his neck.

John didn't argue, since he preferred her right where she was. He went to the chair near the fire, wanting to get her warm, then he'd tend her wound.

"You didn't intend to come to supper. You were going to leave, weren't you?"

"You come to me wounded and bloody and you want to know if I was leaving?" he asked and shook his head that she was more concerned with him than herself.

"I see it for myself. Your sword is sheathed on your back. A cloth packed with food lays on the table. You were leaving."

"And you were?"

"Coming to stop you."

Had that been the reason he had delayed his departure? Had he waited to see if she would come looking for him when he had not shown up at the Great Hall? He had wanted a few stolen moments with her, one last kiss, one last time to hold her in his arms, wishing he'd never have to let her go again.

Damn, what had this wee woman done to him? He had trusted and cared for no one these past two years. How had she managed to make him do both?

"Who did this to you?" he demanded, anger churning his stomach.

This was his fault. If he had shown up for supper as he had said he would, this wouldn't have happened to her. And he intended to see whoever did this suffered a far worse beating.

"He is worse off for it than I am," Sorrell said. "So there is nothing you need to do."

Seeing how she looked, bloody and the wound swollen, he found that difficult to believe, but he hadn't known her to lie. Still, he'd find out for himself and throw the person another beating.

"Did you leave him writhing in agony? Anything less is not acceptable," he cautioned.

Sorrell thought him teasing, but his serious tone and the way his blue eyes seemed as turbulent as a raging storm, she realized he meant it.

"He suffered his fair share."

"I'll see for myself. Who did this to you and don't make me ask again," he warned.

There was that tone again, commanding and sounding as if he was born to it.

"You need not fight my battle," Sorrell said.

John was ready to argue with her. He damn well would fight her battles. However, her wound and the fatigue he saw heavy in her eyes stopped him.

"Let me tend your wound and clean away the blood," he said and this time when he carried her to the bed, she didn't protest. But then she thought she had won the battle, foolish lass.

"You lost your cloak in the altercation?" he asked, after placing her on the narrow bed.

"I did," she admitted, a yawn following.

He wanted to remind her that she had barely recovered from the injury Seth had left her with and now here she had suffered another. Also that she had to stop getting herself into trouble, but she didn't need a lecture right now. She needed someone to look after her, and she damn well needed a husband who would protect her, especially from herself.

Her tremble had turned to a shiver, the cold having settled deeper into her bones. He hurried to remove her boots, needing to get her warm.

"What are you doing?" she asked on a yawn.

"You're bloody, bruised, cold, and exhausted. I'm going to see that you get warm and tend your wounds so when your sisters see you they don't get upset."

"You are kin—"

"I'm not the man you think I am," he said, stopping her before she could finish and tucked the wool blanket around her.

Her eyes were closed when he finished, the altercation and the cold having taken its toll. He went to the door, needing to fill a bucket with water from the rain barrel, and he no soon as opened it than Sorrell called out to him.

"Don't leave me, John, or I'll hunt you down."

He had to smile. That was the Sorrell he knew.

"You have my word, I won't leave you now, Sorrell," he said and he barely heard her whispered words that drifted over to him.

"Not ever."

***

Sorrell winced now and again when John cleansed her wound. He was gentle, but the gash to her head proved painful to the touch. She tried her best not to show it, since every time she did wince, John's blue eyes flared with anger.

Anger not directed at her. It was meant for the person who did this to her.

"Lift your chin," he ordered gently.

She did and he ran the freshly rinsed cloth along her jaw, cleaning off the last of the blood.

"It isn't as bad as I first thought. All the blood made it look far worse," he said, relieved himself. "At least you won't look as bad when your sisters see you."

"They're used to my wounds and bruises." Sorrell yawned again.

"I'm not," he said with a gentle tap to the tip of her nose. "Get some rest. You need it."

"I need to return to the keep."

"After you rest a while," he urged.

Sorrell went to sit up.

John's hands went to her shoulders, easing her back. "You will do as I say and I will wake you before the hour grows late and someone comes looking for you."

"You will not leave?"

"I will be here when you wake."

"And you will stay one more day?" Sorrell asked anxiously.

"I will promise you one more day, no more," he said, though he wished he could promise her forever.

Sorrell sighed and closed her eyes. "Good. I look forward to the day with you."

John waited until she was sound asleep and left the cottage in search of Sorrell's cloak, though he really hoped he'd come across whoever did this to her. The person deserved a good beating and he intended to give it to him.

The light snow had stopped and left a dusting on the ground. The heavy cloud covering was gone, the stars bright in the night sky, and a nearing half-moon cast a good glow, making it easier to see in the dark.

He hadn't gone that far when he caught movement in the shadows. He stilled and listened and once he determined where the noise had come from, he followed it. The person wasn't light on his feet, he stomped through the woods like a troop of warriors on the march.

When the heavy footsteps stopped, so did John. He proceeded slowly and silently, keeping his footsteps light so as not to be heard. He stopped again when he saw someone sitting on a fallen tree... Peter.

He should have known.

John was nearly on top of him when Peter finally realized he was there and he scrambled so fast to get away that he fell back off the fallen tree trunk onto his back.

"Don't hurt me! Please, don't hurt me! Peter begged, trying desperately to scramble away from John.

The lad cringed in fright when John's booted-foot came down on the fallen tree trunk and a crack echoed throughout the woods.

"Sorrell really did lay a beating on you," John said when he got a good look at Peter's face.

Blood still oozed from a sizeable gash on his forehead above his right eye and blood covered his mouth and chin. The white of his other eye was completely red and there was a large bruise on his one shin.

John found himself doing something he hadn't expected, he held out a helping hand to Peter.

Peter eyed him suspiciously.

"I'm not going to hurt you. I only want to talk," John assured him. "Besides, if I wanted to hurt you, you'd be writhing in pain by now."

Peter sighed as if resigned to his fate, though still extended a cautious hand out to John.

John yanked him up and sat on the fallen tree trunk, nodding to the spot beside him. "Sit."

Peter cast his eyes about.

"Run and I promise you'll regret it," John warned, though he understood the lad's instinct to try and escape.

Peter sat and turned to John. "I didn't mean to hurt her. I just wanted to scare her some."

John narrowed his eyes, staring at Peter. "Did Sorrell knock one of your teeth out?"

"Two," he said, sniffling back tears.

"And your eye?" John asked, seeing how it was red where the white should be.

"She shoved her finger in it. It hurt bad."

John saw it for himself but couldn't believe the damage Sorrell had done.

"My da beat me the day I got home and saw the mud all over me and found out it was Sorrell who had done it. He told me I better make her pay for making a fool of me. I thought if I jumped at her from out of the dark, I'd stand a chance against her."

"Stand a chance against her? She's a wee bit of a thing," John said.

"That's what my da said, but you both don't know what she's like when she's roaring mad. And once she gets anything in her hand that she can throw… watch out. She hits her mark every time."

"Is that how you got the gash on your head?" John asked.

Peter grimaced when he touched it lightly, and nodded. "She wasn't paying attention like she usually does. She seemed far away like something was bothering her and it gave me the opportunity to creep up on her. I tripped when I went to throw the first punch, falling into her and sending her tumbling. She went down and hit her forehead on a rock." He shook his head. "She used that rock. He pointed to his two bottom front missing teeth. "Then she got hold of another rock." He pointed to the gash on his head, then stuck out his bruised leg. "Then she kicked me a couple of times. How does a wee woman like her have such a hard kick?"

John was glad that she did and after hearing what Sorrell had done to the lad, he couldn't help but feel sorry for him. No lad or man wanted to admit that he got beaten by a woman, and a petite one at that, and certainly not as badly as Sorrell had beaten Peter.

"I intended to give you a good beaten myself for what you did to Sorrell, but after seeing you, I think you got what you deserved and then some."

"I would have rather taken the beating from you. At least then my da would have been proud of me for going up against a giant of a man."

That gave John a thought. "I tell you what, Peter, you give me your word that you will never bother Sorrell or her sisters again and I'll let people know that even though you lost to me, you fought like a brave warrior."

"I fought you?" he asked with excitement, then shook his head. "Sorrell will never agree."

"She will when she learns that you won't bother Snow again, and I don't need to remind you that if you give me your word and break it, I will break you in two," John said and gave Peter a friendly, though firm slap on the back.

Peter didn't hesitate. "You have my word. I'll never bother any of the Macardle sisters again. I've lost enough teeth to Sorrell already." He spit out another tooth, confirming it.

***

John was a few steps from the cottage when he caught movement to one side, where the small garden sat. The size and shape of the figure, what he could make out in the dark, gave him an idea of who it might be and also that he hadn't sensed any imminent danger.

"Time to talk," came the strong whisper.

"Aye, Erland, it's time to talk," John agreed and disappeared into the shadows.

***

John draped Sorrell's cloak over the end of the bed and took the chair and placed it against the wall to the side of the hearth and sat. He hadn't talked long with Erland, since a long conversation was not necessary. He knew what he needed to do and he would do it. Like Sorrell, he had little choice.

He looked over at her and was glad to see she still slept. He would leave her sleep a while longer before he woke her to return to the keep.

Her wounds did not look that bad, though she would certainly be questioned about them. He would tell her about his talk with Peter. He had no doubt she would agree with it, since it would protect Snow.

Sorrell gave a soft moan as she turned on her side and pulled the blanket up to tuck under her chin.

She was still cold and he wished he could warm her. It would be easy. All he had to do was wrap his big body around her tiny one. His warmth would seep into her and chase her chills away. But he'd want to do more than wrap himself around her, and he'd more than warm her... he'd set her passion burning.

He rested his head back against the wall, though he should have pounded it against the wall for thinking that way. Things were complicated enough for the both of them. Falling in love hadn't been in his plans. It had been the furthest thing from his mind and he was still struggling with it. He wanted to deny it, kept trying to, but he hadn't had much luck. But whether it was love or not, neither of them were free to find out.

Solitude was what he had searched for and what he needed. He found people lied far too fast and far too often, to trust anyone. In solitude, he could dig deep, recall, and discover who had torn his life apart. Then he would find him and have his revenge.

That had been his thoughts for several months. Now his thoughts centered on Sorrell. He found himself smiling more, laughing, looking forward to what the day would bring, since with Sorrell one never knew what might happen, and less about his troubles.

He closed his eyes, warning himself not to sleep. He had to wake Sorrell soon so she could return to the keep. It would do them no good to be caught, appearing as if they'd spent the night together. The consequences could be disastrous. And while sitting in a chair wasn't conducive to sleep, he had found he could sleep standing up if need be. One of the skills he had learned from a long list of other skills he had acquired these past two years, though to be truthful, some he had already possessed.

A moment, just a moment more, then it was time to wake her, he silently warned himself.

***

Sorrell winced as she stretched herself awake. Her body ached and so did her head, then she remembered and bolted up in bed, not her bed. She braced her hands on the straw-stuffed mattress, having set her head spinning from moving so fast. Finally, when things had settled, she spotted John sleeping in a chair, his head resting back against the wall. How he didn't topple over was beyond her.

Fear roiled her stomach when she looked to see light seeping in under the door. It was morning and past dawn, the light bright.

She had spent the whole night here and God help her if it was discovered. She remained as quiet as she could as she rushed out of bed and into her boots. She swiped up her cloak at the end of the bed, though didn't recall having it when she had arrived here last night, her memory sharp of last night's events.

John had seen to tending her and he had done so gently. Her first thought once she had finished with Peter had been John, not Willow who usually saw to tending her injuries. Her only thought had been John and she hadn't hesitated in going to him. He would understand and he would help her without question or a lecture, well maybe a small lecture, and he had.

She looked at him sitting so straight, not a slump to his broad shoulders, his arms tucked close to his chest and his hands resting in his lap. How she would love to crawl into his lap and slip into the crook of his arm, a spot she fit perfectly.

How she wished they…

She shook her head. Wishing didn't make it so. If it had, her parents would be alive, her da would have never gotten ill, and Snow would have never gone blind. She also never would be stuck marrying Seth MacCannish, but James had made it clear of the consequences to the clan if she didn't wed Seth. The reason she had to leave now and hope that no one saw her leaving John's cottage.

She eased the door open slowly, peeked out and, seeing no one about, stepped out just as James and Seth MacCannish came into view.

Chapter Eleven

Sorrell froze where she stood and for a moment so did James and Seth, though not for long. Seth's face turned a startling red and his eyes glared like burning embers, so much so, that Sorrell thought he'd burst into flames.

James tilted his head back and shook it, and guilt stabbed at Sorrell. James was doing his best to see the clan kept safe and from starving this winter. He had even honored her and her sisters' desire to remain nearby, choosing a husband for her from a clan no more than a short horse ride away.

She had not meant for this to happen and she hoped she could somehow salvage the marriage agreement, she had never wanted, for the sake of her family and clan.

"This is all a misunderstanding," she called out. "I've done nothing wrong."

"She speaks the truth."

Sorrell jumped and swerved around startled by John's strong declaration.

His hand reached out and took hold of her arm to steady her and he moved to stand beside her. He didn't once glance down at her. His eyes remained focused on Seth and James.

"Lies," Seth shouted, shaking his fisted hand in the air. "Sorrell was not in the keep when I arrived and James couldn't find her, even her sisters didn't know her whereabouts."

James took a step forward and his eyes narrowed. "You've been injured, Sorrell. What happened?"

"A small altercation, nothing more," she assured him.

"Nothing improper went on here. Sorrell is a good woman," John said in her defense.

"Good woman?" Seth said with a smirk and a snort. "She's bruised and battered from fights she gets into more often than men. She doesn't hold her tongue, never obeys anyone, and pokes a wanderer and who knows how many other men."

"Watch your tongue," MacCannish," John warned.

"That's enough, Seth," James cautioned.

"You're right. It is enough," Seth said. "I only agreed to marry her because of the substantial sum the Lord of Fire agreed to pay me, but I'll be damned if I'll wed a whore."

John went to step forward, but Sorrell grabbed his arm in a silent plea, stopping him.

"You will apologize to my sister," James demanded.

"I will not apologize for speaking the truth. I didn't trust Sorrell from the start and my instincts to have her followed proved wise." Seth pointed an accusing finger at her. "I've been told that this isn't the first time she's been to his cottage, closed in there alone with him. I'm no fool and either should you be, James. She's been poking that good-for-nothing wanderer and probably already has his bairn growing inside her. I'll not wed a wh—"

"You're right," James interrupted. "You'll not wed my sister. You're not worthy of her."

"Worthy?" Seth said with a snicker and another snort. "There's not a sensible man alive who would wed her."

"I'll wed Sorrell," John called out to the shock of them all.

Seth laughed. "A whore and a wanderer, a perfect match. The Lord of Fire will be so pleased."

John moved so fast that Seth was on the ground before anyone realized what had happened, including Seth. He was shaking his head to clear it, and his jaw was already beginning to bruise.

John stood over Seth, his hands fisted tightly at his sides and he looked as if he struggled not to throw another punch.

"Call Sorrell a whore again and I'll rip that lying tongue of yours right out of your mouth," John threatened in a manner that left no doubt he would do exactly that.

Sorrell never knew Seth to back down from a threat. He was the one more likely to threaten, but he had never come up against a man the size of John. She thought it wise of Seth to hold his tongue and not chance losing it.

Seth got to his feet and rubbed at his jaw once he stood. He cast an angry eye at James. "You and your clan will suffer for this and the Lord of Fire as well. I'll not pledge my fealty to him. I'll pledge it to Walsh MacLoon."

Sorrell only realized that she had been leaning against John since he had returned to her side and his arm went around her. It was getting to be a habit with her, seeking him out, leaning on him, and he never refused to offer comfort or support. She needed both right now, since she feared what James had once warned her about—*someday you're going to get yourself into something you can't get out of*—was upon her.

What had she done? What would happen to the clan now? And what would the Lord of Fire do when he found out he had lost the support of the Clan MacCannish?

"You know Walsh MacLoon reached out to a distant relative for help to secure his rights in this land dispute, don't you, James?" Seth asked.

"Aye, I heard it mentioned," James acknowledged curtly.

"He received word the other day that his relative will give him all the help he needs."

"And why should that matter to me?" James asked.

Seth smirked as if about to claim victory. "Because that relative is the powerful Lord Finn Northwick."

James actually paled and Sorrell felt her stomach roil. The Clan Northwick was the most powerful and influential clan in the north and Lord Finn a legend. He had never tasted defeat, not once.

"Lord Northwick let it be known that his son will return home soon and from the tales spreading about him, his time spent away has made him a fiercer warrior and far more ruthless than his father." Seth grinned. "The Clan Northwick will sweep down on you and conquer your clan and the Lord of Fire as well. Tarass may be a fierce warrior himself and have superior warriors, but Northwick far outnumbers him in warriors."

This time Sorrell paled, upset. This was all her fault.

"Good luck to you, James," Seth said and laughed as he turned and walked away.

Sorrell stepped away from John, ready to approach James and offer her heartfelt apology, but he held up his hand, halting her steps.

"Not now, Sorrell. I have to send a missive to Tarass and make him aware of the situation before Seth does, and you both," —James looked from Sorrell to John— "need to prepare to take your marriage vows today."

Sorrell didn't bother to tell him that that was yet to be decided. She would talk with him later about it. She did, however, turn to John, once James walked off, to make it clear he was under no obligation to wed her.

"It is not necessary for you to wed me," she said, still a bit shocked that he had even offered to do so.

That they were attracted to each couldn't be denied and that there was a good chance she was in love with him couldn't be denied either. But she wanted no forced marriage between them.

He rested his hands at her slim waist and with a gentle tug brought her closer to him. "Aye, I do have to wed you. I have no choice."

A tiny pang stabbed at her heart. What had she expected him to say? That he loved her that was why he was marrying her? More dreams that are just that... dreams.

She pulled and turned away from him as that pang grew more hurtful.

"No, you don't," she insisted. "I will speak with James and make him see reason. He can find me another husband."

"Turn around and look at me, Sorrell," John said.

She wasn't used to such a firm tone from him and she turned out of annoyance, about to let him know not to speak to her that way.

"Don't you want to marry me?" he asked before she could say a word.

"Do you want to marry me?" she shot back.

"I wouldn't have said it if I didn't mean it."

With a lift of her chin, she demanded, "Why? Because you feel it's the honorable thing to do?"

"I won't let a lie ruin your life," he said, knowing all too well what such a consequence could bring.

"It won't ruin it. I'll survive," she insisted, though a bit of doubt nagged at her.

"How? MacCannish will spread the lie about us in no time. Tongues will wag and the lie will grow even bigger and more outrageous. It will gain momentum and you won't be able to stop it."

Sorrell remained silent, thinking on his words. As much as she didn't want to believe it, John was right. No one would believe the truth.

"The lie is always a better tale to tell," she said.

He knew all too well the truth to her words. "And easier to believe."

"We must wed. We truly have no choice," Sorrell said, the realization of it sinking in and while in a way she should be pleased, marrying the man she would much rather have as her husband, she also felt guilty.

John slipped his finger beneath her chin as it drooped and lifted it. "What weighs so heavily on your mind?"

"It is my fault Seth will join with Walsh MacLoon and if what he says is true…" Sorrell didn't want to think of what might happen if the powerful Lord Northwick attacked the Clan Macardle.

"You had nothing to do with Seth joining with Walsh MacLoon. That decision was made as soon as he learned who would help him. Seth chose the side he believed had a better chance of victory."

"If that is so then others will side with MacLoon as well."

"It's possible, though from what I hear the Lord of Fire is a powerful lord himself. Lord Northwick may have met his match."

"Sorrell."

A repeated yelp followed Sorrell's and they turned to see Snow as she stopped walking.

"You found them, Thaw?" Snow asked, raising the little pup, she held snug in her arms, to kiss the top of his head.

"He did," Sorrell said to her surprise as she and John walked over to Snow.

"Willow and I were so worried when we couldn't find you, and when I learned what happened I wanted to make sure you were all right and thank John for doing the honorable thing."

"Nothing happened between us, Snow," Sorrell said a bit disappointed that she would believe that of her.

"I never doubted it did. He had no obligation to wed you, but he offered anyway. That's what makes John so honorable, and what makes me so pleased to call him brother," Snow said with a tender smile.

"As am I," Willow said, joining them. "I am pleased Sorrell will have a husband who rescues her without complaint."

"Very funny, Willow," Sorrell said and thought how true her words.

"While there is not enough time to have a festive celebration, we will have a small one for now. We can have a big celebration later," Willow said.

Sorrell made sure to remind her sister of their present food situation. "Much later when there is enough food for all."

"I will make sure there is enough food for your clan," John said.

"Your clan now as well," Willow said.

"Aye, *my* clan." John nodded, claiming it his own.

Willow linked her arm with Sorrell. "Now come. Snow and I will get you ready for the ceremony, and while I take a look at that wound on your forehead, though it already looks well-tended, you can tell me how you got it."

"Another fight?" Snow shook her head. "This must stop."

"It will happen no more, at least with Peter," John said and took a moment to explain what had happened and what had been agreed to.

"You are sure he'll not bother Snow again?" Sorrell asked, turning a skeptical look on John.

"I have no doubt, since I told him I would break him in two if he should break his word to me."

"That should do," Sorrell agreed.

"Now let's be quick," Willow ordered. "James has sent for a cleric from the friary. He'll be here within two hours and all must be ready. James insists this be done as quickly as possible."

"There's no need to rush," Sorrell said. "James says John and I are to wed, so he will be sure to see it done."

"Unless the Lord of Fire objects and decides to pay a larger sum to someone else to wed you," Willow explained. "And while James would prefer to send the missive to Tarass after you and John wed, he knows Seth will see that Tarass learns of what happened immediately."

"Your brother is an honorable man. I owe him much," John said.

"You will be a fine help to him," —Snow smiled— "It is good to have you part of the clan."

"Now, come," Willow urged with a tug to Sorrell's arm. There is much to be done before the ceremony."

"Wait for me," Snow said and, tucking Thaw in one arm, she stretched out her hand and Sorrell took hold and wrapped it around her other arm.

John was glad they would wed quickly. He wanted nothing to prevent this wedding. He intended to have Sorrell as his wife, and he'd let nothing stop that from happening.

Chapter Twelve

Sorrell stood, looking out the window of her bedchamber, still trying to comprehend that in a short time she would be John's wife. Though she was pleased, she was also apprehensive. John was a good man, but would that make him a good husband? And what about the solitude he had seemed desperate to find? He would not have that once he took her as his wife.

"All ready?"

Sorrell turned to see that Willow had entered the room. A twinge of uneasiness ran through her and she reached her hand out to her sister, the person who had always been there for her. The one who had healed every one of her wounds, defended her against anyone and everyone, listened to her complaints, and held her tight in her arms and wept with her when their mum and da died. Willow was the rock of the family and Sorrell was grateful she was her sister.

Willow took hold of Sorrell's hand and pulled her into a tight hug. "I am so pleased and relieved that you will wed John. You will do well together, and I am thrilled that you will make your home here."

Sorrell turned a joyous smile on Willow. "I hadn't realized that benefit of marrying John. We stay together."

"Till I wed, but at least Snow won't be alone now. She'll have you, John, and Thaw," Willow said with a soft laugh.

Sorrell pulled her into another hug. "James promised he'd keep us close. You won't be far from us."

"Aye, but enough about me. It is your day and you look beautiful. That was Mum's favorite garment and it fits you perfectly."

Sorrell ran her hand over the soft green, wool tunic. The neckline, edges, and hem were trimmed with an intricate, gold thread stitching as was the pale yellow shift beneath.

"Mum would be so proud and happy to see you wearing it," Willow said, tears gathering in her eyes.

Seeing the tears in Willow's eyes brought tears to Sorrell's eyes, and the two sisters hugged again.

Repeated yelps announced the arrival of Snow and Thaw before they reached the door.

The little pup came running into the room and yelped as if announcing Snow's arrival, ran back out, and entered again in front of Snow, then ran straight to the hearth to plop down and fall immediately asleep.

"His tiny yelps exhaust him," Sorrell said with a laugh.

"He's sleeping by the hearth, isn't he?" Snow asked, turning her head toward the flickering shadows. "His favorite place." She held up a slim wreath fashioned of heather and lavender. "I made this for you to wear."

Sorrell felt more tears gather in her eyes. "It's beautiful, Snow." She took the wreath from her sister and placed it on her head. Her raging red curls refused to allow it to sit perfectly balanced on her head. No matter how many times Sorrell tried, it tilted to the side.

"Let me," Willow said and moved a few strands of curls to fall gently near the wound on her forehead and positioned the wreath to hold them there, setting it straight.

"How does it look?" Snow asked.

"See for yourself," Willow said and took Snow's hand and placed it on the wreath.

Snow smiled as she moved her hand over it. "Perfect."

Sorrell reached out and drew Snow into a tight hug. "I am so grateful."

"I am too," Snow said, sniffling back tears. "I am grateful you will be staying here with us. I hope you and John have a whole lot of bairns I can spoil."

Sorrell hadn't given that much thought to bairns. Of course she wanted them, but it was Snow who had talked about having a bunch of them and her blindness had stolen that dream.

"I'll do my best," Sorrell said and a slight tingle ran through her, thinking of the night ahead. John and her would do more than kiss tonight and she found herself looking forward to it, though a bit anxious.

Thaw's head shot up and he let out one of his tiny yelps.

"Someone is near," Snow said and turned as a servant appeared at the open door.

"The cleric has arrived. Your presence is requested in the solar."

This was it. It was going to happen. She would become John's wife.

***

John could not take his eyes off Sorrell when she entered the room and he couldn't help but think that this wasn't real. He would wake to find it all a dream. But then none of it was truly real, since Sorrell didn't truly know who he was.

"Could I have a moment with John?" Sorrell asked of James, and he nodded.

John stepped out of the solar with Sorrell and moved a short distance down the narrow hallway, away from the open door.

"Something troubles you?" John asked concerned she might have found a reason not to go through with the wedding.

"I need you to know something before we take our vows."

There was nothing that she could say to him that would change his mind about marrying her. Not a single thing. If only that was true about him.

"I'm listening," he said, though the thought to kiss her and chase away her concerns popped into his head and how in just a short while he'd be able to do both anytime she needed him to.

She drew her shoulders back and brought her chin up a notch. "I need you to know that I'm not an easy woman to have as a wife."

John lowered his head and brought his face so close to hers, she thought he would kiss her.

"Aye that you are, but you're *my woman* and that's all that matters." His kissed her gently, and gave her no chance to say any more. "Now we wed." His large hand closed around hers, almost devouring it and hurried her into the room.

A servant rushed into the solar only moments after John and Sorrell entered.

"The Lord of Fire and a contingent of his warriors are not far off and either is Seth MacCannish and a troop of his warriors," a servant lass said, worrying her hands in front of her.

John turned to the cleric and demanded, "Wed us now."

The skinny cleric turned a nervous glance to James.

"Do as he says and hurry," James ordered.

The ceremony was over in a few minutes after it started and Sorrell felt as though she held her breath through the whole thing, worried that at any moment someone would burst through the door and stop it.

John took hold of her hand as he turned a nod on James. James returned it. "Be quick about it."

"Your bedchamber?" John asked, looking to his wife.

Sorrell didn't understand at first. The Lord of Fire and Seth MacCannish were on their way here, and John wanted to know where her bedchamber was? Then it dawned on her and she held tight to his hand as she led him out of the solar and up to the second floor and into her small bedchamber.

John shut the door, then brought Sorrell into his arms. "I'm sorry it has to be this way, our first time together, but the marriage vows must be sealed, made final so no one can dispute we are wed."

"I understand," she said. "There will be time to see it done properly.

John smiled. "I'm anything but proper when it comes to coupling."

"And I have no experience, so it doesn't matter," Sorrell said with a laugh. She rested her hand to his warm cheek. "What does matter is that you will be my first."

"And your last," he said and lifted her off her feet and kissed her as he walked them to the bed.

Sorrell thought her heart would pound right out of her chest, it beat so fast with excitement. And when they went down on the bed together and he pushed her garments up and his plaid aside and she felt his manhood poke between her legs, her small hands latched onto his thick arms as best they could.

His mouth found hers once again and this time his kiss demanded and Sorrell responded.

John worried that she was too small, his manhood too large for her to take with ease. And he had no time to stoke her passion and make this moment easier for her. He had to be quick, and he hated that he might cause her pain or discomfort.

A repetitive beat of a drum ended their kiss, and they both hurried a glance at the window. The incessant drum beat droned on. It was not far off, which meant either was the Lord of Fire's arrival.

"Hurry," Sorrell urged and tightened her grip on his taut arms.

John didn't hesitate. He plunged into her, meeting less restraint than he had expected, but he mumbled several oaths beneath his breath when she cried out and before he could tell her that he was sorry for causing her pain, she smiled at him.

"You feel so good inside me."

Her response eased his concern and ignited his passion and he smiled at her. "It gets better... much, much better."

And it did.

Sorrell moaned so loud with pleasure that she drowned out the drum beats that had grown louder.

John captured her scream with a kiss when she climaxed, afraid it would echo throughout the keep. The kiss also helped stifle his own moan of pleasure that almost shot with a roar from his mouth, he had climaxed so hard.

"I can't wait to do that again," Sorrell said breathless and hugged him to her as best she could, since her arms didn't fit even halfway around him.

He reluctantly rose up off her, having realized the relentless drum beat had stopped, signaling the Lord of Fire's arrival, and held his hand out to her to help her up.

"We should do that often," she said, taking his hand.

"I couldn't agree more," he said and pulled her up off the bed and into his arms. "I did not hurt you, did I?"

"A twinge of pain no more and a small price to pay for unbelievable pleasure."

He tucked a springy, red curl behind her ear. "Promise me you will always be who you are."

She chuckled. "Are you sure you want that."

"More than anything," he said.

"I promise I will always be me," she said and shrugged. "I couldn't be any other way. And you? Promise me the same, since I think I've come to love you."

She worried when he stared at her as if it was a promise he wasn't sure he could make. Or had she surprised him or upset him with the mention of love? She was relieved when he finally spoke, though it was not what she had expected.

"Remember what I say this day to you, wife. I will keep you tucked in my heart and let no harm ever befall you for all our days. Never forget my words no matter what happens."

For some reason a chill ran through Sorrell as if his words were a portent of things to come and she wondered if being tucked in his heart meant he loved her. A hard knock sounded at the door before she could ask what he meant.

"You must come, the Lord of Fire demands your presence," Willow called out.

"You will remain by my side. Do not leave it, not once," John ordered, taking her by the arm and hurrying her to the door.

There was that commanding tone again, one he seemed comfortable with, and as soon as she got a chance she was going to ask him about it. And let him know he wouldn't be speaking that way to her.

***

Sorrell walked alongside her husband through the Great Hall, somewhat surprised to see it empty. She expected to find the Lord of Fire waiting there for them. When John opened the door and raised voices greeted them from outside, she realized why.

The men no sooner had gotten off their horses, then they were arguing.

She was relieved to see that Willow and Snow remained close to the keep's door, Thaw letting a tiny yelp out each time he got the courage to peek his head out from beneath the hem of Snow's garment, and Willow keeping a firm arm around her.

"You think it matters to me that Lord Northwick sends his son here?" Tarass, the Lord of Fire asked, his blue eyes glaring with anger. "It changes nothing."

Sorrell was familiar with Tarass's commanding nature. Who in the surrounding area wasn't? She had seen large men quake in his presence and women stare in fascination then scurry in fright if he looked their way.

He was a man of fine features and one that could intimidate with one look. He kept his dark hair short at the nape of his neck and at the sides as well. He was tall and lean, but defined with muscle, warning one not to underestimate his strength. She had seen him lay a large man low one day to the shock of all around him. He demanded respect and easily got it, though more out of fear than respect itself. He was a man to watch with caution.

That James had little choice but to pledge his loyalty to Tarass had been obvious. His troop of warriors he had returned home with were far from abundant, but there were whispers that there were more—much more.

"That you run here at Walsh MacLoon's bidding to try and convince James to go against me and join forces with him shows me MacLoon isn't as confident about Northwick's help as he claims to be."

"It is done," Seth claimed, stretching out his chest as if victory was at hand. "Lord Northwick sends warriors."

"He can send all the warriors he wants. It changes nothing and as for your betrayal to our agreement," — Tarass's hand shot up to point an accusing finger at Seth— "I will see you pay for it."

Seth took a step back, though he didn't stand near Tarass. "Lord Northwick will have you bowing down to him."

Tarass took a quick step at the man, causing Seth to stumble as he backed away.

"I bow to no man," Tarass warned, sounding like a snarling beast who dared anyone to challenge him.

Though one seemed to challenge him—Thaw. His small continuous bark could be heard every time Tarass spoke.

"Shut that pup up," Tarass commanded, turning toward the yelping pup. "Or I will."

Sorrell turned ready to protect her sister and Thaw and was surprised to see Snow scoop Thaw up in her arms and take several steps forward.

"If you stopped ranting like a beast, then my pup would not need to bark," Snow called out in anger.

John grabbed Sorrell's arm when she went to stop Tarass from climbing the keep steps and approaching Snow. "Let her see to this. I will let no harm come to her."

Thaw's yelp turned to a growl that sounded mighty threatening for a little pup, and Sorrell wondered if her sister had chosen the right pup after all.

"Silence," Tarass commanded the pup, but Thaw ignored him and continued growling.

"Silence him or I will," Tarass warned again.

Snow tucked a growling Thaw under her arm and stuck her finger out to poke at Tarass's chest. "Touch my pup and I will see you dead."

Sorrell grinned at her sister's courage.

James hurried over to the pair, but Tarass's hand shot out to the side, warning him to stop, and he did, though he spoke up.

"The pup means no harm. Snow will take him into the keep," James said.

"The pup and I both mean him harm if he dares lay a hand on Thaw," Snow warned and jabbed at his chest again.

This time, however, Tarass grabbed her hand. "Silence the pup or do as James says or you will regret it, and never ever think you can speak to me like that or dare poke me. Blind or not, you will pay for it."

Snow yanked her hand out of his, though she felt him release her. Otherwise, she would have never been able to free herself of his strong grip. That thought sent a slight tremble to her, but fearful as she might be, she would let no harm come to Thaw and she would not desert Sorrell.

She raised Thaw to place a kiss on his head, then spoke to him softly. "Quiet, Thaw, all is good. I am safe."

The tiny pup yelped once, then licked her cheek and settled quietly against her chest.

Tarass turned away from her to glare at James. "You were right. No man would want her as a wife."

Snow almost grabbed her chest, his words feeling as if he had thrust a dagger into her heart.

Willow stepped forward. "That was cruel and uncalled for."

Tarass ignored Willow and looked to James once again. "Is there no Macardle daughter who knows how to hold her tongue?"

Sorrell rushed away from her husband before he could stop her and headed toward Tarass, calling out as she did, "We never hold our tongue when dealing with an arse."

"The Macardle sister that caused all the trouble," Tarass said.

Sorrell stopped in front of him, her hands planted on her hips. "That would be you, not me, with your foolish demands."

He shook his head and again looked to James. "I've had enough of the three of them. Do you abide by our agreement or not?"

"Of course he does, you fool. You've given him no choice if James wants to keep our clan protected and well-fed for the coming winter," Sorrell said.

"Good," Tarass said, an angry glare marring his handsome features. "Then you'll wed, with haste, the next man of my choice."

Sorrell grinned up at him. "Afraid that's not possible."

Tarass crossed his arms over his chest, his patience near gone. "Why is that?"

"Sorrell is already wed… to me," John said, coming up behind her.

A burst of laughter had everyone looking to Seth.

"So you wed the nobody that you've been poking." Seth laughed again. "Now there's a beneficial match for your clan."

Tarass walked over to James. "Is this true?"

"Aye, they are wed and the marriage consummated."

"Why did she wed him?" Tarass asked with a dismissive wave to John.

"Because she's been poking him more than enough times that she's probably carrying his bastard bairn," Seth snickered.

John was about to turn, his hand already closed in a tight fist to deliver a forceful punch when the sudden consistent beat of a drum sounded.

All talk stopped and listened as the incessant beat continued. Even the village had gone quiet, no one moving except for those who shivered in fear. The solemn rhythm droned on and fear began to grow since often that type of drumbeat warned of a possible attack or the approach of a powerful clan.

Seth was the only one who was smiling. "Walsh MacLoon was right. He got word that Lord Northwick's son would arrive soon and here he is."

"Seth is here to give you a choice," Tarass said. "Side with him…"

"Or," James asked when Tarass didn't finish."

"Die," Seth said. "From what I've heard his son Ruddock spent the last two years with barbarians. Tales are he did unspeakable things and grew to enjoy it. It's said he thinks nothing of cutting out a tongue of anyone who lies to him and eating it in front of him."

James turned a worried glance on Tarass. "How do we defeat such a man?"

Seth snorted. "You don't. You join forces with him or die."

The drumbeat grew louder and with it the fear in the village grew.

"He won't attack now," Tarass said to James and lowered his voice so no one could hear him. "Hear him out and ask for time."

James saw no sense in that. "What good will that do?"

"It will give me time to see it settled," Tarass said with enough confidence that had James nodding.

"Whatever you're plotting, it won't work," Seth said annoyed he couldn't hear what the two men had discussed.

Tarass signaled two of his warriors and called out. "Escort a small troop of men who approach here to the keep steps. The others are to remain on the outskirts of the village."

The two warriors nodded and turned their horses around and rode off.

Seth laughed and shook his head. "You think they will obey two warriors when there is a troop of them?"

"There is a reason Lord Northwick never lost a battle. He never went in blindly and he stopped many before they even got started," Tarass said.

"How do you know about him?" Seth asked.

"He is a legend. How does one not know about him?" Tarass turned to James, dismissing anything else Seth might have to say. "Lord Ruddock is here to speak with you. I will stand to the side unless addressed. You should send the women inside the keep."

James cringed, knowing what kind of reaction that would bring, and he was right.

The three Macardle sisters shouted out in unison, "No!"
Thaw even joined in with a strong yelp.

The approach of horses turned everyone silent once again and by now most of the villagers had gathered around out of fear and curiosity.

Six men on horses rode behind Tarass's two warriors. An older man was the only one to dismount and approach the keep steps.

He dropped to one knee, bowed his head, then lifted it and looked to John. "Lord Ruddock, it is good to see you again."

Chapter Thirteen

Sorrell's mouth fell open in shock, her eyes spreading open so wide that she thought they would burst from her head, and anger stirred like a bubbling pot in her stomach. That her husband didn't even look at her worsened her churning stomach.

Ruddock nodded at Erland and called out for all to hear, "With my marriage to Sorrell, the Clan Macardle joins with the Clan Northwick. I rule here now and my word is law." He looked to Seth. "Go tell Walsh MacLoon that the land in dispute between the Clan Macardle and the Clan MacLoon is no more since MacLoon and Macardle land now belongs to Lord Northwick."

"That wasn't the agreement," Seth shot back.

"Let Walsh MacLoon tell me that himself," Ruddock said. "And as for you... pledge your fealty now to me or I will see you and the Clan MacCannish wiped out."

Seth paled and, for a moment, appeared as if he didn't know what to do.

"I will hear it now from you on bended knee or you are a dead man," Ruddock warned.

Seth dropped on one knee, words spilling rapidly from his mouth. "I pledge my fealty to you, Lord Ruddock, and the Clan Northwick."

"Come here to me," Ruddock demanded.

Seth approached Lord Ruddock with caution.

"Closer," Ruddock ordered when the trembling man stopped a few steps down from him. As soon as Seth placed his foot on the second step from Ruddock, his fisted hand swung out catching Seth in the mouth.

Seth went tumbling down the steps, blood pouring from the split in his lip.

"I've warned you before about besmirching my wife's good name. Next time, I'll slit your throat as soon as the words leave your mouth. Now get out of my sight."

Seth nodded and hurried down the steps, stumbling as he went, then mounting his horse with difficulty and riding off.

Sorrell shook her head, gathering the last of her wits about her and gave John a jab in the arm. "John or Ruddock or whoever you are, you are no husband to me."

She took off down the steps running.

Ruddock turned to James and Tarass. "I will speak with you both in James's solar, after I speak with my wife."

"I would leave her be if I were you," Willow said, stepping toward him.

"It is imperative I talk with her."

Willow disagreed. "She needs time."

"That is something I can't give her."

"If you speak with her now, you will face her wrath, not her logic. She needs to rant her anger before she can think sensibly."

There was truth to Willow's words, but it was difficult to pay heed to them. Sorrell might need to rant before she could see the situation reasonably, but she also needed his arms around her. Or was it that he needed to feel her in his arms and know things were good between them?

"I need to go to her," Ruddock said.

Willow smiled softly. "I'm glad to hear that, since the man we've come to know as John would let nothing stop him from going after her. I wanted to make certain Ruddock felt the same."

"There is no difference between the two," Ruddock assured her.

"Sorrell might disagree."

"Then I will let her see for herself." Ruddock said and turned away from Willow.

"Lord Ruddock."

Ruddock halted his steps and turned to Willow.

"There will be something else Sorrell questions."

"And that is?" Ruddock asked.

"Did you wed her to gain control of the Clan Macardle, to expand Northwick holdings and power in this area?"

"What do you think, Willow?"

"I got my answer when you told me you needed to go to her, though I warn you, Sorrell may not be so easy to convince."

He walked down the steps, Willow's warning heavy in his thoughts.

"Sir?" Erland asked as Ruddock reached the bottom of the steps.

"Bath and fresh garments," Ruddock ordered as he walked past him and Erland nodded, keeping his smile to himself.

Ruddock hurried his steps, though he didn't run. His hurried steps would far outdistance his wife's rushed ones, and they did.

"Don't dare go into the woods," he warned when he came upon her ready to do just that.

Sorrell stopped and turned to face him, fury raging in her green eyes. "You can't tell me what I can and cannot do. You are nothing to me."

"I'm your husband," he reminded firmly.

"I married John, not Ruddock."

"You married me," he said as if it were law.

"Your true name is not on our wedding document, which means we are not wed."

"My true name is on our wedding document."

"You lie just like you've lied about everything to me," Sorrell said, frustration bringing tears to her eyes.

"You can see for yourself the truth of it. I wrote my true name and rolled up the document to hand back to your brother."

"You knew all along your father was sending a troop of men for you," she accused. "And you said nothing, not a word. You let me continue to believe you were a man of no means, no family. You lied. How can I ever trust you to tell me the truth?"

"I lied about my name, but at the time I spoke about having no one, I didn't have anyone. It will take time to explain—"

"I don't care. I will not have you as a husband."

"You have me as a husband whether you want me or not," he said and saw anger flare like a sparked flame in her eyes. "Hear me out, Sorrell."

"Hear you out? About what? Lies? Deceit? Secrets?"

"Aye, there's plenty of all that in the tale I have to tell."

She shook her finger at him. "A tale is what it is."

"Hear it and then judge for yourself," he offered. "Though I warn you, in the end you will still remain my wife. I'll not let you go."

"Why? With your power you could end our marriage easily." A sudden thought struck her, turning her eyes wide. "Of course, what a fool I've been. You wed me to gain control of the Clan Macardle, to expand Northwick holdings and power. I'm nothing more to you than a means to an end."

"That had nothing to do with it."

"I'm to believe that after all your lies?" she said, annoyed at the tears that were building in her from the hurt that tore at her. She had thought she wed a good man and it broke her heart to lose that man.

"No matter what you think of me, my word means something to me. I gave it when I said I'd wed you today and all the days to come. Besides, you told me that you think you've come to love John. Has that changed? Are you sorry you wed me?"

She wiped at the tears falling slowly from her eyes as she responded, frustrated that she couldn't keep them locked away and annoyed that what he asked hadn't changed. "It is John I love. John who I don't regret marrying. John who I miss at this very moment. John who would not want to see me hurt like this. John the good man who saved me endless times. John who wanted me to remain me."

"Ruddock is no different," he said and took a step toward her and when she didn't move, he took another step. "My name may have changed, but I haven't."

"Why didn't you tell me?" she asked, aching for the feel of John's strong, comforting arms around her. She always felt safe wrapped in them. But would she feel safe now in the arms of a different man, not the man she thought she had wed?

"It is a complicated tale, one I don't understand myself, and that makes it all the more difficult to explain to you. But I will endeavor to do so if you give me the chance."

He sounded more like John, though recalling how he had spoken on the steps of the keep, like a lord that ruled with absolute authority, made her realize he had a side to him that she didn't know at all. So who was this man she had married?

She wiped at her eyes trying to catch the tears before they fell and that tore at Ruddock's heart. He hated seeing her hurt and hated even more that he was the cause. He moved fast, thinking she might stop him, and had her in his arms before she realized he was holding her.

Sorrell looked up at him, ready to order him to let her go.

"I can't stand to see you cry," he said and kissed at the corners of her eyes.

This was John, the man she loved, and she let herself relax against him as his arms closed snugly around her.

"I don't recall the last time I offered an apology to anyone. Northwick men rarely, if ever, apologize and I doubt you'll ever hear it from me again, though something warns me that might not be so, but..." He lifted her chin to look up at him. "I am sorry for any pain I may have caused you. I never meant to hurt you, only to protect you."

"Pain from a wound or an illness I can deal with. I know, in due time, it will come to an end. Pain that touches the heart can be never-ending and the thought of losing John stirs my heart with dreadful fear."

"You're not losing John. You're here in his arms where you belong," he assured her and lowered his mouth to hers only to have her turn her face away from him.

"Am I?" she asked when he drew his head back and she turned her head to face him and seeing the disappointment on his face tugged at her heart. "Will John be helping with the chores tomorrow? Will he listen to Melvin's complaints? Will he reside with his wife in the keep?"

"Those are all things we will discuss."

"And you will decide?" she asked and waited for an answer she already knew.

"We have much to discuss," he said.

Sorrell feared that she would die there and then, feeling as if her heart shattered in her chest. Refusing to answer her was an answer itself. It took all her willpower to step out of his embrace and not think it was like stepping away from him forever.

"That we do, Lord Ruddock," she said, keeping a tilt to her chin and her shoulders squared.

Ruddock didn't care for her demeanor. It seemed as if she had made a decision and not a good one for him. He wouldn't remind her again that they would stay wed, their marriage vows sealed. In time, she would calm, and they would talk.

But at the moment he had managed to clear the first hurdle. His true identity. The second hurdle would probably be difficult as well, since he knew without doubt that she would fly into a rage when she found out that she would not be remaining here with her sisters. She would be returning home with him.

Sorrell remained silent on their return walk to the keep, every spot she glanced at a memory of John and the joy she had shared with him. She had been so lost in those bittersweet memories that she hadn't realized he had taken hold of her hand as they walked. Or that her small fingers had instinctively entwined with his.

They fit, even though his were large and hers small. They fit as if they were meant to be together.

Erland greeted them once they entered the keep and Ruddock was quick to take his leave, reminding her they would talk later.

Sorrell was surprised to see the Great Hall so busy, filled with Ruddock's and Tarass's warriors enjoying the feast that had been prepared for her and John's small marriage celebration. But that was no more, since there was nothing to celebrate.

"My sisters?" Sorrell asked of one of the harried servants.

"Your mum's solar."

She climbed the stairs, unwanted tears filling her eyes, clouding them, and an aching pain squeezing at her heart. She didn't need more tears. She was stronger than that. She had to keep her head clear and her anger—or was it disappointment—at bay, and be wise about this. She would talk this out with her sisters and hopefully it would help to stop the pain of losing John.

Sorrell stood in front of the closed door, took a fortifying breath to keep calm and keep her tears from falling, and opened the door. As soon as Willow popped up from the chair and Snow turned toward the door, Sorrell's name spilling from her lips with worry, Sorrell burst into tears.

***

"How is my sister?" James asked.

Ruddock was pleased that the first thing out of James's mouth when he entered the solar was to inquire about Sorrell. Though, he didn't expect anything less, having come to know James.

"She does well enough," Ruddock said to ease James's concern.

"What you're saying is that it doesn't concern me, but I disagree. Sorrell is my sister and I will see her kept safe."

"That is my task now that I'm her husband."

"And a heavy task at that," Tarass threw in, handing Ruddock a goblet of wine. "She has a penchant for speaking her mind when she shouldn't and for getting herself into unlikely situations... for a woman."

Ruddock smiled. "Life will never be dull with her."

"That's for certain," James said and raised his goblet. "To you and my sister Sorrell, may you know endless happiness."

Tarass raised his goblet. "And may your patience never wear thin, since she will test it endlessly."

They all drank to the good wishes.

"You do know I won't pledge my loyalty to you," Tarass said.

"I never expected you to, though I will ask for your friendship, since we are close neighbors."

"And would your father approve? I assume he has sent you to conquer the area," Tarass said. "Of course, marrying into the Clan Macardle was a bloodless way to conquer. And with MacLoon owing you for coming to his aid, he'd have no choice but to pledge his fealty to the Clan Northwick. As for Seth MacCannish, his land borders mine and with his pledge you have a clan at my doorstep. Quite an achievement with nothing more than the exchange of vows."

"Is that why you came here? To wed one of the Macardle sisters and lay claim to the clan?" James demanded, an angry crease to his brow.

Ruddock shook his head as though the question was absurd. "You truly believe that Sorrell would have been my choice if that were true?"

"He makes a good point, James," Tarass said. "Willow would have been the sensible choice. She is reasonable and adapts to situations quite easily. Snow would not have been a thought since she is blind and would be more of a burden than a benefit."

James turned a questioning eye on Ruddock. "Then what was your reason for coming here?"

"Your clan wasn't my destination. I was searching for someone and that search brought me in this direction. I wanted nothing more than shelter and food from you for a day or two, then I met Sorrell."

"Are you saying it was a coincidence that you arrived here shortly after Walsh MacLoon reached out to your father for help?" James asked skeptically.

"I need not explain myself to you, James. What is done is done."

"And I'm to accept that and entrust my sister to you without knowing the truth of it all?" James argued.

"All you need to know right now is that I would never harm your sister or see her harmed. I will always protect her and the Clan Macardle as well. I will leave men here to help you prepare for winter. They will hunt and make certain your food sheds are full so that no one goes hungry, and they will protect the clan from any possible harm."

"That is generous of you," James said, his shoulders broadening some as if a weight had been lifted off them.

"There is also no need now for Willow to be forced to wed," Ruddock said, looking to Tarass.

"You're right, there isn't. With your influx of wealth to the Clan Macardle, James is no longer in need of my support."

"Willow will wed a man of her choice," Ruddock said.

James smiled. "She will be as pleased as am I. She is a sensible woman and will make a wise choice when the time comes." His smile faltered. "One other thing, you mentioned you would leave men here. Does that mean you and Sorrell will not be making your home here?"

"Aye, we'll reside in my home," Ruddock said.

"And how far is that from her sisters," James asked.

"A good three days' ride," Ruddock said with a slight cringe.

"I see you understand the problem. Sorrell will not want to be that far from her sisters."

"She has no choice," Tarass said.

"We're talking about Sorrell," James reminded them.

Tarass raised his goblet and smiled. "Good luck."

Ruddock didn't want to think about Sorrell's response when she learned she would be a distance from her sisters. There were other matters that required his attention, matters much easier to handle.

"We will talk more before I leave, James, but right now I will have a private word with Tarass."

James nodded. "I look forward to talking more with you."

Ruddock understood that James had more questions and concerns and he would address what he could while other issues would not be discussed. He already knew that would not be a problem with James since he now had what he had been so desperately trying to accomplish, protection and well-being for his sisters and clan.

Once the door closed behind James, Ruddock turned to Tarass.

"I heard the Lord of Fire was looking for me," Ruddock said. "What is it you want?"

"So you are the Ruddock I search for. After I learned that Finn Northwick disowned his son and wanted him dead, I thought you might be the Ruddock I searched for. If you knew I searched for you, why avoid me?" Tarass asked.

"I didn't know what you wanted from me and wasn't about to easily present myself to you in case you should want me dead. So again I ask, what do you want from me?"

"To speak with you," Tarass said, placing his goblet down on the small table.

"Speak with me?" Ruddock asked and took a step toward him. "Is that all you wanted to do?"

"That depends… were you with the barbaric tribe that killed my father and mother?"

Chapter Fourteen

Sorrell felt like she was spinning, her thoughts going round and round, going nowhere.

"There are no easy answers," Snow said, a contented Thaw curled in a ball asleep in her lap. "You won't know until Ruddock confides the truth to you."

"The truth… will he ever speak it to me?" Sorrell asked and felt as if she had repeated it for the umpteenth time since she had entered the room.

"It isn't the truth that disturbs you so much as it is the trust," Willow said. "You trusted him and he didn't return that trust, and so you question endlessly. You'll get no easy answer as Snow said, not even when Ruddock confides it in you. It will only come when you finally believe it yourself."

"You offer me wise words, but not easy ones to digest," Sorrell said, wishing differently.

"John is a good man," Snow said, "He protected you and defended you without pause or doubt, which means there must have been some trust there."

Sorrell reached out to Snow, in the chair beside her, and gave her hand a squeeze. "For a blind person you see more clearly than those who have sight."

"That's because she isn't as stubborn as you," Willow said. "You are wed and there is no undoing it. And the most important thing you need to remember is that you love John, and if I'm not mistaken that hasn't changed."

"Another reason you hurt so badly," Snow said. "You fear you have lost John when he is still very much with you. Though I don't blame you for feeling as you do, since John's true identity has been a shock to all of us. Still, what's most important is that Ruddock had ordered all others to wait while he went after you. You came first to him."

"Snow is right, his first concern was you," Willow said. "I told him not to go to you. That he should let you calm and talk with you later, but he told me he needed to go to you."

Snow chuckled. "Whether the man knows it or not, he is as much in love with you as you are with him."

"He has not voiced it," Sorrell said, wishing he had.

"But he has showed it every day to you, since the day he first protected you from Peter's mud balls," Willow said with a chuckle of her own.

Snow kept her voice low. "You consummated your vows. How did that go?"

"Snow, that's private, between Sorrell and Ruddock alone," Willow scolded, though she was just as curious.

A soft smile lit Sorrell's face. "It was astonishingly magnificent."

Willow and Snow giggled.

"So it felt right?" Willow asked.

Sorrell sighed. "More than right. It was as if—"

"Fate had fashioned you for each other?" Willow asked.

"Are you telling me that you think Ruddock and I are meant to be?"

"Isn't it obvious?" Willow asked.

"I'd like to believe it," Sorrell said, wishing all doubt would simply vanish.

"Then believe it," Snow said. "Or at least give yourself a chance to believe it."

"But no matter what comes of this, there is one thing that will always remain the same," Willow said and the three of them smiled and reached out to join hands. "We always—"

"Always," Sorrell and Snow echoed.

"Have one another," Willow finished.

"Even though you'll be a distance from us, we'll plan long visits," Snow said, "though I do not look forward to bidding you farewell."

Sorrell scrunched her brow wondering what Snow was talking about until it finally struck her. "I must go live with my husband at his home. I hadn't given that thought." She shook her head, looking from one sister to the other. "How do I live without the two of you?"

***

"Why would you think I was with a barbaric tribe?" Ruddock asked, walking away from Tarass to refill his goblet with wine.

Tarass swiped his goblet off the table and walked over to Ruddock and held it out to him. "There were tales of a giant man who was spotted on raids with the barbarian tribes of the far north. I thought them just that tales, until one day I met an old woman who had seen the giant with her own eyes. That's when I began searching for you."

Ruddock filled both their goblets and returned to one of the two chairs in front of the crackling fire.

Tarass joined him, taking the other chair.

"You look for the man who killed your parents," Ruddock said.

"Viciously murdered my parents," Tarass corrected. "A wee bairn was the only one to survive the attack on the small village my parents had sought shelter in for the night. The child kept talking about a giant, but he was so small that most anyone would be a giant to him. I foolishly dismissed him. Then sometime later after hearing the tale grow, I met an old woman who had seen him when a tribe came through their village. Reddock, she called him, though later, as I learned more, I realized she meant Ruddock. The description she gave me fits you perfectly."

"And many like me."

"Except there are few who have gone on raids with barbaric tribes," Tarass said. "So I ask you. Are you the giant who killed my parents?"

"What village?" Ruddock asked, nightmares rising up to torment him.

"Sandvik," Tarass said and his stomach clenched when Ruddock's eyes squeezed shut and his face scrunched in agony.

"That was a bloodbath," Ruddock said as he opened his eyes. "A rogue tribe was responsible for it. Banishment is a form of punishment among the tribes, and if you meet that fate, then no other tribe will accept you. You will be alone, on your own to survive. Those who are discarded often band together and form a rogue tribe. Some of those rogue tribes can be vicious and with no astute leadership they never last. The other tribes usually see to their demise. The rogue tribe you speak of was dealt with swiftly and there had not been any talk about a giant among them. Whoever killed your parents are dead."

"There was a giant among them and he killed my parents, and I intend to kill him," Tarass said in warning.

"Then you waste your time with me, since I took no part of that atrocity. It is another giant you're after."

Tarass shot a heated glare at Ruddock. "I'm supposed to take your word for it?"

"It is the truth. I care not if you believe me, but you waste your time if you don't." Ruddock stood. "I have much to see to before I return home."

Tarass got to his feet quickly. "If you are lying to me—"

"You know where I will be," Ruddock said.

Tarass went to the door but before opening it, he turned and asked. "What makes you so sure that all in that rogue tribe are dead?"

"Because I'm the one who hunted each of them down and killed them."

***

Sorrell needed to clear her head of all the endless thoughts that refused to leave her be. She decided the best way to achieve that was with work. Keeping busy would not give her a chance to think. There were baskets of food in the kitchen waiting to be stored in the new shed. She'd find Melvin and Dole and set them to the task.

She stopped when she entered the kitchen. Several Northwick warriors were busy carrying the food baskets out.

Sorrell walked over to Dorrit. "What goes on here?"

"Lord Ruddock ordered his warriors to see to filling the new food storage shed under my direction. It is almost done. He also ordered his warriors to hunt and see that the meat shed is made full for winter." Dorrit's whole face lit with a smile. "It will be a good winter for the clan. No fear of starving and no worry of battle with Clan MacLoon." A tear touched the corner of her eye. "You did good by the clan, Sorrell."

Sorrell did her best to smile and left Dorrit directing the warriors at their task. She walked through the village bewildered by the busy activity going on and the joy on the peoples' faces.

"It's a miracle it is," Melvin said, raising the tankard he held in his hand. "My good friend Lord Ruddock does well by us."

"Melvin," a man shouted, "come drink with us and tell us more about Lord Ruddock."

Melvin grinned. "You are a good soul, Sorrell. You have done well for the clan."

Sorrell heard it again and again as she walked through the village. Her thoughts had been so busy on John that she hadn't realized the extent of the benefits to her clan that her marriage to Lord Ruddock would bring.

The clan had, and they were rejoicing.

Any thought of ending her marriage was impossible now, not that it had been much of a thought. It was one that had struck her out of hurt and anger. It also had pained her heart to think of never seeing John again.

Ruddock.

It would take getting used to calling John by another name. She feared each time she did that John, the man she had come to love, would slip further and further away from her. That was a good reason to get to know Ruddock better.

Shouts of joy brought her out of her reverie and she saw two Northwick warriors carrying the cleaned carcass of a deer through the village.

"Your husband didn't waste a moment in seeing that the clan is looked after," James said after stopping beside her. "He has also ordered more cottages to be built for the warriors he will leave behind to protect the clan. You have done—"

"I haven't done well by the clan. I married John, a common man who brought nothing with him."

"That's not true," James argued. "John brought honor to our clan by marrying you and not letting your good name be ruined."

"Or I could argue that he wed me to expand his father's holdings in this area."

"Something I questioned myself and asked him, and he claims it is not so," James said. "Will you protest the marriage?"

Did she trust Ruddock had spoken the truth, when there had been so many lies?

"How can you ask me that when you see for yourself what my unexpected marriage has brought to our clan?" She shook her head. "No, I won't protest the marriage. I am wed to Lord Ruddock, our vows sealed, and I will remain wed to him."

James's shoulders sagged in relief. "I know you will do well with Lord Ruddock and just think of how your marriage benefits your sisters. Lord Ruddock has ordered that Willow is to wed a man of her choosing, and Snow will always be protected."

"I am more than pleased for my sisters," she said relieved Willow would not suffer a forced marriage and Snow would be kept safe.

"The Great Hall will fill with celebration tonight. Lord Ruddock has ordered food and drink for all. You should go prepare for it."

She nodded and saw what James meant. Fire pits had been built for the meat that would be roasted over them and torches had been attached to thick tree limbs that had been stuck deep in the ground. Ale was flowing freely and laughter spreading.

All would celebrate her wedding… all but Sorrell.

Night was fast encroaching on dusk when Sorrell entered through the keep's kitchen. She purposely avoided the Great Hall, having heard laughter and song coming from it. She had no desire to participate in the festivities. She preferred what her husband had often wanted for himself… solitude.

She hadn't seen John… Ruddock. Would she ever get used to calling him by that name? Since he had left her in the Great Hall to go off and speak with James and Tarass, he had made no effort to see her at all. She also had made no effort to seek him out. She hadn't wanted to see him, and she still didn't want to see him.

Frustration, anger, disappointment, they all continued to haunt her in various ways. It was better if she were alone. She had no idea how she would receive him if she were to see him. Her bedchamber was where she sought solace when her thoughts overwhelmed her, but if he did look for her, he would surely go there.

Instead, she went to the one place she knew would be empty. A place where no one went anymore… her parents' bedchamber.

She climbed the stairs to the third floor. No other rooms occupied this floor. Her father intentionally wanted it kept private, a place that he and his wife could go to and be alone, separate from everyone but each other.

Sorrell stopped as she got closer to the door, thinking she heard something. She scrunched her eyes when a flickering light at the narrow space at the bottom of the door caught her attention. It couldn't be. It was impossible. No one came to this room. It had stayed closed and untended since her father's death. And though James was entitled to make it his own, he had chosen not to and she and her sisters had been grateful. He had told them that in time, when he wed, he would make use of it. Until then, it sat unused, nothing more than memories to keep it company.

That her parents' sanctuary had been invaded infuriated Sorrell and she rushed at the door, words already on her lips as she swung it open to take to task the person who had the audacity to do such a thing.

The words died on her lips as she stared at her husband rising out of the round wooden tub before the hearth, naked, and water running in rivulets along every muscle and curve of his body.

Chapter Fifteen

Never had Sorrell seen such a finely-toned muscled body. It was as though every inch of him had been chiseled to perfection... even his face.

She stared, scrunched her eyes shut, then opened them again, not sure if she was seeing clearly. His beard was gone and his long hair cut to fall just above his shoulders. She had thought he had fine features upon meeting him, but he was far more handsome, his features far more defined, without the beard. So much so that her breath caught for a moment.

All traces of John were gone. This man was now her husband.

Her breath caught again when her eyes drifted—who was she fooling—her eyes didn't drift, they shot to his manhood. Her first thought was how had it ever fit inside her? The immediate thought that followed was... *he was aroused.*

"I was thinking about you," he said, it being all too obvious at what she was thinking.

That brought her eyes up to meet his.

Why? Why? Why did she have to grow damp? Her annoyance reminded her of the reason she had entered the room in a rush and was grateful it took her thoughts elsewhere. "What right have you to invade my parents' bedchamber?"

"I meant no disrespect to your parents, but we needed a more private place to talk. Your room is much too close to your sisters' rooms to have any true privacy."

Sorrell saw that he had had the room cleaned. Not a spot of dust lingered on the furniture or the floor, several candles were lit around the room, and the bedding had been made fresh.

"I also wanted to be far from the noise of the celebration."

So he wished to avoid the celebration as much as she did. She almost smiled, catching a glimpse of John in Ruddock, and her annoyance settled some.

"You'll catch a chill. Dry yourself," Sorrell ordered in her usual direct manner.

Ruddock picked up one of the towels off the stool beside the tub and held it out to Sorrell. "Dry me?"

Sorrell didn't have to think about it, her response came quick. "You don't need my help."

"I didn't say I needed it. I prefer it."

She was tempted, but uncertain of what to do.

"Too fearful to come near me, Sorrell?" he challenged.

"I wisely keep my distance from strangers."

"I can easily remind you that we're far from strangers." He took a step toward her and stopped when she took a hasty step back.

"We should talk," she said.

Ruddock wanted to roar out his frustration. He was tired of talking. He wanted to take his wife in his arms and make love to her, preferably all night. But she deserved some answers.

He dried himself quickly and tossed the towel aside, leaving some parts of himself still glistening with bath water and went to the sideboard and filled two goblets with wine from the tall decanter and walked over to her.

"You should put something on," she said as he approached.

"No. I'm going to remain naked since when we're finished talking, I'm going to strip you of your clothes, carry you to the bed and make certain you have a proper, possibly not so proper, wedding night." He handed her one of the goblets.

Sorrell took it from him, a slight tremor to her hand. The tremor wasn't from fear or him being naked. She trembled at the thought of making love with him. He was different from John, more so now with his beard gone and his hair shorter, making him more a stranger to her. And how did she make love with a stranger? But how did she deny her husband? Or herself, since desire continued to stir in her.

A knock sounded at the door.

"Do you need anything, Lord Ruddock?" a servant asked.

"Enter and remove the tub," Ruddock ordered.

The door swung open and when Sorrell saw that her husband intended to remain naked in front of the servants, she jumped in front of him, her back keeping his private parts private.

Ruddock liked that his wife intended to keep anyone from seeing him naked. He hoped it was because she wanted to keep him all to herself, though he figured it was more out of embarrassment that she shielded him from anyone seeing his manhood.

He warned himself to behave with her being so close, but how could he not take advantage of the situation. He slipped his arm around her waist and with a slight yank had her locked back against him.

Sorrell caught her gasp before it could slip from her mouth, though she wished he could hear the silent oath she let loose in her head.

"I've missed you, wife," he whispered softly.

Her annoyance dissipated and her eyes drifted closed for a moment, seeing John in her mind, standing behind her, his arm snug around her, and her response spilled without bidding from her lips. "I've missed you as well, husband."

Silence settled between them and not a peaceful silence. It was a silence marked with passion. It built slowly, his arm resting snug around her waist while his hand caressed the slim curve above her hip, and his manhood rubbed and poked at the back of her garment as if demanding entrance.

He didn't kiss her, but he might as well have, since he brought his goblet to her lips, even though she still held her own, far too tightly, and ran the edge of it slowly along her bottom lip before tilting it up just enough for a dribble of wine to touch her lips.

It didn't take long for it to make her grow madly impatient for the want of his lips on hers.

John. John.

This was John. The man she married. The man she loved. Never would she feel such desire for anyone but him.

She rested her hand on his arm and gave it a squeeze and wished that the servants would hurry and finish their task. She could not wait much longer to feel her husband bury himself deep inside her.

Ruddock had intended a playful tease, no more. That hadn't been possible once he started. His passion had already been aroused and it didn't take much for it to swell. Her scent alone could arouse him, a gentle flowery aroma that tickled the nose and roused the senses.

Lord, how he wanted to strip her bare, toss her on the bed, and bury himself inside her until they both exploded in pleasure. But she needed a proper wedding night, a proper introduction to coupling, not another quick poke like he had given her earlier.

God help him. He didn't know how he'd be able to last when his manhood throbbed, more like begged, for immediate release.

The last servant was about to shut the door, when two more entered and placed food and drink on a small table.

"I will not be disturbed until morning," Ruddock ordered sharply and the servant lass gave a quick nod and hastily closed the door behind her.

Ruddock released Sorrell, grabbed her goblet out of her hand, and placed both his and hers aside before scooping her up in his arms and bringing his lips down on hers in a not so gentle kiss.

Sorrell matched his kiss with her own frenzied eagerness, not able to get enough of him.

By the time he reached the bed, he had to tear his lips away from hers for them to take a much needed breath.

"Good God, wife, but I want you," he said with a low growl and lowered her to stand in front of him.

He didn't waste a minute stripping her and was pleased when she joined in, helping him rid herself of her garments. He had worried that she might shy away from him with all that had happened today and how she had stared at him when she had entered the room, like she didn't know him. But then his Sorrell was no coward and besides, she loved him. And though he had feared that might have changed, this moment proved it hadn't.

"I should—"

"Be inside me now," she insisted and fell back on the bed, pulling him down with her.

He made sure his hands hit the bed at either side of her head to keep his large body from crashing against her small one. And it was a good thing he did, since she was quick to swing her legs around his waist and hug him to her.

"Now, John, now. Please, I cannot wait another moment," she pleaded.

That she wanted him so badly heightened his own passion to the breaking point, and she loosened her legs from around him as he moved to balance himself on his knees between them. He grabbed hold of her backside and without hesitation plunged into her.

She let out a long moan and arched against him, taking him deeper inside her.

It was a frenzied, demanding joining as if they would never get enough of each other.

"Don't stop. Please don't stop," she begged, her fingers digging into his arms in a tight grip.

She had no worry about that, Ruddock had no intention of stopping, not until…

Ruddock dropped his head back and roared as a climax slammed through his body a moment after Sorrell shouted out his name as her climax crashed upon her in wave after wave of pleasure.

After he gave a last groan, he realized that Sorrell was wiggling against him and went to pull out of her, afraid he had hurt her.

"No, don't," she pleaded, arching up against him. "I-I…" She moaned, pressing against him.

Ruddock realized she was near another climax and hurried to satisfy her before he grew too soft to do so. It didn't take her long and he enjoyed watching her burst with pleasure once again.

When she finally lay snug in the crook of his arm, her naked body pressed close to his, she sighed. "Lovemaking is far more satisfying than I expected."

He had thought to tell her that she experienced only a small portion of it, but decided he'd show her over time instead.

She looked up at him, her expression serious. "I won't wear you out will I. You'll let me know if you're not up to it."

He couldn't stop the laugh that burst out of him.

Sorrell sat up quickly. "It isn't humorous. I don't want to demand too much of you in bed and have you grow tired of me."

Ruddock couldn't keep from laughing.

Sorrell punched him in the arm, though she did enjoy his hardy, deep laugh, since she had never heard it before. "It isn't funny. I'm serious."

Ruddock snagged hold of her waist and swung her to land stretched out over him, her face close to his, and his laughter fading. "You will never wear me out, never demand too much of me in bed, I will always be up to making love to you, and never ever will I grow tired of you."

She reached her hand up to trace his clean shaven jaw. "You look so different."

"I grew tired of hiding behind the beard and I thought it only fair you saw all of me."

He had cut his beard for her, so she could see who he truly was and that touched her heart. "You didn't have to."

"Aye, I did. There is enough you don't know about me. I would least have you know the whole of my face."

Her stomach took that moment to gurgle quite loudly.

"Have you eaten today?" he asked.

Sorrell had to think about it.

"If you must think on it, that tells me you don't remember when you last ate." He gave her bare backside a soft slap. "Up and off me, we eat."

"But I like being on top of you."

He tilted his head back, scrunching his eyes. "Your innocent remarks, wife, are going to do me in." He slapped her backside not as softly as before. "Up with you, you need to eat and so do I."

She rolled off him then and he quickly slipped out of bed, surprised that he felt an arousal stirring in him. He turned to offer his hand to her but she had already left the bed and was walking toward the food.

Everything had happened so quickly between them once the servants left the room, he hadn't had a chance to enjoy the pleasure of seeing his wife naked. Now that he did, he took his time.

There was a graceful slimness to her petite body and gentle curves and a firmness to her backside, that he had enjoyed gripping as he had plunged in and out of her. Her breasts would fit his hand nicely and her nipples were a rosy color he couldn't wait to taste. Her red hair was a mass of curls that looked to be as untamable as she was and he smiled at the thought.

She turned with a bowl in her hand, piled with meat, cheese, and bread. "We'll share." She walked over to him and tugged at his hand for him to follow her back to bed.

He was glad she was comfortable being naked in front of him after only having wed him this morning. But then there had been a shared comfort between them, an easiness he had not felt with anyone.

She handed him the bowl, then climbed into bed, slipping her legs beneath the blanket and tucked it up to her waist.

He almost groaned with regret. Her thatch of red hair between her legs tempted, since the pleasure that laid hidden there was for him and him alone.

She held her hand out to take the bowl from him and he caught her slight shiver and nearly cursed aloud. He'd been too enamored with her body to give thought that the room held a chill. The cold rarely bothered him, being so big, but she was petite and chilled much faster than he ever would.

After returning the bowl to her, he went to the hearth and added more logs, then to the pegs lining the one wall. He returned to her and held up a green, soft wool shawl.

"I assume this belonged to your mum. I don't think she would mind you borrowing it if she knew a chill ran through you."

"It did belong to my mum. It was a favorite of hers." Sorrell reached up and took it from him and draped it around her shoulders. It was like her mum's arms had wrapped around her, hugging her, and letting her know she was happy for her.

Ruddock joined her in bed and under the blanket, pressing his leg against hers to help keep her warm.

She turned a smile on her husband. "Sometimes I can see John in you, at other times today you seemed a stranger to me. I know not what to make of it."

"Give us time," he said, hoping time would be his friend and not his enemy. He took a piece of cheese from the bowl and handed it to her. "You wanted to talk."

Sorrell took a bite, giving herself time to respond.

Ruddock waited, taking a bite of cheese himself.

"I don't think I want to talk tonight," she finally said.

He was relieved. This time with her was pleasant and he didn't want to ruin it with things he knew would upset her.

"As you wish," he said.

"I do want to thank you for all you are doing for the clan. The people are relieved that the winter won't see a shortage of food. And James walks with a lighter step, his burden having been lifted."

"James treated me well and your clan made no complaints against me. You even offered me a home. Therefore, I return what you so graciously shared," he said, taking the last of the bread from the bowl and holding it out to her.

Sorrell shook her head, letting him know she didn't want it, that he was welcome to it.

"A home is important," she said, thinking of her sisters, James, and even Thaw, the little pup humorous to watch.

"Aye, it is," he said, "but home to me will always be wherever you are," Ruddock said and tapped her playfully on the tip of her nose.

The way she narrowed her eyes and gave a slight tilt of her head had him thinking she contemplated a question that might end their pleasant evening. He was grateful for the big yawn that rose up and prevented any words from leaving her mouth.

"You're tired. You need to sleep," he said, snatching the near empty bowl off her lap and placing it on the small table beside the bed.

She had hoped to make love again with him, but he was right. She was tired, another yawn proving that as did the slump to her body.

Ruddock eased under the blanket with her and before he could take her in his arms, she snuggled against him. He closed his arms around her and the contentment that filled him overwhelmed him. He couldn't recall when he had last felt this content and he didn't ever want to lose it again.

She yawned against his chest, then sighed. "I think my da and mum would be pleased that we spent our wedding night in their bedchamber. They began a happy life here and that holds promise for us. I look forward to more nights in this room with you before we leave for your home."

At least she had realized they wouldn't be remaining here, though he didn't look forward to telling her in the morning that they would be leaving by mid-day.

Chapter Sixteen

Sorrell stretched herself awake and turned to hug her husband only to find herself alone in bed. She sat up to find she wasn't only alone in bed but the room as well. The light from the lone window was no help in letting her know the hour, since it was a gray day.

Why hadn't he woken her, there were the day's chores to see to. He may no longer be doing any, but she still had responsibilities to her clan.

She hurried into her garments and snatched up her boots. She'd stop in her bedchamber to give her face a wash and tie her hair back, for all the good that would do, then find her husband before she saw to the chores.

A bright smile lit her face as she thought how much she had enjoyed sleeping in her husband's arms. His big body had kept the chill away and his arms had cradled her with comfort. She looked forward to all the nights to come with him.

Her smile and that thought vanished when she entered her room to find Willow and Snow packing her belongings in a chest.

"What are you doing?" Sorrell demanded.

"Oh dear, he hasn't told you yet," Snow said and Thaw gave a yelp from where he lay in the center of Sorrell's bed.

"Told me what?" Sorrell asked and didn't care for the sadness she saw in Willow's eyes or the way she hesitated to respond.

"You leave today," Willow said.

Sorrell pursed her lips, narrowed her eyes, dropped her boots on the floor, and marched out of the room.

"She's angry, isn't she?" Snow asked.
"Beyond angry," Willow said.
"Should we try to calm her?"
"No, that's for Ruddock to do now."
Snow chuckled. "Poor man."

***

Sorrell paid no heed to her bare feet as she left the keep, finding no signs of her husband there. She wore no cloak either, the cold air nipping through her garments, but she didn't care. She was on a mission to find her husband and let him know, most emphatically, that she would not be taking leave of her home today.

The wind caught her curls and whipped them around her face, but she paid them no heed as well. She spotted one of her husband's warriors near the stable, ordering Melvin and Dole about and walked over to him, giving him a hard tap on the back.

The tall, broad-shouldered warrior turned with a start and looked surprised to see the petite woman in front of him.

"What are you doing?" Sorrell demanded.

Melvin was quick to respond. "He thinks he can order me and Dole about. I told him we only take orders from you, Sorrell."

The warrior bobbed his head at her. "Pardon me, Lady Sorrell, I didn't know it was you. These men are to see to building a new fence to the east side of the stable."

"That isn't a chore I would entrust to either of them," she said, a bit taken back by being referred to as *Lady Sorrell*.

"Those are my orders, my lady."

"We don't take orders from you," Melvin said, jabbing his finger in the air in his direction.

"Aye, from now on you do," the warrior said. "Or you'll find yourself spending time in the stock.

Dole snickered. "We don't' have a stock."

"You will have two by the week's end," the warrior said.

"What is this, Sorrell?" Melvin asked. "We've never had need of one stock let alone two."

"There must be some mistake. We don't use stocks here," Sorrell said, annoyed that two would be built without her knowledge.

"Lord Ruddock's orders, my lady," the warrior said and looked to Melvin and Dole. "Get to work on that fence."

"They won't be doing the fence," Sorrell said and received a grateful look from Melvin.

"Forgive me, my lady, but I follow Lord Ruddock's orders and he says these two will build a new fence today."

"He of all people should know that these two aren't capable of it."

"Sorrell's right, me and Dole can't do it," Melvin said, nodding in agreement with Sorrell.

"You've addressed Lady Sorrell most improperly several times. You will address her properly from this moment on," the warrior corrected.

"She's just Sorrell to us," Melvin said.

"No more. Lady Sorrell is Lord Ruddock's wife and will be addressed according to her title," the warrior warned.

"I am Sorrell to the Clan Macardle and will remain so," Sorrell ordered in a tone that left no doubt she meant it. "Melvin. Dole. Go see what help Dorrit might need."

"Will do, *Sorrell*," Melvin said purposely emphasizing her name, then quickly took off, Dole close behind him before the warrior could stop them.

She was about to take the warrior to task when she heard a disturbance in the stable and when she saw the cause, a warrior having a difficult, if not impossible time, controlling her horse, Prince, as he escorted him out, anger took hold.

"What do you think you're doing?" she screamed at him and her horse grew agitated.

The warrior tightened his hold on the reins and looked about to argue with her when the warrior she had been speaking with spoke up.

"This is Lady Sorrell."

The warrior immediately bobbed his head in respect. "My lady, your horse is to join our horses for the journey home."

Sorrell walked over to him, seeing Prince grow more agitated, and held out her hand. "Give me his reins."

The warrior didn't know what to do. "I have my orders, my lady."

"He is my horse. Give me his reins," she demanded and Prince pounded the ground with his hoof.

The warrior yanked on the reins, agitating Prince all the more and causing him to rear up.

The other warrior reached out and yanked Sorrell away from the horse while the other warrior tried to get Prince under control.

Sorrell turned on the warrior, giving him a punch in the gut, not that it hurt him, but it startled him enough to release her and knowing the other warrior wouldn't surrender the reins, she charged at him.

She lowered her head as she got near him and rammed him in the gut, and the reins left his hands as the breath was knocked from him, and he tumbled to the ground.

"Easy, Prince, easy," she cajoled. "Everything is all right. No one is taking you from me." It took only a moment to calm him down, though he continued to paw the ground, to let her know he was still upset.

"What goes on here?" Ruddock demanded angrily as he approached with four warriors trailing him.

The warrior on the ground scrambled to his feet while the other warrior actually looked terrified.

Sorrell remained beside Prince, keeping her eyes on her husband. He looked nothing like John anymore. He was striking in his clean, dark green plaid with slim lines of yellow and red running through it, and a pale yellow shirt beneath. It fit snug at his waist, as did the piece that ran across one shoulder and down on an angle to his waist.

He appeared a man of power, though his size and his angry look gave one pause and cautioned one to keep a distance. The thing Sorrell didn't understand was why the warriors appeared fearful of him. You could see it in how they avoided standing too close to him and how they tensed when he snapped orders.

Ruddock turned a glare on the warrior who Sorrell had knocked off his feet. "What were you doing on the ground?" Before the warrior could respond, Ruddock turned to the other warrior. "And why aren't Melvin and Dole working on the fence?"

Both men's eyes went to Sorrell.

Ruddock looked to his wife and when he saw her bare feet, he demanded, "Where are your shoes?"

"In my room where I left them when I came upon my sisters packing my things."

"Go!" he ordered with a raised voice, but not a shout, dismissing his warriors.

"You should have told me last night," she said, walking Prince over to the fenced area next to the stable and freeing him to run out the rest of his agitation.

"I didn't want to spoil the evening," Ruddock admitted, joining her by the fence. "Last night would have been ruined if I had told you and I didn't want that."

Hearing that, she was glad he hadn't told her last night. She would have never had the wonderful memories they had made.

"You're right. I wouldn't have wanted that either," she confessed.

"A wife who admits when she is wrong. I'm a lucky man."

"Not too lucky, since I'm rarely wrong," she said with a teasing smile and thought how easily she calmed around him.

Ruddock gave a quick laugh. "I'll have to remember that." He reached out and eased her close to him. "I wish I could give you more time with your sisters, but it is imperative I return home at once,"

"A few days will matter?" she asked, resting her hand on his chest and recalling what a comfortable pillow it had made last night.

"I wish it wouldn't. I'd like us to spend more time here before taking you home. Unfortunately, I can't delay my return. My father is dying and I don't know how much time he has left."

Sorrell's stomach roiled and her heart hurt for her husband, reminded of her own da's death and the pain it had brought. She wanted to hug him close and ease his pain, but there was no sadness in his eyes or sorrow in his voice. He didn't care that his father was dying. Why? What had happened to make him feel that way?

"I'm sorry to hear that," she said. "Of course, you must leave right away."

"My lord," a warrior called out, interrupting their private moment. "You are needed."

Sorrell contained her annoyance. She needed time to speak with him. It wasn't necessary that she go with him? She could join him later, though the idea left an ache in her heart. Would she miss him too much?

"We leave at mid-day. Hurry and get done."

She took hold of his arm when he went to walk away. "There are things we need to discuss."

"On the journey home."

"No, they need to be discussed here," she said firmly. "I will not see two stocks erected here. We don't punish our clan that way. And you of all people should know that Melvin and Dole aren't capable of building a fence."

"I have no time for this, Sorrell."

"Make time," she snapped.

"Go speak to James, it has already been discussed and agreed upon. Now go prepare to take your leave. The hour will be upon us soon."

He turned and strode off before she could say another word, his commanding manner irritating her.

"Sorrell," he called out without looking back. "Don't ever interfere with my command again."

She was about to go after him and tell him exactly what he could do with his command when she heard Prince's agitated cry. She turned to see a figure on the edge of the woods, bow and arrow in hand ready to release the arrow arched in the air.

The target was obvious... her husband.

She took off running, gaining as much speed as she could while screaming the name most familiar to her. "John!"

He turned just as she hurdled herself into his arms with such force that he stumbled, the arrow grazing Sorrell's upper arm as it whizzed past them.

Chaos broke loose, Ruddock yelling out what sounded like a battle cry and warriors descending on them, some rushing into the woods, others keeping guard around the couple.

"Do you have a death wish, wife, risking your life to save mine?" Ruddock asked, trying to keep the fury and fright out of his voice as he dropped his arm from around her waist, his stomach clenching with fear that he might have lost her.

His heart slammed against his chest when he saw the blood that stained her sleeve. "You're bleeding."

Sorrell was still a bit stunned from throwing herself against her husband. The impact had been hard, though his arm had gone around her fast enough. She turned to give the wound a look and a bout of dizziness hit her as she pulled at the tear in her sleeve. It was nothing more than a scratch. It would be fine, she went to tell him, but her words failed to reach her mouth and everything around her began to fade.

Faint?

No, it wasn't possible. She'd never fainted. She wouldn't let herself, her last thought as she slumped into darkness.

Ruddock caught his wife up in his arms as soon as he felt her body go limp and he let out several oaths as he hurried her to the keep.

***

"She's fine. It's a minor wound, barely a scratch. Some honey and a bandage will see it right in no time."

Sorrell listened to her sister Willow's reassuring voice as she drifted out of the faint. She couldn't believe she'd fainted. She'd never fainted and it annoyed her that she had. It certainly hadn't been the wound that did it. It was throwing herself so hard at her husband and hitting solid muscle that had done her in.

"Does she need to rest? Do I need to delay our departure?"

A day or two, Sorrell thought, giving her more time with her sisters, and guilt stabbed at her. She had heard the worry in her husband's voice. He was concerned enough to delay their departure if necessary. She wasn't one to lie and she wouldn't start now.

"While I would love to have my sister remain a day or two more, the wound does not warrant a delay in your departure," Willow said. "Sorrell would say the same if asked. Sorrell will always speak the truth to you whether you want to hear it or not."

"It's one of the things I admire about her," Ruddock said. "It isn't always easy to keep a truthful tongue."

"Why not?" Sorrell asked, opening her eyes.

She was surprised when James answered.

"Sometimes the truth can cause more pain than it's worth."

Ruddock nodded at James, agreeing and knowing that only someone who lived through the difficulty of undeserved lies could understand the truth of his words.

He went and sat beside his wife on the bed, tucking one of her wild red curls behind her ear. Her hair was as brazen in color as she was in manner. He tapped her gently on the tip of her nose. "Never again put your life in danger to save mine."

"Would you do it for me? A foolish question," she said shaking her head. "Of course, you would and I would do the same for you."

"You will not. I forbid it," Ruddock demanded and heard a low chuckle come from her sisters.

"Why did someone try to kill you?" she asked, ignoring his command and thinking that she had yet to take him to task for his commanding manner with her.

For a number of reasons, he thought, but said, "I don't know, but I plan to find out and don't think you're going to get involved in it."

He heard her sisters chuckle again.

There was no way she won't get involved with finding out who attempted to kill her husband, but for now she would hold her tongue… on that matter.

"I'll go fetch what I need to tend your wound," Willow said, thinking it best the couple had a few moments alone and stretched her hand out to Snow, intending to give her a tug to let her know she should join her, when Snow spoke up.

"I'll go with you," Snow said and scooped up a sleeping Thaw from in front of the hearth and took Willow's hand she felt at hers.

"I'll see how the search goes," James said, understanding what Willow intended and got a smile from her.

"I'll be along shortly," Ruddock assured him.

"James," Sorrell called out just when he went to step out of the room and he turned. "Did you agree to two stocks being built?"

"I did," James said and went on to explain. "There will be curiosity seekers when word spreads about Lord Northwick's power coming to this area. Stocks will be a deterrent to those who flaunt our rules and they will be used with caution. And I hope never to use either of them on any of our clan, but if necessary I will. Your husband is a wise man, don't question him."

Ruddock spoke as soon as he heard the door click closed. "I can think of one person you would have put in the stocks by now and probably more than once, if you had had one."

"Maybe I would have put Melvin in the stocks and more than once," she said grudgingly. "But you can't be that wise if you ordered him and Dole to build a fence after the disaster that happened when you had him repair one."

"The very reason he is building one, to learn he can't get out of chores no matter how disastrous his attempts. And I believe you'll find his building skills improve rapidly."

Sorrell placed her hand on his warm cheek. "You are a wise man."

"I am glad you believe that and now you'll question my decisions no more." He pressed his finger to her lips to stop her from arguing. "What matters to me right now is you."

She eased his finger away from her mouth. "And you matter to me, so please do not keep things from me or I will worry endlessly about you, like now. You've showed no surprise at the attempt on your life. You know something yet refuse to tell me. I would not keep something so important from you."

He hadn't confided anything in anyone in some time. There hadn't been anyone he could trust, until he met Sorrell.

"My father let it be known that he would pay a handsome price to see me dead. His imminent death had him rethinking his decision. I assume some people haven't received word as to my father's change of heart, not that he has one. I will tell you more about it on our journey home."

Sorrell went to sit up and Ruddock's arm reached around her and eased her up. She rested her hand on his arm and gave him a gentle kiss.

"I am so sorry your father caused you such suffering. That is a horrible thing for a father to do to his son, and I am glad I will be with you to protect you from him."

That she even thought she could protect him touched his heart, but then by now nothing she did should surprise him. And the thought that he might have lost her today after having only found her tore at his heart.

"You will not put yourself in harm's way for me, wife, and that is final. I will not tell you again. You will obey me on this." He kissed her quick before she could object, then made a hasty retreat to the door, concerned if he remained he'd want to do more than simply kiss her.

"You'll have a problem if you keep ordering me about and think I will obey," she called out to him.

Ruddock turned. "And you'll have a bigger problem if you don't obey me, for I'll take a hand to your backside."

Sorrell gasped. "You wouldn't dare."

Ruddock laughed. "Oh, lass, the last thing you want to do is dare me."

***

Sorrell stood on the steps of the keep, her sisters to either side of her. The horses waited at the bottom of the steps, departure imminent. She was to ride with Ruddock. He had insisted on it and she hadn't objected, since it would give them time to talk.

Prince, her horse, would follow behind them, if he should be needed. The animal would be good and follow without a problem, seeing that he wasn't being separated from her.

However, she was being separated from her sisters and she was sure her heart would shatter. They had never been apart, and she didn't know how she'd live without seeing them every day. Who would she take her troubles to? Who would tend her when she got ill? Who would laugh with her? Who would hold her tight when she needed comfort?

"Ruddock will be there for you," Willow said as if she had heard her sister's thoughts.

Sorrell grabbed Willow and Snow into a tight hug, fighting back tears, fighting the ache in her heart. "This is more difficult than I thought, leaving you both, leaving my home. It breaks my heart."

"I envy you," Snow said, surprising both sisters. "You go off to start your own home as it should be, have your own children, watch them grow, and fall more deeply in love with your husband. We've talked endlessly about always being together, but I think we knew a day like this would come when fate set us on different paths. We will always be in one another's hearts and thoughts and we will visit often, but as Mum would have told you... it's time for you to live your own life now."

"When did you get so wise?" Sorrell asked.

Snow smiled. "I've always been wise. You just never paid heed to it."

The three sisters laughed as tears trickled down their cheeks.

The three hugged and kissed repeatedly.

"Once I'm settled and see things going well, you'll come visit," Sorrell said.

Willow wiped at the tears that refused to stop falling. "You couldn't keep us away."

"And I'll come back and visit often," Sorrell said, wiping at her own tears.

"My word that you all will see each other as often as you like," Ruddock said, halfway up the steps.

Sorrell tensed and her sisters gripped her hands.

It was time for her to leave.

Sorrell looked to James standing behind them and was surprised to see his eyes glistening with tears.

She went to him. "You will look after my sisters and keep them safe?"

"You have my word, and, Sorrell, believe it or not I will miss you."

Sorrell reached out and pulled him into a tight hug. "And I will miss you, dear brother."

She hurried back to her sisters, more tears falling, and hugged and kissed them one last time. She reached for her husband's hand he held out to her, clinging tightly to it, and a few moments later, tucked firmly against her husband atop his horse, she sent one last wave to her sisters.

Once out of the village, Sorrell buried her face against her husband's chest and wept.

Chapter Seventeen

Sorrell sniffled back the last of her tears and raised her head off her husband's chest to look up at him. "Talk with me."

She wanted to be distracted and Ruddock could easily provide that while solving two problems at once. One, give pause to her pain in leaving her sisters and two, explain to her the rift between him and his father.

"I envy the strong bond you have with your family. I had such a bond once," he said and he hoped to have it again with her and the family they would have together.

"What happened?" she asked, resting her hand on his chest. "Was your father always heartless?"

She was quick to offer him comfort and she had no idea how much it meant to him, having gone too long without it. He'd almost forgotten what it felt like to have someone care and believe in him as she did, defending him by his word alone.

For the first time, he felt comfortable telling someone what had happened.

"It started after my mum died, about two years ago. My mum and da were much in love. Her death was not easy for him to accept. He locked himself away, leaving me to see to the everyday running of the clan and settling any potential problems that affected our clan or land.

"I returned one day from such a mission and was immediately summoned to his solar. His tongue was quick and sharp when he told me that I was no longer his son, never had been his son. He claimed my mum had been with another man and that man was my father. He ordered me to leave and never dare show myself to him again and, as not to sully the good Northwick name, he warned me never to refer to myself as a Northwick again."

"Did he tell you how he came by this information?" Sorrell asked, her already aching heart wrenching for him.

"He told me he had undeniable proof and he hoped that Alida, my mum, was burning in hell for her betrayal." He looked off in the distance, that moment burned in his memory and seeing it unfold again as it had done so many times. "That's when I did something I never thought I would ever do. I hit my father hard enough to knock him off his feet."

"He deserved it," Sorrell said.

Some women agreed with their husbands just to please them, gain favor, or manipulate them. He didn't have to worry about that with Sorrell as Willow had reminded him. Sorrell would always be truthful with him whether he liked it or not. It was plain to see in the sparkle of anger in her green eyes meant for his father.

"So you left home that day and haven't been back since?" she asked.

"Aye," he said, though it was only a partial truth. He had left home, though not entirely of his own accord. But that was better left for another time.

"Did you ever once think it could be true?"

He took no offense to her question. She probed for the truth just as he had and it felt good to discuss it with someone he could trust. "I admit that I gave the idea thought, briefly. I don't recall a day I didn't hear my mum and da claim their love for each other. They always held hands, as if they didn't want to be separated, not even for a moment. My mum would always kiss my da before leaving his side even for a few minutes. It made no sense that she would ever look at another man."

"Did your father at least show you this proof he claimed to have that you weren't his son?"

"No, never. It took time, but I came across the name of the man who first raised the issue with my da... Sterling. From what I've learned, he is a man easily persuaded by coin to say whatever asked of him. I came close to capturing him, but he is a sly one, more so than anyone knows."

"Does that mean you weren't looking for solitude? That your search for this Sterling fellow brought you to our clan?"

"My search did bring me to your area, since I learned the fellow was headed north, near to my home. But solitude was foremost on my mind. I needed a place to find peace, if only briefly, and try to connect the few pieces of the puzzle before I moved forward." He gently tapped the tip of her nose. "You changed all that."

"I'm glad I could be of help," she said with a smile, loving his playful gesture. There was something intimate about it, his way of letting her know she meant more to him than he could say.

"You're more help than you know," Ruddock said and gave her a quick kiss, surprised to see her frown afterwards. "My kiss does not please you?"

She shook her head, frowning. "Your kisses always more than please me."

"It doesn't appear so."

"It is the thought that your father offered money to see you dead. Why, if he wanted you dead, wouldn't he simply kill you instead of sending you away?"

She was far too astute. Whether he wanted her to know the rest of it or not, she would find out. It was only a matter of time. But he wasn't ready to tell her.

"I don't know, perhaps he couldn't bring himself to see me killed," he suggested.

"That would mean he still cared for you whether he believed you his son or not, which is quite odd. Maybe a part of him doubted what he had been told." Her frown deepened. "How is it that none of what you told me is widely known?"

"You think my father wanted it widely known that his wife, he claimed to have loved so dearly, betrayed him with another man and that his only son, heir to his huge holdings, would go to a bastard son?"

"What of the price on your head? I recall no talk of it," she questioned.

"You wouldn't. Only the circle of those interested in such things were informed. My father is a powerful man and can do things even the King can't do."

"Will your father be pleased to learn that you've wed?"

"It matters not to me if he is or not."

"He should be pleased. It means he will have heirs to see his name and legacy live on," Sorrell said, thinking of the bairns she hoped to have one day.

Ruddock grinned. "Many heirs, since my wife is always eager to couple."

"Aye, I am," she said, her grin as large as his.

That she admitted such without embarrassment pleased him and caused a brief laugh. "I do adore your honesty, wife."

"I am glad it pleases you, but it does not please me that we will be sleeping under the stars with your warriors circled around us. We will have not an ounce of privacy, which means lovemaking will have to wait, a dire situation to me."

A slight scowl and not a spark of teasing in her green eyes let him know she was serious.

"I had thought the same myself, so tonight we will take shelter in an abbey where we will have a room, small that it might be, to ourselves."

"You can't be serious," she said with a tilt of her head and her eyes turning wide. "You can't expect me to couple with you in an abbey."

"We're wed. The church expects us to couple and produce children. It would be blasphemous for us not to couple."

"Blasphemous or not, the abbey is a silent place and we are far from silent when we couple," she argued.

He laughed. "At least the nuns will know we are fulfilling our marital duties."

She lightly punched him in the chest, not wanting to injure her hand. "We will not couple in the abbey and that's final."

"Are you daring me, wife?" he asked

"I said nothing about a dare."

"I think I heard a dare in your words," he challenged playfully.

"You most certainly did not."

"Is someone afraid to take on a dare?"

"No, someone knows not to take on a dare she is positive she will lose," Sorrell said with repeated taps to his chest.

Ruddock laughed again. "You are a gem, wife."

"Aye, I am and you will be respectful of my wishes and behave while we're at the abbey," she cautioned. "And I'll have your word on that."

"You have my word I will be a good husband and adhere to his wife's wishes."

"Good," she said, now tell me about your home. I look forward to running the keep and making friends there."

"A steward, Erskine, oversees the running of the keep, since it is such a large chore. All in the keep report to him."

"A man replaced your mum in running the keep?"

"After my mum died, it seemed the wisest choice, since there was no one else who knew the keep as well as Erskine."

"If your mum ran the keep, then so can I," Sorrell said, eager to take on the challenge.

"The keep is large and Erskine did well with it when I was there. You may find it too much to handle," Ruddock said and knew it was a mistake as soon as the words left his mouth.

"We'll see about that," Sorrell said.

Ruddock hurried to retrieve the gauntlet he had inadvertently thrown down and she had quickly snatched up. "You're Lady Northwick now and need not worry about chores or the upkeep of the clan. There are others to attend to that. Enjoy the leisure and freedom you have as my wife."

"A wife has duties and I intend to see to them."

"Duty and obedience to your husband comes first," he reminded teasingly.

She appreciated his playful manner, though she kept hers serious. "My husband will always come first to me."

"As it should be," he said with feigned sternness.

She stretched her head up and kissed him gently. "I do so love you."

Her words twisted his stomach in knots and melted his heart. He loved hearing her say that she loved him. The words were on his lips to tell her the same, but he held them back. It wasn't time yet, just as it wasn't time to free himself of the shackle on his wrist. But soon, he hoped very soon, it would be.

***

The nuns welcomed Ruddock and Sorrell, and only them, into the abbey with solemn faces. Ruddock's warriors were left outside to make camp around the abbey, something Mother Abbess hadn't welcomed.

Night had fallen several hours ago, but they had pushed on to the abbey. Sorrell admitted, to herself, that she was glad they had. It had gotten colder with the descending darkness and a light rain had started to fall. It would have been a cold, wet, uncomfortable night to be outside.

Sorrell followed behind Mother Abbess and in front of her husband down a narrow hall, a cold stone floor beneath their feet, sending a chill through her and the gray stone walls seemed to close in on the narrow space, making it feel more like a prison than a sanctuary. Silence hung heavy, not a sound being heard, giving the impression that the abbey was deserted.

Sorrell was pleased with the room Mother Abbess had led them to. It wasn't large, but not small either and a small hearth burned brightly, heating the room nicely.

"It is because of your father's generous support that the abbey survives. This room is kept for anyone, without question, he sends our way. Your father did not, however, let us know that you had wed."

"My father does not know I have taken a wife. We were wed only yesterday and I wish to surprise him with the good news."

The abbess did not hide her skepticism, looking questionably between Ruddock and Sorrell. "As I said anyone your father sends we accept without question."

"Mother Abbess," Sorrell said as the tall woman turned to walk away. "I am new to my position as wife to Lord Northwick, but I am not new to recognizing rudeness. You obviously think we lie to you and are not wed. That you question my husband's integrity is an insult. One that I believe his father will not take lightly." She turned to her husband. "I will not stay where I am believed to be a whore, and I will be sure to inform your father of our unwelcoming experience here."

Ruddock couldn't have said it better, though he had intended to, but his wife had been hastier with her words. He was pleased to see the Mother Abbess pale, her thought of losing Northwick's patronage no doubt foremost in her mind.

"Forgive me, Lady Sorrell. There had been no news of Lord Ruddock's marriage and I fear I thought the worst of—"

"My husband," Sorrell said with a note of anger.

"My apologies, Lord Ruddock," Mother Abbess said, turning to him. "It was wrong of me to have assumed the worse. Let me make amends and have some of our fine wine brought to you and your lovely wife to enjoy while I lead the sisters in a special prayer session blessing you both and your marriage."

"My wife will decide if what you offer makes amends for your discourtesy," Ruddock said with an air of command.

Sorrell looked up at the tall woman, though by no means felt shorter than her. "I appreciate any blessing offered for our marriage, since it can only help strengthen our love and commitment to each other. And the wine is most welcomed as is the fire in the hearth after traveling in the cold and damp."

"You are a forgiving and generous woman, exceptional qualities, and will make Lord Ruddock a good wife," Mother Abbess said with a respectful bob of her head.

Sorrell stopped her from leaving again. "Where is the chapel located where you and the sisters will pray? I'd like to know so that I may pay a visit before our departure in the morning."

The Mother Abbess smiled, pleased with Sorrell's intention. "On the other side of the abbey and to the front. Any of the sisters would be pleased to show you the way."

"Thank you. I will be sure to ask if necessary," Sorrell said and entered the room.

Ruddock turned a questioning eye on his wife as soon as he shut the door. "Now tell me why you really wanted to know where the chapel is located."

Sorrell dropped her cloak on the lone chair and held her chilled hands out to the warmth of the fire. "I wanted to know how far the chapel was from this room so when you seduced me and had me moaning in pleasure, I would know whether I could be heard or not." She shook a finger at him. "And don't play the innocent with me. You know full well the promise you made was no promise at all. A good husband and adhere to his wife's wishes is what you said when what you meant was you'd do all you could to have me wishing you'd make love to me. Of course, I'd surrender and you would have kept your promise."

"You have too sharp a wit for me, wife," Ruddock said with a laugh, closing the small distance between them with three easy steps.

"A good thing for you to remember," Sorrell warned as he took her in his arms.

He placed a gentle kiss on her lips, then another, and another, until the kisses became hungrier and more demanding.

Sorrell pushed at his chest as she tried to end the kiss, though it did little good. It did, however, had Ruddock halting the kiss long enough to give her a questioning look.

"Mother Abbess is sending wine and I prefer the sister who delivers it doesn't find us naked in bed."

"Why? It's perfectly normal to find a husband and wife in bed," Ruddock said, keeping his arms around her waist.

"In their bedchamber," she countered and took a breath. "Please, Ruddock, the more you kiss me, hold me, the more I want you, and the less control I have over it."

The way his true name spilled off her lips in a soft plea jolted his senses, not to mention how easily he was able to arouse her.

He heard her sigh of relief or was it regret, when he released her and took a step away. "We will not have much time. Bedtime is upon the abbey and strict rules abide here."

"It doesn't matter if it is quick. I only know I need to feel the joy of you inside me."

Ruddock rubbed at his chin as he turned away from her, her words stirring his manhood that had been turning hard rapidly. He was quick to turn back again, pointing his finger at her. "I will have you slow and easy one night soon, wife, and have you know the pleasure leisurely lovemaking brings."

She shivered with the thought. "I look forward to it."

A soft knock sounded at the door and Ruddock was quick to open it and take the tray from the sister standing there red-faced. He sat it on the small table next to the chair and went to fill both goblets.

Her hand on his arm stopped him.

"No, there is no time to waste. We will have it afterwards."

Sorrell went to the bed, dropped down on it, spread her legs and lifted her garments.

As inviting as his wife was, it reminded Ruddock of the days he would give a willing woman, or pay one, for a quick poke, and he shook his head. "This is not how I want it between us."

"It is either this or nothing and that I cannot bear to think about," she said and held her arms out to him. "I love you, want you, need you, isn't that enough?"

That she sounded like she pleaded with him tore at his heart. He went to her, reached down, grabbed her by the arm, and yanked her up off the bed, scooping her up in his arms. Then he brought them both down to lie side-by-side on the narrow bed.

"You should know that I wake with you in my thoughts and sleep with you in my dreams. You are always there. You never leave me and I never want you to. I could make love to you endlessly and never grow tired of you."

Tell her. Tell her you love her. She deserves to know.

Something stopped him from listening to himself. Something buried deep inside him.

"That is good because I am a demanding wife in bed," Sorrell said with a chuckle before giving him a kiss.

"Then we will do good, since I am a demanding husband in bed."

She whispered near his lips. "Show me."

He wished he had time to do just that, but he didn't. He moved off her and she turned to lie on her back, spread her legs and to bring her knees up as he slipped to position himself between them. He knew she would be wet and ready for him, and that grew him harder, and he slid into her with ease.

"Right where you belong," she said on a soft moan.

She was right. He was where he belonged, inside her and loving her.

It wouldn't take long. They were both in need, though he didn't want it to end fast. He wanted time for them both to linger in the enjoyment, in the pleasure that mounted too quickly in them.

"John," she moaned, gripping the bedding beneath her.

She had yet to call him Ruddock when in the throes of passion and he couldn't wait until she did, since it would mean she finally and fully trusted and accepted him as her husband.

Ruddock kept a fast, hard rhythm, knowing time wasn't their friend as Sorrell's moans grew louder.

"John! John!" she cried out.

He knew she was close and so was he. Any moment they would burst with unmeasurable pleasure.

"Lord Ruddock! Lord Ruddock!"

Pounding footsteps came rushing down the hall.

"Lord Ruddock!"

The frantic voice was suddenly steps from the door. Ruddock had no choice. He pulled out of his wife."

Her groan of disappointed echoed in his ears and down to his manhood that throbbed unmercifully.

"I'm sorry," he whispered and hurried off her to help her to her feet.

Sorrell fell against him, the unsatisfied passion coursing through her like a raging fire out of control.

"I promise. I'll make this up to you," he whispered as the pounding at the door sounded as if it would shatter the wood.

He didn't dare kiss her or touch her, worried that he might make it worse for her and fearful he would come right there and then.

He went to the door and flung it open, swearing beneath his breath that whatever Erland had to say better have been worth interrupting him.

"My lord, a barbaric troop descends on the abbey."

Chapter Eighteen

"Stay here. Don't leave this room. I mean it, Sorrell," Ruddock snapped when she went to protest. "I'll have your word on it."

That wasn't fair of him. He knew she wouldn't lie to him.

"Your word," he demanded.

"You have it," she said, having no other recourse and understanding now was not the time to argue with him.

He left without another word and she stepped out of the room to watch Erland trail after him down the dreary hall.

"In the room and stay there, wife," Ruddock called out without looking back.

He knew her too well, but she did as he ordered, slamming the door so he would hear it and know she had obeyed him. She did it, more so, to help him. With a barbaric horde descending on the abbey, he didn't need to be worrying about a stubborn wife.

She paced the small room, her thoughts chaotic. Barbarians hadn't attacked this area in ages. Why would they do so now? Was it women they were after? She paused at the thought. What if she needed to defend herself?

Her eyes scanned the room, looking for anything that might serve as a weapon.

Nothing. She could see nothing that would help her.

"Think, Sorrell, think," she chided herself. "Don't leave yourself defenseless."

She continued searching the sparse room, growing discouraged as she did.

A sound caught her attention. Was that weeping she heard?

Before she reached the door it swung open, slamming against the wall.

A young, weeping nun dressed only in her nightshift, that hung on her slim body like a sack, and barefoot was shoved with such force into the room that she tumbled to the floor in front of Sorrell.

"Forgive me, my lady, he forced me to bring him here," the young nun begged, looking up at Sorrell with terror-filled eyes.

Sorrell helped her up, the young nun clinging tightly to her arm, while she kept her eyes on the barbarian standing in the doorway. He was draped in furs with swaths of cloths around his legs and appeared thick in size, though it could have been the furs that made him appear that way. His hair was long and braided in spots as was his beard that reached to his chest. The two sizeable scars on his aged face and the sneer he wore was enough to frighten anyone.

"You both die," the barbarian said and stepped into the room.

The young nun wailed in fear and the barbarian raised his sword to his side.

Sorrell fell to her knees, taking the young nun with her. "Please, please, I beg you let us pray before we die so that heaven opens its arms to us. Please. Please."

The young nun's slim arm fell away from Sorrell and her hands locked in prayer as she began to pray in earnest, tears pouring down her cheeks.

Sorrell lowered her head. She only had a moment, a mere moment. She didn't let herself think of the consequences. It was her only chance to escape, to save herself and the young nun.

Her hand shot out and grabbed the end of a log the flames had yet to reach, the other end burning like a torch.

She swung it up and at the cloths wrapped around his legs and they instantly caught the flame and climbed rapidly up along the barbarian's clothing.

He roared in fury, it turning fast to screams as the fire caught his flesh and began to consume him.

She grabbed the young nun, frozen with fear, and rushed past the burning man and down the hall.

A roar behind them let her know that he followed.

"Don't look back, run," Sorrell ordered when the young nun went to turn her head. "You need to direct us out of here, to the front where my husband's warriors are camped."

The nun nodded, took hold of Sorrell's hand and ran with all the strength and speed she had, Sorrell keeping pace with her.

They both felt the heat of the burning barbarian grow closer.

"Not far," the young nun said, after a few moments. "The next turn."

It came upon them fast and they almost toppled as they took the turn, but helped each other to remain on their feet. The door was only a short distance away and they rammed into it when they reached it and stumbled out of the abbey into the night and the light rain that fell.

"John! John!" Sorrell screamed as she and the nun righted themselves and kept running.

Ruddock thought he heard his wife shouting for John, but she had given her word she would remain in the room. She would honor that word unless…

He turned away from where he stood talking with the barbarian leader and ran toward his wife's frenzied shouts. Several of his warriors followed, while others remained keeping an eye on the troop of barbarians.

Rage roared up in Ruddock when he saw a man in flames following after his wife and the young nun with her.

The man didn't get far. He collapsed to the ground, the flames completely engulfing him.

Ruddock rushed to his wife and she threw herself against him, and his arms went around her, holding her tight.

"He wanted her dead," the young nun said breathless. "He said so. Lady Sorrell saved us. She set him on fire with a log from the hearth."

Mother Abbess and several nuns came racing toward them. "What happened here? Sister Eleanor, have you no shame being out here in front of these men in your nightshift?"

"Take pity on her, Mother Abbess, she has been through an ordeal tonight," Ruddock warned. "Take her inside and see to her."

Two nuns hurried over to the young nun and wrapped their arms around her and guided her back to the abbey.

"I will have an explanation of what went on here tonight, Lord Ruddock," Mother Abbess said. "I have turned my eyes away from many things over the years, but one of my postulants out in the dark of night only in her nightshift, a man's dead, burning body, and a group of barbarians on the sacred grounds of the abbey, is something I cannot ignore."

"Unless you want to be exposed to more unholy doings, I suggest you retreat inside the abbey," Ruddock said.

"This isn't the end of it, Lord Ruddock," Mother Abbess warned and walked away.

Ruddock cared not what the Mother Abbess thought. He cared only about his wife and what had happened to her.

He looked to one of his warriors. "Have Erland bring Asger to me."

The warrior took off to do his lord's bidding.

"Sorrell." Ruddock said, his hand going to her chin to lift her head. "I need to know you're unharmed."

Her husband's comforting arms had calmed her with their strength and warmth, helping her breathing and racing heart to calm as well.

She smiled softly ready to reassure him. Unfortunately, it turned to a wince, a stinging pain hitting her hand as she went to hug him tight.

"My hand," she said, bringing it around and giving it a look.

Ruddock winced himself, seeing the redness that ran along the side of her left hand."

"A burn, though not a bad one. The skin does not blister," Sorrell said.

"You grabbed a burning log out of the hearth?" he asked, recalling the young nun's explanation.

"Aye, it was the only thing I could think to use and the closest to reach. I grabbed the end of the log that had yet to catch the flame. I must have gotten too close to the embers as I grabbed the log." She tilted her head. "Thinking on it now, why would that barbarian want me dead? It makes no sense. I have no connection with them."

Aye, you do have a connection... it's me, he thought, but said no more.

"I assume you spoke with whoever leads this horde of barbarians. What did he say?" she asked.

"This particular group trades with my clan from time to time. They were returning from there and—"

"Why come this way? Their home is far north and across the sea from here."

"They have trade agreements with other clans and were on their way to speak with one."

"Why would anyone align himself with barbarians?" she asked.

"It depends on the tribe. Some are not as ruthless as people think while others are pure evil."

"You are familiar with the barbarian tribes?" she asked, then shook her head. "Of course, you would be if your clan trades with them."

"My lord," Erland said, hurrying over to the couple. "Lady Sorrell is unharmed?"

"A small wound, nothing more," Sorrell said.

Erland seemed nice enough. He was short, though next to Ruddock anyone was short. His brown hair was beginning to gray and he had a few age lines around his eyes and mouth. He did not appear old yet she recalled Ruddock telling her that he had been his father's longtime friend. He either aged well or never stretched his mouth out in a smile or held a hardy laugh more often than not. He was attentive to Ruddock's every need, but he was reserved with her. Or perhaps like her, he had yet to learn enough about her to call her friend. She would reserve her opinion until she got to know him better.

"Where is Asger?" Ruddock asked.

"He took his leave with his warriors," Erland said.

Sorrell felt her husband tense with annoyance.

"Did you tell him what happened here?" Ruddock questioned.

"He showed no interest," Erland assured him.

"What about his warrior that lies burned to death on the ground? Sorrell asked astonished that his tribe had abandoned him.

"The spoils of battle," Erland said.

Not quite. Ruddock knew Asger well. If he had no interest in the fallen warrior, then that meant only one thing. The warrior didn't belong to his tribe. If that was so, then what barbarian tribe had the warrior belonged to? And who wanted Ruddock's wife dead?

***

After a few words with Erland to see that the sentinels were doubled for the remainder of the evening, Ruddock returned to the abbey and ordered items brought to him.

"I can see to the burn," Sorrell said when he settled her on the bed.

"No, I will see to it," Ruddock said.

The finality of his tone left no room for debate and Sorrell let it be. She noticed that the room had been made clean, bits of debris from the log and the burning cloth having been removed. But the stench of burning cloth and flesh still lingered.

The items Ruddock had ordered brought to him arrived quickly.

"How is Sister Eleanor?" Sorrell asked of the nun who handed the items to Ruddock.

"I cannot say," she said quickly and hurried away with just as much haste.

"Stay put," Ruddock ordered when he saw her about to stand. "You can inquire about Eleanor in the morning."

"She was so fearful at first and willing to accept death far too easily."

"Until you showed her differently," Ruddock said and sat on the bed beside his wife, placing some of the items he needed to tend her hand next to him. The bowl of water and towel he set on the chair he had moved beside the bed.

"I'm not one to surrender easily,"

"A thought that makes me proud and frightens the hell out of me," he admitted, taking her injured hand gently in his. "I fear one day that it may cost you your life, and I do not like to think of life without you."

"You would miss me? I would miss you," she eagerly admitted.

He smiled at how she never held back. That she told him how she felt. It did his heart good.

"I have grown accustomed to spending much of the day with you and now, of course, I get to enjoy the nights with you." She grinned, then winced when he placed her hand in the bowl of cool water, the burn stinging.

"I would miss you too, far more than you can imagine." He dabbed at her hand to dry it so as not to cause her pain.

Sorrell rested her head on his shoulder, a sudden tiredness coming over her. "I think fate brought us together. We were meant to be, nothing can stop it."

"Nothing," he agreed, since he'd kill anyone who tried to take her away from him.

She yawned and the way her body relaxed against his, he realized the exhaustion of the long day and the frightening incident had finally caught up with her.

"You need sleep," he said and finished spreading honey over her wound.

She yawned again. "I would argue with you, but you're right. I can barely keep my eyes open."

Ruddock wrapped her hand in the clean cloth, ripping the last of it to tie around the bandage and keep it in place.

She didn't argue with him when he laid her on the bed fully clothed, explaining that their garments would remain on them in case needed. It also helped not to reignite the passion that had had them so close to climax earlier. She was far too exhausted and his mind far too occupied.

He tucked himself in beside her, covering them with the lone blanket and taking her in his arms. As soon as she laid her head on his chest, she was sound asleep. However, sleep did not come as fast for him.

His thoughts remained on the night's incident and the question that enraged and frightened him. Who wanted his wife dead?

He thought his father might be responsible, but his father knew nothing about their marriage. Who then and for what reason could someone want Sorrell dead?

The more he thought on it the more his rage grew and the memories he kept suppressed surfaced, reminding him of the consequence of such an overpowering fury.

He looked down at his wife cuddled comfortably against him, thought of the love she had for him and the trust she placed in him. There wasn't a doubt in his mind that he would let the barbarian loose in him and kill anyone who harmed her… kill as viciously as he had when he rode with the barbarians.

Chapter Nineteen

Sunrise couldn't have come early enough for her, though it was a gray sky that greeted them. As soon as she and Ruddock woke they were out of bed and ready to take their leave. They had declined the morning meal Mother Abbess had offered them and the woman had seemed relieved that they had done so.

Sorrell now stood by her horse, Prince, talking to him, letting him know they were on their way to a new home as she waited for her husband to finish discussing the day's plan with Erland, when she spotted the young nun, Eleanor. She had inquired about her earlier, wanting to see how she was doing after last night's incident. Mother Abbess had told her that she was praying and could not be disturbed.

She immediately went to the young nun, but as she approached her, Sorrell saw that she was weeping and she wasn't dressed in the drab garments of a postulant. Her shift and tunic were worn and she hugged herself against the chilled air, wearing no cloak to protect her from it.

Sorrell's arm immediately went around Eleanor when she reached her. "What has you upset, Eleanor? You did well last night. You are stronger than you think. And what are you doing without a cloak on this chilly morning"

"Not according to Mother Abbess, my lady," Eleanor said with a sniffle. "She says there is no excuse for me to have been outside wearing only my nightshift in front of a group of men. That I should have immediately sought shelter where I wouldn't have been seen. That my actions revealed my true nature and being I am only a postulant, not having taken my vows, she has said I'm not worthy to do so and has sent me on my way." Tears rolled down her cheeks. "I have no place to go. These garments are the ones I wore when I arrived here two years ago and Mother Abbess took me in. I worked so hard to prove I was worthy to be a nun, so hard." She shook her head. "I have nothing. The abbey was my home and the nuns my family."

Sorrell was furious. How could Mother Abbess treat the poor woman so badly, but recalling how she had judged Ruddock and her, it was easy to understand. You either lived by her rules or you were condemned.

"I know the perfect place for you to settle and call home. A place you will be welcomed with open arms. The Clan Macardle, my home. I will send a message along with you to deliver to James the chieftain of the clan and another message for you to give to my two sisters."

"Truly, my lady?" Eleanor asked, wiping away her tears and looking hopeful.

"Aye, truly. You're a good woman, Eleanor, and you deserve a good home."

"You really think me a good woman?" Eleanor asked, tears trickling down her cheek. "Mother Abbess spent a good portion of the night telling me what a terrible woman I was."

"Mother Abbess is a bitter woman who should better learn to embrace God's love and share it with others."

"Thank you. I am so grateful," Eleanor said, wiping away the tears that ran into her smile. "Is your home far from here? Can I get there soon?"

Sorrell could see the young woman had grown colder, her slender body trembling. She turned and called out to her husband. "Ruddock, a moment please."

Ruddock nodded, spoke briefly with Erland, then joined her.

"Mother Abbess banished Eleanor from the abbey. I have offered her a home with the Clan Macardle and she has graciously accepted. I need one of your warriors to take her there, and she needs a cloak to keep her warm."

"You are too generous, my lady," Eleanor protested.

"Nonsense," Ruddock said, "You were of great help to my wife last night, getting her out of the abbey and explaining to me what had happened. You should be rewarded not punished. I will arrange for you to be escorted to the Clan Macardle. You will depart when we do."

"I am forever grateful, my lord, and I will work hard to be a good member of the Clan Macardle," Eleanor said.

"I have no doubt you will," Sorrell said. "Now let's get you a cloak and I will relay the message you are to give to James and my sisters, though the message to my two sisters, Willow and Snow, is to be given only to them."

Sorrell wanted to let her sisters know that she did well and she missed them. And since an explanation as to why she was sending Eleanor to them would reveal the attempt on her life, she wanted to make sure her sisters knew she was unharmed and well-protected, saving them from worry.

"I understand, my lady," Eleanor said. "I will make certain they alone receive it."

It was only a couple of hours after sunrise that they finally took their leave of the abbey. Sorrell sat atop Ruddock's horse snuggled against him. She needed his warmth today, the strong wind making the chilled air feel colder.

"How long until we reach Northwick land?" Sorrell asked.

"Two days if there are no delays and we maintain our pace, then almost half a day to reach the keep."

"Your father awaits our arrival?"

"My arrival. He has yet to learn I have wed," he reminded.

"What do you think he will say about you bringing home a wife?" she asked, having wondered what kind of welcome the news would receive.

"Are you concerned how my father will receive you?" Ruddock asked.

"Do you really think it matters to me? I care not for me, but how he treats my husband is a different matter."

The wee lass could touch his heart with just a few words. "Ever the defender, wife."

"Forever will I defend my husband and family."

"Of that I have no doubt." He bent his head to kiss her when a crack of thunder sounded as if it had struck the earth with a mighty sword, startling them both.

"Not more rain," Sorrell groaned, knowing a heavy rain would slow them down.

And it did.

Rain continued to follow them. The third day of their journey found them seeking shelter by mid-day, the rain too heavy to continue. They found a cottage, battered and worn, not truly habitable, but sufficient enough to shelter Sorrell and Ruddock.

Sorrell was grateful the fireplace, small as it was, remained intact and that her husband got a fire going. She was also grateful that her husband had sheltered her against the rain the best he could with his body and cloak. Her garments were damp compared to his.

While they settled inside the dilapidated cottage, his warriors settled under the branches of the large trees that surrounded the place.

"I will be glad when this journey is done," Sorrell said, attempting to warm herself in front of the fire. "I would think your warriors feel the same."

"They are well trained to withstand the weather," Ruddock said, slipping out of his wet shirt.

Sorrell stared at his naked chest. She hadn't seen it since their wedding night, though she had rested her head on it the last two nights."

"It will probably take us an extra day to reach home, longer if this weather doesn't improve."

Sorrell smiled. She caught the flare of passion in his blue eyes and how he was doing his best to keep his thoughts busy on things that wouldn't ignite it any further. She thought of teasing him, but she'd only be teasing herself as well.

Lovemaking would have to wait, not a thought that pleased her.

He squeezed the rainwater from his shirt and draped it over a broken chair he'd placed close to the fire.

Sorrell tried to keep her eyes off him but it was impossible. The light from the fire's flames had his damp chest and back glistening and highlighting his hard muscles, which only flamed her own passion.

She focused to keep her attention on her hands, holding them out to the warmth of the fire, not that she needed any more warmth, since her body had begun to heat just from the thought of her husband sinking his manhood deep inside her.

Don't think about that. Don't think about that," she chastised herself silently.

It amazed her that she had found making love to be so wonderfully satisfying that she hoped to enjoy it often. She had worried that it was something she might not like and it would become more a duty, a chore as some women claimed, that she would have to endure.

That she had to endure the lack of it was surprising and frustrating, and if she didn't get her mind off it soon she'd beg her husband to quench her need.

She jumped when he stood next to her, though not close enough for them to touch, a good thing at the moment, and hurried to think of something to say that would drive this unquenched need in her away.

"We have talked little about the incident at the abbey," she said, the memories of how close she had come to dying, taming her passion. "It seems odd that there was an attempt on your life and not long after an attempt on mine. Could the two be somehow connected?"

Ruddock did his best to rub himself dry in front of the flames, running his hands up and down his arms. He was glad his wife's inquiry put at least somewhat of a damper on his passion that had been rising steadily since he entered the cottage. Three days without making love to his wife was taking a toll on him. He had gone without coupling much longer than that, but with his wife, it was different. It was a different kind of need, a different satisfaction he got from joining with her. Maybe it was that she loved him that made all the difference. He didn't know. He only knew that when he slipped inside her, he felt like he was home and he was loved, and it was a glorious and addictive feeling.

"I suppose it's possible," he said, his hand running across his midriff in circles to dry it. "As soon as we get home, I'm going to send a missive to one of the barbarian tribes. I know the leader well from trading with him. He might have heard something, since word travels fast among the tribes."

Sorrell tried to ignore the way his hand glided in circles over his middle, the dampness lapping at his hand as if begging him not to stop, to keep caressing his flesh. And damn if she didn't turn damp when his hand dipped lower as if it would slip beneath his plaid. She tamped down the urge to reach out, push his hand away, and—she squeezed her eyes shut—a mistake. All she could see was herself licking every inch of his middle while her hand slipped beneath his plaid.

She forced herself to gather her thoughts and voiced one, that had been brewing in her head for a while, aloud. "Since there had been no attempts made on my life before I became your wife, I assume this attempt has something to do with me being your wife."

"An obvious observation," he said, turning to her, his hand moving to his chest to continue drying himself, though he would have preferred her hands drying him.

"I love solving puzzles and this definitely is a puzzle, husband," she said, forcing a gleeful smile while fighting the urge to replace his hands with her lips.

"One you will pay caution to," he ordered, running his hand roughly across his chest and nipples to hurry and rid himself of the last of the dampness, though mostly to rid himself of the images of his wife's hands doing it for him.

"Oh for goodness sake stop that!" she snapped at him while slapping at his hands. "You're driving me mad."

His grin was more seductive than joyful that his wife thought the same as him. "And myself as well, since I can't stop thinking of planting myself inside you."

Sorrell backed away from him. "There is little privacy here with your warriors right outside the door that sits barely closed since it is so badly battered. And the hole in the roof allows for sound to escape."

"The rain pounds down loud enough for no one to hear what goes on inside here. Besides, you need to learn to contain your moans and shouts when needed or there will be times we will suffer for it."

One step had him in front of her and he slipped her cloak off and draped it over the leg of the broken upended table. He took her hand, kissed the back of it and keeping it firm in his, as if he feared her pulling away, walked her to the corner of the cottage where shadows dwelled.

She almost hesitated, but as if expecting her reluctance, he tugged her hand hard enough for her to fall against him and the shadows swallowed them both.

Ruddock's hand slipped from hers to cup the back of her neck firmly, holding her head still as his lips came down on hers.

As soon as his lips touched hers, she was lost and she feared as soon as he entered her that her moans would outrival the thunder.

She didn't want to stop. God, how she didn't want to stop him. His kiss was magic, sending the most delightfully sensuous ripple through her. And when that ripple culminated between her legs, she knew she was in trouble. She had to stop him before it was too late.

She took a chance, raising her hands to press at his chest, hesitating a minute, since she feared when her hand touched his flesh and felt his thick, hard muscles, she'd want to do nothing more than caress him, and she wouldn't stop at his chest. She rushed to give him a push, letting him know to stop, yet wishing otherwise.

Ruddock was not going to be denied and he wasn't about to let his wife deny herself either. He took her face in both his hands and whispered, "Trust me, wife."

He didn't give her a chance to respond, at least not verbally. Her body told him with the way she relaxed against him and he kissed her again, his arm circling her waist.

He sunk slowly to the floor and moved his lips off hers briefly to whisper, "Straddle me." And he helped her, his hand going to her backside and giving her a slight boost as he returned to continue kissing her.

Her legs clutched his waist, exactly where he wanted them when his backside finally touched the floor. His hands worked their way beneath her garments, moving them out of the way, and she helped by raising herself up some and not surprisingly moving his plaid aside, not once interrupting their kiss.

He didn't slip into her right away. He let his manhood linger between her legs, shifting his body beneath hers so that she could feel him hard and hungry for her.

She moved her mouth off his, more to take a needed breath than anything, and resting her brow to his murmured, "You tease me."

"No, I enjoy the feel of you and the anticipation of what's to come," he whispered with a smile that promised.

"I can't wait. I can't seem to ever wait when I feel you hard against me." She braced her hands on the wall behind him and rubbed against his manhood and sighed, feeling how it had swelled.

"Shhhh," he warned softly, her sigh loud enough for the wind that swooped down from the hole in the roof to pick up and carry off. He reached up to cup her face in his hands and kiss her again.

She moaned in his mouth and lifted off him enough for his manhood to spring up.

"Slip him inside you," he whispered and returned to kissing her, eager to capture her every moan.

Sorrell reached one hand down, keeping the other braced against the wall, and took hold of his manhood. It was thick and hard and pulsed in her hand as if it had a life of its own and she stroked her hand along it, eager to feel more.

Ruddock tore his mouth off hers and brought his lips close to her ear to whisper, "I will come if you continue to do that and it won't be inside you."

"Another time," she whispered.

Ruddock kissed along her cheek as he drew his head back. "You can count on it, wife."

She positioned his manhood between her legs and after shifting her hips twice, she began to sink slowly down on him. She quickly returned her hand to the wall and dropped her head down, her eyes drifting closed, as she took her time sliding down on him, relishing the glorious feel as she welcomed him inside her.

Ruddock hurried to grab her cheeks and bring her face toward him to catch her lips just in time to capture the moan he had heard building inside her.

Sorrell didn't think making love could get any better than it had, but she was wrong. She wanted to toss her head back and moan to the heavens with pleasure. She went to pull her head out of her husband's grip, but he wouldn't let her go.

She glared at him not with anger but with need.

Ruddock rested his thumb on her lips, holding it firm. "Remember we're not alone," he warned with a soft whisper.

Her eyes went wide, having forgotten their surroundings, so lost was she in passion.

She nodded and when he removed his thumb off her lips, she locked them tight.

Ruddock smiled. He'd need to kiss her again soon. For now, he slipped his hands beneath her garment, grabbed her backside, squeezed her firm flesh, and helped her to ride him.

Sorrell fought with all her might to keep her lips sealed tight, but it was next to impossible with how her passion was building stronger and stronger inside her, swirling around, consuming her, approaching that moment when she'd scream her husband's name over and over as her climax devoured her.

Ruddock kept his eyes on his wife, watching her beautiful face as it twisted and winced in pure pleasure as she rode him hard and fast. He feared he'd burst before she did and that he wouldn't have. She was near, he could feel.

He moved his hands from her backside to her waist, sat up straighter, his back off the wall and whispered, "Grip my shoulders."

She did as he said and he took command of her movements, lifting and dropping her on him, driving his manhood deep and fast and exploding her in a climax that shattered her clear down to her soul.

Ruddock saw her eyes go wide and her mouth drop open and he captured her scream with his mouth, as he spilled his seed into her.

Sorrell shuddered again and again after her body slumped down on her husband. She rested her head on his chest and listened to his heart pound rapidly. It matched her own pounding heart. She didn't want to move. She wasn't ready for him to slip out of her yet, to separate from him. She liked laying there against him and connected intimately.

She smiled and looked up at him when he ran his hand down her cheek. "You earned my never-ending trust with that one." She felt his chuckle deep in his chest, and her smile spread.

"I'm glad it pleased you."

"Pleased?" She chuckled this time. "You went far beyond pleasing me, husband."

He ran his hand slowly down her cheek again. She was so soft, her cheeks warm and flushed from their lovemaking, and her smile generous. "And you give me more pleasure than I ever thought possible."

"Me and only me," she ordered, poking him in the chest with her finger. "Lay with another woman and I will—"

"Bite my cock off." His chest rumbled with another chuckle.

She laid her hands against his naked chest to push herself up and her brow scrunched. "You gave me a thought. Is it permissible for me to taste your manhood?"

Ruddock couldn't answer her fast enough. "Aye. Definitely, aye, and definitely permissible and most welcomed."

"I'll have to try it sometime."

He loved her bluntness. "Anytime you want."

She didn't protest when he lifted her off him, since he tucked her in his lap and eased back to rest against the wall.

"The rain has slowed or has stopped," she said, not hearing it.

"That is good. I am eager to get home and settle us in our bedchamber."

Curious about her new home, she asked, "Is it large?"

"It is a good size."

"Tell me of your home," she said, settling comfortably in his lap to talk.

"It has been two years since I've been home so I don't know how much has changed. You should wait and judge for yourself."

"Lord Ruddock, the rain has stopped. We should be on our way," Erland called out from outside the door.

"Aye, have the men ready," Ruddock said with a loud command.

It wasn't until Sorrell was settled on his horse once again that she thought about what he had said.

It has been two years since I've been home.

Where had he been and what had he done the two years he had been away from home? And what had happened that had earned him the shackle on his wrist?

Chapter Twenty

Sorrell was filled with excitement and anticipation. Up ahead was Ruddock's home and now her new home. She couldn't wait to catch a glimpse of it. A heaviness caught at her heart, wishing her sisters were here to share this with her.

The muscle in her husband's arms suddenly tensed around her and his body grew even tauter against her. She glanced up at him. The bold blue color of his eyes was more intense than she had ever seen it. She couldn't imagine what he must be thinking, arriving home to his father who was dying. A father who not long ago wanted him dead.

"Whatever awaits you, we face together," she said, giving his arm a squeeze.

Ruddock looked down at his wife tucked against him. "You have no idea how much that means to me, wife."

She kept her hand on his arm as they continued toward the keep, letting him know she was there for him.

As soon as they rounded a bend in the road, his home came into view. Sorrell found herself staring in awe, shocked by the size of it all. The keep looked as tall and wide as a mountain. It rose up past the towering, gray stone wall that went on endless, surrounding a sizeable portion of the area. A single dirt path led to the entrance. A distance away to the left side of the wall ran a forest, thick with growth and beyond that a mountain stood majestically. To the right, far to the back of the stone wall there looked to be a waterway of sorts.

"That's the water mill you're seeing," Ruddock explained. "It's fed from the harbor water beyond the back of the castle.

"A harbor?" Sorrell asked, trying to comprehend the breadth and width of his home.

"Aye, it makes trade easier, something my father planned on when he had the castle built."

"It is quite large," she said, trying to take all of it in.

"Those two towers, looking as if they reach to the sky, to either side of the gatehouse are defense towers. The wooden hourds surrounding the tops allow the warriors to drop munitions on the attacking enemy."

"Has the castle been attacked?" she asked.

"Twice, though well before I was born."

They entered through the gatehouse, single file, passing under the timber-framed portcullis overhead. Once that heavy gate was lowered there would be no way out and that disturbed Sorrell. She didn't want to feel a prisoner in her new home.

Her eyes couldn't take in enough as Ruddock directed the horse to take the road to the left. Cottages, nicely kept, sat to either side, until the road widened and they came upon a busy market area. They skirted it, going to the right, and continued to meander toward the keep. The village was massive and Sorrell didn't know how she would ever find her way around.

One thing she noticed that disturbed her was the way the villagers stared at her husband, some crossing themselves, others turning away as if they dared not lay eyes on him, while others glared with their mouths open in shock. Not one offered him a smile or greeting. And his glance never fell on one of them, keeping his eyes on the keep in the distance.

Servants waited at the bottom and top of the keep steps to assist them. They bowed their heads respectfully when Ruddock dismounted.

"You'll stay close by my side," he whispered up to her as his hands settled on her narrow waist and lifted her with ease off his horse to settle her on the ground beside him.

She nodded and coiled her arm around his, and he smiled.

The women servants didn't look at Ruddock, theirs eyes were on Sorrell, and she couldn't believe the shock she saw in them. Did they think her not right for him?

They entered a small area, servants standing in front of benches to either side of a closed door. They took their cloaks and one servant opened the door and stepped aside. Not one of them smiled or offered a welcome home.

His father had done a good job of poisoning them against his own son, and Sorrell intended to change that.

They stepped into the Great Hall, and Sorrell stared in awe. It was massive. Wooden beams crisscrossed overhead, various colorful banners hanging down from them. Numerous trestle tables sat in perfect lines along either side of the room, windows filled one wall, and a huge fireplace occupied the other. A defined path ran between the tables to the dais where a long table was draped in a green and white cloth. Beautiful tapestries hung from the wall behind it and in a chair, fit for a king, sat a man.

Sorrell hugged her husband's arm, letting him know once again that he was not alone. She was there with him.

Erland hurried around them and to the dais to stand behind Lord Northwick, making it clear who he served.

He was loyal to the old lord and Sorrell would remember that. She wondered why the man wasn't in bed if he was dying. As they got closer, she saw that he looked as if he should be.

Lord Finn Northwick was big like Ruddock, though half the weight. His face was gaunt and his long white hair scraggly and looked in need of washing. His bold blue eyes were where you could see the strength left in the man and his eyes also revealed the part of him his son had inherited.

"You bring a whore into my house?" his father said, his fist pounding the table.

Sorrell felt her husband's hand tighten in a fist at his side, and she hurried to step forward and let loose her tongue. "I am no whore. I am his wife, and you will keep a civil tongue in front of me."

God, but he loved his wife, Ruddock thought.

"How dare you speak to me so—"

She didn't let him finish. "I defend my name to any who dares to besmirch it."

Ruddock stepped next to his wife, his hand still clenched in a fist and spoke like a man who would be obeyed or else. "You'll not speak to my wife that way."

His father glared at him and looked about to rise, his hands braced on the table and his body lifting slightly, but he quickly settled in his seat.

Sorrell saw that it wasn't that he had thought better of it that he had remained seated. It was that he didn't have the strength. She should feel sorry for him, but she didn't.

"You summoned me home, Father. Have your say," Ruddock said.

His father was blunt. "I will not die without an heir."

"But you don't believe me your son," Ruddock challenged.

"I'm not sure about that and in case I could be wrong, I want the rightful heir to inherit and carry on the proud and distinguished Northwick name."

"Do you claim me as your son?" Ruddock asked.

"What choice have I?" his father said bitterly. "Besides, you have the strength and courage of a Northwick… you survived."

In spite of you, Sorrell thought, biting her tongue to keep the words from spewing out. This was between father and son, and she would not interfere… not yet.

"We will talk," his father said.

His words struck a pain in Ruddock's chest. Those words had once brought joy to him. His father would say that very thing throughout the years as Ruddock grew from a lad to a man and they would sit in his solar and discuss everything and anything. He had learned much from him. They had been cherished memories for him and it pained him to think that this talk would not be like the others.

"Food waits in your bedchamber and the servants will prepare a bath if you wish. We will talk on the morrow."

He went to stand and Erland went to help him, but he collapsed against the table before Erland could reach him.

Ruddock rushed to the dais, Sorrell hurrying along with him.

"I will see to him," Erland said, blocking Ruddock from reaching his father.

"Who sees to his care?" Sorrell demanded.

"That is not your worry, my lady," Erland said.

"Go, I need no help," his father said, his words etched with pain.

"Nonsense," Sorrell said, pushing past her husband and jabbing Erland to move out of her way.

The man was so shocked by her actions that he moved.

Sorrell felt the old man's brow. It was damp but not feverish. "You are in pain, are you not?"

"Go away," he ordered and winced, answering her query.

Sorrell looked to her husband. "Can you carry him to his bedchamber?"

"No," his father commanded.

Ruddock paid his father's protest no heed. He went to him and pulled his chair away from the table to be able to lift him more easily.

"You'll not touch me," his father demanded.

"You're too ill to do anything, old man. I rule now!" Ruddock commanded and lifted his father in his arms, shocked by how thin he had gotten.

Sorrell followed her husband, wrinkling her nose at the foul odor drifting off the old man, while Erland rushed ahead of them.

"I can walk," his father snapped, then groaned.

"Say what you will, it matters not. It is my word now you will pay heed to."

"You think I will allow you command?" his father argued.

"You have no choice just like you gave me none," Ruddock spat.

His father's blue eyes teemed with anger. "You seek revenge."

"I seek justice, old man," Ruddock said, anger filling his own eyes.

It took several steps to reach Lord Finn's bedchamber, Erland there waiting for them.

"I'll get the brew the healer has him drink to help with the pain," Erland said and rushed out of the room.

Ruddock placed his father on the bed, sitting him up to rest against the headboard of a large bed. He had had it built special to accommodate his large size. Now he looked lost in the massive bed.

"Where does it pain you?" Sorrell asked, approaching the bed.

"That does not concern you," Finn said, turning his head as if dismissing her.

Sorrell went to open the heavy curtains that shut out all light, a good-sized fire in the hearth and a few candles providing the only light in the large room.

"Don't open them," Finn ordered.

"Let him be in his misery and stench," Ruddock said.

"Aye, get out. Let me be," Finn ordered.

Ruddock turned away from his father and walked to the door. "Let me know when you want to talk, old man."

Sorrell caught the glisten of tears in the old man's eyes.

"Be gone with you," he said to her with a nasty growl.

Sorrell turned and joined her husband waiting just outside the door.

They passed Erland rushing up the stairs as they went down, not an easy task with her husband's size.

She scrunched her nose as Erland slipped slowly past her, the smell from the tankard turning her stomach. She didn't know how the old man could drink it.

Once inside Ruddock's bedchamber, she glanced around. It was three times the size of her room back home. There wasn't a speck of dust or dirt and recently made rush mats lay in on the floor throughout the room. The bedding on the large bed was fresh and the blankets folded back.

A table, with an assortment of food sat atop, and two chairs sat beneath one of the two windows. A good-sized hearth, with a hewn mantel above, kept the room cozy warm. A series of pegs ran along one wall, several garments hanging from them.

Sorrell was glad to see that the heavy drapes on the windows had been left pulled back, letting light in the room. Not that there was much since the skies were gray.

Ruddock stood by the hearth, his hand braced on the mantel, staring at the flames.

A knock sounded at the door and Sorrell went to it, seeing that her husband hadn't heard it.

"My lady," a man said with a respectful bob of his head. "Is Lord Ruddock here?"

"Come in, Erskine," Ruddock called out and Sorrell stepped aside to let the man enter.

He went straight to her husband. He was of fair height and slender and he wore his gray hair short. His features were plain and his posture slightly stooped.

"Forgive me, my lord, for not being there to welcome you home. There was a problem in the kitchen," Erskine explained.

"Pay it no mind, Erskine. I didn't expect a warm welcome," Ruddock said. "How long has my father been ill?"

That her husband should ask that of this man made Sorrell think he trusted him.

"Far too long and he grows worse lately."

"What does the healer say?" Ruddock asked.

"She says he has the rotting illness and dies a little each day."

"The clan is now under my rule. You will bring all problems and issues concerning the keep to me," Ruddock instructed.

"The problems and issues of the keep are my duties," Sorrell said.

Ruddock looked to his wife and she was struck by the sorrow in his eyes. This had not been an easy day for him and she would not add to his burden.

"I'm sure with Erskine's guidance and tutoring, I can learn the workings of the keep and in time fulfill my duties so that Erskine and I may work well together."

"I would be pleased to teach you all you need to know and pleased to work with you, my lady," Erskine said.

Sorrell smiled. "I appreciate that Erskine, perhaps we can start tomorrow."

"I will be available when you are ready," he said with a bob of his head.

"In the meantime, do you think a bath could be prepared for Lord Ruddock and for me?"

"It is being done as we speak, my lady. Lord Ruddock's bath waits in his washroom and yours has been prepared in your private bedchamber."

"Thank you, Erskine," Ruddock said as a way of dismissing him.

The man understood and took his leave.

"My bedchamber?" She shook her head. "I sleep where you sleep."

He smiled, reached out, and took her in his arms, wanting to feel her warmth, her love. "This is your only bedchamber, wife. Do what you will with the other room. And thank you for being so wise and working with Erskine."

She pressed her cheek to his chest and hugged him. "He seems pleasant."

"He is a good man. I trusted him once."

She raised her head off his chest to look up at him. "But not anymore?"

"I don't know who to trust anymore, except you." He kissed her briefly.

"I love your kisses," she said with a soft sigh, "and I love you."

His mouth opened as if to speak but nothing fell from his lips.

Sorrell tapped his lips with her finger. "One day, husband, you will say what I already know… that you love me." She slipped out of his arms. "Now let's get to those baths so we can return here and enjoy the food and that bed, and preferably not in that order."

"On that we agree, wife," he said and he hoped that she understood that he meant he agreed with everything she had said.

***

Sorrell couldn't wait to get out of her garments and into the bath water. Four days' travel and much of it in rain had her eager to get clean. She only wished the two, young servant lassies attending her were a bit friendlier. They barely looked at her and whispered far too much between themselves.

By the time she stood in nothing more than her shift, she'd had enough.

"Is there a reason neither of you say a word to me, or refuse to look me in the eye?"

Both women were stunned and stared at her in silence.

"You have no answer for me," she asked when both remained silent.

They both shook their heads.

"Then leave me, you will tend me no more," she ordered, missing her sisters more than ever at that moment.

The two ran from the room.

Sorrell shook her head and went and sat by the warmth of the hearth, her interest in the bath waning. She didn't know what was going on here, but something was amiss. It seemed too much was amiss in her husband's home and with his father. She had watched her mum tend many illnesses since she was young. Never had she smelled anything as bad as that brew Erland was taking to Ruddock's father. And never would she understand how Finn Northwick could treat his son so badly and want him dead.

What surprised her the most is what a good man and husband Ruddock was for what he had been through. He was kind, tender, and passionate with her, and she loved everything about him. She wished he was here now and they could bathe together.

She cast a glance at the round, wooden bath tub draped with cloth, and grinned. He'd never fit in it and if she did bathe with him they'd probably wind up doing more than only washing.

She looked down at her chest, her nipples hard and poking at the shift, and she thought about her husband's mouth on them. The sensation that sparked to life between her legs had her warning herself to stop thinking about him.

The door swung open.

Please, please, let it be her husband, she pleaded silently.

A plump woman, who stood at least a head above Sorrell's height entered the room. Her red hair was a mass of curls similar to Sorrel's and her pretty face was defined by a friendly smile.

"I'm Blodwen, my lady. Erskine sent me to tend you. Surprised me he did, since I'm usually relegated to chores where my chatter doesn't bother or offend anyone, and I'm not one to judge. Well, not too often anyway," she said with a hardy laugh. "And I can hold my tongue when needed or asked, not like most around here."

Sorrell smiled, finally meeting a friendly face. "I am pleased to meet you, Blodwen."

"And I you, my lady," she said with a quick nod of her head after shutting the door behind her. "Now let's get you washed."

Sorrell looked longingly to the door, wishing for her husband, thinking about going to him, not caring about propriety.

"Come, my lady," Blodwen said, "I'll get you scrubbed up in no time."

Sorrell was glad for the assistance and distraction from her thoughts and glad she felt comfortable with the chatty woman

"Up with your arms now," Blodwen said and yanked the shift up and over her head as soon as Sorrell raised her arms up. "You're a wee bit of a thing, if you don't mind me saying so, but you must be a strong one since you wed Lord Ruddock."

Sorrell didn't get a chance to ask Blodwen what she meant. The door swung open, slamming against the wall and there stood her husband… naked.

Chapter Twenty-one

Sorrell stood stunned, unable to move, seeing her husband standing naked in the open doorway. His body glistened with water, droplets sticking to him, not wanting to let him go, and she couldn't blame them, though she was jealous of them. The thought of catching each droplet with her tongue delighted her and made her feel wicked all at once.

He strode toward her and scooped her up in his arms. "We bathe together."

She grinned and swung her arms around his neck and planted a kiss on his cheek, and as they walked out the door she heard Blodwen chuckle.

"There is no one in your bathe chamber is there?" she asked anxiously as they neared the room.

"I chased them all away. It's just you and me, the way I like it."

"The way I like it as well, but you're wet. You bathed already?"

Ruddock shook his head. "I got in the tub and realized something was missing."

"Me," she said and kissed his cheek again.

"Aye, wife, you," he said and entered his washing room and went straight to the massive tub.

"That tub will certainly hold two people," Sorrell said and understood why there was a separate washing room. The tub was simply too large to move.

Ruddock settled them in the tub with ease, the water not hot but more than warm, and she sighed as she sunk into it.

When the water reached her chin, her husband lifted her higher against his chest until it was only at her neck.

"Never would I have thought of sharing a bath with my husband, and now," —she sighed— "I don't believe I'd have it any other way."

"That's good, since I don't intend to have it any other way," he said and hugged her tight.

Ruddock closed his eyes after a few minutes of silence passed between them and rested his head back against the rim of the tub. This was peace and solitude to him, being alone in the quiet, his wife in his arms, and the warmth of the water cradling them both.

Words were not necessary and he was glad she felt the same. After a few moments, or had it been longer, the water having lost a good bit of its warmth, he glanced down at his wife and saw that she slept.

The journey had been exhausting, still she had not complained. He laughed softly. She had complained about one thing… privacy for them to make love. He had planned on doing just that tonight, but it wouldn't be fair when she was so bone-tired.

"Sorrell," he said softly, "the water grows cold. We need to wash and you need sleep.

Sorrell woke with a moan.

"We need to wash, the water grows cold," he repeated in case she hadn't heard him.

Sorrell barely opened her eyes as she nodded her head.

Ruddock realized she was far too tired to do anything but sleep.

He'd get her washed and dried quick, tuck her in bed, and then return to the tub and see to himself.

He started with her hair, tipping her head back for the water to soak through the stubborn strands, then grabbed the soap from the small ledge on the outside of the tub and lathered her hair. He loved her wild, red curls that did whatever they wanted. They suited her. When the sun shined on them, she looked as if her hair was ablaze and as fiery as her nature.

He rinsed the soap from her hair, running his fingers through it. When that was done, he went to work on her body, not an easy task and one that produced an arousal in him that kept growing.

He hadn't had a chance to touch her all over, get to know every inch of her intimately, but not this way. He wanted her awake, participating, and enjoying. With strength he feared wouldn't last, he ran the soap over her chest, turning her nipples, that bobbed in the water, hard.

Damn, if he didn't want to taste them, but he would be good and honorable. Or so he told himself.

He ran the soap down over her midriff, along her narrow waist, and lifted her against his chest to scrub her back and backside, loving the feel of her firm cheeks. And all she did was sigh and moan and seek his chest to lay her head on.

He left between her legs for last, intending to hurry and be done with that spot and have her out of the tub before he lost his senses.

Her legs were easy to reach, since she was so petite including her feet. He was almost done with her. He rubbed the soap over the red curls, his fingers getting entwined with them and his thumb accidentally connecting with her small bud of pleasure.

Leave it be. Leave it be, he silently cautioned himself.

Paying mind to his warning, he slid his hand down between her legs that had remained slightly spread after washing them. He ran the bar of soap over her, not letting his fingers touch her as torturous as it was.

"Enough," he mumbled to himself and placed the soap in the holder.

He slipped his arm under her legs, his other arm at her back, and went to stand when he felt her hand press at his chest.

"I'll have you here and now after torturing me the way you have."

"You weren't asleep," he accused with a hint of a smile.

"You think I could sleep while you touched me so intimately?" She didn't wait for his response. She moved out of his arms and situated herself between his legs. "My turn to wash you."

She reached past him to grab the soap, her breasts brushing his chest and faintly skimming his warm cheek.

"Tease me like that, wife, and you'll find me inside you fast enough."

She frowned. "You would rob me of the pleasure of touching all of you as you did me?"

Ruddock closed his eyes and groaned at the thought of her small hands exploring him. He kept them closed when she began to rub his chest with the soap, slowly, methodically, even more so when she ran her palms over his nipples.

"Sorrell," he said with a passion filled growl.

"Shhh," she said near his lips. "I'm enjoying myself."

The next thing he knew, her hand had slipped between his legs and taken hold of his manhood that had already swelled to a tormenting ache.

She stroked it, tugged playfully at it, but when she moved closer and rubbed it against her entrance, he lost it.

His hands were at her waist as his eyes sprang open and he landed her down on his manhood with such accuracy that she gasped when she felt him rest deep inside her.

She rushed her hands to grip his shoulders as he began to slide her up and down on his manhood, his rhythm picking up speed as he went. She wouldn't last long. She didn't want to.

She dropped her brow to his and he quickly captured her lips with his, catching a moan that escaped her.

Ruddock couldn't slow down, didn't want to slow down. He had driven himself mad washing her and with her hands having tormented him, he couldn't hold on any longer to his sanity. And he was sure she felt the same.

Sorrell tore her mouth away from his and with an anguished plea moaned, "Ruddock."

That did it for him. It was the first time she called him by his given name when they made love and it sent him over the edge. And he took her with him.

Sorrell groaned so loud, it echoed off the walls and Ruddock couldn't stop himself from letting out a roar.

Other satisfying groans followed until they tapered off and Sorrell fell limp against her husband. It took a while for the last ripple to fade away and that was when it struck her. If she thought she was tired before, it was nothing to how she felt now.

Ruddock locked his arms around her as her body grew more limp against him. This little tryst had more than exhausted her.

"You need sleep," he said and kissed her brow.

"I can't move. I don't want to move," she pleaded.

Ruddock lifted her off him, moans of protest coming from her, and placed her in his arms. He climbed out of the tub and placed her feet on the floor and resting her body against him, he hurried and toweled her dry.

She licked at his chest. "I thought of licking the drops of water from you when you entered my bedchamber." She sighed. "Next time."

"Promise?"

"You have," —she yawned— "my word."

He wrapped a dry towel around her and carried her to their bedchamber, to place her in bed, and tuck the blankets around her.

"You aren't joining me?" she asked with a pout.

"As soon as I dry myself."

She gave a brief smile, sighed, and pressed her head against the pillow as she curled up beneath the blankets.

Ruddock dried himself while watching his wife's eyes drift close and drift off to sleep. He wasn't ready for sleep yet. He was hungry. He went to the table with the food, sat, helped himself to some meat, and filled a goblet with wine. He needed to think about what obstacles he might face with claiming himself in charge of the clan.

It was obvious his father was no longer capable of ruling. He was too ill, to close to dying. Ruddock needed to see the state of the clan's affairs and make certain all was well. And where once he would have wanted to redeem himself in the eyes of the clan, now it didn't matter to him. He had done nothing wrong. What he had done had been forced upon him. He had been given no choice and he'd be damned if he was made to pay for it any longer.

He only hoped his clan would not treat Sorrell poorly because of him, though if anyone did, they would learn fast the consequences.

What was most important to him was finding out why an attempt was made on his wife's life and if the attempt on his life had any connection. He intended to send Asger a message. He had left too quickly that night at the abbey and he wanted to know why.

He helped himself to cheese and bread and more meat and refilled his goblet twice. He didn't feel as burdened as he once did even though his burdens had yet to be lifted completely. It was his wife that had brought some peace to him. Having her by his side, knowing she would always defend him, always love him, made a difference.

He swallowed the last of the wine, went to the bed, and slipped beneath the blanket to gently tuck himself around his wife. Content with her in his arms, he fell asleep soon after his head rested on the pillow.

***

After having breakfast with her husband the next morning, Sorrell decided to see how his father fared before she started her day. There was something amiss with Finn Northwick and the only way she could find out was to talk with him, as cranky an old man as he was. But she'd dealt with crankier men than him.

The door was open to his bedchamber when she reached his floor and she quietly went to stand behind it and listened, the voices inside loud enough to hear.

"I have no choice, Erland, I refuse to die without an heir. Son or not, Ruddock will inherit all that is mine. And with him wed, there is a good chance that she will be with child soon and the Northwick name will carry on."

"You can still continue to rule until then. It isn't necessary for you to turn over command of the clan to Ruddock just yet," Erland argued. "And as far as his wife, she is but a wee thing. How will she ever birth a bairn?"

"As long as the bairn lives that's all that matters. Ruddock can always find another wife."

Sorrell's temper almost had her marching in there and telling them both bluntly what she thought of them, but she wisely remained where she was and continued to listen.

"This illness has taken its toll and will eventually take my life. I will see that Ruddock is capable of leading the clan and doing right by it."

"How can you trust him or even forgive him after what he did when you proclaimed him illegitimate?" Erland asked incredulously.

"He will answer to me for that," Finn snapped. "You will be my eyes and ears and tell me everything he does."

"What if—"

"I will decide his fate," Finn said with finality. "Now go and see what my son is up to."

Sorrell quietly moved into the shadows in case Erland closed the door and was relieved when he went straight down the stairs. She waited, not wanting Ruddock's father to know she had heard them talking. It infuriated her that he did not trust his son and was having Erland watch him, and that Erland did not want Finn to abdicate command to Ruddock yet. What was most curious to her was Erland's reference to something Ruddock had done that Finn should not trust or forgive. Also that Finn intended to hold him accountable. She'd find out for herself.

Feeling confident enough time had passed, she quietly made her way to the stairs, went down a few steps, and hurried up them, humming a melody so that Finn believed she had just climbed the stairs.

"How do you fare this morning, Finn?" she asked, entering the room.

"Did I request your presence? And you'll address me properly, Lord Finn or my lord," he scolded with a scowl.

"Not until you truly recognize my husband as your son," Sorrell said and went to the window and threw open the curtain, sending a glorious stream of light into the room.

"Close that!" Finn shouted at her, holding his hand up to shade his eyes.

"No," Sorrell said and walked to stand at the end of the bed, her hands on her hips.

"The light is no good for my illness. Now close it," Finn ordered.

"Who told you such nonsense?"

"My healer who knows more than you."

"She can't be much of a healer if she thinks light will bring you harm. Light can't be harmful if the plants, the trees, the animals look to it for growth and strength."

"I didn't ask for your opinion," he snapped.

"I know, but I'm giving it anyway," she said, then sniffed the air and scrunched her face. "When was the last time you bathed?" He went to speak and Sorrell held up her hand, stopping him. "Don't tell me, the healer says bathing is no good for your illness."

"Be gone with you or I'll have you removed," Finn commanded.

Sorrell ignored him and walked around to the side of the bed, picking up the near empty tankard and wrinkled her nose. "This is godawful. How can you drink it?"

Finn dropped his head back on the pillow, his strength fading. "It keeps the pain away for a while at least."

"Ruddock has your eyes," Sorrell said, amazed at how identical they were. It was like looking in Ruddock's eyes.

"Don't think to play games with me. I never lose," Finn warned.

"I don't play games," Sorrell said, "but if I did you would taste defeat."

"Is that a challenge?" he demanded, determination sparking in his eyes.

"You feel up to it?"

"My body may betray me, but my mind is as sharp as ever," Finn said, his chin jutting out stubbornly.

Sorrell was quick to dispute him. "That's not true. A man who is sharp in wit would never let himself stink as badly as you do and blame it on the healer."

"I blame no one and you better learn to watch that tongue of yours, lassie," Finn threatened.

Sorrell paid no heed to his threat, her mind too busy with memories of her da that rose up to taunt her and tears sprung up to glisten her eyes.

"Don't think tears will do you any good with me," Finn warned.

Memories she tried so hard to keep locked away suddenly broke free and rose up to torment her. Her legs grew weak, no longer able to support her and she hurried to sit in the chair beside the bed.

The words seemed to rush from her mouth as if by doing so she would rid herself of the painful memories.

"My da took ill." She shook her head and rubbed at her chest, trying to ease the ache in her heart. "We all realized too late that his mind had betrayed him. One moment he was the da I remembered, strong and loving, and the next…" Sorrell wiped at a tear that trickled down her cheek. "He was a good father and I loved him dearly, and I miss him to this day." She reached her hand out to rest on Finn's arm and though she felt it tense beneath her, she didn't pull away. "Your son is a good man, talk with him before it's too late."

She stood and grabbed the tankard of the godawful brew. "I will see that a bath is prepared for you."

"That's my decision, lassie. You don't tell me what to do," Finn said with a snappish tongue as Sorrell walked to the door.

Sorrell turned when she reached the door. "You may be a stubborn old fool, but foolish you're not."

She hurried off, not waiting for a response and went in search of Blodwen. She was directed to the wardrobe room, two floors above her private bedchamber.

"My lady," Blodwen said with a bob when Sorrell entered the room.

It was filled with several chests, a small fireplace, a single bed, and had one lone window to emit light.

Blodwen continued when she saw that Sorrell glanced around. "The room is meant for your personal servant and the chests store linens and garments. I came to fetch some garments that could be stitched to fit you. I have a fine hand with a needle."

"This is your room then?" Sorrell asked.

Blodwen's face registered surprise. "If you'll have me as your servant, though truth be told most believed I would not last the day with you."

Sorrell smiled. "More fools them, since I declare you my personal servant, making this room yours."

A tear tickled at the corner of Blodwen's one eye. "I am so very grateful, my lady. There are not many who want me around."

"I want you around. I believe you will be of great help to me."

"Anything, my lady, I would do anything for you," Blodwen said, nodding her head and confirming her words.

"Good since I have a question for you. Do you know of anyone who could tell me the contents of this godawful brew?" Sorrell asked, holding out the tankard in her hand.

"The healer makes it and brings it to Lord Finn."

"Is there anyone other than the healer who might be of help to me?"

Blodwen stepped closer and lowered her voice. "The woman in the woods would know. There are some who prefer to seek her skills rather than Wilda, the clan healer."

"Will you take me to her?" Sorrell asked.

"Aye, if you want, my lady, but you should know that most think the woman in the woods a witch."

Chapter Twenty-two

"For the third time, no, you cannot go into the woods to see this woman," Ruddock said, looking over a map in front of him on the large desk in his father's solar.

Erland stood beside him, paying her no mind.

Sorrell planted her hands on her hips, better there then around her husband's neck since she felt like strangling him. Not that she ever would, of course, frustration causing the thought. Besides, her hands would never fit around his thick neck.

"You do realize I asked you out of curtesy. I intend to go whether you grant me permission or not."

Ruddock leaned back in the large chair and grinned. "I am more than familiar with your willfulness, wife, which is why I have assigned two warriors to follow you wherever you go outside this keep."

Sorrell burst out laughing, causing Erland to stare at her in shock and her husband to shake his head.

"You truly believe I can't outsmart two of your warriors?"

Ruddock's smile vanished and he stood and planted his hands on the desk in front of him and glared at his wife in warning. "You better not even try to outsmart them."

Sorrell walked over to him and slapped her small hands down on the desk in front of his hands and brought her face close to his. "Then let them escort me into the woods to see this healer or I go without them."

"She is no healer. She a witch, my lord, an evil witch," Erland said. "You mustn't let her go there."

"Leave us, Erland," Ruddock ordered.

"I meant no disrespect, my lord," Erland apologized and made no move to take his leave.

"And none was taken, now leave," Ruddock ordered sharply and Erland bobbed his head and scurried out of the room.

Ruddock walked around the desk to stand in front of his wife. "The only reason I stop you is because of the attempt on your life. Until I can learn more, I prefer you remain in the confines of the castle's walls."

"Then send a troop of warriors with me," Sorrell suggested.

"Why is it so important for you to see this woman?" he asked and his eyes suddenly turned wide. "Are you ill?" He reached out, his arm circling her small waist.

"No, I'm fine," she assured him, seeing the worry that sprang in his eyes. "I want to ask her about the brew that the clan healer has been giving your da. There's something troubling about it to me and I believe she may be able to help."

Ruddock's hands went to her waist, lifted her, and sat her on the edge of the desk, planting his hands on either side of her.

"I know you wished you had realized sooner that your da was ill and that there had been more you could have done for him. But my father's illness has been openly known. He is dying and there is nothing you can do to save him."

Sorrell placed her hand on her husband's warm cheek. "You're probably right, but I need to do this for me, not your da."

If Sorrell hadn't been sleeping in his arms on their journey here, then she had been chatting endlessly and he had enjoyed learning more about her and her family. He had realized that she felt that she had failed her da by not recognizing his illness sooner. Of course, she hadn't, but she would continue to blame herself until she finally accepted the truth. And perhaps saving his father would make amends for not saving hers. Not that she would be able to save Finn Northwick, but if he didn't let her try, what then?

"I'll take you," he said, "but it will not be until tomorrow morning."

She grabbed his face in her hands and kissed him. "You are the most wonderful husband."

"And you are the most challenging wife," he said and lifted her off the desk. "Now go and don't get into any trouble."

She smiled and hurried to the door, calling out, "I'll try, but I can't promise."

Ruddock shook his head as he returned to sit behind the desk.

"You should obey your husband. You have no idea how dangerous a man he is," Erland whispered, waiting outside the solar.

Sorrell would not hear such nonsense. "I know my husband and he is a good man."

"He is not a good man… he is evil," Erland whispered harshly and hurried to enter the solar, closing the door behind him.

Why would Erland think Ruddock evil? There were far too many things that didn't make sense and it was time to find out why.

***

Erskine had suggested that Sorrell be shown the keep and become familiar with it before he began explaining the running of it, and she agreed. She requested that Blodwen be her guide since she was certain Erskine was too busy for the task and he had eagerly agreed.

"I'm so pleased to have been given this task, my lady," Blodwen said as she entered Sorrell's private bedchamber.

"I am as well, Blodwen," she said and went to a peg on the wall and grabbed two cloaks, handing one to Blodwen. "But first a walk through the village for some fresh air."

Blodwen nodded and took the cloak and once out on the keep's steps Sorrell stopped and cast a glance out over the castle grounds. The size of it amazed her. There were cottages neatly lined up beside one another and on both sides of the various roads that ran through the village. Patches of good-sized gardens could be seen behind the cottages. There was even a church that sat on a small mound of land in the center of the village, cottages around all sides of it and two roads leading from it.

"I've never seen a village the size of this one," Sorrell said. "And so well kept."

"It does surprise some when first seen. Lord Finn insists the village, the keep, everything here be well-maintained, he wouldn't have it kept any other way."

Yet the man didn't bathe. So was it the strength of the healer's influence or Finn's strong desire to live that made him follow the healer's orders without question?

"Can you take me to the healer's cottage?" Sorrell asked.

"Of course, my lady, this way," Blodwen said and turned down a road a few steps from the keep.

Sorrell smiled at the various people they passed, ready to call out greetings, but most turned away from her. Some avoided looking at her at all. A couple of woman who appeared ready to respond to her greeting were yanked by their arms and given a tongue lashing by their husbands. Several women wouldn't even let their children near her, calling out to them to return home when she got near them.

It was quite puzzling, since none there knew her. How then could they judge her?

A couple of cottages up ahead stood a man a few feet from his cottage door. His red beard was as thick as his long hair and the same color, and even from a distance one could see anger stirring in his dark eyes. He looked to have been a sizeable man at one time, but no more, his garments appearing to hang on him and though taller than most other men, though not as tall as her husband, there was a slump to his shoulders that made him appear shorter. His left arm hung at his side at an odd angle and as Sorrell got closer she could see the arm was lifeless.

"Come in, Hugh," the woman who appeared at the door urged.

"No, Lana, I want to see the harlot who wed the devil," Hugh said, looking straight at Sorrell.

"Hugh!' Lana scolded. "Come in at once before you make matters worse."

"We should turn the other way, my lady," Blodwen said just as the two warriors following Sorrell stepped around them.

"Enough, Hugh. Keep a civil tongue around Lady Sorrell, or you'll be in the stocks," one of the warriors warned.

"Hugh, please," his wife begged teary-eyed. "I don't want to lose you."

"Pay heed to your wife's worries, Hugh, and go inside," the one warrior cautioned.

"What difference does it make?" Hugh asked with a huff. "I'll be in the stocks soon enough once the devil finds out I called his wife a harlot."

"You spoke up knowing the consequences. You have no one to blame but yourself," Sorrell said, stepping around the two warriors.

"There's plenty of blame and it doesn't fall on me," Hugh spat.

"Are you implying that the blame falls on my husband?" Sorrell asked.

"You know nothing," Hugh challenged. "If you did, you would have never wed him."

"Please, my lady, he's into his cups. He means no harm," Lana pleaded, taking hold of her husband's good arm and trying to pull him into the cottage.

Sorrell agreed with her. He did appear to be into his cups and the fear on the wife's face seemed genuine.

"Leave me be, woman," Hugh said, yanking his arm away from his wife. "I'll hold my tongue no more."

"Then you'll wind up just like Lander if you don't weigh your words," his wife cautioned anxiously.

The reminder turned Hugh's eyes wide and Sorrell wondered what had happened to Lander that frightened Hugh.

"Good day to you, my lady," Hugh said and entered his cottage.

His wife closed the door behind him, but not before she turned a pleading glance on Sorrell. She was begging Sorrell not to let any harm come to Hugh.

Sorrell fell silent as they continued walking, the two warriors returning to walk several steps behind her and Blodwen. Something was very wrong here. She had thought that the people hadn't greeted or even acknowledged Ruddock's return because they had believed the lies that he wasn't Finn's son and had no right to return. But after meeting Hugh, she realized there was far more to it than that.

She was about to ask Blodwen, who had strangely remained silent since Sorrell had exchanged words with Hugh, about what had happened to his arm and also about Lander, when the young woman spoke.

"This is Wilda's cottage, my lady."

Sorrell stepped up to the door and knocked, but got no answer.

"Wilda is probably out somewhere tending someone," Blodwen said.

Sorrell nodded and stepped around the side of the house. Spying a garden in the back, she walked over to it. There wasn't much to see, the last harvest having cleared nearly all of the garden. If she was hoping to find something that would explain the reason for Finn's awful smelling brew, it wasn't here.

"You wish something from me, my lady?"

Sorrell turned while Blodwen jumped at the soft voice behind them.

"I wanted to meet the clan healer and come to know her if ever I should require her skills," Sorrell said, looking over the older woman, surprised by how frail she appeared.

She had perhaps a bit of height over Sorrell, but not by much, and she was rail thin, her skin pale and the single braid of her long, gray hair rested over her shoulder and on her chest. Her dark eyes, however, appeared to tell a different story. They were bright, alert, and watchful.

"It will be my pleasure to come to know you, my lady. Unfortunately, I have no time to spare today. I only returned here to gather more items to tend those in need."

"Another day then," Sorrell said.

"Of course, my lady," Wilda said with a nod.

Sorrell stopped in front of her when she went to walk past her. "I was curious as to the brew you make for Lord Finn. What is in it?"

"Several herbs that help him tolerate the pain that grows by the day. Now if you will excuse me, my lady, I must go. There are those in need of my care."

"Until next time," Sorrell said and walked off.

"Much luck in getting to know Wilda, my lady," Blodwen said, after taking a few steps away from the healer's cottage. "She keeps much to herself."

"How long has she been the clan's healer and how can one healer provide for such a large clan?" Sorrell asked.

"I believe Wilda has been with the clan five years now. There was another healer, but she died about six months ago. She had been with the clan for as long as I can remember. There's also two women who tend to the births. Lady Alida, Lord Finn's wife, had provided healing for the clan along with Esta, the older healer who passed. All loved Lady Alida. She was a good woman." Blodwen gave a look to the sky. "We should return to the keep, my lady. It grows colder, the gray sky darkens even more and rain will follow soon."

The two warriors drifted off when Sorrell reached the top step of the keep, their chore done.

"A hot brew would do well before we begin exploring the keep," Sorrell said as Blodwen opened the door.

"I'll see to it right away, my lady," Blodwen said.

Sorrell hesitated a moment before entering, thinking she heard someone cry out. When it didn't sound again and Blodwen didn't seem to notice, she stepped inside. It came again as the door closed behind Blodwen and this time it sounded more like a plea.

"Your cloak, my lady," Blodwen said and went to reach for it.

Sorrell shook her head. "See to the hot brew. I'm chilled."

Blodwen bobbed her head and hurried off and Sorrell stepped back outside.

She went down a few steps and this time it was clear.

"Please, please, Coyle, I'm sorry," a woman's voice begged.

Sorrell made it quickly to the bottom of the steps and followed the voices.

"You'll do as I say, woman."

Sorrell cringed when she heard the hard slap, almost feeling the woman's pain.

"No! No! I beg you, Coyle. I'll be good. I give you my word, I'll be good," the woman pleaded.

Sorrell realized the voices came from beyond the castle walls, and she spotted a door that sat open, leading outside the wall. She hurried through it to see a fair-sized man dragging a woman toward the stream of water that fed the water mill

"Let her be!" Sorrell shouted, halting the man.

He turned and glared at Sorrell. "This doesn't concern you, woman. Be gone with you."

"Coyle, no, she's La—"

Coyle slapped the woman across the face, her head swinging back from the blow, and blood spewing from her mouth. "Didn't I order you not to speak?"

Sorrell's eyes flared with anger and she didn't think twice, she searched the ground and finding several rocks swiped them up.

"I'll not tell you again to let her go," Sorrell ordered.

The woman didn't open her mouth again, too fearful of what the man would do.

"And what are you going to do about it?" His sneer marked with a short laugh.

Sorrell didn't wait she aimed and threw and hit her mark, sending a good-sized rock hurdling at his arm and hitting it with enough force that it caused him to release the woman as he shouted out in pain.

"You bitch!" he screamed and headed toward her.

Sorrell fired rock after rock hitting him in the leg, almost bringing him to his knees, his head, stunning him a moment, and she saved the largest one for last, sending it hurdling to hit between his legs. That one did it. It felled him like a tree toppling and crashing to the ground.

She hurried around him to the woman. "I'll get you to safety."

The woman clung to her, nodding as Sorrell helped her to her feet. They had almost reached the door when Sorrell was yanked back by her hair.

"Get help," Sorrell called out to the woman as she was dragged away from her.

"Don't you dare go anywhere, Miriam," Coyle ordered and the woman froze.

Pain and anger warred in his eyes while blood ran down the side of his face from the wound on his head and he was hunched over some from the pain that probably still radiated in his nether region.

"You're going to pay for this lass," he snarled and dragged her toward the rushing stream.

Sorrell tried to dig her heels in the ground, but he was too strong. She wouldn't give up. It wasn't in her to give up. She would get away from him.

He dropped her to ground, but she had no time to escape. He grabbed her by the back of her neck, his fingers digging into her flesh, and dragged her the short distance to the stream. He plunged her face into the cold water and held it there until she couldn't hold another breath, then he yanked her head up.

She gasped for breath as he roughly pulled her up to her feet and before she could get a decent breath, he swung his hand, slapping her across the face and sending her tumbling to the ground.

"You'll learn not to interfere with me and my wife again," he said, fisting his hand this time to deliver another blow.

She gathered her wits fast enough when she felt a sharp jab to her side after landing on the ground. *A rock*. She hurried to grab it and swung it just as he went to lean over her, his fist raised to deliver a stinging blow. It caught him hard in the jaw and he stumbled back, blood gushing out of his mouth.

He coughed and spit out blood and a tooth came out along with it.

"You bitch," he screamed, wiping at his bloody mouth with the sleeve of his shirt.

Sorrell had gotten to her feet and was running for the door in the castle wall. She saw that the woman was gone and prayed that she had gone for help. If not, as long as she could get inside the castle wall, she could get help.

She heard his footsteps pounding closer and she ran faster and just as she reached the open door, her husband stepped through it, and she threw herself at him.

Ruddock locked his arms around his wife as he glared with fury at the man who stopped abruptly when he caught sight of him.

"You dared to lay a hand on my wife," Ruddock roared.

The man paled. "I have just returned the castle. I didn't know she was your wife. She interfered with me reprimanding my wife."

"You mean beating your wife."

"Miriam got what she deserved," Coyle argued.

"Then you will get what you deserve as well," Ruddock said, his anger turning to a raging fury when he saw his wife's red cheek and that her hair was wet, it having soaked part of his shirt.

Sorrell was quick to assure him, seeing the concern that rose in his eyes. "I am unharmed."

"That red welt on your face tells me differently as does your wet hair. Did he hold your face under water?" Ruddock demanded, his muscles tightening as he tried to keep hold of his anger.

Sorrell attempted to reassure him. "I am fine."

"Did he hold your head underwater?" Ruddock demanded again.

Sorrell saw a fury in his eyes like she had never seen before and she was quick to answer. "Aye he did."

"Blodwen, take Lady Sorrell and tend to her," Ruddock ordered and the woman stepped from behind Ruddock.

Sorrell went to protest, wanting to stay with him.

"Not a word, wife. You'll go inside and stay there," Ruddock ordered with such an icy resolve that Sorrell shivered and left his arms without protest as he eased her away.

"Come, my lady, you're wet and need to get warm," Blodwen said and after walking through the open door, six warriors filed through it behind her to fan out on either side of Ruddock.

Sorrell halted her steps, forcing Blodwen to do the same.

"My lady, Lord Ruddock ordered you inside," Blodwen said.

"You need to know that I don't take well to orders," Sorrell said and went back to peer past the frame of the door and watch.

Coyle wisely dropped to his knees. "Forgive me, my lord, I beg you."

"Did my wife beg you to stop," Ruddock demanded.

"Not once, my lord, not once."

Ruddock stepped in front of him. "Well, I'm going to make you beg."

The first blow lifted Coyle right off his knees and before he hit the ground the second knocked a couple of more teeth out of his mouth and the third blow knocked him unconscious.

Ruddock dragged him by the back of the shirt to the stream and grabbed him by the throat and held his head under until he woke. Then shoved it in the water again and again and again.

"How many times?" he roared at Coyle. "How many times did you push her head under?"

Coyle coughed and sputtered. "Once. Only once."

Ruddock shoved his head under again, Coyle staring up at him through the water, his hands grabbing frantically at

Ruddock's hand that squeezed at his throat, begging him to let him go.

He yanked Coyle out of the water and threw him to the ground, then turned his eyes on the open door and called out, "Sorrell get in the keep now."

Sorrell jumped, wondering how he saw her. Her head was barely visible from that distance. She didn't move even with Blodwen's urgings, until she saw her husband grab Coyle by the shirt and give him a kick to the backside.

"Start walking," Ruddock ordered. "It's the stocks for you."

Sorrell hurried away from the door and up a few steps of the keep, Blodwen following.

When Ruddock passed close by the side of the steps, he called out, "I mean it. Sorrell, get in the keep and stay there."

When Sorrell didn't budge, Blodwen pleaded with her, "Please, my lady, I don't want to see you hurt."

"I want to see what my husband does," Sorrell said.

"He will be angry and punish you," Blodwen said teary-eyed.

Sorrell stared agape at her. "You think my husband would hurt me?"

Blodwen nodded.

"Ruddock would never hurt me, not ever," Sorrell said. "He is a good man."

Blodwen bit at her lower lip as if to keep herself from speaking.

Sorrell didn't notice, she was too busy stretching her small neck past the steps to the left of the keep where she had spotted the stocks upon their arrival here.

People started gathering as the warriors placed Coyle in the stocks, while Ruddock stood and watched. A sizeable crowd had formed by the time the warrior finished securing Coyle.

Ruddock stepped forward and raised his voice for all to hear. "This man will remain in the stocks until I decide whether he lives or dies. He dared to take a hand to my wife. Anyone who dares such a thing or even speaks disparagingly to or of her will suffer the same fate. I do not care what you think of me, but you will treat my wife with respect."

Sorrell couldn't take her eyes off the peoples' faces. They feared her husband even more now. She watched them gather in groups and whisper, many shaking their heads. She was so engrossed that she didn't see her husband had neared the steps.

"Hurry, my lady, Lord Ruddock draws near," Blodwen whispered.

Sorrell looked to see her husband nearly on top of her and she didn't hesitate. She ran to him.

Ruddock scooped her up in his arms when she reached him and hugged her tight against him. "What am I going to do with you, wife?"

Sorrell lifted her head off his chest and smiled. "Love me."

Chapter Twenty-three

"Have a hot bath prepared for my wife, Blodwen," Ruddock ordered, the servant remaining on his heels as he carried his wife through the keep.

"Aye, my lord," she said and hurried off.

"Do you fear *anything*, wife?" Ruddock asked.

She tapped his chest. "Losing you."

"And I fear losing you, so you will take pity on your husband and not take such chances with your life ever again."

"Is that a command?" she asked as they were about to leave the Great Hall.

"Must I make it one?" he asked, a slight warning in his tone.

"Lord Ruddock, a matter that needs your immediate attention," Erland called out as he entered the room.

"Go," Sorrell said as if granting him permission, and kissed his cheek. "I'll be good."

Ruddock reluctantly placed her on her feet when he would have rather kept her in his arms.

He ran a tender hand over the welt on her face and anger sparked in him again. "You are always good, Sorrell, always ready to defend. That's what worries me."

"Go see to your duties and worry not about me."

"That is impossible, wife," he said, shaking his head slowly, then kissed her gently before going to Erland.

Erland kept his voice low. "The two warriors who guard your wife need to speak with you. They await you in the solar. I must see to your father."

He turned to ask his wife what else she had done that brought the two warriors to him, but she was gone. She could frighten the hell out of him at times while also making him proud. It wasn't so much her fearlessness that worried him as it was her sense of injustice. She refused to standby and do nothing when confronted with it. She was a true warrior.

Ruddock entered the solar and looked from one warrior to the other. "Did the task I give you of guarding my wife prove too difficult?"

Both warriors had similar responses, their words tripping over each other. "No, my lord. No. Not difficult."

Ruddock stared from one warrior to the other until he pointed to the shorter and thick-chested of the two. "You're Hollis."

"You remember, my lord," Hollis said surprised.

"I could never forget such a skilled warrior."

Ruddock's praise brought a proud smile to Hollis's face.

"You're Bruce," Ruddock said, turning to the other warrior, tall and lanky in stature. "You have skill with a bow and arrow."

Bruce nodded. "You remember well, my lord."

"I don't forget those who rode and fought with distinction beside me." He walked over to stand in front of his desk. "Now is there a problem with my wife?"

"No, my lord," Hollis assured him. "There was an incident we felt you should know about."

"Concerning my wife?"

"Aye," Bruce said, sending Hollis a quick glance that had neither man speaking up.

"An incident you both seem reluctant to tell me about," Ruddock said.

"We don't think any harm was meant, but after what happened with Coyle, we thought it wiser to tell you about it," Bruce said.

Ruddock folded his arms across his chest and waited.

"It concerns Hugh, my lord," Hollis said.

"Hugh," Ruddock repeated pleased to hear his good friend's name, though truthfully he had been more like a brother.

He and Hugh had been inseparable since they had been wee lads. Hugh was the only one who openly defied Lord Finn, accused him of telling lies when he claimed Ruddock wasn't his son. Hugh had defended him to the very end and would have left with Ruddock when he had been banished if he hadn't been wed to Lana.

Ruddock had thought Hugh would have presented himself by now and since he hadn't, he got the feeling something was very wrong.

"Tell me," Ruddock ordered.

Bruce delivered the news as fast as he could. "Hugh called your wife a harlot and you the devil."

Hollis was quick to add, "He was well into his cups, my lord."

Ruddock shook his head, it difficult to believe what he'd just heard. What had happened that had changed things between them? He had never thought, not once, that Hugh would turn against him.

"Why?" Ruddock asked, looking from one to the other.

Bruce and Hollis stared at him speechless.

It was easy for Ruddock to see that they knew something, yet neither spoke.

"Bring Hugh to me," Ruddock ordered since he was the one man who would speak the truth.

Ruddock poured a much needed drink while he waited for the two warriors to return with Hugh. Hearing that Hugh turned against him was like the final blow. All this time, he believed he had one loyal friend, someone who would never doubt him. Now even he was lost to him.

He had tried to imagine who would do this to him. Who would want to rob him of his life? And after all this time, he still didn't know.

Anguished tears from outside the door interrupted his musings and he wasn't surprised to see Lana precede her husband into the room. She was still the pretty woman he remembered, though she had grown thin and lines marred her face for one so young. What did surprise him was that she dropped to her knees in front of him and begged for no harm to befall her husband.

"Please, please, my lord, don't harm him. He meant your wife no harm. The ale caused his tongue to be foolish. Please, I beg you, please."

"Get up off your knees, wife. You'll not beg to him for me," Hugh said, raising his chin to glare at Ruddock defiantly.

Ruddock tried to hide his shock at seeing the changes in his friend. He was half the man he remembered, his body lacking the girth it once had and his face gaunt from what he could see of it, a bushy beard covering half of it. His left arm hung loose at his side and it was obvious it was lifeless.

"Do as your husband says, Lana," Ruddock said and gave a nod to one of the warriors who walked over to help the woman up.

Hugh took a step forward. "I will apologize for calling your wife a harlot, but I won't apologize for calling you the devil."

Ruddock looked to the two warriors. "Both of you escort, Lana, to the Great Hall and see that she is provided with a hot brew and food while she waits for her husband."

Lana felt hopeful. He would not have her wait for Hugh if he intended to place him in the stocks or worse, at least she hoped not.

Ruddock filled a goblet with wine and added more to his own goblet and walked over and handed Hugh one.

He took it without hesitation and took a quick swallow.

Ruddock had endless questions to ask him, but first he needed to know one thing. "You think me the devil?"

"Only a devil can rain destruction down on his friend that was like a brother to him," Hugh accused, casting a quick glance at his useless arm.

Ruddock looked from Hugh's arm to him. "I know not what you mean."

"You lie," he spat. "You did this and more. Lander and I were the only ones to survive the attack, the rest of the troop was slaughtered. And Lander's lost his tongue. They cut it right out of his mouth."

"Who?" Ruddock snapped.

"The barbarian troop you sent to attack the Northwick troop."

Ruddock shook his head, his brow wrinkling. "You're making no sense. What are you talking about? I never sent any barbarians to attack a Northwick troop."

"You're going to stand there and deny joining with the barbarians after you were banished from here," Hugh accused, his tone growing angrier with each word, "riding with them, raiding with them, *slaughtering* with them?"

Shock turned Ruddock silent for a moment. Lies. More lies. He was forever surrounded by them. It was time for the truth. "I didn't join the barbarians, my father *sold me* to them. I was their captive, their slave. I had no power to command any raid and I certainly wouldn't have ordered a raid on my own people. I would have died first. You above anyone should have known that and never questioned it."

"The barbarian claimed it was you as he cut Lander's tongue from his mouth."

"You believed the word of a barbarian opposed to that of a friend you knew since you were a wee bairn?"

"He pointed to a man on a horse up on a hill. He wore the Northwick plaid and I thought it was you."

"You actually thought I would not come to your defense? That I would let harm befall you? We made a pact when were lads and gave our word to always defend each other. I would never dishonor my word and I believed the same of you, since you defended me against my father to the very end."

Hugh shook his head. "I have struggled with this since it happened. I refused to believe it when your father announced you joined with the barbarians… until the attack."

"My father announced to the clan that I had joined the barbarians?"

"He did. Not long after the troop was viciously attacked. Anyone who had once believed you falsely accused did so no longer. And that I saw you—thought I saw you— there in your plaid on a horse watching it all and doing nothing, turned the entire clan against you."

"My plaid was taken from me shortly after they captured me and they made it clear that my father had sold me to them. I didn't want to believe them, but then I never thought my father would disavow me."

"What happened, Ruddock?" Hugh asked bewildered. "One day all was fine and the next our lives were torn apart and hell descended down on us."

"I don't know what happened. I don't know who caused this or for what reason, but I intend to find out."

Anger left Hugh's words and sorrow filled his eyes. "You are right. I was a fool to even think you would have stood by and let any harm befall me. The barbarians proved victorious not only in battle that day but also in making your best friend doubt you and cause you even more damage. I am truly sorry and I hope you can forgive me and let me help find out who is responsible for the lies and deceit that has nearly ruined this clan."

"I could use the help and I could use a true friend."

"I will give you all the help you need. And it is more than a true friend you have," —Hugh placed his goblet on the desk and held out his hand— "I miss the brother I once had and I welcome him home."

Ruddock took it and pulled him into a tight hug, giving him a friendly slap on the back, feeling for the first time since arriving that he'd been welcomed home.

"I hope the same, for I had looked forward to seeing you again," Ruddock said, stepping back. "Now go and enjoy a brew and some food with your wife. We'll talk again soon. I have a matter to see to."

"Thank you, my lord, and Ruddock… I truly am sorry," Hugh said and hurried off.

Not fast enough though, since Ruddock caught the glisten of tears in his friend's eyes and that he had called him by his name, like he had always done before this mess, jabbed at Ruddock's gut. He hadn't been the only one who had suffered due to the lies. The pain and harm had extended far beyond himself and continued to spread.

Ruddock intended to see it stopped. He would start at the beginning and find out where all the lies started and the only one who could tell him that was his father. But first, he had to go to his wife. He couldn't let her hear these lies. She had to know the truth and he was the only one who could tell her that.

***

It wasn't until Sorrell relaxed in the tub after washing her hair that she recalled what had happened earlier with Hugh and asked, "Blodwen, who is this Lander that Hugh's wife had mentioned and what happened to him that put enough fear into Hugh to finally have him hold his tongue?"

Blodwen paled and looked too frightened to speak.

"Why is it that I see nothing but fear when it concerns my husband? He has done nothing to deserve it." Sorrell's brow shot up. "Or do the people believe he has?"

Blodwen avoided looking at her.

Sorrell would not be denied an answer. "Tell me, Blodwen, I need to know. Why did Hugh call my husband the devil?"

Blodwen shook her head. "It is a horrible tale, my lady."

"All the more for me to hear it," Sorrell encouraged.

Blodwen sighed and worried at her lower lip a moment before she spoke. "It was a terrible day, my lady, that Lord Finn accused his son of not being his son and disavowed him. Hugh was the only one who spoke up for him. Lord Ruddock and Hugh had been like brothers since they were wee bairns. Lord Finn and his son had a fierce argument. Some thought it would come to blows. Then Lord Finn ordered Lord Ruddock off his land never to return."

"This just happened all of a sudden. There was no talk of it beforehand?"

"Rumors were spreading, though I didn't think it fair that Lord Ruddock was not here to defend himself. He was off on a mission for the clan," Blodwen said.

"So Lord Ruddock knew nothing about this until his return?"

"Nothing, my lady."

Sorrell's heart hurt for her husband. She could not imagine him returning home to a father he believed loved him to suddenly be denounced. "It must have been a terrible shock to Lord Ruddock."

"I have heard some say that he looked as if his father had stabbed him in the heart and others say he simply stared at his father and said nothing, at first. He was expelled that day from the clan, sent off with nothing, not even food, or a horse, and ordered never to return again."

"I don't understand," Sorrell said with a slight shake of her head. "Why would that have the clan fearing Ruddock?"

Blodwen shivered. "It's what happened only a short time after he was forced to leave. A troop of our men were returning from a mission. They were not far from the keep when they were attacked by a group of barbarians. Most of the troop was savagely killed. Hugh's wound was so bad that it left his arm lifeless. Lander…" She shivered. "Lander had his tongue cut from his mouth."

Sorrell's stomach roiled. "That's horrific, but what has that to do with Lord Ruddock?"

Blodwen worried her lips again.

"Please, Blodwen, I must know."

Sorrow not only filled Blodwen's eyes but was also heard in her voice. "Lord Ruddock joined with the barbarians after leaving here. He sent the barbarians to attack the troop. All died except Hugh and Lander. It's believed Lord Ruddock ordered that Hugh's life was to be spared since they had been friends and Lander's tongue to be cut from his mouth since gossip claimed Lander was the one to start the rumor about Lord Ruddock not being Lord Finn's son."

The water splashed over the rim of the tub as Sorrell hurried to get out. This couldn't wait.

"Hurry, Blodwen, I need to dress and tell my husband this."

Blodwen looked bewildered, standing there staring at her.

Sorrell grabbed a towel. "Don't you see? Ruddock would never do something like that. He protects. He doesn't destroy."

"He was seen on the hill during the attack," Blodwen said.

Sorrell shook her head. "Never! Something is amiss here."

Blodwen was too bewildered to speak or move, that is until the door to the bedchamber swung open and Ruddock entered.

Chapter Twenty-four

"Leave us," Ruddock ordered.

Blodwen hurried out, quickly closing the door behind her.

Sorrell rushed to her husband, towel in hand. "There's something I must tell you."

"There's something I must tell you first," he said and took the towel to wrap around her. "You'll chill." He didn't want her to get a chill, but he also worried that he wouldn't have the strength to ignore her nakedness, since he not only found peace when he held her or was inside her, but he also felt loved.

Sorrell adjusted the towel under her arms, tucking it in at the side to keep it in place as she said, "Mine cannot wait. You are accused of joining the barbarians after leaving here—such nonsense—I don't know how anyone can believe it. And what's even worse and more senseless is that your clan believes you ordered an attack on a troop of your warriors where Hugh—which gives reason why he spoke to me the way he did—lost the use of his arm and Lander lost his tongue, poor man. If that isn't enough, and even more ridiculous, it's claimed you ordered the attack and were seen there." She shook her head. "How could anyone believe such nonsense? We need to find out who is to blame for these outrageous lies."

Ruddock found himself speechless. His wife never doubted his innocence, never once believed him guilty. She trusted him explicitly. It was time for him to do the same… trust her enough to know the truth and hopefully still love him.

Sorrell tapped at her chin, her eyes narrowing in thought. "The thing that puzzles me is what had someone seen to make him think that you where there when the attack took place on the Northwick troop."

Ruddock took hold of her hand. "Let's go to our bedchamber. There is something I must tell you."

Sorrell's heart gave a flutter of worry when she saw concern mar Ruddock's handsome features. "Whatever it is," —she stretched up on her toes to kiss his cheek— "never forget that I am here for you always. That I love you… always."

"Something I should have voiced myself when we wed, since it is the very reason I wed you," — the words fell easily from his lips— "I love you. Sorrell. I love you more than I ever thought possible. I believed I had lost the ability to love, even care… until you came along. You changed everything."

Sorrell's heart swelled with joy, hearing him finally declare his love for her, and her eyes grew misty. She knew this moment would come, though she underestimated how much it truly would mean to hear it from him.

"I believe I fell in love with you when I saw you pelt Peter with those mud balls. Who wouldn't want a wife who could throw with such accuracy," he said with a growing smile and placed his hand at the curve of her back. "I wed you because I love you, Sorrell. I've wanted to tell you, probably foolish that I haven't, and a poor excuse as to why I haven't."

"You were afraid, afraid to trust me with your love since so many who claimed to love you had betrayed you. And once you told me you loved me, you feared I would do the same, especially once you revealed everything about yourself to me." She poked him in the chest. "I should be angry at you for not believing that my love for you is far too strong to let anything interfere with it, let alone rob me of it." Her hand went to rest on his chest. "What you failed to realize is that I have known from the moment you stepped in front of me to shield me from Peter's mud balls that you are a good man with a good heart, and nothing—nothing in this whole world—will ever change that." She grinned. "Now tell me you love me again. I like hearing it and since you waited and wasted time not telling me, you have to make up for it."

Ruddock chuckled. "You are a remarkable woman and the best wife, and I love you with all my heart and always will. And I will make sure you know it every day from this day on."

"I will hold you to that, husband," Sorrell said with a playful poke to his chest.

"I have no doubt you will, wife." He kissed her, a faint one at first as if tempting her, seducing her to reach out for more, and she did. Her lips pressed against his with playful urgency and he returned the same in kind, until the kiss turned hungry and more demanding.

Ruddock forced himself to end the kiss and step away from her, not that he wanted to, but it was necessary. He had to tell her all of it so she knew the truth, knew what she was defending.

"I need to talk with you. It is important."

The glimmer of desire remained strong in his eyes and stronger than ever within her since finally declaring his love for her. She pulled the towel off from around her to drop at her feet. "Nothing is more important than having you inside me."

Ruddock groaned beneath his breath, his wife's petite, curvy body too luscious to ignore or deny. He reached out to grab her waist and pull her too him but her sudden sharp grimace had his hands falling away.

"What's wrong?" he asked anxiously.

Sorrell turned her head, her eyes able to catch the edges of a bruise at her side and to the back. "I forgot about this. It's just a bruise, nothing to worry about, but it is tender to the touch."

Ruddock turned her gently and winced seeing the sizeable purple bruise that spread in a circle from her side to her back.

"I'm actually glad to see it. If it hadn't been for the rock I fell on that gave me this bruise, I wouldn't have been able to fend Coyle off as I did."

Ruddock shook his head, not knowing what else to do and thinking he'd be shaking his head a lot when it came to his wife.

"I should leave you be and see that your bruise is tended to," Ruddock said and snatched her up, his hand avoiding the bruised area, so that she instinctively wrapped her legs around him. "But I won't because I want to be inside you as much as you want me there."

Sorrell had been ready for him as soon as he had told her that he loved her. She needed this to truly seal their union, their love binding them as one.

Ruddock took her to the bed and dropped her down on it, going down with her since her legs remained locked around him. He pushed his plaid out of the way and settled his manhood between her legs.

"Don't keep me waiting," she urged, raising her hips in welcome.

He didn't. He slipped into her.

Sorrell moaned at the slow ease in which he entered her. It was sheer pleasure feeling him slide little by little into her, waiting for that moment when he was fully sheathed in her, and the ride would start.

"You feel so good," she groaned, gripping the sheets to either side of her, then biting down on her lower lips as he sank deeper and deeper inside her.

"Good God, I do so love you, wife," he said and pulled out to slide slowly inside her again.

"That's mean," she said with a moan.

"That I love you?" he teased.

"That you torture me with such divine pleasure," she said and groaned again as he settled once again deep inside her. "I am on the verge, please don't be cruel and make me wait."

"Never," he whispered, and he didn't.

It may have been a short and quick lovemaking, but it had been far from disappointing. It satisfied not only her body, but her heart as well. And when her husband threw back his head and roared, she smiled, knowing he felt the same.

They lay side by side afterwards, their hands joined.

When she shivered, Ruddock pulled the blanket over her.

"I hope your seed takes root fast, so I may give you a son this summer," she said.

"What if I want a daughter?" he asked jokingly.

"She can follow not long after."

He liked the thought and grinned. "You plan to keep me busy in bed."

"In bed and anyplace else that strikes our fancy," she said with a wink.

"You are a wicked woman, wife, and I love you all the more for it."

A knock sounded as he kissed her, both unable or unwilling to respond to it.

"I'm so sorry, my lord, my lady," Blodwen apologized, opening the door and entering after she had received no response. "I thought the room was empty. I came to see that the bathing tub was emptied and removed."

"See to it," Ruddock ordered and pushed himself off the bed, to lean down, wrap his wife snug in the blanket, and lifted her in his arms.

"We'll be in our bedchamber," Sorrell called out as he carried her to the door.

"Bring a comfrey soak for my wife's bruise," Ruddock ordered.

"I have it all ready. I'll bring it at once, my lord," Blodwen said and hurried the four stunned servants into the room to see to emptying the bath, their eyes focused on their lord carrying his lady from the room wrapped in a blanket.

Once in their bedchamber, Sorrell slipped on a soft wool robe lying on the bed. Blodwen probably having left it for her. It was too large for her, but it was warm and soft and that was all that mattered to Sorrell. She snuggled in it as she curled her feet up under it when she sat herself comfortably on the bed.

"My mum's robe," Ruddock said, joining her on the bed to sit beside her.

"Would you prefer I didn't wear it?" Sorrell asked, her hand going to the belt at her waist.

"I prefer you naked to clothed anytime, but I don't begrudge you wearing my mum's garments. She would be pleased that you made use of them, though they will be large on you."

"Blodwen can see to that and thank you. I will enjoy wearing them."

"My mum was thoughtful to a fault and honest, always honest, which reminds me, I need to confess something to you. Something I should have told you sooner."

Sorrell leaned closer to him and placed her finger to his mouth for a moment, warning him to hush, then whispered, "I haven't told you everything about me either."

"Really? And what is it you hide from me?" he asked curious, thinking there wasn't much he didn't know about her.

"You first," she challenged, settling against him to listen.

He accepted, wanting to be done with it.

"I was stunned when my father claimed I wasn't his son and ordered me from my home, my clan, never to return. At first, I didn't know what to think or what to say, then when I realized he'd never see reason, we got into an awful argument, ending with my banishment. I left that day with nothing but the garments I had on. I was so shocked I didn't know what to do, where to go. I recalled a small cottage in the woods, a bit in disrepair, but shelter nonetheless. I was making my way there when a troop of barbarians seemed to come from out of nowhere. With nothing to defend myself, a wise move on my father's part, I was taken captive.

"The leader of the tribe I was taken to, let me know that my father sold me to him. I was his property. I believe he expected the news to somehow defeat me and make me more pliable to his commands. It made me the opposite, and I received more punishments and beatings for failing to obey him."

Sorrell could only imagine the horror of his situation and the courage it had taken to survive it, after what had been lost to him. She slipped her arm around his and gave it a squeeze, so he would know he was not alone anymore. She was there for him now and always.

Ruddock appreciated her comforting and loving touch and silently thanked the heavens for her.

"It wasn't until the tribe was attacked and I battled along with the barbarians that the leader told me that I could remain a slave or I could ride and raid with them and earn my freedom."

"Naturally, you chose to join them so you would be free," Sorrell said.

"Free to kill for them," Ruddock said bluntly. "That was the price of my freedom. Kill as many of their enemy warriors as I could and, when the leader deemed I killed enough, he'd set me free." He paused a moment, his hand caressing her arm that coiled around his. "I've fought many battles, some more disturbing than others, but nothing compared to the ferocity of the barbarians."

"You did what you had to do and I'm glad for it or you would have died and I would have never gotten to know and love you," she said.

"I sometimes thought death would be preferable, since there was no honor in what I did."

"No honor?" she asked incredulously. "No honor is your father selling you to the barbarians, making you their slave, robbing you of your life. He didn't count on your courage to survive and I doubt he ever expected you to free yourself."

Ruddock's glance went to rest on her lovely face. "I killed many."

"As any warrior does in battle. You are a courageous man more so for returning to a father that treated you horribly."

"This is my home, my birthright, and I thought of it every day while away, wondering how I could finally make it home again... until I met you. It was the first time I truly felt I could build a new home for myself with you. Then Erland showed up and told me my father was dying."

"And you had to return. You had to find out the truth."

"It has eaten at me since my father banished me. I don't believe I'm not my father's son and I can't understand why anyone would want to bring such harm to me and my clan."

"Did you ever think that maybe it wasn't you this person wanted to hurt?" Sorrell asked.

"But I was the one who was made to suffer…" Ruddock gave thought to the realization he had had when speaking with Hugh. "I haven't been the only one to suffer. My banishment brought suffering and sorrow to the entire clan."

"Someone wanted more than only you to suffer. Someone wanted to see the clan destroyed."

"Be left without an heir and left ripe for someone to claim," Ruddock said, the realization setting in. "I've been looking at this all wrong. I thought it was all about me. It isn't."

"I would say it's about someone who wants to destroy your father."

Chapter Twenty-five

"You're going to have to speak with your father, and it must be before we leave for my visit with the healer in the woods," Sorrell said, spearing a small piece of meat with her knife off the platter in front of her and Ruddock.

They sat at a table in his solar enjoying the morning meal in private. She was beginning to understand his preference for privacy, though it was more solitude he sought. He had grown accustomed to it after leaving the barbarians and now saw no other way. It would take time, but that would change. It already had changed some, he having enjoyed meals with her and her sisters.

"And why is that?" Ruddock asked, spearing a larger piece of meat.

"The healer should have left your father's malodorous brew by now and I'm hoping there's just enough in it to take to Sage, the healer in the woods, to see if she can tell me what's in it."

"You still think someone is trying to poison my father?"

"Or perhaps making him suffer by drinking that horrific stench," she said wrinkling her nose. "Besides, it's time you talk with him. Time for you to learn the truth."

"I thought I knew the truth. Anyone that knew or even saw my mum and da together could easily see they loved each other. "I remember thinking how someday I wanted to find a love as strong as theirs. That's why none of what happened made any sense."

"Then confront him," Sorrell encouraged. "And I'll be there with you."

Ruddock scrunched his brow. "I don't know if that's good or bad."

"It's good, husband," Sorrell said with a sweet grin. "I'm always good."

"I could argue that," he said with a laugh.

She kissed him quick. "You would have me no other way."

"Naked, wife, I would always have you naked," he said and grabbed her face in his hands and kissed her, not quick and not gentle.

"That's not fair, husband," she complained, "though you satisfied me quite thoroughly upon waking, you stir me again now. And I need to get to your father before he drinks that entire brew."

Ruddock chuckled. "You are insatiable."

"No, I'm in love with my husband."

Ruddock's smile slowly faded as he brought his face close to hers. "And I am madly in love with my wife. She has my heart and I sometimes wonder if she has my soul as well."

"She has all of you," Sorrell whispered and brushed her lips faintly across his twice.

Ruddock leaned in for more than a faint kiss and met nothing but air. He opened his eyes to see that his wife was out of her chair.

"Time to talk with your father."

"That's not fair, wife," he complained.

"No, it isn't, is it?" she said with a smug grin.

"You're going to pay for that," he said, a spark of playful warning in his eyes.

"I can't wait." She winked and hurried to the door as he hurried to his feet.

She squealed with laughter when his arms closed around her before she reached the door.

"You can't get away from me, wife," he said with a teasing nip at her neck.

She craned her head back to look up at him. "I don't want to."

A knock interrupted them just as their lips met.

"My lord, your father wishes to see you," Erland said.

"It's time," she reminded him again in a whisper and stepped out of his arms to take his hand.

***

"I didn't ask to see you," Finn said, pointing a finger at Sorrell as soon as she entered his bedchamber.

"And yet, my wife is here and she is staying here with me," Ruddock said, leaving no room for debate, and came to a stop at the foot of his bed.

"You need a woman to help you face me?" Finn challenged.

Ruddock returned the challenge. "You needed my mum by your side every time you dealt with something?"

"You're not here for us to discuss your mum," Finn snapped and raised his arm up to block the light that shot in the room as Sorrell pulled the window covering back. "Close that!"

"The light will do you good," Sorrell said and spied a tankard on the small table beside the bed. "You should get out of bed now and again and sit by the window."

Finn sat up straight, away from the pillows he leaned against, and pointed his finger again at her. "You need to learn to obey."

Ruddock laughed. "That's not likely."

Sorrell turned a soft smile on her husband. "My husband knows me well and loves me anyway."

"You love her?" Finn asked surprised. "Erland told me you wed her to save her name from being soiled."

"I would not have her name ruined since she had done nothing wrong, but I wed Sorrell because I love her, like you did when you wed my mum unlike your other two wives."

"You had two previous wives?" Sorrell asked surprised, since having heard nothing of them, though she hadn't been here long enough to hear much gossip. Given time she probably would have learned about it.

"I did, but it doesn't concern you," Finn said annoyed.

"Maybe not, but it makes me curious, but that's all right. If you don't want to speak about it, I'm sure I can learn it all from servant gossip," Sorrell said with a shrug as she walked around the bed to stand near the small table the tankard sat atop.

"Your wife needs to learn her place and mind her tongue," Finn said, shaking his finger at Ruddock.

"My wife knows her place… it's beside me. As for her tongue, she'll never mind it and that's one of the things I love about her."

Finn leaned back against his pillows as if in defeat. "You'll not learn the truth from gossiping tongues."

"I'm listening," Sorrell said, an eager smile lighting her face.

Finn spoke, if not reluctantly. "I was young, barely ten and nine years when I married for the first time. It was an arranged marriage and we got on well enough. She died in childbirth a year into our marriage, as did the bairn. My second marriage was also arranged, three years following the first, and we dealt well enough with each other. She lost one child she carried shortly after learning she was with child. Two years later she died in childbirth, the bairn as well."

He seemed lost in memories as he continued, "I thought myself cursed and refused any marriage arrangements proposed to me. I didn't want to lose another wife or bairns, two wives and three bairns were enough to lose. But then I had never truly fallen in love, until Alida came along."

Sorrell wondered if he knew he smiled when he spoke her name.

"She arrived at the village alone and in need, a widow and childless. Some would think her plain, to me she was beautiful and older than my ten and eight years by five years." He laughed softly. "It was madness. I fell in love with her at first sight. Nothing mattered but her. She was all I wanted, all I needed. It took her a while to even look at me, thinking I wanted only one thing from her. I wanted so much more. I wanted a whole life with her, yet I also feared it, frightened she would die like the others had. I chased her until she finally gave in and we wed, even though our union was met with some disapproval. I was shocked and worried when she became pregnant. She was surprised herself since she had never had any children with her first husband. She was so happy and I was so frightened I'd lose her."

Sorrell saw his eyes turn misty and from his tone and the way he spoke about her, there was no denying he loved her beyond reason.

"She was the perfect wife and as her delivery time grew close, I grew more frightened." He shook his head and smiled. "To my great relief, she delivered the child without difficulty. It was such a joyous day. The whole clan celebrated. She gave me a son or so I thought." He shook his head again. His smile gone. "How could she betray me?"

"How could you believe she would?" Ruddock asked with a bite of anger. "Mum loved you beyond measure. How could you think otherwise? And what proof do you have that she cheated on you and that I'm not your son? You never even gave me a chance to defend myself against the false accusations."

Finn shot forward, looking as if he would lunge from the bed. "How could I when it came from your mother's own mouth?"

Ruddock glared at his father in shock, then in the next moment he was ready to plummet him for speaking such an awful lie. "What nonsense do you speak?"

"Your mum confessed all to Father Andrew on her death bed. She wanted absolution for her sin. He told me as he lay dying, wanting no sin on his soul for letting a bastard inherit my title and holdings. He also told me that he was not the only one who heard it. Lander had entered the room, having fetched something for the cleric and heard Alida beg for forgiveness for her adultery and for lying to me that you were my son."

"I don't believe it. Mum would not do such a thing and if she had anything to confess it would have been to you and no one else, not even a cleric. Mum was like Sorrell; the most honest person I know. She would never have cheated on you and that you believe such lies disgusts me."

"Father Andrew would not lie on his deathbed. He would not condemn his soul like that," Finn insisted.

"And Lander thought he was justified in spreading a deathbed confession he supposedly heard?" Ruddock asked, fighting to contain his anger.

"You made sure he paid for that, having his tongue cut out so he could say no more," Finn accused.

"How dare you accuse me of that when it was you who sold me to the Wolfen Tribe and made me their slave… made me a barbarian. So watch your lying tongue, old man, or I'll cut it out myself."

"Ruddock," Sorrell cautioned, seeing the anger that had fired to a rage in her husband's eyes about to erupt.

"Leave us," Ruddock ordered, casting a scowl at his wife. "And do not argue with me on this."

Sorrell nodded, understanding there came a point where it was between father and son, and swiped the tankard off the small table before leaving the room.

"Now you lie," Finn accused once Sorrell was gone. "I never sold you to those savages, you joined them of your own accord and showed your true colors by attacking a Northwick troop, brutally killing all but two, yet leaving both cruelly scarred. Then when your savagery became too much even for the barbarians, they sent you away. That's when I knew you had to be stopped and I offered a reward for your death."

"You believed I could do such horrible things, Father?"

"At one time no, but when you joined the barbarians and I found out you raided with them, I wondered if a barbarian was your true father and you had embraced your true heritage."

Ruddock turned away from him, shaking his head, then looked back with disbelief at his father. "I rode with them to win my freedom."

"So you dishonor yourself and raid with the barbarians?"

"Do you recall what you said to me when I was young and on a hunt with you and suffered an injury that would have left it nearly impossible for me to get home on my own?"

Finn nodded. "I told you that a Northwick is no coward and would do anything to survive."

"I am no coward, Father, and I did what I had to do to survive. What I didn't think I would survive was your betrayal, and not to me, to your wife. My mum isn't here to defend herself against these atrocious lies, but I am. And I will get to the truth, for I know without question that your wife, my mum, would never have laid with another man. She lived to love you and only you, and you are a fool if you believe otherwise." He walked over to the side of the bed and glared down at his father, staring boldly up at him. "When I find the person responsible for these lies, I will kill him with my bare hands, and then, old man, I will come for you."

"Unless the devil gets me first," Finn spat.

***

Concern for her husband had Sorrell pacing in front of the hearth in the Great Hall. She wished she could hear what father and son discussed, but Ruddock would tell her. If not all at first, then eventually.

"Something troubling you, my lady?" Erskine asked, glancing around. "And why isn't Blodwen in attendance?"

"All is well, Erskine. I impatiently wait for my husband and Blodwen tends me well and is presently seeing to a chore I set her to."

"I am glad to know that, my lady. Is there anything you and Lord Ruddock might need?" Erskine asked.

"No, we won't be needing anything. We go for a walk in the woods. I'm curious about the healer there. Do you know of her?"

He bobbed his head. "I know of Sage, though I've not met her. The women seek her out. If it is a good healer you need, my lady, Wilda is a skilled one."

"I will keep that in mind should the time come I need one."

"Is that all, my lady," he asked and went to grab the tankard off the table by Sorrell.

Sorrell snatched it up before his hand reached it. "I do need one more thing, Erskine, a small sack to hold this tankard."

"As you wish, my lady," he said and summoned a servant with the flick of his hand to see to the chore, then gave a respectful nod to Sorrell and turned to take his leave.

"Erskine," Sorrell said and the man turned. "Are you responsible for the keep's accounting?"

"Aye, my lady I record it all and report it to Erland monthly."

"And who sees to all the other accounting?"

"Erland, my lady. He keeps excellent records of all that goes on."

Sorrell smiled. "I learned something about the keep already."

"A good start, my lady. Now if you need no more from me—"

"Go," she said shooing him away as the servant returned and placed the tankard in a small sack. "I did not mean to keep you from your chores."

He bobbed his head and left, as did the servant, and Sorrell turned to the hearth, her mind churning with thoughts. If Erland kept excellent records would that mean he kept a record of whatever was exchanged with the barbarians when Finn sold his son to them? It might not have been recorded so blatantly, but something might be there that suggests a trade of some sort.

"Come, wife, we go see the healer in the woods," Ruddock said, entering the room and Sorrell eagerly joined him, tucking her thought away to revisit later and grabbing the small sack off the table.

***

Sorrell wasn't surprised to see six warriors follow along with them. Her husband would take no chances, especially outside the confines of the castle. She also wasn't surprised that he remained silent as they walked, though it didn't last too long, and she was glad for that, since she was finding it difficult to hold her tongue, eager to hear what his father had said.

"He says he never sold me to the barbarians."

"Do you believe him?" she asked, the puzzle accruing more pieces, or more lies, and making it that more difficult to fit them all together.

"I always believed my father an honorable man, so it has been difficult to believe he had sold me to savages. It would be a relief to learn it was a lie. But with so many tales, I don't know where the lies begin or if they ever end."

"What is one thing you believe without doubt?"

Ruddock didn't even have to think on it. "My mum would never cheat on my father."

"Then that is what you base all else on," Sorrell said. "You had told me you searched for a man you thought a culprit in all this. How did you conclude that?"

"From someone I met chained to in a prison cell."

Sorrell's eyes shot wide. "Where you got that iron cuff?"

Ruddock raised his arm and nodded at the shackle. "Aye, where I got this."

"I believe I have waited forever to hear about this," she said with excitement.

Ruddock stopped suddenly and grew quite.

Sorrell heard nothing but the whisper of the trees from the crisp breeze and the sound of a bird or two.

The next thing she knew Ruddock let out a ferocious roar, that shivered her deep down to her bones, and he drew his sword from the sheath at his back. His warriors did the same as he grabbed her by the arm and practically dragged her in front of a large boulder.

"Stay put," he ordered, the murderous look in his eyes warning her to obey.

That was when she heard a thunderous roar that ran her blood cold and what she saw had her stomach churning with fear. Warriors, stripes of white paint crossing their faces, furs draped over their bodies, cloths and furs strapped to their legs, and battle axes raised in the air, came charging through the woods at them.

Sorrell saw the fear and despair on the faces of the six Northwick warriors. It was as if they were already defeated. But they stood their ground, ready to fight and face imminent death.

What happened next shocked all but Ruddock.

Another group of barbarians seemed to come out of nowhere, their faces marred with blue and white markings.

"Northwick warriors," Ruddock yelled, "get behind me. Protect my wife."

Not one hesitated, they rushed behind him and formed a half circle in front of her, shielding her.

Sorrell had to peer between them as best she could to see what was going on and her heart slammed in her chest as she watched her husband run forward, letting loose with a ferocious roar, and raising his sword to meet the barbarians head on.

She had heard grand stories of battles, but being caught up in one was far from grand… it was terrifying. A wounded barbarian, blood pouring down his face from a head wound, split so far open she wondered how he remained on his feet, stumbled toward the warriors protecting her.

Hollis didn't hesitate. He stepped forward and swung, felling the warrior in one blow. After that the other Northwick warriors rallied and began stepping forward to take on any warrior that got too close.

Swords clashed, axes felled limbs, screams of pain tore through the air and blood seemed to be everywhere.

Sorrell had faced many a situation but never one as horrible as this one. Rocks were not weapons that would help her here, nor would she have the strength to fend off the large, gruesome barbarians. This was one situation she would not escape on her own, and the thought terrified her.

She did the only thing she could. She prayed. Prayed for her husband. Prayed for the Northwick warriors. Prayed for the barbarians that fought alongside her husband. Prayed for the clash of metal to stop.

Not able to take it anymore, she turned her head and that's when she saw the barbarian on top of the boulder, his sword ready to strike down at her. Instinct had her letting out a scream she didn't think she was capable of and it also had her yanking her cloak off and tossing it at the sword as it came down towards her.

She heard the tremendous roar that seemed strong enough to splinter the earth. Her husband appeared to fly through the air towards her, his warriors falling to the ground to avoid him. His one hand shot out, shoving her away, and his other swung his sword with such fierce force that it severed the barbarian's head from his body. It toppled back behind the boulder, as his head fell and rolled along the ground to come to a stop not far away from her, the eyes open wide glaring at her, and she screamed.

Instinct had her beating at the hands that reached for her while she continued screaming.

Fight. Fight. Don't surrender. Was all she could think.

"Sorrell! Sorrell!" Ruddock yelled through his wife's chilling screams. He grabbed her face, forcing her to look at him and his heart slammed against his chest seeing the terror lodged there. "You're safe, Sorrell. It's over. You're safe."

It took a bit for her to hear his words over the screaming until she realized that it was her own screams, echoing in her ears, and she stopped. She looked around and saw that he was right. It was over and the barbarians who had helped him were all gone and the ones who had attacked them were all dead. Gratefully, not one of the Northwick six warriors were dead or looked to be injured.

She turned to stare at her husband, splotches of blood marred his garments and was splattered across his face.

"You are safe," Ruddock said again, her eyes still wide and her body still trembling.

Sorrell tried to speak, but found it difficult. It was hard to breathe, hard to speak, hard to stop hearing the screams even though they were silent now.

As much as Ruddock wanted to take her in his arms, he knew doing so now might not prove wise. The fear and shock had yet to leave her and reason was nowhere in sight.

Sorrell looked around again, then back at her husband. "I want to go home."

Ruddock nodded, thinking it wasn't Northwick keep she meant.

Chapter Twenty-six

Ruddock had no choice but to let Blodwen see to his wife's care when they returned to the keep. She had kept herself at a distance from him as soon as they had started walking and had remained silent the entire walk back to the castle.

He stood and watched his wife hurry up the steps to the keep, away from him, and he worried she would run even farther away.

The tolling bell drew his attention and he turned to Bruce who stood with Hollis, at their post, ready to follow Sorrell if she should leave the keep.

"Bruce, stop them from tolling that damn bell. We're not under attack," Ruddock ordered and the warrior hurried off.

"You brought the barbarians down on us."

Ruddock turned to see his father standing on the top step of the keep, leaning on Erland.

"Take him inside, Erland, *now*," Ruddock ordered.

Finn looked about to explode his face turned so red and before he could open his mouth Ruddock was up the steps, standing in front of him.

"Accuse me again of something I didn't do, old man, and I'll show you what the barbarians taught me." He looked to a startled Erland. "Now get him inside before I drag him in there myself."

Finn had no chance to argue, a pain had him doubling over.

"Hollis," Ruddock called out and the warrior ran up the steps. "Help Erland get my father inside."

The tolling bell had gone quiet as Ruddock turned away from the trio and walked down the steps to see that several of the villagers had gathered there. Fear and some tears marred most faces. The blood that covered a good part of him didn't help. He needed to put their fears to rest.

"Listen well," he said his voice raised with a strength that echoed out into the village. "There is nothing to fear. The castle is not under attack by barbarians. A small band of renegade barbarians was responsible for the attack on our troop. They were defeated, with help from a barbarian tribe we trade with. They will bother us no more. I will let no harm come to the clan. You are safe. Worry not."

"The barbarian tribe you joined?" someone challenged and sudden silence fell over the crowd.

"Since your wagging tongues have already spread lies about me, I owe none of you an explanation," Ruddock said, his voice remaining strong. "But keep spreading lies and I will have more stocks built to accommodate the liars. Now return to your chores and mind your tongues."

Ruddock went to turn away when he spotted Hugh and his wife. They appeared to be arguing with some of the villagers, shaking their heads and pointing toward him. He would have wondered if his once good friend was defending him, if he hadn't already spoken to him. That they both had missed their friendship had been obvious and he was relieved they were repairing it.

Hollis passed him on the way out of the keep. "Lord Finn awaits you in his solar, my lord."

Ruddock nodded. "You did well today, Hollis. All the warriors did well against the savages."

"Because of you and your bravery, my lord. All the warriors there today now know your lordship protects the clan with his life and every one of us are proud to stand with you."

"I'm honored to have such courageous men by my side," Ruddock said and after giving a respectful nod, Hollis held his chin high with pride and took his leave.

Ruddock went to his father when he would have preferred to go to his wife. He was worried about her. He sometimes wondered if battle was easier to endure than what followed it. The memories forever haunted, never leaving your thoughts. The faces of the dead and dying invaded dreams, producing endless nightmares. A battle never ended, it lived in the mind forever, and that was something he never expected nor wanted for his wife.

Then there was the attack itself. His wife once again was targeted as in the abbey. Only this time, all were meant to die. Someone wanted him and his wife dead.

If it hadn't been for Asger signaling, warning him, and being there to help him, the attacking barbarians would have succeeded. But what had Asger been doing here? Ruddock's message to him couldn't have reached him yet, so what had brought him here? And what had really brought him to the abbey? Also what had the attacking barbarians been doing there in the woods? And had they come upon him, Sorrell, and the troop by sheer coincidence or had they been waiting for such a moment?

Ruddock entered the solar, *his* solar. "Leave us Erland."

Erland looked to Finn.

"It is my command you'll obey, not his," Ruddock warned.

"I'll wait outside the door," Erland said.

As long as Erland obeyed his command, Ruddock didn't care if he felt the need to let the old man know he'd remain nearby. Ruddock recalled his father telling him to always trust Erland. He would do what was right for the clan.

Ruddock got the feeling that Erland didn't believe he was right for the clan.

He went to the sideboard and filled a tankard with ale and drank it down, then went to where his father sat in front of the fire. A tankard sat beside him on the table and it wasn't the foul-smelling drink that filled it. It appeared he had needed a drink as much as his son had.

Ruddock stood in front of the fireplace and glared at his father. "Did you order mine and my wife's death?"

Finn looked genuinely shocked. "What are you saying? Someone is trying to kill the both of you?"

"It seems that way. This is the second attempt on my wife's life," Ruddock said and detailed the one at the abbey.

Finn shook his head. "I know nothing about that and I certainly wouldn't pay, nor would I trust, a barbarian to carry out any deed for me. I trade with them, nothing more. You can see that for yourself in the impeccable accounting Erland keeps for the castle."

"I've gone over some of it with Erland. He does his job well."

"He is invaluable to the clan and serves me well as he will you. If you are honest with him."

His father's innuendo that he was less than an honest person prompted a question. "Tell me, Father, did I ever give you reason to think I lied as I matured?"

"Never," Finn answered without hesitation and to his own surprise.

"Then why would you think I lie now?"

"Shame. Regret," Finn said, looking for a reason.

"I believe your hatred for me far outweighs any love you may have ever had for me."

Finn leaned forward in the chair, an angry grumble to his voice. "Blame that on your mum."

"You hate her as well as me?"

"She destroyed the most precious gifts Fate gave me, her love and a son."

"You told Sorrell that you fell in love with my mum as soon as you laid eyes on her. It seems your hate for her came just as quickly."

"Prove otherwise as you said you would and I will claim you my heir and seat you as the rightful heir to Clan Northwick. And do it before I die or I will bestow the title on someone else."

"It doesn't matter who you chose to inherit over me. I would unseat him moments after you spoke his name. I will let no one take what is rightfully mine. So you would do well to hold your tongue about that."

Ruddock remembered that spark of pride he would see in his father's eyes when he did something to make him proud. It was something that Ruddock had strived to earn again and again. He thought he saw that spark now. Or had he wanted to see it and had only imagined it? And why would he want to see it after what his father had accused his mum of and what he had done to him?

He got annoyed at himself. For a moment, he had reverted to that young lad who wanted his father to be proud of him.

"Are you familiar with the barbarian tribe that attacked you?" Finn asked.

"Renegades similar to the mercenaries that sometimes fought with you in your earlier days," Ruddock said.

"Warriors for hire," Finn confirmed. "The question is who paid them?"

A knock sounded at the door and Erland entered.

"Forgive the intrusion, my lords. Wilda is here with your brew and you know how she insists you rest while taking it."

"I'm sure you have plans to—"

"Add extra sentinels to the barbicans and defense towers and keep the warriors on alert and weapons at hand."

"We will talk tomorrow, so—" Finn bit back the word, not letting it slip from his mouth and said no more as he walked out of the solar.

For a moment, they had conversed as they once did, as father and son, and for a moment Finn had thought of him as he once did… his son.

"Erland send a servant to me," Ruddock commanded as the man assisted Finn.

"Aye, my lord," Erland said.

Ruddock went and filled a tankard once again with ale. He had much to do and much on his mind, his wife his most important thought. He worried how she was doing and he worried that she had not sent for him. His biggest worry was that she would tell him she wanted to return home… home to her sisters, not him.

He wouldn't let her go. He couldn't let her go. It wasn't only because she was his wife; it was because he didn't want to live without her. He loved her far too much, would miss her far too much.

He smiled briefly. Life would be far too dull without her.

Ruddock turned, hearing approaching footfalls and when the servant stopped at the open door, he said, "Send the warrior Hollis to me, I have a task for him."

Ruddock needed someone to be his eyes and ears throughout the clan, someone he could trust as his father trusted Erland.

He hoped he was right in choosing Hugh.

***

Blodwen went to answer the knock at Sorrell's bedchamber door. She bobbed her head, and stepped aside. "My lord."

Sorrell remained in the chair by the hearth, her feet tucked up under her and the soft wool robe wrapped snugly around her as she turned her head. Her eyes widened a bit seeing Lord Finn approach her.

He didn't appear as frail to her as he usually did, but at the moment anyone appeared stronger than her. Propriety called for her to stand and it took all her effort to move just a little.

"Don't get up," Finn ordered. "I came to see how you were doing. It was quite an ordeal you went through." The vacant look in her eyes told him what he needed to know. "For a warrior battle can be exhilarating, the aftermath not so much."

"I never saw anything like it," Sorrell said, letting out a breath that had been trapped in her.

Blodwen placed a chair by Sorrell and Finn sat.

"The grunts, the roars, the screams, the clash of swords, and the blood, so much blood." She shook her head and whispered, "And so much death."

"You survived that's what matters," Finn said. "Whatever difficulty you meet the only outcome is to survive it, and often survival itself takes courage."

She stared at him and tilted her head, as if trying to make sense of something. "Survived. Ruddock became a savage to survive. There was no other way for him, and I saw that savage in him today. He felled more barbarians than all the others and he took a man's head off in one swing of his sword." Her whole body shuddered.

Blodwen was quick to tuck a blanket around her.

"My husband kept his word to me. He kept me safe as he said he always would. He is a good and honorable man."

"And you, Sorrell, are a courageous wife?" Finn asked.

She turned her head away, shaking it. "That I'm not."

***

"You want me to be to your counsel as Erland is to your father?" Hugh asked stunned.

"I do," Ruddock said without an ounce of doubt. "I need someone to see and hear what I don't and not be afraid to tell me I may be wrong. Someone who can learn things from others that would not be discussed in front of me. Someone I can trust with my life."

Hugh stared at him too stunned to speak.

"And since you agreed to help me learn the truth of what is going on here, it would make it easier with this position for you to do so. Of course, you'll have to clean yourself up, cut that beard some and the hair as well."

"The hell you say," Hugh complained and smiled when he caught the grin that surfaced on Ruddock's face.

"I will speak my piece to you," Hugh warned bluntly, feeling life being restored in him, like he could be the man he once was even with a lifeless arm.

"I'd have it no other way, my friend."

Hugh stretched out his hand. "I wouldn't either, Ruddock.

Ruddock gripped his hand, giving it a powerful shake, then pulled him in for a hug.

"I'll serve you with dignity and honesty, my lord," Hugh said.

"Ruddock to you."

"Only when we're alone, otherwise I pay you the respect you deserve."

Ruddock nodded. "Get yourself a new plaid from the weavers and anything else you and Lana need. And no heavy drinking, Hugh. I need you alert to everything that goes on around the castle. I'll also need you to make some discreet inquiry regarding certain people, but we'll discuss that tomorrow."

"I look forward to it," Hugh said.

"Do you know anything about the healer in the woods?"

"I don't, but Lana has gone to see her."

"Lana is ill?"

Hugh appreciated the concern he heard in his friend's voice. "No. We remain childless and Lana has gone to see her in hopes she can be of some help. What reason have you to ask?"

"What we discuss is to be held in the strictest of confidence," Ruddock said.

"You have my word."

"My wife believes the drink Wilda gives my father is poison and she wants to see if the healer in the woods can tell her about what's in the brew."

"Wilda poison your father?" Hugh shook his head. "She can be a strange one, but I would never think that of her."

"I would never think that my father would denounce me as his son."

"Things have been strange here for a while now," Hugh admitted.

"Can you say when it first began?"

"Lana and I were discussing this after you and I spoke. She made mention of something not being right here. I think it was when you and I were away for a month on your last mission. Let me speak to her and talk with you tomorrow about it."

"Lana can tell me herself if she'd like."

"She just might, since she is so pleased and relieved that you've forgiven my foolishness." Hugh grinned. "I can't wait to see her face when I tell her about this."

"Then go and celebrate with her and I will see you tomorrow."

"You will tell me then about the attack, since people will expect to hear the truth from me once they learn of my new position."

"I will explain that and more to you."

"Until tomorrow," Hugh said and turned to leave but stopped. "Your wife, Lady Sorrell, is unharmed?"

"Unharmed, but battle scarred."

"A scar that can't be seen and never heals."

***

Ruddock made sure to bathe and rid himself of the stench of battle before going to his wife. He stood at their bedchamber door, not sure if he would find her there or if she remained in her private bedchamber where she had been the last time he had spoken with Blodwen.

If she did, she would not be there long. He would not let her put distance between them, not now when she needed comforting… not ever.

He opened the door and stepped into the room.

Chapter Twenty-seven

Ruddock exhaled his relief with a brief breath when he saw his wife standing by the fireplace. She was staring at the flames and he could only imagine what she might be seeing or thinking. She hadn't heard him, since she hadn't moved.

He didn't want to frighten her, so before taking another step he gently called out her name. "Sorrell."

She turned, her eyes wide and her face pale, and he was sure he saw tears shimmer in her eyes. That was enough for him, he went to step forward and go to her, comfort her, when she rushed toward him.

"Ruddock," she cried out, a tremble in her voice.

He hurried to her, catching her up in his arms, and she threw her arms around his neck and pressed her face against his naked shoulder. He carried her to the bed and sat, moving them to the middle and resting his back against the headboard before settling her comfortably in his lap.

He felt her tears fall on his bare chest, and whispered, "I'm so sorry you had to go through that. I would have done anything to spare you that terrifying ordeal."

Sorrell raised her head, shaking it. "No, you kept your word and kept me safe. It is I who failed you. I always thought myself strong and capable of anything. Today I discovered that wasn't true. I was so frightened and trembled with such fear, that I did nothing to help myself or you. How could I not be courageous enough to help you, the man I love? I'm so ashamed I failed you."

Ruddock stared at her in disbelief. She was more worried about what she hadn't done for him than what she had been through herself.

Ruddock ran a tender caress down her cheek and along her jaw. "That is utter nonsense, wife. You were braver today than I have ever seen you. It takes courage to stand there while fighting goes on around you, not knowing what will happen, and taking quick action when a sword is about to claim your life. The way you flung your cloak and caught it on his sword made it easier for me to strike with one blow. We stopped him together."

"You are a good husband to say that."

"I speak the truth."

"The truth is that you fought those savages without fear while I trembled in fright," she argued.

"Fear is instinctive. It resides with every warrior when entering battle. It's what keeps a warrior fighting to survive and conquer death, as you did when you flung your cloak. You were no different from every warrior there."

"Do the screams go away?" she asked.

"I would like to tell you they do, but I've found they hide and creep up on you when least expected."

"I feel a coward for asking, but I don't want to leave your arms tonight," she said.

"You are not a coward and I will not hear such nonsense. In my arms are where you will remain all night long." Her eyes suddenly turned away from him and he could see she struggled with whatever it was she wished to say. "Sorrell, you can tell me anything."

"I don't want to disappoint you, but I fear I'm not up to making love tonight. I simply want to lay here with you wrapped around me."

"I have you in my arms and that's all that matters," he assured her, though wondered how he got so lucky to find such a loving and giving wife.

He was relieved to feel her body begin to relax against him and to help ease her even more he told her about the discussion he had with Hugh.

"I think Hugh will be a great help to you and I believe he is still a loyal friend to you, even more so now with the truth coming to light. The more the truth is revealed, the more secrets will be discovered."

"It is good to have a friend again," Ruddock admitted.

"Hopefully you will have a da again as well."

"I fear that is impossible. There is nothing that can bring my father and me together."

"But there is… the love you both have for your mum. As much as your da doesn't want to admit it, he hasn't stopped loving your mum. That could be the very thing that helps solve this mystery and brings you both together again."

"Quite unlikely," Ruddock said, though silently wished otherwise.

"I thought it would take time for your da to care anything about me, but he paid me a visit to see how I was and sat and talked with me. He told me I was a courageous wife."

"He did?" Ruddock asked surprised, though pleased that his father had been thoughtful to Sorrell.

"Aye, he offered me words of comfort and I believe he meant them and that they came from his heart."

"He doesn't have a heart, at least not for his son."

"Perhaps he had hardened his heart from the pain of losing the woman he loved, then thinking he had also lost the son he loved."

"He should have never doubted either," Ruddock argued.

"Forgiveness can be difficult, but we all do foolish things, some more foolish than others. Your da needs to see how foolish he was before he can ask your forgiveness."

"My father would never ask for forgiveness and I wouldn't forgive him."

"Like father like son," she said on a yawn.

"You need to sleep," he said, trying not to think on her words. He was not like his father. Or was he?

"I fear I will have nightmares," she said with a shiver.

Her shiver rippled over him and he hugged her, wishing he could reassure her that no nightmares would invade her sleep. Unfortunately, he couldn't, since nightmares almost always followed battle.

"You will be here tucked safely in my arms," he said.

She yawned again and Ruddock eased them down on the bed and pulled the blanket over them.

"Sleep. I'll not leave your side," he assured her.

She snuggled against him and tried to fight sleep, frightened of what awaited her, but exhaustion claimed her and she fell into a deep sleep.

They won't survive. They couldn't with so many barbarians descending on her and her husband and no one to help them. He slayed them one after another, but they kept coming. They didn't stop. Sorrell turned and in the distance stood a man and another figure not far from him. The one figure was blurred, too difficult to make out, but there was something familiar about the man. He was too far away for her to see him clearly, and yet, she knew he smiled as he watched her and her husband about to meet their death.

She grew angry, a rage surfacing in her, and suddenly she had a sword in her hand and she turned and fought alongside her husband. She fought until there were no more barbarians left to fight, then turned to her husband just as a sword struck him in the back and he fell to the ground.

Sorrell let out a blood-curdling roar and swung her sword...

"Sorrell! Sorrell! Wake up! You are safe!"

Ruddock. Ruddock called to her. He wasn't dead. She had to get to him. Save him before the man came after him again.

"Sorrell!" Ruddock said sharply and shook her, to free her from her nightmare.

Her eyes popped open and she labored for breath, but that didn't matter. Her husband was alive.

He hugged her tight, kissed her about the face, and repeated. "You're safe. You're safe. You're here with me."

Sorrell snuggled tight against her husband's warm, strong body, his arms locking around her. It had been nothing more than a nightmare. Or had it been a warning?

***

Sorrell was pleased that Ruddock asked her to join him, Hugh, and Lana, Hugh's wife, in his solar.

Lana appeared much different than the last time Sorrell had seen her. She wore a pleasant smile and her dark, long hair was neatly braided whereas before it had been unkempt. There was no fear in her soft green eyes and the slump to her shoulders Sorrell recalled seeing was gone, making her appear much taller than Sorrell remembered. She stood a good head over Sorrell.

Hugh also looked far different. His beard was trimmed short and the sides of his hair were neatly braided. He stood tall and proud in his clean garments and wore the Northwick plaid well.

"We are so grateful for your generosity, my lord," Lana said.

"It's not generosity, Lana. I trust Hugh and I'm in need of that trust and his friendship," Ruddock said and smiled. "And I'm glad to see you cleaned him up nicely."

Lana chuckled. "It was a chore, but I managed."

"You two better not start picking on me again," Hugh said, smiling.

Sorrell beamed with her own smile. "You are all friends."

"Aye," Ruddock said, "longtime friends."

"Since we were wee bairns," Lana confirmed with a nod.

"Lana claimed at five years that she would wed me," Hugh said with a laugh. "I did everything to avoid that—"

"Though I knew it was inevitable," Ruddock boasted.

"Hugh was the only one who didn't see we were fated to be together," Lana said.

Ruddock laughed. "Until he came to his senses."

"I was doomed from the start, Lady Sorrell, completely doomed," Hugh said dramatically.

"Aye, that he was," Lana agreed, her smile wide.

"We will visit and talk, Lana," Sorrell said. "I must hear all about Ruddock when he was young."

Ruddock was quick to say, "She's sworn to secrecy."

Sorrell turned a sweet smile on her husband.

"I know that kind of smile." Hugh laughed. "Now you're the one who's doomed, Ruddock."

Ruddock took his wife in his arms and kissed her. "I was doomed the first day I laid eyes on her when I watched her throwing mud balls at her foe."

"Mud balls?" Hugh and Lana asked in unison.

"Oh, you must tell me about that," Lana said.

"And I will tell you about the time Ruddock saved a man from me biting his cock off."

Ruddock shook his head.

Hugh burst out laughing.

Lana said, "I definitely want to hear about that."

"Enough," Ruddock said, still shaking his head. "We have important things to discuss."

They all gathered in the chairs Ruddock had the servants place near the hearth and conversation turned serious.

"Tell me what happened between my absence and my return here after the mission that had me gone for a month."

"I believe it all began with the stranger that arrived here. Slatter was his name," Lana said.

Sorrell saw a slight change in her husband. The name was familiar to him, but he said nothing.

Lana continued, "He was a handsome one and a charmer. Had plenty of women sniffing after him and a few believing his wily tongue. You can always count on a man with a smooth tongue to be a liar. He was here only a few days, yet he seemed to bend every one's ear."

"My father's?" Ruddock asked.

"I don't believe so, but he talked enough with Erland. It was just a day after he left, I should say disappeared, since no one saw him take his leave, that whispers began circulating. I finally found out what the gossipy tongues were saying and was shocked." She shook her head. "There was no way—no way—your mum would have even looked at another man. Her heart belonged to your father. You could see the love in her eyes by the way she looked at him." Lana smiled. "It's the same way Lady Sorrell looks at you."

Sorrell beamed. "I'm glad everyone can see that I love my husband with all my heart."

Ruddock felt his heart swell with joy. He had the best wife and he wanted all to know how he felt about her. "I love her even more."

Lana smiled. "You have found a love as strong as your father's," —she paused and shook her head— "I don't understand how your da fell prey to the lies. He was always so cautious, needing proof before he would even pass judgement on anyone in the clan."

"Did this Slatter speak with Father Andrew?" Ruddock asked.

"I saw him coming from the church a couple of times, but I can't say if he spoke with Father Andrew," Lana said. "I did see him speak with Wilda a few times."

"Ruddock told me you're familiar with the healer in the woods," Sorrell said.

"Sage," Lana said with a nod. "She has been here three years now and the women trust her. She is pleasant unlike Wilda."

"Though Wilda is a wise healer," Hugh said. "My arm may be useless, but she refused to remove it when others insisted I would die if she didn't. And as long as it is there, I can hope that by some miracle it may be useful again one day. She also saved Lander's life after losing his tongue."

Lana shook her head. "And she claimed that liars get what they deserve. Lander avoided her after he healed."

"Did he start the rumor about me not being my father's son?" Ruddock asked.

"So many tongues were wagging, I couldn't say for sure who started it. I do know it spread fast."

"So my father had time to at least make an attempt to find out the truth," Ruddock said.

"His word was good enough for everyone and once he disavowed you, there were few who didn't believe him. Unfortunately, when Hugh's troop was attacked and he and Lander claimed to have seen you on the hill watching, then there was no one who doubted Lord Finn's claim."

"Except Lana," Hugh said, reaching out and taking her hand. "She continued to believe in you, her friend. She told me over and over again that I couldn't have seen you. That you would never have allowed anyone to harm me. She never gave up on you."

Lana looked to Ruddock. "I was there when you and Hugh made that pact with your blood. I knew that you both would die before letting harm come to each other. There was no way you would have stood by and seen Hugh hurt."

"You know my husband well," Sorrell said more than pleased that someone had continued to believe in him.

"I appreciate the faith you have in me, Lana," Ruddock said. "Is there anything else that you recall about that time that might help us solve this puzzle?"

"Things changed rapidly once Slatter was gone. Your father had not been well and it began to show on him. People were divided. What were they to believe? Their beloved Lady Alida had been marked a..." Lana would not repeat what Lady Alida had been called. "Then Father Andrew got sick and died. Your father turned terribly angry after that.

"I am grateful for you sharing this with me," Ruddock said. "There is one other thing, Lana. Is there any reason why the healer in the woods doesn't come to the castle?"

"Wilda told her she's not welcome here and to stay away," Lana said.

"Then she would come if I summoned her?"

"I don't see why not," Lana said.

When Ruddock stood, signaling that the meeting had ended, Sorrell looked to her husband, "A word with you, please?"

"I'll see my wife out and wait in the Great Hall for your summons," Hugh said.

"I will pay a visit soon," Sorrell said with a smile to Lana.

"I look forward to it, my lady," Lana said and took her husband's hand as they left the room.

Ruddock rested his hands on his wife's waist, lifted her, and walked with her feet dangling above the floor to sit her on the edge of the desk. He planted his hands to either side of her and kissed her.

"You feel well, wife?" he asked, having been concerned after she had detailed her nightmare to him over breakfast. And how adamant she had been that the nightmare had warned there were two people out to see them both dead.

"I do very well," she reassured him.

"Then what troubles you?" He kissed her again.

She draped her arms over his shoulders and leaned close. "That your kisses make me forget what I wanted to ask you."

Ruddock laughed and kissed her quick. "You have too sharp of a mind for that to happen."

"You underestimate the power of your prowess," she said with a wink.

"I never underestimate that, wife," he whispered near her lips, then kissed her with the prowess that was so very familiar to her.

A knock sounded at the door and Erland called out, "Sorry to disturb, Lord Ruddock, but the morning wanes and there's work to be done."

"A moment, Erland," Ruddock called out.

"I'll make certain to demonstrate my prowess to you later," he said and lifted her off the desk.

"I'll hold you to that," she warned.

"Not to worry, you won't need to," Ruddock said with a grin.

Sorrell turned to leave, then quickly turned back around. "Now I remember, see your kisses do distract me. I got the sense that Slatter was a familiar name to you."

"Aye," Ruddock said and raised his arm. "Slatter was the man at the other end of this iron cuff."

Chapter Twenty-eight

Sorrell entered Lord Finn's bedchamber, a tankard of hot cider in her hand. "How do you feel today, Da?"

"I see there's no use in telling you not to call me that," Finn said, his protest a weak one.

"I can't stop myself. You reminded me of my da when you offered me words of comfort after the attack, and it feels only right to address you as such."

"I suppose I can't stop you," Finn grumbled.

"No, you can't," she said with a smile, knowing full well he could. All he had to do was ban her from his bedchamber and not speak to her, but it was easy to see he enjoyed their visits. Something he would never admit to.

She placed the tankard on the small table beside the bed, then went to the window and drew the drapes back a bit, a concession they had agreed upon. However, he had refused to stop drinking the smelly brew Wilda continued to give him.

Sorrell wondered if she could be wrong about the brew since there were times Finn appeared more fit, but then he had his good and bad days.

She returned to the bedside and sat in the chair that was already waiting for her, a sign that he had been expecting her."

"Things are remarkably different since the attack two weeks ago," she said.

"How so?" Finn asked curious as he reached for the tankard.

"The villagers now smile at me and Ruddock and offer greetings. The warriors hold their heads up with pride at having such a brave and honorable leader. Many say how much Lord Ruddock is like Lord Finn... fearless."

What she didn't tell him was that most people had begun to question the possible falsehood of the accusations that Ruddock wasn't Finn's son.

Finn ignored her remark, though it remained in his thoughts as he asked, "How does Coyle do since his release from the stocks. Men like him need to be handled forcefully."

"As soon as he was released, he not only spoke badly of Ruddock, he beat his wife again. It landed him back in the stocks and where before some sided with Coyle, this time no one cares if he is left there to rot."

Sorrell had a feeling Finn knew full well what went on with his clan and within the castle grounds. Erland spent a couple of hours with him every day, no doubt keeping him apprised of everything.

"Have you learned your way around the keep?" Finn asked.

She had been detailing her exploration of the keep to him and was pleased with the advice he had offered her. "Enough of it. A few twists and turns still confuse me, but mostly I can find my way around. I meet with Erskine today to learn more about the workings of the keep."

"It's a good system that's been established. Don't go messing it up. There is far more to running a keep this size than you can handle alone. Erskine doesn't even do it on his own. Various sections of the keep have been broken down into individual parts and someone runs each section and reports to him. You would be wise to let Erskine continue what he's doing and report back to you. Any major changes or issues can be discussed between you both, and make sure you take rounds of the keep with Erskine at least once a month."

"Ruddock told me his mum ran the keep on her own. How did she ever manage it?"

"Surprisingly with ease," Finn said, fond memories bringing a smile to his face. "She's the one who devised the system Erskine follows now. I placed him in the role when Alida became too ill to continue with the heavily responsible chore."

"How did you come to choose him?"

"I had Erland choose, since I had no wont to do it with Alida being so ill. I have no regrets with his choice."

"Regrets can be difficult to live with. You should speak with your son before it's too late."

"You tell me that every time you speak with me."

"And you ignore me every time I do," she reminded him.

"Do you know where your husband is at this moment?" Finn asked.

His sneer told Sorrell he knew and wasn't pleased. "I know he's not within the castle's grounds, but where he's gone I don't know. However, I've no doubt you plan to tell me."

Finn didn't hesitate. "He's meeting with a barbarian."

"Wonderful!" Sorrell said with a clap of her hands. "Finally, he may discover the truth or uncover something that can shed some light on the attack and who wants us dead."

"You defend him at every turn," Finn snapped, irritated.

"As should you, since you raised him to be an honorable man," —she raised a finger to silence him when he went to speak— "whether he's your son or not doesn't matter in this argument. That you raised him to be a decent man is what matters."

"However did your father deal with such a blunt and stubborn daughter?"

"Carefully," Sorrell said with a laugh.

***

Ruddock sat on a downed tree speaking with Asger. He was a brute of a man, thick in weight and sizeable in height. He had good features to spite the scar that ran across his cheek. Gray dominated his blond hair, and his eyes were a softer blue compared to Ruddock's bold color, but the man was anything but soft. He was one of the fiercest and most respected warriors throughout the barbarian tribes.

"I never got to thank you for your help the other day," Ruddock said.

"No need. I owe you," Asger said.

"No more, the debt is settled."

"No," Asger said with a quick shake of his head. "You saved my wife and sons from death."

"It was the right thing to do."

"Not all would feel that way and until I know you and your wife are safe my debt to you is not settled. Don't bother to argue. My wife told me not to come home until you and yours are safe."

"I think I may have a wife similar to your Vera."

"Then you are a fortunate man," Asger said.

"On that we agree, now tell me something you have refused to reveal to me. Who sold me to you?"

"From what I was told it was your father, but I spoke only with a messenger never directly with your father. It was made clear that it was never to be discussed with anyone other than the messenger. I realized why when I heard that your father had announced you joined with us."

"Yet you said nothing," Ruddock accused.

"What did it matter to me?" Asger asked with a shrug. "I paid a good sum for you and I got a good slave who turned out to be a courageous warrior and proved himself invaluable. Whatever went on between your father and you had nothing to do with me."

"I know you didn't attack that Northwick troop that left all but two dead. Do you know who did?"

"A rogue troop and don't bother to seek revenge. You already did and with great success."

"The Sandvik slaughter?"

Asger nodded, "Though it would seem they were more renegades than rogues, having received a good sum for that attack and the one on the Northwick troop, and many others."

"What about the attack on my wife at the abbey? What do you know about that?"

"I knew nothing about it. I left quickly that night to make sure no barbarian troop lay in wait ready to attack. I found nothing. Though, I'd say the warrior had to have been following you if he knew you were at the abbey. Unless someone forewarned him"

"I was wed barely a day."

"Perhaps your wife wasn't the one intended and it was your marriage to her that marked her for death."

Ruddock returned to what Asger first said. "Who was the messenger who delivered my father's orders to you?"

"The warrior who lost this tongue."

***

"Running this keep is quite a task and you do it remarkably well, Erskine," Sorrell said.

"Thanks to Lady Alida. She devised the plan that works so well. I simply follow what she had designed," Erskine said.

"Did you know Lady Alida well?"

"Unfortunately, no. She was quite ill when I arrived here."

"What brought you to Northwick Castle?" Sorrell asked, amazed by the size of the preserving room. She was certain it had to be the size of her bedchamber back home.

A woman stood in front of a large wooden box filled with salt. She was rolling a sizeable chunk of meat in it. Another servant was stringing mushrooms and onions to hang along with the already salted and smoked carcasses on a pole that ran along three sides of the room. Other servants were busy pickling vegetables.

"Erland," Erskine said with a smile. "He had sent a missive to the counsel of Chieftain Thomas of the Clan Tuschet to see if he knew of anyone capable of running a large keep. The steward there sent me here with a recommendation and, thankfully, here I stayed."

"Were you surprised at the size when you arrived? I certainly was," Sorrell admitted.

"I expected large, but not this large," Erskine said, "though thanks to Lady Alida's thoroughness, my responsibilities proved much easier than I had first thought."

"Lady Alida seemed to be well-loved by the clan."

"Until the truth surfaced," Erskine said and shook his head. "Forgive me, my lady, I did not mean to speak ill of her, but I watched the clan suffer when the truth came to light and it did such damage to the clan."

"It was lies that damaged the clan not Lady Alida," Sorrell corrected. "And you would do well not to spread lies."

"Pay heed to my wife's warning or you will find yourself in the stocks and no longer needed here."

Sorrell turned with a smile and Erskine with an apology.

"Forgive me, my lord, I meant no disrespect to Lady Alida," Erskine said.

"It didn't sound like that to me," Ruddock said, raising his hand when Erskine went to speak. "I'll hear no more. You've been warned."

"Aye, my lord," Erskine said with a bow of his head.

Sorrell had not made a move. She didn't want to disturb the silence that her husband's presence had brought. No one had moved or spoken. They all stood in silence, staring at Ruddock.

"Get back to work," Ruddock ordered and held his hand out to his wife.

Sorrell looked to Erskine as she reached out to take her husband's hand. "I look forward to learning more about the keep tomorrow."

"I will await you, my lady," Erskine said with a nod.

Once in the Great Hall, Ruddock took his wife in his arms. "I have gone too long without seeing you."

"I was thinking the same and planned on finding you as soon as I finished with Erskine."

"Erskine needs to watch his tongue," Ruddock said annoyed.

"Blodwen told me that there is much gossip among the servants and your father mentioned I wouldn't learn the truth of his previous marriages from the servant's wagging tongues. So the keep would be a good place for someone to start lies."

Ruddock placed his hand to Sorrell's back and guided her to his solar. "Privacy is preferred for what I have learned."

"Tell me," she said with eager anticipation.

"I have learned that it was Lander who was the messenger between my father and the barbarians."

"We should speak to him." Her eyes went wide. "He can't speak." She grew more excited when a thought hit her. "The reason he lost his tongue, so he couldn't tell what he knows."

"He can still manage to communicate."

"Then his tongue was cut out as a warning of what else he would suffer if he told anyone anything," Sorrell said. "And what better way to accomplish it and to confirm what all were told about you joining the barbarians then to have the Northwick troop attacked."

"And leave my friend who was as close as a brother not only harmed enough to hate me, but to have him believe he saw me watching the whole vicious ordeal," Ruddock said.

"Someone has to hold a tremendous amount of hatred to do such a thing."

"Even a little hatred can go a long way over time," Ruddock said.

Sorrell rested her hand on her husband's chest. "You have no time to hate any longer. You have me to watch over and keep safe."

"A chore in itself," he said with a chuckle.

"Aye, and one that will forever keep you busy," she said with a smile that dripped sweetness.

A knock sounded.

"Hugh no doubt, since I asked him to bring Lander to me," Ruddock said, then called out, "Enter."

Hugh walked in, his brow scrunched. "Did Erland just leave here?"

"No," Ruddock said.

"He was outside the door when I approached and scurried off in a rush, almost as if I'd caught him by surprise."

"He was no doubt listening to see if he could learn anything new to take back to my father," Ruddock said.

Hugh shrugged. "Then he should have stayed around to hear that Lander can't be found anywhere. I've had a few warriors searching the entire village and he hasn't been seen."

"If he ran after learning I was looking for him, that tells me he has something to hide," Ruddock said. "Keep the men searching and extend the search outside the castle."

Hugh grinned. "I already did. I figured that's what you'd want."

"The reason you're my counsel. You know me well."

"Also Sage, the healer from the woods should be here shortly," Hugh said.

"She wasn't expected until tomorrow," Sorrell said.

"Lana tells me Sage is coming here today to see one of the women who will give birth in the next month or two and isn't doing well. She is pleased to be able to visit the woman, since you let her know she is welcome here." Hugh looked to Ruddock. "Though, I've heard that Wilda made it clear to all that Sage would not be allowed to see Lord Finn."

"That's not her choice," Ruddock said.

"Maybe not, but I believe it was Lord Finn who issued the order."

***

Ruddock made his way to his father's quarters, having left Sorrell to visit with Sage when she arrived. His father was sitting up in bed, his head resting back on the pillows and his eyes closed when he entered and for a sheer moment he thought his father had passed.

The thought tightened his gut. He didn't want his father to die, not before they settled things between them, and not if it couldn't be helped. He was relieved to see his eyes flutter open.

"Something important brings you to me?" Finn asked.

"Did you order Wilda to let it be known that Sage, the healer in the woods, was not to come near you?"

"I did," Finn said firmly. "She's a witch and I'll not have her around me."

"What if she can help you?" Ruddock argued.

"She can't and I'll hear no more about it," Finn snapped sharply.

Ruddock went to argue with him.

"You can command others all you want, but you will not command me."

Finn's firm, terse tone had Ruddock holding his tongue. It was the same tone his father had used when he had been younger, stronger, and in command. And oddly enough, Ruddock was pleased to hear it.

"I trust Wilda and no other to tend me," Finn ordered.

"If that is your wish, and there is no reason otherwise, I will abide by it."

"It is," Finn confirmed with a nod. "Is there anything else to tell me?"

"Hasn't Erland reported back with whatever he has learned?"

"If my son would confide in me, Erland wouldn't need to sneak around," Finn accused.

Son was all Ruddock had heard.

"It's been two years since you've called me son," Ruddock said, a heated glare in his eyes. "I'd prefer that you mean it when you call me that."

"Then find me the proof that you are my son," Finn said.

"You really need proof, Da?" Ruddock all but growled at him.

"I'd prefer you mean it when you call me da," Finn said.

Ruddock left the room, anger simmering in him. Da had slipped from his tongue without thought just as son had slipped from his father's tongue. He promised himself that when this was done, he'd give his father what he deserved.

***

Sorrell wasn't as knowledgeable when it came to healing as her sister Willow. She knew some rudimentary practices, but no more. She wished Willow were here now to speak with Sage, but then if she had been here, there would be no reason for her to speak with Sage, since Willow would probably know what was in that malodorous brew. The thought reminded her of how much she missed her sisters.

"I am so pleased to finally meet you, Lady Sorrell," Sage said with a bob of her head.

"And I you, Sage," Sorrell countered with a smile and pointed to a chair before the hearth in her husband's solar for the woman to sit.

Sorrell glanced over her as she did. She was fairly tall, slim, her face touched with few wrinkles and she wore her pure white hair in a long braid. She spoke softly and maintained a pleasant smile and her garments were clean and well-mended.

"Lana has told me how skilled you are in delivering bairns," Sorrell said after sitting.

Sage's face glowed with a wide smile. "You are with child already?"

Sorrell shook her head. "No. No, I'm not with child."

But could she be? She hadn't given it a recent thought and her bleeding time was near. The thought that she might be thrilled her.

"I'm sure you will be soon. From what I hear, Lord Ruddock is a virile man," Sage said.

Sorrell grinned. "There is no doubt about that."

"Is there another reason you wished to meet with me?"

Sorrell reached for the tankard she had taken from Finn's bedchamber this morning. "I was hoping you could tell me what's in this brew."

Sage took the tankard and sniffed.

Sorrell didn't expect to see the anger that flashed in the healer's eyes, and her brow wrinkled in surprise.

Raised voices beyond the closed door drew both women's attention.

"Let me in now or I will go to Lord Finn and see you punished."

Sorrell went to the door and opened it to find Wilda arguing with Hollis. She rushed past Sorrell into the room. Hollis entered as well, but stopped from going after Wilda seeing Sorrell shake her head, though he remained in the room.

"Lord Ruddock may be foolish enough to have you here, but I'm not. You're no healer and I'll not let you touch any member of this family," Wilda threatened, her aging eyes wide with anger.

Sage stood, her own anger showing. "I'm no healer, you say? You are no healer. No healer would give Lord Finn poison?"

Chapter Twenty-nine

"You are not to go near my father," Ruddock ordered Wilda after being summoned to his solar and told what had happened.

"I can prepare a brew that will prevent any more damage the poison has already done," Sage offered.

"Lord Finn does need something to help with the pain," Erland said anxiously.

"You trust that she tells you the truth?" Wilda challenged.

"Lord Finn's own body is poisoning him," Erland argued. "He suffers with the pain of his illness and needs something to ease that pain."

"Is my father ill or is it the poison that has made him ill?" Ruddock asked, looking to each of the healers.

"I cannot say since I have never tended, Lord Finn," Sage said.

"I am not sure," Wilda admitted.

"Poisoned or ill, Lord Finn suffers and needs relief from the pain," Erland argued.

"Neither healer will tend my father," Ruddock announced to the shock of everyone.

Erland spoke up, anger in his words and worry in his eyes. "But Lord Finn requires a healer to help him."

"I will see that my father gets what he needs," Ruddock said, making it clear he would hear no more.

"Or will you see he gets what you think he deserves?" Erland accused.

Hugh stepped forward, having entered the room with Ruddock. "Watch your tongue, Erland."

"Why? Will he cut it out like he had done to Lander? How do you defend and serve such a monster?" Erland asked with disdain.

Sorrell stepped forward, shaking her finger at Erland as she walked over to him. "Don't you ever call my husband a monster again." She jabbed Erland in the chest. "Ruddock is a good man and you above all, the man who has counseled Lord Finn through the years, should know that Ruddock is a good man because he was taught by a good man." She jabbed him in the chest again. "So don't *ever, ever* speak disrespectfully to my husband again or you will know my wrath."

"I'd pay her heed," Hugh advised with a smile. "From what I've heard, Lady Sorrell is a force to be reckoned with."

Erland turned a troubled glance on Ruddock. "Lord Finn is who I serve and who I protect and I will make no apology for it."

"Then you serve my father well," Ruddock said, "but I decide what is best for him now."

Erland turned to pleading. "He needs a healer, my lord."

"And he shall have one," Ruddock said.

"Which one?" Erland asked, glancing from Wilda to Sage.

"Neither." Ruddock raised his hand to prevent Erland from speaking. "Enough, go see to my father and you will be informed about the healer who will tend him."

Erland left, his annoyance obvious the way he marched out of the room.

"I will take my leave, my lord," Sage said with a gentle smile and a bob of her head. "If you have need of me, I'd be only too glad to help."

Ruddock gave her a brief nod.

"Lord Finn will not be pleased with your decision. He wants me as his healer," Wilda said, as soon as Sage left. "It is imperative that I am able to tend him."

"Why?" Ruddock asked. "Another healer can do as you do."

"Only a knowledgeable healer," Wilda argued.

"Isn't Sage a knowledgeable healer?" Ruddock asked.

"I know only that she is skilled at birthing bairns. That does not make her a healer. Therefore, I would not chance her tending Lord Finn."

"You fight hard to tend my father and to keep him safe," Ruddock said. "Or is it you fight hard to do him harm?"

"You should ask yourself who is the one who has suffered the most from all of this," Wilda said and walked out of the room.

Hugh shook his head. "I don't know if I'd trust either healer."

"The reason I have a healer, I trust completely, arriving soon," Ruddock said. "Now go and make sure the two healers keep their distance from each other."

Hugh gave a nod to Ruddock and another nod to Hollis to follow him out, closing the door behind them.

Sorrell went to her husband, slipping her arms as far around her husband's waist as they would reach. "I have questions for you."

"Why is that not a surprise?" Ruddock chuckled, his arms going around his wife.

She grinned. "It is nice to have a husband who knows his wife well. Now how will you keep Wilda from tending your da when he insists that she be the one to tend him?"

"When he learns that she may be poisoning him, he might think differently."

"Or he may be stubborn like his son and refuse to believe it."

"My word will be final."

"I imagine your da thinks the same," Sorrell said and laid her finger to his lips when he went to respond. "You had to have sent for another healer before meeting Sage. Did you have doubts about Sage's healing skills that had you send for another healer? And if so, where did those doubts come from? Or is it Wilda's skills you doubt?"

Ruddock kissed her gently. "I can think of better things for us to do than talk."

"I have no doubt you can, but we won't be doing any of that until I have some answers," Sorrell warned him.

"I could prove you wrong," Ruddock challenged, his hand drifting down over her backside and giving it a squeeze.

Sorrell shut her eyes a minute, fighting the images that came rushing to mind, her husband was naked in every one of them as was she.

"Not fair, husband," she said, opening her eyes.

"One more question," Ruddock said, "then we go to our bedchamber."

"You answer my questions about Sage first, then I get to ask one more question."

"You drive a hard bargain, wife," he said and kissed the tip of her nose.

"And you make it even more difficult, thinking of the pleasure that awaits me. So hurry and let's be done with this."

Ruddock was quick to oblige her. "I know no more than you about Sage or her skills, and I don't know how skilled Wilda is as a healer... since many seem to avoid her. Though that could be because of her abrupt nature. To be cautious, I thought it wise to seek the opinion of someone I trust."

"What healer do you have such trust in?" As soon as Sorrell asked her eyes turned wide and a huge smile broke out on her face. "You sent for Willow."

Ruddock didn't get a chance to confirm it, Sorrell rose up on her toes, threw her arms around his neck and planted kiss after kiss all over his face.

"Thank you! Thank you! Thank you! Than—" She stopped suddenly. "Is Snow coming too?"

"I left that up to them to decide, though I invited both. They should arrive tomorrow or the next day."

"And you weren't going to tell me?" she asked, feigning a pout.

"It was meant as a surprise."

"You are the best husband," Sorrell said and planted a quick kiss on his lips.

Ruddock wanted more than that from his wife and went to nibble along her neck when she stepped away from him.

"Do you think Wilda believes the same as we do? That this whole horrible ordeal was meant as revenge against someone. She did say that you should ask who suffered the most with all that happened." She held up her hand, closing all fingers but her thumb. "You suffered." Another finger went up. "Your father has suffered." Another finger followed. "Hugh suffered." A fourth finger went up. "Lander suffered." She spread all five fingers. "The clan suffered." She shook her head and looked at her husband. "Do you see it?"

Ruddock planned to let his wife have her say, then he intended to sweep her away to their bedchamber and have some time alone with her. That all changed after hearing his wife count off who had suffered from this ordeal. It brought things into perspective.

"Someone wants to destroy the Clan Northwick, piece by piece," Ruddock said.

"Your father has made enemies through the years. Can you think of any who would want such revenge?" Sorrell asked.

"Not this way. Clans settle things through battle to proclaim their strength and courage. What is being done here has been planned and slowly executed."

"So the suffering extends over time, producing more suffering." Sorrell reached out to rest her hand on her husband's arm. "Not only does someone have to hold a tremendous amount of hatred to want so many to suffer, but also patience to see it done."

"Patience would be the easy part for him, since he would revel, feel powerful, in seeing what he put in place succeed little by little."

"Where could this hate have been born?" Sorrell asked, then squeezed her husband's arm. "You should speak with your da and explain what you believe is going on here. He might not realize he holds some pieces to the puzzle."

"I will speak with him, though I believe Lander holds the missing piece. He was the messenger between the barbarians and whoever sold me to them."

A sudden worrying thought had Sorrell's eyes rounding. "Do you think Lander could have run off, afraid this person who had ordered his tongue cut from his mouth would do him more harm?"

Her question alarmed Ruddock. "If that is so, then it means the culprit resides within the castle and lives amongst us."

A quick chill shivered Sorrell. "It could be anyone, since the person wouldn't reveal his true nature. He'd have to have patience to carry out the plan and he'd have to get to know the workings of the castle. That would take time and that would mean he has resided here for many years."

"It also means no one is safe," Ruddock said, pulling his wife into his arms. "You will go nowhere without me or a guard and you will not argue with me on this. And you will be alone with no one, not even Blodwen."

Sorrell went to argue. "Blodwen would never—"

"I thought the same of my father," Ruddock reminded. "I need you to be mindful and cautious of what we are up against. In a way, it is a ghost who walks amongst us that we search for."

"Is there no one we can trust?" Sorrell asked.

"Each other."

"That goes without question." Sorrell smiled. "Willow. We can trust Willow." Her smile suddenly faded. "Will she be in harm's way here?"

"I'll have a warrior guard her."

"How do we trust the warriors if we are to trust no one?" Sorrell asked, not liking the implications of her own question. "There must be some we can trust, like Hugh and Erland. Hugh has been friends with you since you both were bairns. Erland has served your da faithfully since both were young. Surely neither wish the clan harm."

"I suppose you're right, though having my father turn against me leaves me suspicious of everyone."

"Not me," Sorrell reminded and stretched up to kiss him gently.

"Never you," he said, brushing his lips across hers after the kiss finished.

A knock sounded and Ruddock bid entrance.

"Your father demands to see you," Erland said. "I believe you know why."

Sorrell felt his reluctance to let her go. "I will be mindful and extra cautious. Go talk with your da and see if you can learn something that will bring an end to this puzzle."

Ruddock didn't want to leave her, since she had a habit of getting into troubling situations. "You should come with me."

"Your father demanded you come alone," Erland said.

Ruddock almost forgot the man was there. "I no longer bow to my father's demands."

"Go," Sorrell urged. "I will be safe."

"Of course you will," Erland said, "unless you do something foolish, I believe a habit of yours and a worry to your husband who presently has enough to contend with."

"Speak disrespectfully to my wife again and I will have you permanently removed from the keep," Ruddock threatened.

Erland paled and was quick to apologize. "Forgive me, my lord, my concern for your father has me—"

"That's no excuse," Ruddock said, not letting him finish.

"Aye, my lord. It won't happen again," Erland said.

"Go. I will be there shortly," Ruddock ordered and once the door closed he turned to his wife. "Stay away from Erland."

"As you say," Sorrell said.

"You agree too fast, wife."

"I don't believe Erland is the culprit or that he means me any harm. He defends your da like I defend you. But I will do as you say so you don't worry about me."

Ruddock shook his head. "An impossible task."

***

Sorrell sat in the Great Hall, a tankard of cider in hand and her mind busy with thoughts. She couldn't get Wilda's words out of her mind. She had listed who had suffered the most from all that had happened, and yet, she had a feeling she was missing someone. Would Wilda have the answer? Or was Wilda part of the problem? Was she poisoning Finn?

Tomorrow couldn't come fast enough for Sorrell, hoping that her sister would arrive. She saw things with more reason than Sorrel. She might see something Sorrell was missing. In the meantime, though, she couldn't wait. She needed to talk with Wilda.

"Some food, my lady?" Blodwen asked.

Sorrell had been so engrossed in her thoughts that she hadn't heard Blodwen approach. "You were born here, weren't you, Blodwen?"

"Aye, my lady," Blodwen said with a nod, "and grateful I am for it. When my da died, my mum and I had no worries, since Lord Finn looks after all in the clan."

"You're loyal to the clan," Sorrell said.

"Without question, my lady. I would take up arms to defend it and give my life if needed," Blodwen said, a worried look in her eyes. "Did I do something to make you think otherwise, my lady?"

"No. No, Blodwen," Sorrell assured her, realizing how her questions must have sounded. "Just wondering if most of the clan was born to it or migrated here."

"I can tell you about most here, my lady," Blodwen said with a relieved smile.

"Good," Sorrell said and stood. "You can do that as we walk."

"Night has fallen and with it a light snow, my lady," Blodwen warned.

"All the better. I have yet to walk the village in the evening and I love snow," Sorrell said with a grin and proceeded to tell Blodwen about her sister Snow.

"Your sister sounds like a remarkably strong woman," Blodwen said as they walked down the keep steps. "And what a perfect name she picked for her pup... Thaw."

When they reached the bottom, Sorrell turned in the direction she wanted to go. She was glad Blodwen followed without question and hadn't taken notice that Hollis and Bruce were not at their posts. She assumed both were engaged in the hunt for Lander. She was also glad she hadn't given her word not to leave the keep. Otherwise, she would be stuck inside. She didn't intend to take long and hoped to be back in the keep before Ruddock discovered she was gone.

"Tell me of those in the keep not born here," Sorrell said as they walked. "Like Erland, he was born to the clan."

"No, my lady," Blodwen said, shaking her head. "From the stories I've heard of the days before Lord Finn became a lord, Lord Finn conquered Erland's clan. Defeated, the men had no choice but to pay allegiance to Lord Finn. Erland and Lord Finn became friends through the years. Some wonder how Erland can serve the man who defeated his clan and robbed him of his land and birthright."

Surely, Ruddock knew of this, but why hadn't he questioned it?

"I thought you might come to see me," Wilda said, jolting Sorrell out of her musings.

Blodwen stepped between the two women. "Lady Sorrell enjoys a walk."

It wasn't lost on Sorrell that Blodwen didn't hesitate to shield her and that alone proved to her that she had no cause to believe Blodwen would harm her.

"I'll have a word with Wilda, Blodwen," Sorrell said, the young servant bobbed her head and moved aside.

Wilda turned and walked toward her cottage door and Sorrell followed.

A short walk and Wilda turned up the path to her door, where she stopped and turned to face Sorrell. "Lies and secrets. They are everywhere."

It sounded like a warning and Sorrell agreed with the old woman. Lies and secrets were everywhere. They had hurt her family and had led to the death of her mum and da.

"A question is on your lips," Wilda said.

Sorrell let it spill, anxious for an answer. "You made mention to look at who suffered the most from all that has happened. Many have suffered, in different ways, but have suffered nonetheless."

Wilda leaned close and whispered as if revealing a secret meant for Sorrell alone. "But only one is different from the others and that one holds the missing piece."

***

Ruddock wanted to smash his fist into something. His father hadn't been at all cooperative. He argued endlessly about Wilda, and how Ruddock had no right making any decision for him. He wouldn't listen to anything Ruddock had to say. He had dismissed Ruddock's claim that revenge was the cause of all the lies as absurd. His father insisted that anyone who sought revenge against him would do so on a battlefield like any respected Highland warrior would do.

If he hadn't taken his leave when he did, Ruddock feared he would have punched his father, though he had to agree that his father was right about one thing. Any Highland warrior would seek revenge on the battlefield. Still, his father was far too stubborn for his own good. He wondered how his mum had tolerated him for all those years.

She loved him.

Something he couldn't get out of his head no matter how hard he tried. He remembered one time how he had laughed, teasing her about how often she had told his father she loved him. She had smiled at him and told him that one never knew what the day would bring, and she didn't want to miss out on a chance to let her husband know that she loved him in case she never got another chance.

It reminded him that he hadn't told Sorrell he loved her when they had last parted, and his stomach clenched. With all that was going on, he wanted that first and foremost in her mind.

His father forgotten, he went to find his wife to tell her that he loved her. With night having fallen along with a light snow, it would be a perfect evening for them to spend alone in their bedchamber.

Ruddock began to worry when after searching his wife's bedchamber, their bedchamber, her solar, his solar, he had yet to find her.

"Erskine," Ruddock said, entering the Great Hall. "Is Blodwen with my wife?"

"I couldn't say, my lord, I haven't seen either of them."

"I have, my lord."

Ruddock felt a sense of relief, turning to the servant off to his right. He recognized her. The short, round woman had been a favorite of his mum's. "Fern, you saw my wife with Blodwen?"

Fern nodded. "Aye, my lord. Lady Sorrell and Blodwen left the keep some time ago. I believe a walk was mentioned."

The relief Ruddock felt vanished in an instant. He should have made Sorrell give him her word that she would remain in the keep for the remainder of the day.

"Has Blodwen done something wrong, my lord?" Erskine was quick to inquire.

"No, Nothing. You may return to your duties."

Erskine nodded and left the Great Hall.

What had made his wife leave the keep? The question he intended to ask her when he found her, after he gave her a good tongue-lashing.

Ruddock stepped into the entrance space between the Great Hall and the outside door just as Hugh stepped through the front door. One look at him and Ruddock knew something was wrong. Fear gripped his heart and he said a silent prayer that it wasn't his wife.

"What is it?" Ruddock asked.

"Lander has been found and Coyle is dead. Both have been murdered."

Chapter Thirty

Hollis and Bruce appeared from out of nowhere and hurried Sorrell and Blodwen toward the keep. They would answer none of her questions that she asked with rapid speed. Her stomach roiled thinking of what could be wrong and she prayed it had nothing to do with Ruddock.

When she saw him on the keep steps, she rushed past the two warriors and up the steps to her husband.

Ruddock caught sight of her, his heart slamming in his chest as he rushed down to lift her in a hug.

"What happened?" Sorrell asked and a horrible thought hit her. "Nothing happened to Willow, did it?"

"No," he assured her, having sent a large troop to escort her here. "It's Lander. He's been found... dead. Coyle is dead as well, both murdered."

Sorrell found herself speechless.

"I need to go see to this and you need to go inside the keep and stay there, and on that I'll have your word," Ruddock said, making sure she would do as told.

"I'll go with you," she said, latching on to his arm.

"No, Sorrell," he said firmly. "I will spare you seeing any more horrid death."

She thought to argue, but bit her bottom lip instead. Did she want more horrid images to haunt her as the ones from the battle with the barbarians continued to do?

"Let it be, Sorrell. I will tell you all when I return."

She nodded relieved he had denied her this. "I will have food and drink waiting in our bedchamber."

He turned to go, then turned back, kissed her cheek and whispered, "I love you, wife."

Sorrell's heart still fluttered when he'd tell her that. "And I love you, husband."

She watched him disappear into the dark night and the softly falling snow before she retreated into the keep.

***

Sorrell paced in front of the bed, the hour growing late or though it seemed. Food and drink sat waiting on the table, not that she was hungry. That two men had been murdered within the confines of the castle made Sorrell think that whoever was responsible for this atrocity had done so out of fear of discovery.

Lander had to have known who the person was, but what had Coyle to do with it? And how could anyone have been so ruthless to kill Coyle while defenseless in the stocks? She also couldn't stop thinking about what Wilda had said.

But only one is different from the others and that one holds the missing piece.

Who was different from the others?

She shook her head, not able to think clearly, her mind too busy trying to sort the pieces and fit them together. She would share it with Ruddock and see if he understood what Wilda meant and if not him, then Willow. She could reason things far better than most.

The door suddenly opened and for a moment Sorrell froze where she stood. Her feet took flight as soon as she saw her husband. She threw her arms around him, hugging him, and when she turned a smile on him, it quickly faded seeing the annoyance in his eyes.

Sorrell took his hand and tugged him to the table to sit and filled a goblet with wine for him. "Tell me."

Ruddock swallowed half the wine before he responded. "I was told that Coyle had begged anyone who passed by him to fetch Lord Ruddock. He had something to tell me that couldn't wait. Every one ignored him, thinking it was a ploy to get his release. I assume he saw something concerning Lander, possibly the person who killed him, and that was what he wanted to tell me and why he was murdered."

Sorrell disliked Coyle, but she detested that someone killed him in such a cowardly fashion. He had had no chance to defend himself.

"That Coyle didn't trust anyone to share with what he knew, tells me something," Sorrell said.

"I reached the same conclusion. He didn't think anyone would believe him, which means the person who killed Lander and has wreaked havoc on the clan is a trusted and possibly high-regarded individual."

"So the culprit does walk among us." Sorrell shook her head. "One person couldn't inflict this much damage."

"We think alike, wife. There is more than one person responsible for this madness."

Sorrell left her seat to plant herself in her husband's lap and he welcomed her, his arms going around her to tuck her close.

"I had things I wanted to discuss with you about all that has gone on, but I find myself not wanting to talk about this anymore tonight."

"I've had enough of it myself," he admitted. "I sometimes think I would have preferred to have remained at your home and lived a simpler life. Unfortunately, life is never simple."

"It can be for one night. Nothing has to exist but you and me tonight. Tomorrow is soon enough to face the problems at hand."

He cupped her face with his one hand. "First, you will promise me that you will not go anywhere outside or within the confines of the castle walls without Hollis or Bruce accompany you. Also, you will be cautious while in the keep and not place yourself in any position that could prove dangerous."

"Like here on your lap?" she asked, turning a sweet, wicked smile on him.

His whispered 'aye' fell like a gentle breath on her lips before he kissed her.

She never failed to get lost in his kisses. Whether a faint brush of the lips or a tangle of tongues, each and every one was magical and reminded her just how much she loved him.

Of course, they also turned her wet.

She grew excited so fast that they couldn't often linger in their lovemaking and she was feeling that way now. She needed to be as close to him as she could and the only way was to have him deep inside her.

Her lips left his long enough to say. "I need you." She returned to the kiss that had her stomach fluttering madly and her desire sparking out of control, which had her saying between her teeth tugging at his lower lip, "I always need you."

Ruddock cradled her in his arms as he stood and walked to the bed. He set her on her feet and slipped off her robe and before she could get her hands on his garments, he scooped her up and placed her on the bed. Then he hastily disrobed and climbed in bed to stretch out over her, his hands braced to either side of her head to keep his large body hovering just slightly over her.

"I want to taste all of you tonight," he whispered and buried his face in her neck to start there.

"I won't last," she protested.

"Then I'll bring you to climax again and again."

She groaned, his hard manhood brushing teasingly between her legs, letting her know the pleasure that lay in wait for her. While she could easily slip her hand down to tease him, make him surrender quicker than he planned, she found she enjoyed him exploring her body with his lips.

He brought her nipples to attention with his tongue and teeth, showering them with playfulness, and moans and deep sighs spilled with pleasure from her lips. But it was what his frisky tongue did to the small tight bud nestled in her triangle of red hair that had her screaming out his name and demanding she needed him inside her right that very moment... or else.

Ruddock brought his face to hers while he tormented her nether regions with his manhood. "Or else what, wife? You'll climax? Go ahead, since I intend to make you climax again and again and..."

He pressed himself against her, his manhood tormenting that small bud beyond sanity and Sorrell couldn't hold back any longer, she burst with pleasure, groaning deep and what seemed like forever as ripples of satisfaction coursed through her.

Ruddock watched her and damn if feeling her body arch against his as if she couldn't get enough of him and the way pleasure rolled off her lips with each ecstatic moan, he almost climaxed as well, a good reason to slip inside her before he did.

He sheathed himself deep within her and her body bolted up to swallow the last of his manhood whole.

"I need to come again," she cried with an agony of impending pleasure.

Ruddock needed to as well, his passion near ready to explode and he moved within her with an urgency he had never imagined. Her pleading cries of '*don't stop, please don't stop*,' fueling his passion even more.

Sorrell gripped his arms and screamed out his name, a thunderous climax taking hold of her and refusing to let go as it set off a growling rumble in Ruddock's chest that erupted in a deep groan of pure pleasure as a climax rocked him down to his core.

"I love you, Sorrell," he said later after his senses returned and when they were wrapped around each other and tucked snugly under the soft wool blanket.

"And I you," Sorrell said on a yawn, head resting comfortably on her husband's chest.

Ruddock laid awake as his wife slept soundly in his arms. As much as he didn't want to think on what had happened, if only for tonight, he couldn't stop his thoughts. Lander had been found in the woods, his throat slit. Coyle had suffered a fatal stab wound and with no one paying heed to him of late, it had gone unnoticed.

It made Ruddock wonder if it wasn't what Coyle had seen but what he might have known that got him killed. He had been away when Ruddock had returned home. Where had he gone and for what reason? Could he had been asked to do something for someone? Had he seen that person with Lander and when he learned Lander was dead, murdered, had he feared for his life? Most importantly was the person responsible for all the lies, starting to get rid of anyone who could identify him?

Coyle's wife, Miriam, had been too distraught to talk with him. However, tomorrow he intended to speak with her and see what she knew about her husband's time away.

His busy thoughts tired him, his eyes drifting closed and his last thought before he fell asleep was that nothing mattered more than keeping his wife safe.

***

Sorrell joined her husband in his solar to talk with Miriam the next morning. The woman's eyes were red and puffy from copious tears, though Sorrell wondered how she could weep over a man who had treated her so badly. She still carried the bruises he had last inflicted on her and here she sat mourning his death.

"What took Coyle away from the clan recently?" Ruddock asked.

Miriam sniffled and shook her head. "I don't know, my lord, he didn't tell me, though before he left he did mention something about extra coin for market day." A tear slipped down her flushed cheek. "I am a bad wife. I hoped he wouldn't get the coin since I knew he'd spend it on drink and he'd raise his hand to me."

"You are not a bad wife," Sorrell said.

Another tear rolled down Miriam's cheek. "I am no more."

"Did he say where this coin came from?" Ruddock asked.

She shook her head. "Not once in the four times he went away for the sake of the coins did he make mention of it. And after asking him once about it and getting a beating, I never asked him again."

A rap on the door had Hugh entering with a smile. "Our troop approaches."

Sorrell held her excitement, not wanting to show her joy in front of the heart-broken woman.

"Have Miriam escorted to her cottage," Ruddock ordered.

The woman stood and followed Hugh.

Sorrell shook her head. "How can she mourn a man who treated her so badly?" A crazy thought hit her. "Do you think she shows us what we expect to see? Do you think she could have gotten tired of the beatings and killed her husband? And this has nothing to do with Lander?"

"I suppose anything is possible, but logically I think it more likely Coyle is somehow connected with Lander." Ruddock grinned, his hand going to rest at his wife's slim waist. "Shouldn't you be more concerned that your sister is about to arrive?"

Sorrell let out a squeal of delight and grabbed her husband's hand. "Hurry we must be there to welcome her."

***

Sorrell bounced up and down on the soles of her feet while stretching her neck to catch sight of her sister as the troop approached the keep. She broke out in a smile when she caught sight of her riding between two burly warriors. She didn't see any sign of Snow and wasn't surprised. Snow felt safe with the familiarity of the Macardle keep and village. Leaving that familiarity would leave her vulnerable and she was vulnerable enough.

Sorrell ran down the steps as soon as the horses drew near and as soon as the horses came to a stop, Willow didn't wait for anyone to help her off the animal. She dismounted and ran to her sister.

They hugged each other, tears fell, and laughter rang.

"I am so glad you're here," Sorrell said, curling her arm around Willow's. "How is Snow?"

"She thought of making the journey, but I think she was just too fearful and I can't say I blame her. Though, I also think she believed she'd be a burden on me. Home she can maneuver around on her own, not so in unfamiliar surroundings."

"In time, when her sight improves more," Sorrell said, praying it would be so.

"Lord Ruddock," Willow said with a bob of her head as Ruddock stepped beside his wife.

"It is good to see you again, Willow."

"I am surprised, though grateful, to see that you have survived my sister," Willow said with a grin.

Ruddock chuckled. "It's a chore, but I manage."

Sorrell jabbed her husband in the side, which had him laughing harder.

Willow waited until his laughter calmed, then asked, "I hope I can help you with your problem. You made mention of needing my healing skills and while I have some, I don't consider myself a healer."

"Nonsense, our mum taught you the most about healing and you have helped many with your skills," Sorrell said. "We need you to see if you can identify what's in a brew that's being given to Ruddock's father."

"I will do my best and I would love to meet your father," Willow said.

Sorrell shook her head. "No you don't. Lord Finn is a cranky old man."

"He is a dying old man and you should have more respect for him," Erland said as he approached them.

Ruddock went to defend his wife, ready to throw Erland out of the keep for good this time.

"You must forgive my sister her rude behavior. She often speaks before thinking," Willow said and turned a glare at Sorrell.

Sorrell felt the familiar sting of her mum's reprimand in Willow and did what she would have expected. "My tongue can get away from me. I meant no disrespect to Lord Finn. I actually like the cranky, old man."

Willow shook her head along with Erland.

Ruddock smiled.

"This is my sister Willow, Erland. She will be tending Lord Finn."

"I know you have just arrived and I don't want to impose, but Lord Finn is in pain, having gone without his healing brew nearly a whole day now. Could you please see what can be done for him?" Erland asked.

"Of course," Willow said and looked to Ruddock. "Is that all right with you, my lord?"

"Of course it's all right with him, that's why he sent for you," Sorrell said and her sister shot her another reprimanding glare.

"I'd also like to speak with the healer who has been treating him," Willow said.

Sorrell was quick to inform her. "She may be poisoning him."

"Good Lord," Willow said, her eyes turning wide.

"Wilda helps Lord Finn. His body is poisoning him," Erland corrected.

"I think Willow should decide for herself what goes on with my father." Ruddock turned to Hollis, standing a short distance from them. "Go bring Wilda to my father's bedchamber and tell her to bring the brew she gives my father."

Hollis took off and Sorrell led the way up the steps, her arm hooked comfortably with her sister's, and her husband and Erland following.

***

"Get out! Get out or I'll have you thrown out," Lord Finn yelled as soon as Willow was introduced to him. "I have a healer and I'll have no other tend me." His arm rushed to grab at his stomach and he let out a heavy groan.

"I am so sorry my visit has upset you," Willow said softly. "And I understand that you would want your own healer. I have asked to meet her and she is on her way here with your brew."

Finn's head shot up. "Wilda brings my brew?"

"She does and I would love to know what she gives you to help you with your pain. It could assist me in helping others who are in need like you."

"You are well-mannered and know your place. Not like your sister," Finn said and turned a scowl on Sorrell.

"You have to admit, Da, that you've grown to like me, if only a bit," Sorrell said, smiling.

Finn looked to his son. "You should have wed Willow. She will make a good, obedient wife."

"I'm afraid that wasn't possible, Lord Finn. Your son and my sister fell in love when they first met and neither had eyes for anyone else."

"You're stuck with me, Da," Sorrell said, her smile growing.

"I suppose I am," Finn said grudgingly.

Willow caught the flash of admiration in his eyes for Sorrell and that pleased her.

"I'm here, Lord Finn. I'm here," Wilda said, entering the room and stopping abruptly when she saw every one.

"The brew," Lord Finn said, stretching his hand out for it.

Ruddock grabbed it out of Wilda's hand as she walked past him and handed it to Willow before anyone could say a word.

"He needs the brew," Wilda pleaded, looking to Willow.

"Just a quick sniff," Willow said and wrinkled her nose, though kept sniffing.

Wilda crossed her arms over her chest and raised her chin, ready for an argument.

"I believe I can improve on the taste and scent," Willow said, handing the tankard to Finn.

"I would be forever grateful if you did that." Finn took a good swallow, wrinkling his nose as he did.

"I'd like to see you try," Wilda challenged.

"Let her try," Finn ordered, after taking another large gulp and gagging.

"I will see what I can do, Lord Finn, and you are lucky to have such an excellent healer," Willow said. "Now why don't we let you rest and I will look in on you later if you and your healer allow me to."

"It is my decision alone to make and you are welcome to visit me any time you wish," Finn said most empathically.

"Good, then I will see you later, Lord Finn," Willow said, then slipped her arm around the old healer's arm. "I could learn much from you. We should talk."

They all settled in Ruddock's solar, Erland included.

"You know, don't you?" Wilda said, her eyes on Willow after the women sat.

"Aye, it was easy to detect," Willow said with a nod.

Wilda's shoulders slumped. "Easy only for a skilled healer."

"What goes on here, Willow? Ruddock demanded. "You would never let my father drink poison."

Sorrell was about to ask the same.

"Wilda isn't poisoning your father," Willow said. "Her brew is saving him from being poisoned."

Chapter Thirty-one

"I don't know when it started," Wilda explained. "And by the time I did realize it, I feared it was too late. I started him on that brew in hopes it would fight the poison."

"Why didn't you tell me?" Erland asked, appearing bewildered by the news.

"And what if you're the one poisoning him?" Wilda asked and shook her head. "I wasn't about to take the chance and confide in anyone. I didn't know who to trust so I kept it to myself."

"How is he ingesting the poison?" Ruddock asked.

"That's the problem." Wilda shook her head. "I don't know. Food would be the most likely guess or the drink."

"Didn't you tell my father what you suspected?" Ruddock asked.

"Not at first since I wasn't sure myself. It wasn't until I tried various brews that confirmed my suspicions were correct that I finally told him. He was skeptical at first, thinking I was wrong, thinking he was dying, and that's all there was to it. Then something changed. I don't know what, but it was around the time he sent for you. He finally began to suspect that I might be right."

"Which is why he got so upset when I wouldn't let you see him," Ruddock said. "He believed your brew was fighting the poison."

"We need to find out who is doing this before it's too late. From what you say, Wilda, it would seem the kitchen is the likeliest place the poison would be added," Sorrell said.

"Or someone who serves it, since he would have time to add the poison without anyone seeing him," Willow suggested.

"Lander worked in the kitchen," Ruddock said. "Hugh told me he asked to work there about eight or nine months ago."

"Can we speak to him?" Willow asked.

"He's dead, murdered, and if he were alive it would be difficult to communicate with him since a barbarian cut out his tongue," Sorrell said.

Willow shook her head. "How do you get yourself mixed up in such things?"

"With great ease," Sorrell admitted with a bit of a smile.

"If he was the one poisoning Lord Finn, then perhaps the poisoning has stopped," —Erland frowned— "but his pain continues."

"It would take time for the effects of the poison to wear off and that he continues to take Wilda's brew would only help him heal faster," Willow said. "As long as someone doesn't try to speed up what he hoped to accomplish… to kill Lord Finn."

Erland hurried out of his chair. "Lord Finn takes a small meal at this time. I should go and make sure no one touches it."

"Keep a watchful eye, Erland, and let me know if you spot anything," Ruddock said.

Erland gave a bob of his head and rushed out the door.

"You should have come to me with this, Wilda," Ruddock said.

"I didn't know if I could trust you, and I gave my word to your mum to keep your da safe. She knew you would do well, find a woman to love and have a family. Your da gave your mum all his love, there'd be none left for another woman. He'd be alone and your mum knew it, and it tore at her heart."

"Did his mum ask anything else of you or confess anything before she died?" Sorrell asked, reaching out to where Ruddock sat in the chair beside her and took hold of his hand, though it was more that his large hand devoured her small one.

"As usual she talked of Lord Finn and her son and how much she loved them and how proud she was of the fine man her son had become. Her confession she gave to Father Andrew, though it couldn't have been much of one since she was a good woman, not a blemish on her soul," Wilda said with a nod. "And those were Father Andrew's own words after leaving her side."

"You were there when Father Andrew heard my mum's confession?" Ruddock asked, rising out of his chair to stand.

"I arrived just as he was coming out of your mum's bedchamber."

"Did anyone else leave my mum's room?"

Wilda shook her head. "No. How could anyone else be there? The confessional is private. No one but Father Andrew can hear it."

***

Sorrell and Willow sat in Lady Alida's solar, having gone there after Ruddock left his solar to speak with his father. Blodwen had brought two hot brews for them and had stoked the fire, making the room toasty warm. After introducing Blodwen to Willow the young servant took her leave.

"I never expected to find you engaged in such a dangerous situation," Willow said. "And I will admit that the main reason I came here was to see that you were unharmed. After what Eleanor had told Snow and me about the barbarian attack, we worried endlessly over you."

"How is Eleanor?" Sorrell asked.

"She is a kind woman and works hard. James gave her a position in the keep and she also helps me with Snow, which let me take my leave without worry. And don't think averting our discussion will work. I'm too used to that tactic of yours. You will tell me all that has gone on here so I can help you solve this horrendous situation and let me return home without worrying over you. If that is even possible."

"I knew I could count on your help. Besides, people seem to trust you more easily than me."

"And why would that be?" Willow asked.

"You are kind, understanding, patient, reasonable—"

"I'm not a saint," Willow snapped.

"You could fool me."

"Perhaps one day I will. Now tell me everything."

Sorrell explained it all, Willow stopping her every now and again, confirming things, since the telling seemed more of a tale.

"Ruddock's da sold him to the barbarians?"

"Finn denies it," Sorrell said.

"Ruddock rode with the barbarians?"

"He had no choice."

"Ruddock's mum confessed cheating on her husband on her deathbed and claiming Ruddock isn't Lord Finn's son?"

"So claims Father Andrew," Sorrell said.

"Who is dead and can't confirm it," Willow said and Sorrell nodded.

"I thought Wilda an unpleasant woman when I first met her," Sorrell said.

"She does have a prickly nature especially for a healer. It seems like people irritate her."

Sorrell was glad to know her sister thought the same as her. "Yesterday Wilda said some odd things to me. She told me that lies and secrets are everywhere."

"Unfortunately, both are common among families, even ours," Willow said sadly. "Lies and secrets tend to work together and often bring far too much heartbreak than they're worth." She raised her finger. "Lies and secrets can also produce hatred and revenge."

"Which I believe is what goes on here," Sorrell said. "The question is revenge against who? Wilda told me to look at who suffered the most from all that has happened. I told her many had suffered, in different ways, but suffered nonetheless." Sorrell leaned closer to Willow as if imparting a secret, the way Wilda had done with her. "She told me that only one who suffered is different from the others and that one holds the missing piece." Sorrell threw her hands up in the air. "I have no idea who she refers to."

"Who are the ones that suffered?"

Sorrell counted them on her fingers as she had done when talking with her husband. "Ruddock, Lord Finn, the clan, Hugh, and Lander."

"You left one out. One who is different from the others," Willow said.

Sorrell got annoyed. Her sister couldn't have solved it that fast. "Who else suffered and how is he different?"

"*She* is different because she is dead... Ruddock's mum. She suffers with her name being besmirched, and her heart would break if she knew what happened between father and son. But worst of all there is nothing she can do to clear her good name, even her husband turns against her."

Sorrell popped out of her chair. "Good Lord, it's Ruddock's mum the culprit is out to destroy; her name, her husband, her son, her clan." Sorrell dropped down on the chair a look of shock on her face. "What if Ruddock's mum hadn't taken ill? What if she was poisoned like Lord Finn?" She rested her hand to her chest, her heart already hurting for her husband. "What could she have done that warranted such revenge?"

"Lies and secrets," Willow said. "Perhaps there are things Ruddock doesn't know about his mum."

"But if it was a secret she kept through the years, how do we find out now with her gone?"

"With great difficulty."

Sorrell popped out of her chair again. "I just realized something. Sage, the healer in the woods. She claimed that Wilda's brew was poisoning Lord Finn."

"That's odd," Willow said. "Any skilled healer would never claim that."

"I need to tell Ruddock about this. We need to talk with Sage again."

Sorrell grabbed her sister's hand and rushed her out of the room.

After searching several areas, she found Ruddock in the Great Hall speaking with Erskine.

"I've been looking for you. I thought you went to speak with your father," Sorrell said.

Ruddock was pleased to see his wife. With his father being poisoned, it meant the culprit was close, too close, and he worried over Sorrell's safety.

"My father sleeps peacefully and Erland ask that I not disturb him, since he rarely has a peaceful night sleep."

"He needs his rest," Willow said.

"The sleep will do him good. Besides, we need to talk to Sage again," Sorrell said.

Ruddock turned to Erskine. "That will be all, Erskine."

Erskine bobbed his head and walked away.

"I'm having Blodwen removed as your servant. Erskine has informed me that he's been told by other servants that Blodwen has insisted on serving you your food and no other. She's been adamant to the point of arguing with the cook about it."

"You will do no such thing," Sorrell said. "Blodwen wouldn't hurt me."

"Don't be foolish, Sorrell," Willow warned. "You don't know that for sure."

"You could be right, wife, but I'm not going to take that chance with your life," Ruddock said. "If it proves otherwise, Blodwen will be returned to her post."

"You leave me more vulnerable without her," Sorrell argued.

"Not with Willow here," Ruddock reminded her.

"Where is Blodwen?" Sorrell demanded.

"She is being confined to a room in the keep until I say otherwise," Ruddock said, seeing anger flaring in his wife's eyes. "You will leave this be, wife, and I'll have your word on that."

"No, I'll not give you my word."

Willow backed away from the couple.

Ruddock stepped closer to Sorrel. "Do not defy me on this."

"Then do not demand something of me you know I will not obey. I told you Blodwen was no threat to me."

"And as I've said, you could be right, but again, I will not take the chance with your life. Blodwen stays confined until I decide otherwise. Now give me your word, you will leave this be."

"No, and it is Sage you should be concerned with. She lied about Wilda's brew being poison."

"I recalled that myself, that's why I've dispatched warriors to bring her to the keep. She should arrive soon." Ruddock reached out and took his wife's hand, then gave a nod to Willow. "Follow us."

Ruddock took the two women to his solar and wasted no time in explaining. "Tongues have begun to wag rapidly with Lander and Coyle's death, and as more is revealed they will wag even faster. Whoever is responsible for this madness will realize it's only a matter of time before he is discovered. Desperate, he may strike out and I don't want him striking out at you, wife."

Sorrell hurried to hug her husband.

Ruddock's powerful arms went around her, returning the hug, and wishing he could keep her attached to him until this madness was settled.

A knock on the door had Ruddock shaking his head and reluctantly bidding the person to enter. He longed for the solitude he once had as long as he could share it with Sorrell.

"Forgive the intrusion, my lord," Erskine said. "Erland wants you to know that your father is awake and knows you wish to speak with him."

"Go and have a good talk," Sorrell said, keeping her thoughts about the possibility that this could all center around his mum to herself. He had enough to discuss with his da without throwing more at him.

Ruddock left after giving his wife a kiss, eager to speak with his father.

"My lady, Erland also requested that you meet with him in the keep's chapel. He says it's important," Erskine said.

Sorrell turned to her sister.

"Don't even think of going without me," Willow said.

"I thought you might need to rest. After all, you arrived only hours ago and I know how tiring that journey can be."

Willow laughed softly. "To be honest, I miss all the things you used to get into. You made life interesting. The day was never dull with you around. I enjoy being part of that again."

"I miss having you to talk with and to tend my wounds. So we must make the most of our time together." Sorrell took hold of her sister's arm and grinned. "Let's go have an adventure."

Sorrell wasn't surprised to see Hollis trailing behind them. Her husband loved her and intended to keep her safe and with all that was going on, she had to admit she didn't mind having Hollis follow her.

The two women were busy chatting when they entered the small chapel. It came to an abrupt end when they spotted

Erland on the floor near the altar. They ran to him, shocked to see his chest covered in blood.

Willow dropped to her knees beside him.

Sorrell turned to Hollis who had taken a guarded stance by the door and saw him sprawled out on the floor, blood spilling from his head and Erskine standing over him with a dagger in his hand.

Sorrell glared at him, stunned. "You?"

"No one pays attention to servants. They're invisible to most. I knew you'd be a problem before you got here since the attempt on your life failed. How does a woman your size defeat a man the size of Otis, the barbarian at the abbey? Then I met you and realized you would be a far bigger problem than I imagined."

"Lies and secrets."

Sorrell and Willow both turned, shocked to see Wilda, a dagger in her hand as well.

Sorrell shook her head, confused. "I don't understand."

On the other hand, it was clear to Willow. "How ingenious. You played the part well, the unpleasant healer, keeping people at bay so they couldn't figure out what you were doing. Yet also the caring healer who did all she could to protect Lord Finn and remain in his good graces."

"But what of that horrendous brew?" Sorrell asked, trying to comprehend it all.

"That was quite clever," Willow said. "You made sure Sage got the brew that contained the poison and I got the brew that combated the poison, which you alternated giving Lord Finn so that you could keep him alive and suffering."

Wilda smiled. "I realized the extent of your skill as soon as you told me you could make it smell and taste better. I knew we couldn't wait any longer, especially when I saw the small troop head out of the castle to fetch Sage."

"You ruined our plan," Erskine said, pointing his dagger at Sorrell. "You're coming with us, though I have no use for your sister." He looked to Wilda. "The boat is ready?"

"Everything is set."

"Good. We finally go home,' Erskine said.

Boat? Home?

Sorrell couldn't let them hurt Willow and she definitely couldn't let them take her on a boat, but what could she do? There was no time to think, no time to plan. Wilda delivered a vicious blow to Willow's head and Sorrell reached out to try and catch her sister before her body dropped to the ground.

Erskine yanked her arm away just as her sister was about to fall in her arms. Sorrell watched as Willow's body hit the floor, her head landing by Erland's shoulder. Rage ran through her like a fire out of control and she clenched her hand tightly and brought her fist around with a fierce force, swinging it straight at Erskine.

He was much faster. His fist slammed into her jaw, knocking her out.

Chapter Thirty-two

"Your suspicions grew after Wilda told you about the poisoning, didn't they?" Ruddock demanded, standing at the foot of his father's bed, though didn't wait for a response. "And it got you thinking that all you'd been told could very well be lies. The problem was you didn't know who to trust. But if it was all lies, then you could trust your son. Your true son. So you had me brought home, though still not sure of what to believe, you continued the ruse until a time you could reveal the truth. Is that time here yet?"

Finn was bone tired. He barely could lift his arms and he could barely look at his son, but he did. "Everything deteriorated after you left."

"You mean after you banished me," Ruddock corrected.

"I lost my way after your mum died."

"I think it's your mind you lost," Ruddock said.

"I did," he agreed, nodding. "I didn't want to go on without my Alida. I hate waking without her by my side and getting in an empty bed at night. I hate that I can't hold her in my arms anymore or listen to her gentle snore as she sleeps. I hated God for taking her from me, and my hate turned me foolish."

"Mum would have never cheated on you. She loved you too much."

"When my head and heart began to clear, I realized my mistakes and I also realized that if someone wanted me dead, then that person just might want you dead as well. And if that was so that meant someone was out to destroy the future of the Clan Northwick. And that person had no intentions of doing it on the battlefield."

"So you let me continue to think you hated me," Ruddock said.

"I didn't know what else to do, son. My mind is far from clear. At times, I did hate you. I did believe the lies told to me. Then other times I knew it couldn't be true. I knew your mother would never betray me. I wanted you home. I needed you home. I needed your strength and courage. I needed you to save the Clan Northwick."

Finn suddenly doubled over in bed, grabbing his stomach.

"Da!" Ruddock cried out and went to his side.

"Have Erland get Wilda," Finn struggled to say.

"Erland!" Ruddock shouted sure that he lurked beyond the closed door. When no response came, he went and opened the door. Erland wasn't there.

"Get Wilda," Finn barely got out, grabbing at his stomach again.

Ruddock raced down the stairs, stopping the first servant he saw. "Have you seen Erland?"

"No my lord," the young lad said. "We can't find Erskine either. He's nowhere to be found in the keep."

"My wife? Her sister?"

"I didn't see either of them anywhere in the keep while searching for Erskine," the lad said.

Fear clenched Ruddock's stomach and he was screaming Hugh's name before he reached the Great Hall.

Hugh hurried in just as Willow stumbled in.

Ruddock was quick to scoop her up. "Sorrell?"

"They took her on a boat. Going home." Willow winced in pain but kept talking. "Erskine and Wilda."

Ruddock and Hugh repeated the two names, shocked to hear them. "Erskine and Wilda?"

"Aye, you must get to the chapel, Erland is badly wounded. Hollis too."

Hugh hurried off.

Ruddock sat on a bench, holding Willow in his arms. "Sorrell would not go easily with them."

"I doubt she did, since I collapsed in front of her." Willow winced when she placed her hand to the back of her head. "You should know that Wilda was poisoning your father while also giving him something to stop the poisoning, making him suffer until the time came she would poison him for good."

"He is in terrible pain now."

"Did he drink another of Wilda's brews?" Willow asked anxiously and tried to hurry out of Ruddock's arm only to grow dizzy when she got to her feet.

"Sit," Ruddock ordered, helping to ease her down on the bench.

The door opened and to Ruddock's relief Bruce escorted Sage into the Great Hall.

Ruddock turned to Willow. "We can trust this healer?"

"Aye," Willow confirmed. "Wilda made sure she got the poisoned brew and I got the brew to combat the poison."

"Do you need my help, my lord?" Sage asked, stopping in front of Ruddock.

"I do, Sage, and Willow here, a healer herself, will tell you what help we need." Ruddock stood. "I need to go bring my wife home."

Willow reached out and grabbed his hand, tears stinging her eyes as she said, "Bring my sister home safe."

"You have my word," Ruddock said and walked out of the Great Hall.

***

Sorrell sat bundled in furs and still a chill ran through her. The sharp cold air off the North Sea stung her cheeks and the sway of the ship as it sliced its way through the water had her stomach roiling.

Ruddock would come for her and that was what Erskine was counting on. She was safe until then, at least she hoped she was. She would stay strong and survive like her husband had done when taken by the barbarians.

When she had first come to, she wondered what she was doing on a barbarian's boat, then she recalled what had happened and her thoughts went to Willow. Wilda had hit Willow hard enough to knock her out, but no blood was lost with the blow. It had to have been on purpose as was the exchange between Erskine and Wilda about the boat and going home. They wanted Ruddock to follow. At first thought, she worried how her husband would know how to find her, then she realized the boat had to have been at port, the barbarians trading with the Clan Northwick and the tribe known to them.

"Tell me why," Sorrell said when Erskine approached her.

He looked far different in the furs wrapped tight around his body. He stood straight and held himself with pride, the slight stoop to his shoulders gone. That he was in command was obvious.

"I was going to wait until your husband arrived to face his fate to tell you both, but I am eager to tell the tale that has been kept a secret far too long."

"Is it Lord Finn or Ruddock you seek revenge against?" Sorrell asked, as eager to hear the truth as he was to tell the tale.

"And here I thought you intelligent enough to understand Wilda's clue."

"Then it is Alida who you wished to see suffer."

Erskine smiled and turned to call out, "She did understand your clue, Wilda."

"Actually, it was my sister who figured it out," Sorrell said loud enough for Wilda to hear, and giving Willow her due.

"Of course, that Willow is a smart one," Wilda said.

"What has Alida to do with barbarians?" Sorrell asked.

"She's one of us, half one of us, though I doubt her mother ever told her that," Erskine said. "Her mother was a slave to my family and bore my father a child... Alida, not her birth name. My father was a great leader, feared by many, and for a good reason. He could be a brutal man in and out of battle. Our tribe thrived under his leadership. Until Alida's mother attacked my father one night nearly killing him. She took Alida and ran before my father was discovered close to death. He survived, though he wouldn't agree with that. He was nowhere near the man he had once been.

"I was young at the time, but the memory of that night lingers. Wilda was older and remembers it well. She helped our mother tend our father. His one arm was left lifeless, his speech was never the same, and the scars on his face left him looking like a monster. Unable to defend the clan he was removed as the leader. We barely survived, no one caring to help us.

"I promised my father I would get revenge for what was done to him. What was done to our family. It took years, but Wilda and I were determined. On my father's deathbed, Wilda and I renewed our vow of revenge to him and he managed to tell us with his last breath how proud he was of us. It took time and I was disappointed when I finally found Edina, Alida's mother. She was dead, but her daughter wasn't. And imagine my delight when I discovered she was wed to the mighty warrior, Lord Finn, leader of the powerful Clan Northwick."

"A joyful moment." Wilda's laugh drifted off on the wind.

"Wilda took residence at the clan first, killing off the old healer so Alida would need to seek her skills. I bided my time, though I admit I grew impatient. Then Alida told me that Erland had sent a missive to another clan in search of a steward for the keep. I intercepted the man before he arrived, killed him, and took his place.

"Our revenge would be greater than I ever imagined. I was, however, disappointed that Alida was ill and would not suffer as much as we wished her to, though Wilda did see that she suffered more than she needed to before she died."

Sorrell shook her head slowly. "I cannot believe that you wasted both your lives to avenge a brutal man? How very sad for you both."

Erskine backhanded her across her face.

Stunned for a moment, Sorrell shut her eyes and when the blood filled her mouth, she opened her eyes and spit it at Erskine. "Like father like son."

"A compliment I'll gladly accept," he said and with the back of his hand wiped away the blood that had splattered on his face.

"How did you get Father Andrew to lie for you?" she asked, eager to know everything.

"You would think a holy man wouldn't fear death, not so Father Andrew. Wilda told him she had been poisoning him and if he did this one thing for her, she would save his life. I suppose he thought to lie to appease her and reveal the truth after she saved him. A foolish thought. Sadly, he died unable to repudiate his lie."

"And what of Lander and Coyle?"

"Lander served me out of fear, since I was the one that had his tongue cut out so that he couldn't tell anyone that I'd been the one who sold Ruddock to the barbarians. Of course, I never expected Ruddock to gain his freedom. I had planned on buying him back when the time came. With that not a possibility, Wilda began planting doubt in Finn's mind that all he had been told about his son could have very well been lies. Between the poison and believing the lies were false, Finn would trust only one person and send for him."

"His true son," Sorrell said.

Erskine grinned. "And he did just that. One problem I didn't expect was Lander to fear Ruddock more than he did me. If Ruddock got a chance to ask Lander anything, he would confess it all. As far as Coyle, he collected information for me on Ruddock. Coyle learned from a thief called Daggit who once frequented this area that Ruddock was at the Clan Macardle. Not trusting Coyle completely, I sent Otis to keep a watch and prevent anything that would interfere with my plan."

"Me," Sorrell said, thinking the arrow she had thought meant for her husband had actually been meant for her.

"You," he confirmed with a sneer. "Who would think a wee woman like you, with her endless chatter and questions, could destroy in a few short weeks what took me years to plan. You deprived me of making Alida's family suffer the years of hell my family suffered. So, before I do to Ruddock what was done to my father and send him home to live in agony, a mere shell of the warrior he once was, like my father had been forced to do, Ruddock's going to know that you will serve me, in every way possible, for the rest of your life while he lays unable to lift a hand to help you."

"My husband will kill you," Sorrell said with certainty.

"Your husband will do anything to save you. I saw for myself how much he loves you. He will surrender himself in exchange for your safe return home."

"He wouldn't be foolish enough to believe you would honor your word."

"Love makes men foolish. He'll do whatever it takes to keep you safe."

"You forget one thing," Sorrell said.

"What?"

Sorrell smiled. "Ruddock is a barbarian too."

***

"What's taking him so long?" Erskine asked, pacing outside the hut.

"It's only been two days," Wilda said and laughed. "Or maybe Ruddock decided she wasn't worth coming after."

Wilda's laugh sounded like a cackle to Sorrell. She did have to agree with Erskine, though. What was taking her husband so long? She was growing weak from barely given any food to eat and the food she was given she was barely able to stomach. A constant cold ran through her, chilling her down to her bones at times. Or it might have been the exhaustion she felt in her bones since Wilda had her doing chores from the time she woke until the time she dropped down on her sleeping pallet.

After the boat had docked, she was brought to this campsite. Temporary shelters had already been constructed and within an hour or so barbarians began to arrive until it seemed like an army had gathered.

Erskine had planned well.

When dusk settled for the second night on the land, Sorrell almost cried. She wanted her husband. She wanted to go home. She wanted to know Willow was all right. She wanted to stay strong. She wanted to survive.

A light snow began to fall and Sorrell prayed it wouldn't turn into a storm or Ruddock wouldn't be able to reach her.

Erskine scurried to his feet when one of the men came hurrying toward him.

"Torches spotted on the sea. Two boats head this way."

"He arrives at night. What a fool." Erskine laughed and the man joined in with him.

"Ruddock is a sly one, be careful," Wilda warned.

"I know what I'm doing," Erskine snapped.

Wilda scowled. "You better. This is our last chance."

"Prepare the men and no torchlights to welcome them. I'll not reveal the strength of my men until it's too late," Erskine ordered and the man ran off.

Wilda stood and grabbed Sorrell by the arm, squeezing it so tight she winced.

"Keep a good hold on her. I don't want her running to her husband," Erskine ordered.

"You're not going to let them have a last good-bye?" Wilda asked with a laugh.

"How sad that your father taught you only hatred and you never got a chance to know love," Sorrell said and let out a sharp cry of pain, Wilda digging her fingers into her arm.

"Our father loved us," Wilda said. "He was proud of us."

"Aye, his last words to you," Sorrell said, recalling what Erskine had told her on the boat. "Proud that you would risk death to avenge him, but not a word of how proud he was of you otherwise."

That got her another painful squeeze to her arm and kept her tongue quiet. She was weak as it was from lack of enough food. She didn't need her arm sore in case she got a chance to grab a weapon, even a rock.

Sorrell's stomach roiled when she saw the amount of barbarians waiting on the shore. There were too many. They would slaughter Ruddock's men. What was Ruddock thinking, bringing only two boatloads of warriors to fight barbarians?

He wouldn't.

He would bring barbarians. Sorrell watched the boats approach and prayed she was right.

"The boats are stopping," one of the men called out.

"What do you mean they're stopping?" Erskine asked and stepped closer to the shoreline.

"The torchlights haven't moved. They bob in place," the man said.

Sorrell stared out at the torchlights and saw that he was right. They didn't move forward or back, though they did bob up and down with the boat.

"I don't need them... *yet*."

The deep powerful voice had the barbarians scurrying to turn around and eyes turned wide when they saw nothing, until...

Ruddock stepped out of the darkness.

Chapter Thirty-three

Sorrell almost didn't recognize her husband.

He was a barbarian. Furs hugged his shins while his upper thighs were naked and a swatch of cloth rode low on his hips, covering his manhood and backside. A large animal fur was draped over his shoulders, the head of the wolf it was taken from still attached, the beast's teeth bared, looking as vicious as the look on her husband's face. His face was painted with blue and white stripes, and his eyes raged with an anger so hot, she thought fire would burst from them. And at his side, clutched in his hand, hung a two-sided battle axe.

"I've come for my wife," Ruddock said, though made no move to go to her.

Erskine stepped past his men and laughed. "And I should turn her over to you? One lone barbarian whose men fear to bring your boats any closer?"

"Do you really think I'd be foolish enough to come alone?"

Sorrell didn't understand the word Ruddock cried out, but she got its meaning when suddenly torch after torch lit behind Ruddock, appearing as if they went on forever.

Ruddock had brought a bigger army of barbarians with him.

Erskine was quick to yank Sorrell away from his sister and plant her in front of him. "She'll die," he threatened with a dagger to Sorrell's throat.

"Kill her and I will slaughter you piece by piece for your men to watch so they know what awaits each and every one of them," Ruddock said. "Fight me and your men go free."

Erskine's men answered for him. They walked away from him to stand to the side to watch.

"Release her... *now*!" Ruddock ordered. "Or are you too much of coward to fight me without help?"

Erskine pushed Sorrell away from him and she stumbled, one knee scraping the ground.

Ruddock didn't make a move to go to her. He stretched his hand out to her. "Come to me, wife."

Sorrell had already gotten to her feet and hurried as fast as she could to her husband. She was surprised when his hand reached up not to pull her into his arms, but to cup her face tightly in his large hand.

"Are you unharmed? Did he hurt you?"

She knew what he was asking. "He didn't touch me."

"Vera," he called out and a tall, blonde woman stepped forward, an axe in hand, and her face also painted with blue and white stripes. "Go with her, wife."

Sorrell realized that he was showing strength in front of the barbarians and while she ached for him to hold her, if only for a moment, she bowed her head and said, "Aye, my husband, as you command." Though she whispered as she walked off, "Don't count on ever hearing that again."

Ruddock had to keep from smiling, pleased that his wife had remained strong and was her usual courageous self. He yanked off the fur draped over his shoulders and threw it aside, the wolf head landing on the ground to stare straight at Erskine.

Erskine threw his dagger aside and picked up a battle axe a warrior had left on the ground for him. "I will avenge my father."

"I care not why you do it. I only care that tonight you will die."

Erskine was so furious that after all this time, all the planning, all the years of living as he and his sister had, with the enemy, Ruddock cared not to know why, and he charged at him.

Ruddock sidestepped him and whacked him on the back as he flew past, sending him stumbling to his knees.

"That's for shoving my wife," Ruddock said. "Now fight like a man, not like a coward."

Ruddock raised his battle axe and with a roar that sent what felt like thousands of tiny bugs rushing over Sorrell and prickling her skin, he charged at Erskine.

Erskine proved to be adept with a battle axe and Sorrell watched fascinated and in horror as the sharp blade came close several times to severing different parts of her husband's body.

The blades weren't the only things swung, fist landed blows, and the hilt of the battle axe was jabbed at arms and backs. Both men were quick with their moves, but there was no denying that Ruddock's strength far surpassed Erskine's. And it showed with the way Erskine began to stumble and his swings began to falter.

Ruddock delivered a blow with his fist to Erskine's face and he fell to his knees.

Wilda came from out of nowhere, running to her brother and dropping down over him to shield him with her body. "No! No! I beg you, my lord, have mercy."

"Get off me," Erskine yelled and pushed his sister away after she tried to hug him tight.

Wilda crawled away crying.

Erskine got to his feet, gripped his battle axe in two hands, raised it, and let out a roar as he charged Ruddock.

With one hand Ruddock brought up his battle axe, ready to defend, ready to end this.

Erskine was nearly on top of Ruddock when a grin spread across his face.

Ruddock didn't hesitate. He took a wide, hasty step to the side and Erskine's axe came down on his sister's shoulder just after she threw a long-bladed knife, landing it in her brother's chest.

They fell to the ground, Wilda screaming in agony from her shoulder that hung off her body or from the pain that her brother lay dead beside her, killed by her hand.

A victorious roar rang out among the barbarians and Sorrell ran to her husband. She didn't care what the barbarians thought, she wanted her husband's arms around her. She ran at him with such speed that he had no choice but to grab her up in one arm and hold her tight. And his mouth came down on hers in a fierce kiss, letting her know she was right where he wanted her.

Things turned hectic after that. Sorrell stayed locked in her husband's arm, at his side, as he talked with the barbarian called Asger and his wife, Vera.

"It is settled between us now," Ruddock said. "You helped me save my wife's life."

Vera shook her head. "Not the same. We stood here doing nothing as did our warriors. You killed six men on your own to save mine and my sons' lives. Asger will be there if you need him."

Sorrell looked up at her husband. There was still much she didn't know about him and she was glad they would have the rest of their lives together for her to find out.

Erskine's men were made to take his body with them and they dragged him away, but they wanted no part of Wilda. Vera had her people take the woman, though there was no hope for her. She would not survive her wound.

Sorrell was relieved when the boats arrived and they finally took their leave. She sat snuggled against her husband, furs piled around them against the cold and a light falling snow.

She finally got to ask the one question she feared to ask. "Willow?"

"She's good. A bump on the head. When I left, she was helping Sage tend Erland, Hollis, and my da. They all do well, though it will take some time for Erland to heal."

Sorrell released a sigh. "I am so glad to hear that."

"And I'm more than glad to have you here in my arms," Ruddock said and hugged her tight.

"You saved me," she whispered softly. "You always save me."

"No, wife, it is you who saved me and I'm grateful every day for having found you."

Their kiss was soft and tender and when it ended, Sorrell said, "There is much for me to tell you and for your da to know."

"It can wait. Right now I want to sit here with you in the quiet with the snow falling and know how lucky I am that you're mine."

Sorrell cuddled against him, resting her head on his chest, his big body keeping her warm as she listened to the splash of the water against the boat as it sliced through the sea.

After only a few moments, Sorrell looked up at her husband. "About the quiet, I don't think that's going to work for me."

Ruddock laughed. "I was wondering how long you'd last without talking... not long."

She poked him in the stomach, smiled, and said, "You're a barbarian."

"Sometimes," he said with a chuckle.

"No, you are a true barbarian," she said and began to explain.

Chapter Thirty-four

Two weeks later

Sorrell hugged Willow, tears running down their cheeks.

"I am so going to miss you," Sorrell said.

Willow reluctantly stepped out of the hug. "And I you."

"Tell everyone I love them and we will see them—"

"After winter," Ruddock said. "Travel will be too difficult before then, especially with snow falling so early this year."

"Safe journey," Sorrell said and hugged Willow again and leaned against her husband as she watched her sister disappear through the village with a troop of Ruddock's warriors to keep her safe.

"Your sister is a good woman and a skilled healer. She deserves a good husband. Find her one, son," Finn ordered from the top of the keep's steps, Sage's arm wrapped around his.

"You're looking so much better, Da," Sorrell said pleased to see him healing nicely.

"Because I had two wonderful healers," Finn said and looked to Ruddock. "And a wise son who is much like his da."

Sorrell had noticed that Finn referred to Ruddock as his son often and also talked about how much his son was like him. He wanted all to know he didn't doubt Ruddock was his son, and she suspected he wanted to rectify the awful mistake he had made in thinking otherwise.

"You said your good-bye to Willow, now it's time to rest," Sage said.

Sorrell was pleased with their new healer. Willow had told Sorrell that Sage was a wise healer and that she should trust the woman. With how easily she handled Finn, Sorrell had to agree.

"See you at supper, son, and don't forget to mind your tongue, Sorrell," Finn said.

"That's not possible, Da," Ruddock called out, laughing and got a jab in the ribs from his wife.

"I'm so relieved that all is well between you and your da and that he's recovering nicely and not dying," Sorrell said. "All is good now.

"Not quite," Ruddock said and took her hand. "Come with me."

Sorrell went along with her husband and was curious when he led her into the barn where Prince and a couple of other horses were kept. She wondered why they were there until she spotted the anvil and hammer.

"Your shackle," she said.

He raised his wrist. "It's time."

She took hold of it, running her finger around the iron cuff. She had felt it against her naked skin endless times. And endless times she asked him to remove it. He would tell her not yet or it wasn't time. She was glad it was finally time.

"That day Lana mentioned the name Slatter—"

"You told me he was the man at the other end of your shackle."

"I had discovered that a man named Slatter had been given substantial coins for using his tongue to charm some folks in the Northwick Clan. I discovered this Slatter had been taken prisoner by a chieftain whose wife Slatter had seduced. I tried to free him, was caught, and chained to him. After a couple of days of talking with him, I discovered he wasn't the Slatter I was looking for and I freed us both.

"The shackle reminded me that I would never be free of the lies until I proved them false and claimed what had been mine since birth. Until I accomplished that, the shackle would remain on my wrist."

Sorrell smiled, took her husband's hand and walked over to the anvil with him. She watched as with one forceful swing, the pin and shackle itself broke in two and fell off his wrist with ease. Her heart swelled with relief for her husband. He was finally free.

Ruddock dropped the hammer down on the anvil and reached out to snag his wife around the waist and yank her to him.

"We should celebrate," she said, draping her arms around his neck and cast a glance to the horse stalls. "A ride."

"You want to go for a ride?" he asked, having a different thought in mind.

"Aye," she said, reaching down to take his hand as she stepped away from him. "I want to ride fast and hard." She led him to an empty stall and turned a smile on him. "Do you think you'll be able to keep pace with me?"

Ruddock laughed and scooped her up in his arms. "Another challenge, wife?"

"Are you up to it?" she asked teasingly.

"Always," he said and brushed his lips across hers.

"I do so love you, husband," Sorrell said, resting her hand to his face and running her thumb faintly over his lips.

He nipped at her thumb. "And I you, wife... always."

"I'm impatient for that ride," Sorrell whispered.

"Believe me, wife, when I tell you, it will be a ride you'll never forget," Ruddock said and stepped into the empty stall piled with hay, the shadows swallowing them up.

Titles by Donna Fletcher

Macardle Sisters of Courage Trilogy
Highlander of My Heart
Desired by a Highlander, July 2019
Highlander Lord of Fire, November 2019

Macinnes Sisters Trilogy
The Highlander's Stolen Heart
Highlander's Rebellious Love
Highlander The Dark Dragon

Highland Warriors Trilogy
To Love A Highlander
Embraced By A Highlander
Highlander The Demon Lord

Cree & Dawn Series
Highlander Unchained/Forbidden Highlander
Highlander's Captive
My Highlander A Cree & Dawn Novel

For a listing of all titles, to learn more about Donna, or subscribe to her newsletter visit her website.

www.donnafletcher.com

Printed in Great Britain
by Amazon